Praise for *Dare to Know*

Named One of the *Times'* Best Books of 2021
A September 2021 Indie Next Pick

"A razor-smart sci-fi corporate noir nightmare. *Dare to Know* is what happens when Willy Loman sees through the Matrix. A heartbreaking, time-bending, galactic mindbender delivered in the mordantly funny clip of a doomed antihero."   —Daniel Kraus, coauthor of *The Shape of Water*

"A voraciously readable page-turner of a novel, part creepypasta, part thought-experiment."
          —Cory Doctorow, author of *Little Brother* and *Radicalized*

"A fascinating, compulsively readable thriller."   —*Guardian*

"Imagine Donna Tartt's *The Secret History* getting a good edit at last, and you glimpse something of this book's occult power. Essential reading for the gathering dark."   —*Times Saturday Review*

"An entertainingly mind-bending read."   —*Financial Times*

"A surreal premise and an unconventional revelation fuel a cosmic journey. . . . A wholly original novel that's bound to frustrate just as many as it entrances."   —*Esquire*

"Audaciously clever and well-written . . . a quite superb piece of storytelling: vivid, thought-provoking and unsettling."   —*SFX* magazine (5 stars)

"A creepy thriller that reads a little like Stephen King writing *Glengarry Glen Ross*."   —*GeekDad*

BRIDE
OF THE
TORNADO

ALSO BY JAMES KENNEDY

Dare to Know
The Order of Odd-Fish

BRIDE
OF THE
TORNADO

A NOVEL

JAMES KENNEDY

QUIRK BOOKS
PHILADELPHIA

LIBRARY OF CONGRESS CATALOGING-IN-PUBLICATION DATA
NAMES: KENNEDY, JAMES, 1973- AUTHOR.
TITLE: BRIDE OF THE TORNADO : A NOVEL / JAMES KENNEDY.
DESCRIPTION: PHILADELPHIA : QUIRK BOOKS, [2023] | SUMMARY: "IN A MIDWESTERN TOWN, A HIGH SCHOOL GIRL'S LIFE STARTS TO CHANGE AS THE ADULTS IN TOWN BEGIN TALKING ABOUT A MYSTERIOUS EVENT KNOWN AS TORNADO DAY AND THE GIRL FINDS HERSELF DRAWN TO THE STRANGE BOY KNOWN ONLY AS THE TORNADO KILLER"—PROVIDED BY PUBLISHER.
IDENTIFIERS: LCCN 2023004796 (PRINT) | LCCN 2023004797 (EBOOK) | ISBN 9781683693277 (PAPERBACK) | ISBN 9781683693284 (EBOOK)
SUBJECTS: LCSH: TORNADOES—FICTION. | LCGFT: HORROR FICTION. | NOVELS.
CLASSIFICATION: LCC PS3611.E5633 B75 2023 (PRINT) | LCC PS3611.E5633 (EBOOK) | DDC 813/.6—DC23/ENG/20230203
LC RECORD AVAILABLE AT HTTPS://LCCN.LOC.GOV/2023004796
LC EBOOK RECORD AVAILABLE AT HTTPS://LCCN.LOC.GOV/2023004797

ISBN: 978-1-68369-327-7

PRINTED IN THE UNITED STATES OF AMERICA

TYPESET IN ROTIS, SABON LT PRO, TRIXIE, AND BURFORD RUSTIC

DESIGNED BY PAIGE GRAFF
COVER PHOTO BY PONGSTORN PIXS/SHUTTERSTOCK
PRODUCTION MANAGEMENT BY JOHN J. MCGURK

QUIRK BOOKS
215 CHURCH STREET
PHILADELPHIA, PA 19106
QUIRKBOOKS.COM

10 9 8 7 6 5 4 3 2 1

TO LUCY AND INGRID

CONTENTS

THE TORNADO KILLER

They called it Tornado Day but none of us knew what it was about. Mom and Dad wouldn't tell us. Neither would our teachers. I never remembered having a Tornado Day before and neither did Cecilia or any of our friends or anyone at school.

All that week leading up to Tornado Day, Mom and Dad didn't let us eat much. I wasn't even supposed to feed Nikki. Breakfast was, like, one piece of dry toast. Lunch was a hard-boiled egg. Dinner was nothing. Late one night Cecilia and I were so starving we snuck some blueberry Pop-Tarts to eat in her bedroom, but they tasted wrong. I felt guilty somehow and ended up throwing most of mine out.

I fed Nikki anyway.

All that week we weren't allowed to watch TV. We couldn't even listen to the radio. Dad unplugged everything—the VCR, the stereo, the microwave, the alarm clocks, all the way down to the toaster and the coffee maker. He and Mom took the batteries out of the flashlights, the boom box, my Walkman, and even old toys Cecilia and I hadn't touched in years. They unscrewed the light bulbs and put them in a box along with the batteries. The refrigerator was cleared out.

Mom and Dad stopped talking to us. It was the same with everyone else's parents. Someone said it's what you had to do to prepare. Prepare for what?

Nobody would tell us.

A killer was coming to town.

That's what we heard from the other kids. We were all scared. We asked, is the killer coming for us?

The adults wouldn't say.

The day before Tornado Day all the stores closed early. We didn't have to go to school. The house was quiet except for the patter of rain and Nikki meowing in the kitchen.

It wasn't much of a holiday.

———

Growing up, when there were tornadoes, Mom and Dad and Cecilia and I would all run down to the basement with candles and food grabbed from the kitchen, and when the electricity blacked out we'd light the candles and set them all around the cold gray basement until it flared up like a cathedral. The candles pushed back the darkness and made it dance, colors multiplied, became richer and warmer. We'd hear the tornado raging outside, pounding at the doors and windows, shrieking like it was mad at us personally, but I felt safe, locked down in the concrete basement, cozy and cared for, but just dangerous enough for me to feel a thrill.

I liked the tornadoes because they forced Cecilia and Mom and Dad and me to hang out together. We played Monopoly and Clue, we listened to our little transistor radio, Dad told funny stories—I wanted more tornadoes, more thunderstorms, because I wanted us to be close like this all the time.

But when the lights flickered back on, when the all-clear siren sounded, Mom and Dad would get up from our game too quickly, "Finally!" they'd say; Cecilia, too, would bolt up the stairs, and then I would be left alone on the basement's concrete floor with the abandoned game, surrounded by old exercise equipment and Halloween costumes and yellowing paperbacks, feeling a little disappointed because it was finally my turn and nobody wanted to play anymore.

———

It was still dark outside when Mom woke us up. It was a raw April morning, black and wet. Drizzle and fog and low, heavy clouds.

It was four a.m. Way too early. The electricity was back on, but after a week without it the light from the hallway looked jarring on the carpet, it cut too bright and hard through the dark. I stayed under my blankets. I had secretly put new batteries in my Walkman and it was under my pillow and the headphones were still on my ears. I'd fallen asleep with it on again. Nikki was awake but she was just staring at me with her yellow slit eyes. I stroked her and she purred but I already knew it was going to be a bad morning. Rushing my shower while Mom banged on the door. The bathroom stinking of Cecilia's toxic hair spray. Everyone fighting.

A normal day.

Not normal, though. Usually, Dad was already off to work before any of us woke up—I never saw him in the morning, I'd just come into the kitchen and see his bowl of milky cereal dregs in the sink, which always depressed me for some reason. But this morning was wrong, everyone's schedules collided. Dad was clunking around in the kitchen, blinking at us like he was still half asleep. Mom usually slept in, but this morning she was up and ordering us around, looking frazzled in her ratty blue robe and huge curlers.

She'd laid out two dresses for Cecilia and me to wear to school for Tornado Day. I'd never seen these weird dresses before. They were old-fashioned flower-print things with puffy sleeves and lace trim. Like something a pioneer girl would wear in an old movie.

Cecilia slammed her bedroom door. There was no way she'd wear that crappy dress to school, she shouted at Mom. Everyone would make fun of her, she said.

I didn't want to wear mine either. The dresses smelled sour, like they'd been boxed up somewhere for a long time. But I put it on anyway. I cleaned out Nikki's litter box as Mom and Cecilia yelled at each other. I kind of hated myself for it, but whenever Cecilia fought with Mom, something in me wanted to be really good, to balance the family out.

Cecilia won. Mom said go ahead—fine, don't wear the dress! But you'll be sorry! Now I was the only one wearing an ugly, stale-smelling dress but the bus was already pulling past our house, way too early. There wasn't time for breakfast, not even to grab a bite on the way out. Cecilia and I had to run to the corner to catch up with the bus. We got on and its doors hissed shut.

The morning was still as dark as night.

———

It turned out everyone had dressed up for school that day. All the boys wore awkward suits and all the girls wore old-fashioned dresses.

Cecilia stuck out in her normal jeans and her pink sweater. She went to the girls' bathroom and stayed there. Mr. McAllister asked Mrs. Bindley to go in and get her. Some of the popular girls were snickering at Cecilia. I happened to be standing near them when Mrs. Bindley came out of the bathroom, pushing Cecilia along by her elbow.

As they walked past us Cecilia said to me, "You just keep on laughing."

We were going to meet the tornado killer.

What tornado killer? None of us knew about any tornado killer. That's how you know he's a good tornado killer, the teachers said— when's the last time you even saw a tornado? We had to admit, not since we were little. But, we said, you always heard about tornadoes in other towns! Exactly, the teachers said. But not here. Would we recognize the tornado killer? They said no, it's against the law for the tornado killer to actually come into town. He does his work outside city limits. But today is a special occasion, they said. Today is Tornado Day.

Some of the younger kids were scared. They begged their teachers, please, please, no, we don't want to meet the tornado killer.

Everyone meets the tornado killer, was the firm reply.

We went to our homerooms to wait for the tornado killer. Mrs. Bindley turned off the lights and told us to put our heads down.

Ridiculous. We were sophomores. I hadn't been told to put my head down since fifth grade. But there's only one big school building in town, so even though our high school was in a different part of the building than the elementary and junior high schools, the teachers still sometimes treated us like children.

The dim classroom smelled like wet coats, old shoes, and body odor. The radiator clanked. It felt like we were in some kind of trouble.

"*Tomato* killer," said someone.

Some kids snorted.

"Cuthbert Monks," said Mrs. Bindley, "another word and you've got yourself detention."

I glanced over at him. Even Cuthbert looked surprised at this. It wasn't like Mrs. Bindley to overreact. But it seemed like she hadn't slept much either. She kept touching her necklace, turning it over and over.

Cuthbert Monks smirked across the room at Ned Barlow but put his head back down. Cuthbert and Ned had been separated months ago, and Jimmy Switz, he'd been moved over to Mr. Pedrowski's homeroom entirely.

They were all obnoxious.

I kept my head down. My desk was near the window. I looked out at the dark, gray, wet day. Cecilia was in Mr. McAllister's room downstairs—she was a year ahead of me, a junior, but I was thinking maybe I could go down to her room, to let Cecilia know that I hadn't actually been laughing with those other girls, and maybe I could offer to switch clothes with her, or maybe we could even call Mom and have her bring in Cecilia's dress for her—and then I saw lights moving outside.

The lights got closer. Wobbling out of the dim woods, coming toward the school. I couldn't see very well through the watery windows, but there were about a dozen men, the white beams of their flashlights sweeping through the darkness, swinging and clashing. Like a little parade, though nobody seemed very happy to be in it. They were coming toward the school.

They were carrying a box.

———

I had so many friends when I was younger. Cecilia and I had been in a group with Lisa Stubenberger, Sadie Hughes, and Danielle Lund who roamed around town and hung out at each other's houses. There was an end-of-childhood in-between time that almost lasted into my freshman year, when we would goof around with dolls but also play truth or dare, when we'd discuss what boys were cute but also pretend to have superpowers. We had our fights but they never lasted. We'd all known each other since I was in kindergarten. We had always just hung out.

Then everyone became a little more individual. Lisa started dressing like she was a preppy and Sadie began dressing what Mrs. Bindley called "provocatively" and they competed over the same boys. Cecilia got into Archie's clique and began saying mean things about the others, and Danielle started working at her mom's restaurant all the time and treated us like we were immature. Everyone went their own older way. I was left behind.

It was around then that I found some trashy books at the library. I never checked them out, I just read them in the stacks, alone. In those paperbacks, people didn't act like anyone I knew, these people were more heartless, more brutal, but friskier and more alive, and it was while reading these books that I started to think that being an adult might be better than just being me. The adults in my own life were boring, but the adults in these books were hungry and fascinating and daring in ways that didn't feel allowed.

I didn't always get what was happening in those books. They always seemed like they were building to some huge revelation, some exhilarating emotion. But when the crucial time came, it seemed the story would skip that revelation, that emotion. I didn't understand what happened when the book was silent, the secret action that seemed to change everything.

The teachers made us get into lines and walk down to the gym. The bleachers were pulled out and there was a small stage with a lectern, like we were about to hear from some motivational speaker or somebody who was going to tell us stay off drugs.

Nobody told us anything about what was going to happen next. Kids whispered to each other, but then the teachers would shush them and give them hard looks. The fluorescent gym lights buzzed. It felt too early to be in the gym. Everything had the remote tingle of a dream.

I hadn't eaten since yesterday. I could feel my blood sugar running down, not exactly like I was going to faint, but I felt weak and kind of detached from what was happening around me. I just went along with it. The teachers separated the girls from the boys for some reason. Cuthbert Monks found Barlow and Switz in the crowd and they were shoving each other and some other kid until Mr. McAllister broke it up. But it wasn't as rowdy as usual. It felt like everyone was a little nervous.

People chattered with anticipation around me. I felt like I could go straight back to bed. In the muddle I got separated from the rest of my homeroom and I ended up having to sit with a bunch of freshman girls I didn't even know.

I spotted Cecilia up the bleachers. She was sitting with the same junior and senior girls who'd been snickering at her before. Now they were all together, whispering in a conspiratorial way. I tried to catch Cecilia's eye. One of the laughing girls saw me and murmured something. Cecilia said something out of the corner of her mouth and they all laughed so hard Mrs. Lubeck had to shush them.

Come on, Cecilia. I'm on your side.

＝＝

Sophomore year was a disaster so far, but Cecilia just said to me, "The reason you don't have friends is because you don't put yourself out there," and I was like, put myself out *where*? But maybe Cecilia was right. When I was younger I had liked being in plays . . . maybe I could be a drama club kid . . . In January there were auditions for the big spring musical. I went to try out.

I didn't know anyone at the auditions. I sat in the dark back of the auditorium. All the girls got up one by one to sing a song from the play, which was *Oklahoma!*. I realized too late that I should have prepared. Like, actually have read the play. One after another, girls got onstage and sang, "*I'm jest a girl who cain't say no! Kissin's my favorite food!*" as I sank deeper and deeper into my seat. I got up and left before they even called my name.

Cecilia was right, though. I see the drama kids messing around together all the time. They are always having a ball.

———

The men came into the gym.

I didn't recognize them. Even in a town as small as ours, you don't know exactly everyone. The men had put their flashlights away but they still had the box.

The strange box was as large as a refrigerator, wooden and old and complicated, with carvings and handles and rails, and you could see it had been painted over a hundred times, because where one color had flaked away there was another color under it, and another color under that, and the paint was bubbled and faded and cracked.

The men set the box down on the stage. All of them walked away except the tallest man. That man put a key in the box and unlocked it.

Then the tall man also walked away, very fast.

None of us said a word.

The lid of the box started to move.

Something was trying to come out.

I held my breath. Everyone in the bleachers around me did too.

Nobody knew what it would be.

But of all the things we had expected—of all the things any of us imagined might've come out of that box—we were all wrong.

It was a boy.

He climbed out. He blinked and squinted at us.

I thought, They had to be joking.

This was a tornado killer?

When Cecilia began going out with Archie, she got mean. Which made no sense, because Archie himself was so nice—like, too-good-to-be-true nice. Still, going out with Archie raised Cecilia to a new level of popularity, and it unleashed something merciless in her. For some reason she went scorched-earth against the rest of our old group, calling them boring sluts and stuck-up bitches. And there was enough awkward truth in what she said about Lisa and Sadie and Danielle that it was unforgivable.

As Cecilia's sister, I wasn't forgiven either. We were both frozen out. Unfair but whatever. Cecilia did let me hang out with her new friends in Archie's popular clique, even though they were all juniors and seniors. I was just a sophomore.

One year makes a difference, though.

So I spent that year mostly alone. I played video games at the bowling alley alone and my high scores stayed on the machines unchallenged. I swam in the quarry alone, even though people had drowned there, but plunging down to the bottom of the cold water felt so good. I went to the thrift store alone and I bought clothes that felt haunted, and books that felt forgotten, and knickknacks that seemed from another planet, and I couldn't understand why I was the only one from school who'd get stuff there.

I hung out in the library alone, reading those books I was too shy to check out. One of them had a girl who was a beautiful runaway. I kept going back to that book. The girl's parents were nice, her life was fine, but she ran away and the book was on her side. I liked that. This girl was innocent but kind of heartless. Cutting straight through her life, using and taking.

I thought about what I read. I did a lot of thinking back then. I liked being in my own mind.

When you're alone, everything feels more intense. But it also feels like you're only half experiencing it.

The tornado killer stood onstage.

He seemed like he was about my age.

Some of the kids were giggling and murmuring. Not just Cuthbert Monks and his buddies. Even the girls around me seemed skeptical.

I guess I'd expected a tornado killer to be older. Or bigger. Or maybe not even a person at all. But this boy could've been someone from school. A year older than me, tops. Maybe a few inches taller. His sandy-brown hair was mussed and his clothes seemed like they were from ten years ago, a purple and green plaid shirt that didn't fit him and gray corduroy pants that didn't match. He didn't look comfortable in them.

He looked like some shy animal that'd been flushed out of its hiding place.

I glanced at Mrs. Bindley. She was touching her necklace again. There was going to be trouble. I could feel it around me. Now that everyone realized that the tornado killer wasn't much different from us, that he was just some kid—they felt cheated.

The tornado killer must've sensed this. When he'd first stepped out of the box and looked up at us, it was as if he'd expected us to welcome him. Like clap or something.

Nobody had clapped.

Missing breakfast was catching up with me. I felt far away from everything in the gym, my stomach hollow. The tornado killer shuffled through some multicolored three-by-five note cards. He was peculiar looking. He had a wholesome but uneven face, almost kind of like an all-American midwestern boy, but then he'd turn his head and he looked raw, on the edge of ugly. Something not fully formed.

He glanced up at us, scanning us row by row. My head buzzed as if there was some tiny thin noise just outside my hearing. But the gym was quiet, everyone waiting for the tornado killer to begin. The tornado killer went back to his cards and fumbled one. It fell to the floor. He stared at it, for some reason not moving to pick it up.

Jimmy Switz said, "*Tomato* killer."

Such a stupid joke. Technically it wasn't even his. But it got a laugh. Not because it was funny. But because the crowd wanted to send the tornado killer a signal. They didn't like him. People were beginning to talk openly. The teachers were losing control.

I felt distant from all of it, a little light-headed from a week of eating almost nothing. The tornado killer shifted his weight and glanced over at his box, like he wanted to go back in. Yeah, he didn't want to be here, okay, I felt for him. I wouldn't want to be up there either.

The tornado killer took a breath. He looked at his cards again, then back up at us—whatever it was he'd come to say, okay, he was going to go ahead and say it—he leaned into the microphone and announced:

"I AM YOUR CHOSEN ONE!"

Silence.

Someone yelled, "Dork!"

"But what was I chosen *for*?" said the tornado killer, reading off his note cards. "What mysterious aristocracy do I belong to, that no man may look into my eyes without sublime terror?"

"Ass."

"For this reason: I am the tornado killer!"

"Ass!"

"But how did you know I was your, ah, uh, chosen one?" said the tornado killer, faltering a little. "Take your pick from the multitude of signs and wonders that attended my birth! There was, of course, the matter of my unsettlingly beautiful *eyes*."

What the?

"Or my uncanny ability—"

"—to be an ass," said Cuthbert Monks.

Snickering. The tornado killer coughed stiffly, read on:

"Or my uncanny ability," said the tornado killer, staring at an index card. "My uncanny ability—"

"I have the uncanny ability to finish a sentence," remarked Cuthbert Monks.

More laughter.

"My uncanny ability," pushed on the tornado killer, "my uncanny ability to soothe the winds—or whip them into a fury—ever since I was a small child—simply by the, the sound of my voice, the twitch of my, uh, my eyes—"

Somebody threw a pencil at the tornado killer. It bounced across the stage, past the lectern. He acted like he didn't notice. It'd taken only a minute for the tornado killer to turn everyone against him. He didn't seem to get that. My heart kind of went out to him. He obviously didn't want to make this speech.

Still, he was pushing through it. He put his hand in his chaotic hair and slowly raked through it, his hand remaining on the back of his neck as he stared down at the card. Then he smiled a little, as though he knew this was ridiculous.

"For many years I have dwelled alongside you," read the tornado killer. "With these legs I have walked the land around this town, circling you. With these eyes I have watched over this town, contemplating you. With these hands I have warded tornadoes away from this town, protecting you. And now today, at last, I am allowed to come among you, and meet you face to face."

He looked up from his cards.

"*I am the tornado killer.*"

Most everyone had stopped listening. It didn't help that up until now, the tornado killer read these words without conviction. His eyes hunted through the crowd again, as though looking for somebody in particular. A wobbly feeling crept up from my stomach. Around me people were just blatantly talking. Tornado killer? I couldn't imagine this kid even beating up another boy, much less killing a tornado, whatever that meant. Maybe, a girl near me was saying, this was all some kind of comedy thing? But the joke didn't make sense.

"The day that I was birthed into the world," the tornado killer went on, gaining steam, "my raw powers instinctively grappled with the radio waves that flow and pulse around us all, bending them to make every radio in town broadcast my newborn cries. Purely by unconscious ability, I reached into the heavens and pulled down hailstones as large as chicken eggs, smashing windows and denting roofs. And thus I put it to you all: if my powers can even shape your airwaves, if my powers can even dominate your unruly skies, what might I do to a tornado? *What might I do?*"

"You might shut up?" said Tina Molloy, loud enough for the tornado killer to hear but not so loud the teachers could pinpoint who'd said it.

But the tornado killer was going for broke now. Maybe he was nearing the end of his weird speech and just wanted to get it over with.

But something felt wrong, my heart was racing, why?

"Only the pure can kill a tornado," the tornado killer declared. "For this reason I must remain outside city limits. For this reason I must live alone. For this reason I have not walked among you, not until this sacred day. Although I have watched all of you from afar."

He looked up at us again, his eyes scanning the crowd again.

Awkward silence.

"Wait a second," shouted Cuthbert Monks.

"Pipe down," said Mr. McAllister.

"No, no," said the tornado killer, as if relieved. "By all means, I welcome some Q and A."

"What do you mean, *watched* us?" said Cuthbert Monks. "Like spying? You've been peeking into windows and stuff?"

The tornado killer looked down at the lectern.

"I have watched all of you," said the tornado killer softly. "Even you. I have watched you ever since you were a small boy."

Cuthbert Monks crowed with delight.

"Okay dude," he said. "Gay."

A lot of kids laughed.

The tornado killer looked up, and stared at Cuthbert Monks.

The laughter died in everyone's throats.

The tornado killer hadn't truly looked at us before. Not like this. Not with these eyes: one a deep glittering green, the other a fierce and furious blue. It was like the eyes of two different murderers had been stuck in the head of one boy, almost glowing, throbbing as if at any moment they would leap out in two different directions. They were hypnotizing. They were terrifying. But nobody could look away.

The tornado killer stared at Cuthbert Monks with his nightmare eyes for a long time.

Then he said:

"If you know of a better way for me to understand the town I have protected ever since I was six years old—killing tornadoes for the sake of you and everyone you know on essentially a daily basis—then by all means, I'd love to hear about it."

Cuthbert Monks and the tornado killer stood, eyes locked.

An agonizing second passed.

"Sportsman, Cuthbert?"

It took me a moment to register that the tornado killer had used Cuthbert Monks's name. How did the tornado killer know his name?

Who *was* this kid?

"What?" said Cuthbert.

"I asked you, Cuthbert Monks: *are you a sportsman?*"

Cuthbert Monks didn't answer.

"Captain of the wrestling team," yelled Jimmy Switz. "He's all-state."

The tornado killer didn't acknowledge Jimmy.

Another second ticked by.

"I wonder," said the tornado killer, "I wonder what *sport* you were playing at the quarry, with your friend Jimmy Switz over there, on June seventeenth last year."

An off-balance moment. What the tornado killer said was so

specific and yet so vague. But seeing how Cuthbert's face changed, it was damning. Still, I didn't understand why Cuthbert did what he did next—and trust me, I don't want to know what Cuthbert and Jimmy were up to at the quarry last summer—but at that moment, several things happened.

Cuthbert Monks rushed the stage.

The tornado killer looked up.

His eyes fell upon me.

Then locked on me. Like he recognized me.

The bottom dropped out of my stomach.

The electricity went out. The gym was plunged into darkness.

And then we heard the rising, grinding wail of the storm alarm—the siren that meant a tornado was near.

<hr>

Darkness, confusion, everyone shouting, pushing—

Chaos at first, all of us scrambling to get off the bleachers in the pitch black. I was bumped and shoved. Somewhere in the darkness Mrs. Bindley and Mr. McAllister were saying things but I couldn't understand what, I couldn't understand anything over the yells echoing throughout the gym, I think they were trying to calm us down but there was only so much they could do in the dark.

"It's all right," Mr. McAllister called out over the noise. "The tornado killer is here. Right now this school is actually the safest place in town."

But Mr. McAllister's voice sounded flattened and far away, somehow wrong. I felt wrong. When the tornado killer looked right at me it scrambled something in me. Like his eyes went into me the wrong way.

I didn't know where the tornado killer was now. I didn't know where anyone was. It was an unsettled darkness, some littler kids were crying and teachers were trying to soothe them but everything felt jumpy, intense. Some kids were excited, the way people get excited by any disruption to school. I kept bumping into others in the darkness and my body felt like it was full of that thin noise just on the edge of hearing, a noise about to break through. Nothing electric seemed to function: the microphone had cut out, the emergency lights didn't switch on, the men's flashlights apparently didn't work anymore either. I heard the wind whipping around outside, the clunking and rattling of things getting tossed around, a mounting noise like a jet engine howling, and the wailing alarms. I was looking for Cecilia, looking for someone I knew, but I couldn't find anyone. I stumbled over a book bag. All the students in the school were packed in the gym, from kindergarteners up to seniors, and I heard Archie's voice nearby, he was comforting some younger kids, being jokey with them ("Wait, *what* time is it? Almost six? Oh man! Yeah, I'm usually not even awake at six either! What do you like for breakfast? Raisin Bran? Aw, me too!") and that was classic Archie, being helpful without being prissy about it, he was just naturally decent, why was he so into Cecilia, who frankly could be a weird bitch sometimes? Kids sat and whispered in little groups, some boys were sneaking around and causing trouble, and Jessica Hauser and Bobby O'Brien were totally making out under the bleachers. I felt knocked out of place, whatever my place was.

I heard a muffled sound nearby.

Cuthbert Monks said, "Lock this fucking freak up."

"Yessir, we're safe as houses," declared Mr. McAllister over the alarms. "Isn't that right, tornado killer? . . . Eh, tornado killer?"

I heard what sounded like the tornado killer, not far from me in the darkness. A strangled shout. The tornado killer—

I stumbled toward where I thought the sound was coming from. There was nobody there.

Then I heard maybe him behind me, grunting and struggling, like he was being dragged away.

"Probably already out there right now, wrestling those tornadoes." Mr. McAllister chuckled nervously. "Okay, settle down, guys."

I shoved through the crowd, trying to find the tornado killer, trying to find Cuthbert Monks—I thought I heard the tornado killer try to call for help again, then he was silenced, it seemed they were headed for the stairwell but now I was pushing the wrong way through everyone, bodies closed in around me, I couldn't get at him and I heard the tornado killer struggle and shout, and then a door slammed and I couldn't hear him anymore, I didn't know where I was either, I was blundering through some elementary schoolers, I plowed into a little boy by accident, he started crying, I tried to comfort him but I was also trying to get a teacher's attention, to tell them the tornado killer wasn't out there fighting tornadoes, that Cuthbert Monks had him for some reason, he was taking him somewhere, to lock him up and there was a mounting rushing sound in the darkness all around me, a buzzing like something huge and invisible swooping in, I tried to find Mrs. Bindley or Mr. McAllister or any teacher, I unexpectedly found Cecilia, I grabbed her—

"What? What?" said Cecilia.

Then the tornado hit, I felt myself lifted up on pure air, and then we were all blown out of the gym like we were made of paper.

* * *

I was blasted out into the main hallway, books and papers and desks and a kid flew past me, hurtling down the corridor, locker doors

were torn from their hinges, walls collapsing, windows cracked and
shattered and bled down the hall in glittering streams, a flying chair
clipped the side of my head and I flew out of the school and up into
the sky as though I'd been shot out of a gun.

I tumbled through the churning air. The world came at me in
flashes. I blacked out and then I was flopped out on the grass, on
the playground behind the school, staring up at the monstrous
spinning tornado.

There were others sprawled in the field all around me. I didn't
know if they were alive or dead. The roar of the tornado was
deafening. My head throbbed from where the chair hit me. I was
surrounded by floating papers and fluttering scraps of books and
heaps of desks, staring at our school and how the tornado was
already relentlessly taking it apart, whipping around faster and
faster, a tremendous howling blur, ripping the roof into ribbons
that went flying into the air, strips of roof fluttering up like tentacles
reaching to the sky and waving around—then the entire roof lifted
off the school, the school just shrugged it off like it didn't need
a roof anyway, and then the tornado was rabidly feeding on the
school, tearing off bricks, slurping out the plumbing, chewing the
girders, the entire building getting bent, twisted, liquefied, gurgled,
and spit into the sky.

I was going to die. We were all going to die together. We were
too close to this uncontrollable killing thing. The tornado whipped
around with vicious energy, chewing through the wreckage, tearing
apart the jumbled tables and cracked chalkboards, but almost
with a kind of furious intent, like it was hunting for a retainer it'd
accidentally thrown away. I lay among the shredded book reports
and wrecked dioramas, my head ringing, too terrified to move.

Our school was destroyed.

Except for one thing.

A stairwell of the school still remained. Plus a little bit of the third floor hallway jutting out of it, where the janitor's closet was. But there was no third floor anymore, no second floor, no school—just the stairwell's shell of bricks and girders supporting the janitor's closet, three stories up in the air, alone.

I saw the door rattling.

Someone was in there.

Lightning shimmered in the dark green sky around us. Everything felt unreal. I tried to scramble up, to run away—

The tornado churned forward and engulfed the stairwell and the janitor's closet, swirling around it as though ravenous.

It ripped the door off.

The tornado killer was inside the closet, crumpled against the wall. His face was bloody. He held up a trembling hand as if to say: please, no more.

The spindly mortar and metal structure that held up the closet collapsed. The tornado killer fell out.

He dropped two stories and hit the ground.

His body lay in the grass. Not moving.

The tornado blasted toward him.

The ringing in my ears had receded enough that I could hear the little kids crying and the teachers shouting. The tornado killer was about to get shredded. Someone should've helped him. Nobody did. I stared at the tornado killer. This boy was all there was between us and this monstrous spinning funnel roaring out of the darkness. The tornado killer stirred. Other kids looked away. As unpopular as he had made himself, nobody wanted to see what they all knew would happen next. What would happen to all of us.

We were all wrong.

The tornado killer raised his head from the dirt.

Shakily, he lifted his left hand.

The air *changed*.

The tornado staggered back—still swirling, but woozily swaying, dipping back and forth—and the tornado killer leaped up. Keeping his left hand raised, he sliced his right hand through the air.

The tornado *reeled!*

I felt the air change, prickly and hissing. The tornado killer advanced on the tornado, waving, pointing, and punching. His face was cruel and his eyes shone.

The tornado wobbled, staggered, *screamed!*

I choked, I couldn't breathe, my body felt as if it was floating.

The tornado killer then raised both hands—gathering up the whirling tornado into a frenzied, narrowing cone—he stretched it taller, narrower—thinner—like it was a string of taffy—thinner—a long, thin, frantically spinning column—the tornado killer drew his hands closer together—the column tightened, spun faster—faster—closer—the tornado was a wildly wobbling, infinitely lengthened thread—the tornado killer clapped—

POP

And there was nothing left of the tornado but the stirring of grass at our feet.

Silence.

The tornado killer stared at all of us with brutal eyes. I was afraid he would look at me again.

He didn't.

"An easy one," he said.

Then the tornado killer limped away.

Nobody followed him.

But I wanted to.

THE GIRL WITH THE CAT AND THE KNIFE

I grew up here, in the middle of what you'd call nowhere. There isn't really any other town for miles, just the highway and cornfields and midwestern plains. Sometimes, when I'd see our one bus station out near the edge of town, I'd think about what would happen if I got on a random bus and left.

Not tell anyone. Nothing was stopping me.

I'd never been out of town. Not even for vacation. It's not like I hated home, though. I didn't hate my family. I didn't hate my life.

But waking up in the middle of the night, sweating, why did I feel so panicked, short of breath, I didn't know why, what was wrong with me?

Then I met the tornado killer.

———

There was a radio station I listened to late at night.

It was from a city a hundred miles away. The DJ called himself Electrifier. He had a low purring voice and the music he played was alien, intense, unlike any music anybody around here listened to. Sometimes the music felt frightening, I didn't know why. Or it felt goofy but I didn't get the joke. Often nobody sang in these songs, or if they sang it was in a foreign language, or the voices were samples from movies, and the music sounded like a machine pulsing and the repetition put me in an expanding trance, especially late at night, it made my brain open up and feel different. The way Electrifier talked between songs wasn't how most DJs talked, he spoke in shadowy fragments about things I didn't understand but it was soothing and mysterious, like there was a secret party in the city happening somewhere without me, but maybe I'd find out about that party if I went to the city, and when I listened to Electrifier's show I imagined I was in the city, I'd close my eyes and think about walking down the city streets at night, different lights blazing all around me, strangers passing me, and maybe I would catch some stranger's eye and we'd feel each other's weirdness for a moment and then we'd move on, and the late-night radio felt like that to me, anonymous and risky and intimate.

Nobody at school liked that kind of music. I didn't like their music either. They wanted slow songs about feelings that they could cry to while they clung to each other at dances.

I wanted something clean and robotic, empty and chilly but full of power, not for my brain to listen to but my body to move to, that I could dance alone to in a dark room somewhere, or a room full of other people dancing alone but watching each other. I thought of that bus station, of getting on one of those buses and running away to that exhilarating somewhere, as I was dancing alone in my room, feeling a little stupid, but it also felt important, like I was practicing.

Ever since Cecilia's and my group broke up I biked around town alone, listening to Electrifier shows I'd taped off the radio over Dad's cassettes of crappy classic rock. He never listened to those tapes anymore anyway. Sometimes where I started and stopped recording there'd be a gasp of Dad's music, or I'd hear it echoing faintly underneath.

There was one song that Electrifier played a few times that I didn't exactly like, but I couldn't stop listening to. The name of the song was a girl's name. A man sang it and the words seemed to be about something wild and thrilling, but he sang them in the flattest way, weary and jaded. I listened to that song again and again.

I wore those tapes down to nothing, trying to figure the songs out.

I listened to Electrifier on my Walkman while I biked around the forest trails. I liked being in the woods, not just because of the trees and ponds and quiet calm, but because I saw that other people came into these woods at night. I'd see like a rotten old mattress with bottles and wrappers around it, some dirty clothes left behind, and I wondered who would come here.

I broke into abandoned houses. There were isolated empty houses from when more people used to live around here. I wondered about those broken-down houses because I've never seen anyone move out of town. Or move into town, for that matter. Sometimes I'd find old clothes and books in those houses, or there would be antique ovens and refrigerators, and all of it would be overgrown with weeds and crawling with insects.

I took stuff from those houses. A glass doorknob like fancy crystal. A red leather photo album with faded pictures of some generation-ago family. A little pearl-handled knife I began to carry around.

I figured out how to get into the storm drains. I climbed to the top of the water tower. I didn't know what I was looking for, but I liked the feeling of looking.

I had a private mystery I was trying to solve.

Sometimes, in little hidden places around town, I would see a strange symbol. Once I discovered the symbol, I began to notice it in other places, or different versions of it. I'd happen upon it unexpectedly: it would be carved into a tree, or written in the margin of a textbook, or spray-painted under a bridge, and although there were variations, there were always four parts that looked like a diagram of a flower, or the features of an alien face, or a sketch of some biological system, or something obscene—a kind of big rounded figure above, a smaller similar rounded figure with something inside it below, and, coming out of them on the sides, two arcing pipes of unequal length, both ending with a kind of knob or cap or circle.

Here are some of the symbols I found around town that I copied into my notebook:

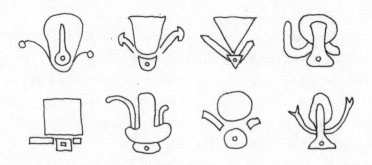

Some seemed like they'd been graffitied recently, or just a few years ago. Others were carvings in wood or stone that looked like they could've been from before I was born.

I didn't talk about this with anyone. I didn't want anybody else to know about it. I wanted it to be a private puzzle only I was invited to understand. I started tagging places with my own version of the symbol that I'd designed. I'd draw it next to others' symbols, or in whatever out-of-the-way place I felt needed it. This was my symbol:

I'd carve it with my pearl-handled knife. As if to tell whoever was putting up these symbols: This is my contribution. I know about this, too. I'm part of your club.

But I didn't know what it was.

I wasn't part of any club.

There was an abandoned convenience store out at the edge of town. It still had its cash register and a broken counter and the aisles were empty except for some old magazines lying around, a few dusty dented cans, collapsed racks, empty bottles from the kids who drank here at night, and a tree growing right up out of the side, busting through the roof. There were animals living in the basement, or I thought there were, because sometimes I heard noises coming from down there. But I never went into that basement.

Until a year ago. I was biking past the abandoned store at dusk when I heard a racket coming from inside. A horrible yowling and shrieking.

A shape flashed out of the store, streaking away into the woods. Then the store was silent.

I didn't want to go in. But something drew me toward it. I ended up going in, I couldn't help it, I just wanted to see what had happened. Inside, the store looked pretty much like I remembered it did during the day, only darker, more shadows. I had never ventured in there so late before. I peeked down the basement stairs.

I heard a soft mewling.

I wished it wasn't so dark. I crept down the stairs anyway, testing each one with my weight in case they were rotten, until I came to the bottom and looked around the dim basement.

Something awful had happened here.

The concrete walls and dirt floors were splattered with guts like a couple of animals had exploded. Blood on the walls. Scraps of fur strewn all around the floor. Tiny organs unraveled and torn. Awful smell.

Something had come in here and killed everything.

I saw a dead mother cat and her litter of dead kittens. One surviving kitten was hiding in a narrow space under a collapsed cabinet, her yellow eyes blinking at me.

I got close and held out my hand. The kitten shied away. I spoke softly, I made the kind of sounds I thought a kitten would like. The kitten just stared. At one point it kind of crept forward, but when I moved my hand slightly toward it, it drew back into its space.

We did this for a long time.

The smell of dead animal all around me was turning my stomach. And it was really getting dark now. So I left the kitten in its hiding place, and went back up the stairs, and got onto my bike.

I heard the little mewling again.

The kitten had followed me out.

After a minute it let me pick it up. I put it in my bike basket and took her home. Mom and Cecilia didn't like the idea of having a cat. Dad didn't say much, but the next day he took me to the vet and the kitten got her shots and when the vet asked me her name, I named her after that song Electrifier always played that I never quite understood.

——————

I had Nikki and I loved Nikki, but that was it. After our group of friends broke up, I didn't have anyone else to hang out with. I didn't understand what I was doing wrong, why people occasionally made comments about how I dressed, I had always dressed like this. I didn't understand why I got teased about my hair sometimes, I hadn't thought of my hair being any other way, it was just my hair.

But I did get it. I had to pick a specific style. I had to start being intentional. Okay, was I an athlete? Uh, no. A preppy? I didn't look like one and I couldn't afford the clothes. A skater? Please. A burnout, a princess, a punk, an art freak? Nothing worked. And I didn't understand why, whenever people did get into a particular group, they began to laugh at things that clearly weren't funny, why they got excited by things that obviously were boring.

I couldn't figure out where I fit in. Maybe I had never fit in and I just hadn't noticed it until recently. If I stayed in this town much longer, I thought, maybe I wouldn't even fit in with myself.

I wanted out.

I wanted out of our house. Cecilia and I used to have friends over, until our house began to feel dingy compared to their houses. When Dad's tire shop went out of business everything started to slip. The broken furniture that Dad half-assedly tried to repair, then banished to the basement. The stained carpet that never got cleaned or replaced. Mom and Dad used to talk about college, but even though it was already the spring of Cecilia's junior year, they weren't mentioning it so much anymore. Neither was Cecilia.

I wanted out.

Some small part of me said: why not run away?

It would be my own adventure, I thought. The world owed me an adventure. I could even run away for just one summer and come back, if I wanted. That way I wouldn't even miss school.

It was a stupid idea. Even still, I saved my allowance, hiding the money in a shoebox in my closet, adding to it little by little. Like it was a game to see if I could really save enough for a bus ticket to the city. But the more money piled up in my shoebox, the more real running away felt. My money was getting bigger, stronger. My money had weight. My money was ready to do its job. Where are your guts? said my money.

Maybe I did hate this town. Maybe I did hate my life.

That was the summer I had planned to run away.

But that was the summer of the tornado killer.

I should've run.

⚬

The night of Tornado Day there was supposed to be a small party at Archie's house.

This party had been planned for a while, actually, just a little dinner thing for Archie and Cecilia and their little group. Archie's family was moving to Canada in a few weeks so I guessed we'd never see him again. It was supposed to be a kind of going-away party, but it also signaled the end of the popular clique Cecilia had burned her bridges getting into.

But after the tornado destroyed the school, Archie's party transformed into something bigger. Because school was more than out—school was erased. Summer vacation was already here, even though it was only April. Everyone was shocked and freaked out by what had happened, there had been a lot of tears and emotion, and now people wanted to get together and talk about it, they needed to be together, to see each other. Somewhere along the line Archie or his parents changed the terms of the party. Now it was a big school's-out bash and everyone was invited.

It was months ago when Archie had first told Cecilia he was moving to Canada. Cecilia had made a big crying scene about it. The two of them had been going out for almost a year, ever since last summer. But even though Cecilia enjoyed the popularity she gained from being with Archie, I sensed she was bored of him. I think she was just impatient for him to move already. Maybe they were both only acting the parts of their stale relationship, waiting for the move to do the work of breaking up for them.

It was already dark when Cecilia and I went to the garage to get our bikes to ride over to Archie's house for the party, and Cecilia looked at me and said, "No. Please. You're not bringing that cat to the party."

I already had Nikki in my bike basket. "Why not?"

"Because people don't bring their cats to parties, do I really have to explain this?" Cecilia gave me one of her looks. "Especially since that thing still has its claws. It'll slash up somebody's face."

"It's cruel to declaw a cat."

"We all get it, you're the freak who bikes everywhere with headphones on and a cat in your basket. You've established that fascinating persona. Take tonight off."

I just stood there.

"Okay, look." Cecilia exhaled. "Do you really want everyone at the party to be touching Nikki? Asking to pet her and whatever?"

"Fine, fine." I put Nikki in the breezeway behind the garage. I didn't like to do it, though. Neither did Nikki. As soon as the screen door tapped shut, she immediately began meowing.

"She'll miss me," I said.

"She'll stop crying as soon as you leave," said Cecilia. "Nikki is a master manipulator."

"Sure."

"You don't even know, that kitten has levels," said Cecilia. "Wheels within wheels on that kitten."

"And people say I'm the weird one."

"And ditch those headphones too, okay? You can go a night without your beep-boop music."

"You've never even listened to my music."

"God, I've tried," said Cecilia. "It sounds like porn music for computers."

In her freshman year Cecilia had figured out, observing the upperclassmen, that she could get more social power if her jokes were dirtier. She'd say crass stuff to me but then later on, when she was with the group, she'd toss off polished versions of the same lines, as though she'd just come up with them.

"Oh, does it?" I said.

"Yeah, like computers literally getting each other off. Rubbing modems on their floppies."

"Gross," I said. "Also, dumb."

"Your music is like listening to a disk drive jack off," said Cecilia, enjoying herself. "Spraying zeroes and ones everywhere."

"There's a joystick joke somewhere and you're passing it up."

"So funny. Let's go."

Cecilia's problem was that she was secretly too wholesome to do those kinds of jokes right. They didn't come off as dirty, just strange. Cecilia didn't want to be strange, she wanted to be popular, and in the end she was good at shaving off her awkward edges, she was good enough at pretending.

‡

So Cecilia and I biked over to Archie's.

It was a beautiful night, it was warm and the dark felt welcoming, you could smell and feel it all around you, wind blowing through the trees, spring sliding into summer, and my bike was flying through it, shooting me forward on pure air. The wind smelled like fresh-cut grass, rushing water, deepening night. I saw Archie's house just ahead, alone at the top of a hill, its windows throwing out warm yellow squares of light.

I was still buzzing from everything that had happened today. A tornado had destroyed my school. Then I had watched as a strange boy somehow killed the tornado. It already felt like a dream. The rest of the day had been a flurry of panicked parents and reporters trying to interview us and intense phone calls and just seeing each other walking around the neighborhood and saying "Could you believe that?" and "So you're going to Archie's, right?" and now summer vacation was suddenly here, astonished at itself, months early, and I felt like anything could happen—Archie's house might blink its dozens of luminous window-eyes, unfold giant wings, and flap up into the sky. I had fresh skin, new eyes, new ears. I was ready.

I was thinking about the tornado killer.

The way he had looked at me, the moment before the lights went out.

Maybe I'd imagined it. I didn't know how it made me feel. It wasn't a pleasant feeling. In fact it didn't make me feel good at all. The way the tornado killer had looked at me didn't fit into the world I knew, like how I felt when I read those library books I didn't understand, or didn't want to understand.

Cecilia said the tornado killer was "cute."

Not the word I'd use.

Cecilia's bike darted in front of me, she cut me off with a whoop and I pumped the pedals to catch up and then we were racing, weaving back and forth, crisscrossing, leaning on our handlebars, laughing. Cecilia pulled ahead, her hair flying out behind like streamers, and we were slicing between cars, whirling down the street, just feeling happy, like we were before she'd started up with Archie.

I hadn't been to Archie's house for months.

There was a reason.

———

I had always known about Archie's house, but I hadn't actually been inside it until this past year. I had been curious about it since I was a kid, though, since his house was so much older and bigger and more ornate than every other house in town. Obviously we had trick-or-treated at it, and Archie's family was famous in town for going all out at Halloween, like putting up over-the-top decorations, and one year even making it so you had to go through a kind of elaborate funhouse tunnel to get to their doorway. But I had never gone inside until Cecilia began going out with Archie. Even though Cecilia put me down, she also looked out for me, in her big-sister way, and maybe to make up for causing me to lose my friends, she eased me into Archie's clique, like I was somebody, or a somebody-in-training.

Until then Archie's house had been like school dances, something mysterious I only observed from a distance. Cecilia went to every school dance, I never went. I didn't have anything against dances in principle, though, and when I once went along with Mom to pick Cecilia up from her winter formal, I saw from our car that her dance was completely different than the awkward eighth-grade dances I

despised—it was at a rented hall, not our nasty cafeteria, and from
the car I saw silhouettes of people coming out of the colored lights
and I heard the distant booming music and the buzz of laughter and
talking, and I thought, okay, sure, this seems glamorous, maybe I
want to experience it, and maybe being in Archie's group would be
like that, and give me a way in to that world, even though I knew
the others in Archie's group didn't care about me. That was fine. I
could handle being on the edges of things.

And I loved Archie's house.

Archie's house was separate from the neighborhoods where
everyone else lived, an elaborate mansion so big and sprawling
that parts of it went unheated in the winter, a hundred rambling
haunted-feeling rooms, many of them filled with stuff it seemed no
one had touched in years.

Last summer, when Archie and Cecilia first started going out,
their clique hung out at Archie's almost every day, with me kind
of tagging along, and the scene was clean-cut in a typically Archie
way, all of us playing casual games of softball in his huge backyard,
and eating apples from his orchard, and watching horror movies
late into the night, sleeping over in the maze of attics. Sometimes
the boys and girls secretly paired off to make out, often in different
combinations, like they were all just sampling each other. But
nobody gave me an inviting eye. No hand touched my leg. I kept
watching TV and pretended not to notice.

I remember last Fourth of July we shot fireworks off Archie's
roof, special fireworks his dad had bought out of town, fiery green
and purple birds that flapped and smoked and shrieked, six-foot-
tall robots with flaming eyes that marched in circles and fell apart
into sparkling jumbles of melting arms and legs, scarlet rockets that
screamed off into the sky and burst so bright and spread across the

stars so lush and red that when I looked up, it was as though the whole universe had bloomed into a gigantic rose for me, bleeding across the sky and spreading beyond my eyes, and even though I really didn't belong at Archie's, or with this group, nevertheless I felt lucky, at that moment I was right where I wanted to be, alone in the giddy gorgeous center of the universe.

Cecilia and I rolled our bikes up Archie's driveway to the porch. It was already kind of dark. Cecilia rang the doorbell. We could hear shouts and laughter from inside and then Archie's mother opened the door.

Archie's mother stared at us in her broken way, like she wasn't really seeing us. As though she hadn't actually expected anyone to be there. Always a little smaller than I remembered her. She didn't move from the doorway at first, just gazing past us, gray and quiet.

I never understood why Archie's dad had married her. Archie's dad used to run an engineering company but now that he was retired, he mostly puttered in his barn, building and fixing stuff, a big man with a big mustache, and we all liked him. Sometimes I secretly wished *he* was my father, instead of my own dad, which was unfair but I couldn't help it. Archie's family was just kind of perfect, not in that they acted like they were better than you, but you just felt lucky to be around them, you wanted to be them.

Except for his mother. Nobody in their right mind would want to be her—a nervous, mousy lady with a vaguely pious air, scolding us over things we didn't understand, but then other times overly friendly and icky sweet. I felt awkward around her. So did Cecilia and I think everyone else, but nobody said anything. We kind of passed over the topic of Archie's mother in silence, to be polite.

We didn't really see Archie's mother that much, actually. She only appeared every once in a while, in the background of a party or a sleepover, hovering around in her meek way and making puzzling comments. The snacks she made always tasted sour and odd. Luckily Archie's dad did most of the cooking, and while we helped him out in the kitchen chopping up vegetables and laughing and listening to music, Archie's mother would retreat into the creepier parts of the house and quietly lock herself away.

Those parts of the house weren't explicitly off-limits. But Archie never took us down those dustier, less-frequented hallways, and we hesitated to pry because it felt like bad manners. Sometimes, though, by accident, I'd come upon certain locked rooms. I'd try the doorknob, I'd knock on the door, and there'd be silence for a moment, and then Archie's mom's voice would come, faintly: "I'm in here . . ." like she was in the bathroom. But I don't think it was a bathroom. Those rooms always seemed to be locked, even when nobody was inside them.

The last time I was at Archie's was New Year's Eve, four months ago, just a few weeks before Archie told us he was moving to Canada. The party was over, we had rung in the new year, auld lang syne and everything, and we were all sleeping over and Cecilia and I had our own room, sharing a bed, when late in the night Cecilia touched my shoulder and whispered to me, "One of those locked rooms is open. I want to go see."

I was still half asleep. I could hardly see Cecilia in the dark.

"It's so weird, my heart's going so fast—I can't sleep!" She grabbed my hand. The house was cold but she was sweating. I pulled my hand away. Cecilia's eyes flashed in the darkness.

She let me go, smiling strangely.

We slid out of bed and crept down the long, high-ceilinged hallways of Archie's house. It was freezing cold, and outside the windows we could see the snow flying silently, speeding past the house and spinning in the wind, as if the snowflakes were tiny stars and the house was airtight and flying through space. The snow piled up outside against the walls, huge drifts of dead stars glowing blue-white by the lights, fading into the vast darkness.

"This way," whispered Cecilia.

We turned and went down a long hallway. Then another. Cecilia clutched my hand hard. I didn't get why Cecilia was doing this, usually I was the one who wanted to snoop around Archie's house, I'd actually discovered a few secret doors on my own, some weird rooms, I'd even seen that strange symbol engraved here and there, in a cabinet or bedpost, and one time I carved my own secret symbol kind of in response, not where anyone would ever see it but Cecilia caught me and said what the hell are you carving, don't do that, it'd be so embarrassing if they knew what you were doing, I'd just die—but this time poking around was her idea, not mine, she had this maniacal witchlike look, it was her urging me on, and Cecilia and I ran and turned and whispered and my body pounded with excitement and then she pointed at the end of a long hallway.

"There."

A jeweled line of light cut across the floor through a cracked-open door at the end of the hallway. I'd never been to this particular hallway before. I couldn't see what was in the room, but that little crack was blazing, like there were galaxies of light inside, dazzling, flashing, shimmering gold, rubies, emeralds—too many colors, too many lights, too much fire and glitter.

A strange, low voice spoke.

I'd never heard a voice like that before.

I turned to Cecilia. She stared ahead, her eyes hot and hard. As if there was something behind that door that she wanted badly.

We crept closer to the door.

Smoke curled outside the crack, hanging in the hallway, smelling sweet and heavy, stinging my eyes.

We edged closer.

There were two voices in the room. The first was Archie's mother's voice.

The other was that other strange, low voice.

Cecilia froze.

I tugged her hand. Cecilia didn't move. She was just staring ahead, at that door. Her face changed, as though she wished we hadn't come. Paralyzed, like something terrible was about to happen. But we'd come this far. I wanted to know. I pulled her forward.

We peeked through.

Two women were there. They looked at us as though they'd been waiting for us. Their stares were hard and empty.

One of them was Archie's mother. She looked severe and composed, nothing at all like the anxious old housewife she usually was.

The other woman was out of a nightmare. She was huge—not fat but out of proportion, her neck and arms and legs too long and thick, even her head swollen to over twice the size of any other woman's head, draped and wrapped in colored robes and sashes like the queen of some faraway country, with a red headscarf and gold jewelry dripping with green and blue gems so pleasingly smooth and polished that I wanted to put them in my mouth. She held a curved knife with a jeweled hilt and her brown eyes were unblinking and both of her enormous breasts were exposed, slicked up with shiny oil, so monstrous I couldn't stop staring, and even though I had never seen this woman before, I knew that she lived right here in town, and that she always had.

There was faint, solemn music playing. The room was packed with candles and lights and shelves of little statues and jewelry and gold and brass boxes and jars. The nasty-sweet incense hit me with an immediate headache. There was something scary and cramped and somehow *in bad taste* about the dizzying complicatedness of the tiny room; but a queasy feeling, that the universe itself might somehow really secretly be in bad taste, made me want to enter the room and sit down at the feet of these two women; I took a small step toward them, and felt a powerful, dirty thrill.

Cecilia pulled me away, and then we were running down the hallway, running away from the suffocating room, running out through the cold lonely hallways and vast wide-open ballrooms and disused parlors, out to where everything felt bigger and freer and fresher and colder and I had a rushing, emptying feeling, like escaping from a tiny hot vicious universe made just for me into a whole world made for nobody at all.

<hr>

I hadn't been back to Archie's house since that night. Cecilia still went, of course, to see Archie and hang out with Archie's clique. I guess it was her clique now.

And then Archie said he was moving to Canada.

Cecilia didn't talk about what we'd seen that night. If I brought it up she would change the subject, almost like we'd done something wrong. After a while I tried not to think about it. It almost felt like something I imagined. Maybe it hadn't even happened. It made me not want to go back to Archie's, though.

But I was back at Archie's tonight.

<hr>

The party was in Archie's backyard. It felt like a graduation party even though it wasn't. Red and orange paper lanterns were strung up and glowing all around and there were tables with catered food, pizza and hamburgers and that kind of thing. There were already dozens of people there. Everyone had changed out of their weird dresses and suits from Tornado Day and they were back in their shorts and jeans and T-shirts and whatever. We looked like ourselves again.

As soon as we came into the backyard Cecilia went off to find Archie. I got some pop and walked around, not knowing who to talk to or what to do. I always felt lost at parties.

Lisa Stubenberger was there, and Keith Merkle on crutches (sprained ankle; he was one of the few who got hurt in the tornado), and Darlene Farley was telling a story to some girls and they were laughing. I think everyone was trying to feel normal, trying to reestablish our world after watching our school get destroyed just a few hours ago. It was good that Archie's family had opened up the party to everyone, we all needed it. I saw Archie's dad was stringing up a piñata, although I didn't understand why, that seemed like kid stuff. It was a piñata of a tornado, which seemed a bit gruesome and maybe insensitive, but then again somehow nobody died when the tornado hit, so in the end I guess it made sense, after all today was still Tornado Day. But what even *was* Tornado Day? It was like everyone knew what was going on but me, as if there'd a been a big meeting beforehand I hadn't been invited to. I was still shaken up by the destruction of the school, by the way the tornado killer had looked at me, by the whole day. I just wanted to be on the same page as everyone else. People were talking about the tornado killer, I overheard them, about the tornado killer's weirdo speech and also the way he had seemingly destroyed that tornado. But it was so out of everyone's normal experience that it was hard to talk about. The conversations were peculiar anyway because it was a peculiar mix of people.

Cuthbert Monks, even. When I saw Cuthbert come into the backyard with Jimmy Switz and Ned Barlow I was surprised. Archie never hung out with lowlifes like Cuthbert. But Cuthbert smirked around the party like he belonged there, like he owned it. I spotted Archie with Cecilia—they'd found each other, and then I saw them catch sight of Cuthbert, and they both went over to Cuthbert and Jimmy and Ned, and then all five of them moved off into the dark, toward the barn. Something passed between them.

I knew it: Cuthbert had alcohol.

I left the lights behind and went off toward the barn. I drank whiskey once with Cecilia and Archie and a couple other kids in Archie's attic. I didn't like it, it tasted metallic and medicinal, but I did like the feeling of doing something secret together. Whatever secret thing was going on, I wanted in on it.

I had my own secrets. Last spring, when I was still a freshman, I secretly went out with a senior, Roy Hetzler. He was kind of a loner, he wasn't in any of the defined groups, he had zits, but he was almost good-looking and he had a car. It felt weird to go out with him since he was so much older. But I was also starting to catch on that what people said not to do and what they actually did could be totally different, and anyway when it's just two people who want the same thing and are smart about it, it doesn't really matter. No one can stop you. When I found this out, I saw everyone at school differently.

Maybe everyone had a secret like mine.

Going out with Roy was exciting because my parents and Cecilia had no idea. Whenever I came home I felt my secret tight and real inside me. He didn't seem in a hurry for anyone to know our secret either. He was probably embarrassed to be going out with a freshman. The thing was, we didn't even go anywhere interesting in his car, we'd just go to fast food drive-throughs or to miniature golf on the other side of town. But when I was riding around with him, I felt like I was trying something on, I was trying on being older, and I liked it, it suited me. I knew how to be older. I could do it.

I was better at it than Roy. He talked too much.

He was my first kiss. It wasn't great. There was something gross about his limp lips. I kept on kissing him in his car because I figured I had to get used to it: so this is kissing, I thought, okay, fine. That summer I went to camp, and so Roy and I were separated for three weeks, and we promised each other we'd get back together when I returned. But when I did return from camp, I didn't call him. He didn't call me either. All the stuff that had happened between us in his car, we both separately seemed to decide, had just been practice, and when I saw Roy at the drugstore a few weeks later, I pretended not to. He didn't say hi either. There were no hard feelings. We were just finished with each other.

Millions of stars were out but the night was dark. The paper lanterns in Archie's backyard had made a little island of light and in that island everyone seemed prettier, happier, more interesting than they were at school, but I was leaving them, moving out of that bright island now, moving into the darkness around Archie's house. Music played behind me and Eric Zenderman was blindfolded, swinging the bat at the piñata while a group cheered. Others were dancing, Archie and Cecilia and Cuthbert had slipped back into the party, flushed, laughing too loud, Bobby O'Brien took Jessica Hauser and danced with her, she giggled at him to stop but he dipped her and it was okay, everyone was surprised to be there at all, the school was destroyed and yet we were all somehow alive and then I saw someone watching us.

Someone in the shadows.

A silhouette of a boy.

He was standing near the barn. Almost invisible in the dark. He might have been watching the party for a long time, as silent and motionless as a lamppost.

Looking straight at me.

The tornado killer.

The tornado killer looked different from that morning in the school gym. Stranger, more adult. He didn't smile. He didn't say anything. He just watched me. His green eye and his blue eye locked on to me and I felt their separate sharpness. No boy had ever looked at me like that. As if he was not looking at me at all, but at something else about me. Not a friendly look.

It felt like an invitation.

The teachers had said it was illegal for the tornado killer to come into town. Except on Tornado Day.

He drew back into the dark.

I moved toward him.

A hand gripped my shoulder—Archie pulling me back, laughing, whiskey on his breath, "C'mon, it's your turn!"

I was too startled to stop him, and then Archie pulled me back into the party fully, back into the bright little island. I tried to twist away, but actually, I didn't really resist as much as I could've. Even though everyone's eyes were on me now, and I couldn't leave anyway—Archie was announcing something—even though I didn't like being the center of attention, maybe I kind of let Archie pull me back into the party.

Maybe I was frightened by that invitation.

Archie had my elbow now, he was guiding me through the crowd. "We were looking for you, you're the only one who hasn't gone yet!" he said. Something triggers inside you when a popular person actually stops to focus on you; you let yourself be led, you laugh when you usually wouldn't, your body obeys, or maybe it was the authority of the booze on Archie's breath that meant he had more experiences than I had, a smell that promised interesting experiences for me, if only I did as I was told. The way Archie steered me along made it feel like he was doing me a favor.

I looked out into the dark.

The lights dazzled me.

I couldn't see the tornado killer anymore.

Archie's father put the aluminum baseball bat in my hand. His mother was coming at us with the blindfold. I was in front of that tornado piñata, which had already been smashed up pretty badly. Most of the other kids had had their turns. You could see holes in it, the candy glinting inside. It wasn't totally broken open yet, but it wouldn't take much to finish it off.

But I wasn't thinking of that.

I was thinking: the tornado killer had been looking at me again. Looking at specifically *me*.

I tried to peer out beyond the party, to see if the tornado killer was still there, but then Archie took me by the shoulders and turned me away from the darkness, he made me face the piñata. Suddenly Archie's body felt too close. He smiled loosely, looked me in the eyes. His own eyes were glassy.

Archie's mother gave him the blindfold.

Archie was telling me the rules, he was getting the blindfold ready. It still seemed dumb to me. I saw everyone in the crowd around me, Lisa Stubenberger talking with other girls, Bobby O'Brien's arm around Jessica Hauser's waist, Cecilia staring at me almost angrily—well, I didn't like how close Archie was to me either, the way her boyfriend kept touching me unnecessarily, but what was I supposed to do?—and there was Cuthbert front and center, also staring at me in a way I didn't like, and Ned and Jimmy too, for a moment it seemed like everyone at the party was leering at me, as if they all knew something I didn't—

No, it was that they were drunk!

Cecilia, Cuthbert, all of them—didn't Archie's parents notice that most of the kids at their party were obviously wasted? Definitely Archie was drunk. Then again, Archie's dad was a "cool dad," the kind who turned a blind eye to borderline stuff, which was probably why Archie seemed so much more experienced and adult than the rest of us . . . and then, just before Archie slipped the blindfold over my eyes, the last thing I saw was Archie's mother.

Staring at me too hard.

Blackness. The blindfold was on me now and Archie tied it tight, knotting it behind my head. I couldn't see anything. I held the aluminum bat loosely. I was definitely not into this. Why did I always go along with everything? Archie turned me around once, twice, three times and said "Okay, go!"

Was the tornado killer still watching me?

It sounded like everyone around me was cheering and hooting. I didn't want to be doing this, but I guess everyone else had done it. Okay then, just get it over with.

I swung. Missed.

Scattered groans. Oh come on, what did anyone expect? Whatever, who cares, I never said I would be good at this stupid game.

Then Archie was behind me again. I couldn't see him but I felt him trying to help me, his hands fumbling over me. He positioned me with his hands on my shoulders, which I didn't like, it felt creepy, he held my shoulders too long—and he whispered too close to my ear, "Don't listen to them, okay, you can do it."

I swung again, confused.

This time I did hit the piñata. But just a tap. More disappointed sounds from the crowd, almost mocking. I sagged but Archie put his hands on my waist and said, "Just swing straight across," but wait, what was he doing, where were Archie's hands?

Was my sister's boyfriend actually on the verge of sort of feeling me up in front of everyone?

It was gross. He was gross.

I swung the bat, half hoping I'd hit him.

I hit air.

Someone in the crowd shouted something I couldn't understand, but wait, what were Archie's hands doing now?

On my stomach, on my skin.

I almost dropped the bat then, and tore off the blindfold, to give him a piece of my mind, but then Archie gripped my arms, he was behind me again saying, "One more time, you can do it, take it easy," and he guided my hands in a practice swing, and then he let go and said, "Now you do it, you can do it," and his popular-kid magic worked, because now I thought to myself, Archie hadn't been groping me, of course not, he was just drunk and clumsy, and now he was even giving me this extra fourth chance at the piñata, because he truly was a nice guy, because he didn't want me to embarrass myself—and in fact, when I swung this time, I was certain, in mid-swing, of precisely where the piñata was—my bat connected with it cleanly, I felt the bat rip through the piñata, the thing came apart and shouts erupted all around me as candy fell to the ground.

I heard everyone running up to grab some. I dropped the bat and pulled off the blindfold. Nobody was paying attention to me anymore. I looked into the night for the tornado killer.

I didn't see him.

Was he there, though?

Maybe.

I could've gone into the darkness then. Nobody would've stopped me. Nobody would've known. I could have gone and found the tornado killer in the dark.

I didn't.

But after the party, at home that night, when I couldn't sleep, lying in bed, staring at the ceiling, thinking of his eyes, that look, that invitation, I thought to myself: I should have gone.

THE MAN AT THE LONELY HOUSE

That week the white strings went up.

They looked just like ordinary white strings, stretched between wooden stakes, zigzagging across fields, fluttering in the breeze. The adults said they were for security's sake—that the white strings marked the boundary between the safety of town and the danger of tornado country.

At first I only saw the white strings here and there, in out-of-the-way places, far out at city limits. But as spring deepened into summer, more and more of them went up, until the white strings started linking to each other, making a perimeter, fencing town off from the outside.

We weren't allowed to go beyond the white strings, the adults warned. If we did, the tornadoes would chew us up.

We said that we'd never seen these white strings before, and the adults replied of course, that's because the weather was changing fast, this was going to be a bad summer for tornadoes, in fact the worst, so you better get ready, and anyone who wanted to leave town, well, they better clear out now, because once that final white string went up, once town was totally closed in, that's when tornado season would hit for real, you can bet on that, there'll be no going anywhere for anyone, it'll be total lockdown.

The strange thing was, after Archie's family left, nobody else actually left town. Or nobody I knew. Maybe because nobody really believed the tornadoes would get that bad, not as bad as they got.

We discovered something cool about the white strings.

The adults didn't know we did it. I would ride bikes with Cecilia and the remnants of Archie's clique on the edge of town, and we'd follow the white strings through the meadows, looking for a place with nobody around. I would sometimes spot Archie's house in the distance as we rode, a dark hulk perched alone on a bluff. It'd been weeks since Archie's family had finally moved away. I guess Archie was off in Canada now. But nobody had moved into his house yet, it was locked up and empty. It had always been a weird place for a house, actually, isolated from everyone else's. But when Archie was still around, his house felt like the center of everything.

Now that center was gone. Everything felt knocked off its moorings, the social world was up for grabs. Our group had changed. Cuthbert Monks had somehow wormed his way in—that never would've happened under Archie, but after Archie moved away, Cecilia sort of inherited leadership, and she didn't care who joined us. She didn't have the power to shut Cuthbert out anyway. Jerks are always popular.

But without Archie and his magic house, our clique didn't feel so special. We were busted down to the same status as all the other kids, just randomly biking during evenings to the windy edges of town, where the gray clouds piled up-huge and heavy, smelling of pent-up electricity, always threatening rain but never actually raining, and we'd dare each other to run at the white strings.

I don't know who discovered this. But when you ran close to

the white strings, when you came to the border of tornado country, you'd feel a strange shiver. The shiver felt good, a tingling gush all up through your bones. So we'd leave our bikes in the grass and take turns running at the white strings, because the closer you ran to tornado country, the more you felt that addictive tingle— even though when you did, the winds would also blow harder, and an actual tornado would begin to rise up just beyond the strings, whirling up out of nothing, almost like you'd awakened that tornado and it was angry at you about it, but now you were running straight at it, you almost couldn't stop, terrified—and yet it was worth it because then you'd feel that juicy, terrible shiver.

The closer you ran to the strings, the harder that shiver pulsed, the stronger the wind blew, almost picking you up, your feet leaving the ground, the dark tornado growing and looming before you as the shiver ripped through your guts, glorious, electricity shooting up from the small of your back to the top of your head, a wild beautiful gush, you were blind, dizzy, no, too much, the tornado was trying to eat you, you had to turn back, turn back *now*, but the tornado had you gripped tight in its invisible jaws, it was dragging you toward the white string, the shiver hurt, you'd panic, the tornado was actually devouring you, all your friends were shouting at you to run, run, run, and you really had to run, you had to run *hard* away from the tornado to overcome its sucking pull— until you broke free, running and stumbling, and then you were back in your friends' arms, gasping, shaking, your body exhausted, everyone around you yelling and laughing.

We all ran at the white strings that summer.

I did it dozens of times.

But no matter how many times I ran, that last part felt just as nightmarish. I'd think, as I was running away from the tornado, as the delicious shiver tore through my body, oh no oh no, *this* was the time I wouldn't be able to run fast enough, *this* tornado wouldn't let me go, and I promised myself I'd never do it again, absolutely not, no matter how good it felt, because I knew I'd be whisked far up into the clouds, faster and higher, watching my friends dwindle below as I was devoured by the sky.

That is the absolute last final time, I'd promise myself.

Twenty minutes later I'd do it again.

Nobody told their parents we ran at the white strings. It wasn't allowed. But all it took was feeling the shiver once and you'd be back. I never went alone, always with a group of friends, and sometimes not even friends. I just didn't want to go alone in case I ran too close to the white strings and got dragged into tornado country. None of us had actually crossed the white strings, but we got dangerously close. And at first we didn't even see any other tornadoes, aside from these tornadoes we provoked into existence when we ran at the white strings. But the sky was darkening every day, distant thunderclouds swelling. The adults said, Oh, just you wait, the really big tornadoes are on the way.

Then we did start to see the big tornadoes. The really gigantic twisters, far off in the distance, gliding back and forth across the horizon.

Like they were watching us. Waiting.

I was waiting.

Feeling myself being watched.

I didn't tell anyone at first about the watched feeling. It wasn't the kind of thing I wanted to tell people. But I wasn't going to run away, I thought. Not yet. I'd changed my mind, for now.

More white strings went up every day, crisscrossing like a spiderweb, like our town was an insect hive spinning a protective layer around itself. Hunkering down for bad weather. Wrapping us in a cocoon.

If I really intended to run away, I realized, I'd better do it soon. Before the circle around town was completed, before the white strings blocked the last way out, I had to get on my bus and leave.

But then I'd see his faraway eyes, burning at me.

═══

Two months after Tornado Day, on a Friday night, right before dinner, I went down into our basement to get some cat food. When my parents redid the basement a few years ago, they made part of it look like a saloon, "for company," with three high stools and a bar with a big mirror behind it and all kinds of liquor, which was weird because Mom and Dad hardly drank, so those bottles just stayed there untouched.

Until now. Cecilia was already down there, pouring vodka into her bike's plastic water bottle.

"Hey," she said. "I just talked to Darlene, everyone's going to the white strings at seven, over by Mr. Z's, so."

"Have fun."

"Allllll right." Cecilia closed her bottle and stuck it in her backpack. "Staying in for Scrabble night with Mom and Dad?"

"I don't know."

"What's up with you lately?"

"Are you going to drink all that?"

"I'm splitting it with Darlene and Jessica." Cecilia narrowed her eyes. "You've got a secret."

"Not really."

"You're the worst liar."

"When do you think Mom and Dad are going to notice you're stealing drinks?"

"They never even come down here." Cecilia slung her backpack over her shoulder. "Don't even pretend you don't want to come out. We'll get trashed and you can get molested by Cuthbert Monks."

Ew ew ew. "Not funny."

"Sorry. You can get gloriously and enchantingly made love to by Cuthbert Monks."

"Still gross."

"I've got it. You're staying in because you're waiting for your hair to grow out."

"I like how you cut my hair."

"Really? Because I was trying to make you look like a whore," said Cecilia, and then she kept repeating it, with a weird rasp: "Whore. *Whore.* WHORRRRRRRE," in imitation of Ms. Shatley, the girls' gym teacher, which, listen, first of all, if you're going to be a high school teacher, don't have the word *shat* in your name, and Cecilia's class had mocked Ms. Shatley so much about it that this grown woman finally broke down, and shouted WHORRRRRRRE at Jessica Hauser, seemingly out of nowhere, it's not like Jessica was even doing anything whorish, I mean how could you even technically be a whore in gym? Anyway Ms. Shatley yelling WHORRRRRRRE got her fired, and she became legendary in a way, but now Mom and Dad were calling us to come upstairs for dinner so Cecilia just said to me, "Seriously, come out, I miss hanging out with you," and I said "Maybe" and Cecilia added, as we started upstairs, "I know you've got some juicy secret, like you're secretly banging the tornado killer," and it was a good thing Cecilia was ahead of me on the stairs, that she couldn't see my face, the way I froze up when she said that.

Cecilia had cut my hair because I won some concert tickets.

I was listening to Electrifier's station a few weeks ago, not during Electrifier's late-night show but during the day, and the afternoon guy, who was nothing like Electrifier, he was too shouty and jokey, announced that the fourteenth caller would get two free tickets to the outdoor music festival that was in the city, a concert I thought I'd never have a chance to go to since it sold out immediately, not like I could afford it anyway, but I called and somehow I won.

Electrifier was going to be part of the festival.

The afternoon DJ was disappointed that I didn't scream with joy. That's what he wanted me to do. How do you feel? he kept shouting, irritated that I wasn't playing ball. But it embarrassed me when people screamed for stuff they won on the radio.

The tickets were mine. No screaming.

The radio station mailed the tickets to me. I didn't tell anyone that I'd won until I opened the envelope, until I actually held the tickets in my hand. These weren't cheap tickets run off a computer printer either, these were fancy passes with a dusky sunset of oranges and yellows fading up into a dark blue background with metallic stars popping out over a city skyline and a silhouetted multicolored crowd with the logo of the radio station embossed over all of it. Tickets I'd save in a scrapbook, if I had a scrapbook.

When I first showed Mom and Dad the tickets they said, No way. Can't go. Forget it. But Cecilia and I kept bugging them, the subtext being, we get it, our family is broke, we never go on vacation, maybe we're not even going to college, so how about at least letting us go to this one concert in the city? But I didn't say that outright, because then Dad would start speculating about how our money problems might turn around, and Mom would talk about scholarships we could apply for, and we'd lose the thread, which was: to get to that concert.

In the end I wore Mom and Dad down.

They gave in.

This won me a new respect from Cecilia. She didn't care about music really, or at least, not about good music. But she definitely liked the idea of us going to this concert.

"We are going to rock this," said Cecilia confidently, and that was when she sat me down in the basement and cut my hair, "because if we're going to this concert, we're going to do it right," by which she meant we were going to look good together. She had a strategy for my hair, my clothes, my makeup, and even though I wasn't a hundred percent on board at first, I liked that Cecilia had an agenda for me, that she was thinking about me. It feels good to be at the center of someone else's plan.

"*Blank* on a triple word score—that's one-two-three, four, five, six, K on a double letter is seven-eight-nine-ten-eleven, twelve-thirteen-fourteen-fifteen-sixteen, times three is forty-eight, and then *be*, that's four, fifty-two."

"Ugh. I completely opened you up."

"Play the board, not the rack," Dad said serenely.

It was dim and windy outside when Cecilia and I were cleaning up after dinner. There was an old black-and-white movie on the TV and sure enough, Mom and Dad were at the kitchen table playing Scrabble. Every once in a while Cecilia and I would pass behind one or the other and see the letter tiles on their racks, we'd suggest words (Dad had M, S, N, G, I, T, E; did he see he could extend it to the other triple word score with *blankets*, with *blanking*?). We were all talking happily, joking around, it was one of the good nights, though Cecilia was itching to get out and go running at the white strings.

Cecilia said to Mom, "What'll you two do while we're at the concert tomorrow?"

"Oh shopping, walking around," said Mom.

I was only half listening. Cecilia had been right: I did have a secret. I washed the dishes, looking out the window into the night overlaid with our reflections.

I expected to see him in the distance.

I didn't see him yet.

Nikki slunk around my ankles, meowing for a shrimp snack. I kept a bag of these cat treats next to the sink, freeze-dried shrimp about as big as nickels that Cecilia refused to even touch. ("Dude, they look like tiny Martian penises and you know it, wait a second, holy crap, I just realized, you secretly like it.") I threw Nikki a handful of shrimp snacks. She pretended to ignore them but that was just her way. Nikki preferred to keep some dignity. She'd stalk away as if insulted, but then a minute later come ambling back, and pretend to notice the snacks as if for the first time, and act mildly surprised, and then she'd eat them.

I loved Nikki so much.

But Cecilia was right, those shrimp snacks did look like tiny gross Martian penises. I watched my reflection in the window, waiting, listening to Cecilia and my parents talking about the tornado killer.

Everyone talked a lot about the tornado killer those weeks after Tornado Day. Wondering where he lived. Who he hung around with. What he'd been doing all those years that nobody had seen him. What was his name, even. But nobody had any answers, not even adults. And nobody had seen him since Tornado Day.

Except for this nobody.

"Maybe we should stay out of town," said Mom. "Take a vacation. You know, just for a few weeks. Or a month."

Dad scanned his rack of letters. "You know we can't."

"We could. You've built up your vacation days."

"It's too late for that." Dad put his word on the board and wrote down the score. "We'll sit it out. It won't affect the girls anyway."

"I'm done, can we go to Darlene's now?" said Cecilia.

Mom said, "I just didn't expect everything would shut down so suddenly, that it would all begin so quickly."

"We'll be fine," said Dad. "Yes, Cecilia, you girls run free, you've got an extra-long summer, have fun while you can. Home by nine for both of you."

Mom said, "The Hausers got a tutor for Jessica, since there's no school . . ."

Dad said, "Let the girls hang out with their friends."

Cecilia said, "Darlene's parents were saying Deacon Terry was talking about the tornadoes after church. That things were going to change."

A moment went by, then Dad said, "There's a lot of nonsense going around. I really didn't expect the Farleys . . ."

"I don't see why we can't go on vacation," insisted Mom. "I just think it's best to stay away from all that. I don't like it, Mrs. Bindley with that necklace every day."

"As long as she keeps that nonsense out of the classroom, she can wear whatever she wants," said Dad.

I wasn't really listening. I was half hypnotized staring at my blurry reflection in the window. For a few seconds I had that feeling, the way you feel sometimes when you look at yourself in the mirror for too long, for a moment you don't even resemble yourself, you're someone else.

I was someone else.

In the two months since Tornado Day, I had changed. Or maybe I'd already been changing all this year and hadn't realized it. But when Cecilia cut my hair, it brought the change out, made it more striking. I didn't look like a kid anymore.

I looked like a girl who knew what she was doing.

A girl who could credibly hang out with Cecilia.

I finished the dishes. I just wanted to get out of the house. I didn't particularly want to go with Cecilia to the white strings, but I did want to go somewhere. The phone rang—for Cecilia, as usual. I already had my jean jacket on, so I headed out alone.

I thought of the concert tickets tucked into the side of my bedroom mirror. Cecilia had already chosen what she and I were going to wear tomorrow. She had a whole plan for us. I think she wanted to meet some boys. That was fine.

I just wanted to dance to Electrifier.

I stepped out into the backyard. The setting sun's burned-out glow cast everything in melancholy shadow. Nikki zipped out ahead of me and prowled around the edge of the yard. I scooped her up and put her in my bike basket and closed the top, but left it unlatched, the way she liked it, so she could peek out.

I kept watching the horizon.

I still didn't see him. I didn't feel it. Not yet. But it would happen when I was outside. It'd start almost imperceptibly, like the kind of feeling you get when someone is watching you but you can't see them. Like when you're in a car, and you sense something, and you turn and the person in the car next to you is staring at you.

I knew he was watching me.

And when I felt him watching me, I'd scan the distance and I'd find him.

There. Now.

Far off in the direction of Mr. Z's house. A tiny blue and a tiny green light burning in the distance. Two pinpricks of color. For a long moment I stood there, feeling myself being gazed at.

Then, blink—the blue and green were gone.

As soon as the lights were gone, I felt their absence. At first I thought it had to be just my imagination. The tornado killer couldn't really be watching me. How could I even see his eyes from so far off, it was probably just some car's headlights . . . But no, I knew because I felt it, with the same butterflies in my stomach as from Archie's party, the same feeling as in the early-morning gym. When I saw those tiny blue and green lights far away, I felt his eyes touch me.

At night, before I went to bed, I would open my window. Sometimes even then I would see the blue and green lights shining at me. I didn't know why the tornado killer was watching me.

But I did not dislike it.

A dozen of us biked out that night. Cecilia and the older girls rode ahead, while Cuthbert Monks and some other boys and girls and I brought up the rear. I had Nikki in my basket, her head barely peeking up, nudging the basket's lid open, her eyes looking out sternly, as if she was the real driver. My headphones were loosely ringed around my neck and my Walkman was on.

I had my stuff. I felt good.

We came out on the top of a little hill. From there we could see the white strings snaking across the dim gray fields where wind harassed the long weeds, going past Mr. Z's house.

Mr. Z lived alone in a funny little bungalow on the edge of town. It was almost the opposite of Archie's house. Nobody I knew had ever been inside Mr. Z's. His yard was overgrown with tall grass, his windows boarded up, his front porch half rotted away and thick with soggy, unopened newspapers, but the thing that bugged me most was that Mr. Z's phone was always ringing. You could always hear it ringing, even from outside, it never stopped ringing, he never answered—but come on, who wanted to talk to Mr. Z so badly? Whenever I rode past his house I'd think, Just pick up the phone already, talk to whoever it was, or leave it off the hook, I mean, didn't the constant ringing bother Mr. Z?

It bothered me.

I didn't understand Mr. Z. He seemed to hate everyone, especially us kids, and we hated him right back. Mr. Z yelled at us whenever he saw us, he chased Theo Wagner around the grocery store one time, he kicked Tommy Haskins's dog when it wandered onto his property, another time he actually stole Keith Merkle's bike and hurled it into a ravine—Keith was only like ten at the time—and the most irritating thing was, when we complained to our parents about Mr. Z, telling them about how Mr. Z had shoved one of us down at the library, or slapped one of us for no reason on the sidewalk, none of our parents ever did anything about it. They'd just shake their heads, and maybe wince, and simply say that Mr. Z had done a lot for our town, actually, in the old days, that he was a distinguished citizen whom we should try to respect.

We didn't respect him.

We baited him. We'd go running at the white strings near Mr. Z's house on purpose, just to rile him up. Because eventually Mr. Z would always come shambling outside, a shriveled wreck of a man always in the same yellowed nightshirt and creepy old-man dark glasses, shouting crazy threats—barking that tornadoes were nothing to mess with, that by running at the white strings and aggravating the tornadoes like that, we were putting the whole town in danger, that if he caught us, why, he'd teach us a thing or two—

We always got away in time, laughing.

⸺

It was almost dark. Someone had brought a six-pack of beer, and Cecilia had that vodka, and it was all getting passed around as we took turns running at the white strings. Standing around in the dim field, waiting for my turn, everyone looked shadowy to me, except when they lit a cigarette and for a moment their face flared up like a demon's.

I hadn't really wanted to come out tonight. But when I saw the tornado killer's eyes gleaming at me from the direction of Mr. Z's house, I thought that maybe he might be around here. That maybe, if I came out here, I would catch a closer glimpse of him.

Maybe he'd catch a closer glimpse of me.

I didn't see him yet. That was okay. Most times, hanging out with the group, I'd just put my headphones on, blast music into my ears, and watch. With a soundtrack everything seemed more intense and meaningful. Even people I didn't like seemed almost okay.

Cecilia had told me to cut it out. I wasn't doing myself any favors, she had said. Bringing Nikki everywhere in my bike basket was weird enough, but listening to headphones while hanging out with the group was kind of insulting to people and how could I expect to make any friends if I isolated myself like that, if I made it so nobody could even talk to me?

So tonight I kept the headphones around my neck. I still had the music playing, buzzing quietly on my collarbones. My turn to run at the white strings was coming up. I asked for a cigarette from Irene Bellardini, a small dark-haired girl who didn't smile much, but sometimes gave me a nod, which made me feel she was on my side. Irene handed me a cigarette. I lit it with her lighter, and it made me feel more comfortable. I had a place in the group. I was with the smokers.

Nikki poked her head out of the bike basket. She gazed at Mr. Z's dark house, not far away. She almost nodded, as if to say, okay, that all checks out. Mr. Z's phone was faintly ringing, as always.

Nikki glanced up at me. I'd never smoked in front of her before. She looked a little judgmental. I could tell Nikki didn't want to be out here, not tonight. She seemed skittish, like she wanted to hop out of the basket, so I closed the top and latched it. She didn't mind being cooped up if it was only for a little while.

My turn next.

I stood astride my bike, watching Darlene Farley running back from the white strings, her hair flying, squealing with thrilled terror. Wind swept over me, the fresh wet smell of a coming rainstorm. Everyone was laughing and cheering but I felt wobbly, the jitters I always felt when it was almost my turn, especially tonight— because what if I got hurt, and we all got caught, and then we'd get in trouble, and then I couldn't go to the concert tomorrow, and I was almost wondering if there was some way I could back out of running at the white strings when I overheard Cuthbert Monks say, "So when did Cecilia's weird-ass sister get hot?"

I pretended not to hear.

But I knew he meant for me to hear it.

When Cuthbert got into our clique, he seemed to be surprised that I was already a kinda-sorta member. He flirted with me, but Cuthbert Monks flirted like a bully, and I hated that he'd taken it upon himself to loudly announce that I was now "hot," and that the other guys were loudly agreeing, in a self-consciously generous way, as if they were being super gentlemen, doing me a favor by making it a matter of official public record that I'd gone from "weird-ass" to "hot."

I turned and glared.

"Aw, come on," said Cuthbert Monks, and I wished I hadn't glared, because now Cuthbert had an excuse to stroll over. "Learn to take a compliment."

"Thanks for the compliment."

"I mean, admit it, you got hot this summer. What happened?"

"I don't know. I guess I just got so hot."

"It wouldn't kill you to smile."

I just stared.

"Fuck, lighten up." This conversation wasn't going the way he wanted. I'd seen this happen with other girls. Now he was going to punish me for not following his flirt script.

"Come on." Cuthbert leaned over my handlebars. "I've seen you watching me."

I said, "Don't touch my bike."

"I'm just trying to be friendly," said Cuthbert in a hurt voice, and I'd seen Cuthbert do this too, swinging from bullying to self-pitying. Soon he'd be back to bullying. He looked at my headphones. "What're you listening to?"

I said, "You wouldn't know."

"Sounds like Electrifier's show."

Damn him for knowing about Electrifier.

"You should learn how to smoke a cigarette," said Cuthbert.

"I know how to smoke a cigarette."

"No you don't. You're just puffing."

He couldn't really see me blush in the dark, I thought.

"You look ridiculous," said Cuthbert in a matter-of-fact way, like he was just offering a neutral observation, a helpful FYI—and then he actually plucked the cigarette out of my mouth.

"Hey—"

"Don't worry. I can teach you how." Cuthbert took a drag on my cigarette, but here's the masterstroke, he didn't blow the smoke in my face, because Cuthbert's trick was always to go right up to the line of being a jerk, but not over that line, so that if you got mad, *you* were overreacting, *you* were being too sensitive, couldn't you take a joke?

"It's no secret." Cuthbert took another drag. "You just have to learn how to suck."

Stupid, obvious, crass. The other boys were laughing. This wasn't flirting anymore. This was a power move.

I said, "Give me back my cigarette."

"You mean Irene's cigarette. You never have your own." Cuthbert Monks ran his hands over my handlebars. "I like your bike."

"You need to stop touching my bike right now."

"Isn't it your turn to run, though?" Cuthbert's hands strayed down to the basket. "You want me to take care of your cat while you're away? Can I see your kitty?"

I tried to yank the bike away from him.

Cuthbert gripped the handlebars, stopping me.

I said tightly, "Let me go."

"I just want to see your *pussy*cat," said Cuthbert, which of course made some of the boys whoop like idiots, though it definitely turned some of the girls against him, ugh, and this was part of why I wanted to get out of town, because of pricks like Cuthbert Monks and everyone like him . . . The other girls were just giving sour looks but nobody was actually sticking up for me. I knew Cecilia would defend me, for all her faults, but she was off somewhere else, and so I only managed to say, my voice catching, "Can I go back to being weird-ass?"

Cuthbert's eyes were amused. "Don't flatter yourself."

"You're the one who said I was *so hot*."

"You're just trying to get attention."

"I want your attention?"

"You sit there with your headphones on with your quirky cat in a basket. You think that makes you fascinating."

Everyone was looking at me now. Out of nowhere I wanted to cry—but no, no, that would be the worst, breaking down in front of everyone just because of the dumb crap Cuthbert Monks said, and I kept looking around for Cecilia and my voice trembled, I hated that it trembled, "What the hell, what'd I ever do to you?"

Cuthbert Monks grinned. He knew he was under my skin now. "I'm just saying it's mean to keep your kitten cooped up."

"You don't know what Nikki likes."

"So her name's Nikki?" said Cuthbert innocently, and I inwardly kicked myself, because now he knew her name—

Cuthbert opened my basket.

Nikki was scrunched up in the corner of the basket. Her eyes went wide when she saw Cuthbert reaching down for her. She drew back further, hissing. Startled, I twisted the handlebars, turning the basket away from Cuthbert.

That was all the opening Nikki needed.

She leaped out of the basket.

Then she was dashing across the field.

"Nikki!" I shouted, and Cuthbert laughed, because of course

this was hilarious to him. A few other kids were yelling something at me, yelling warnings, but I had already thrown my bike aside, I was shoving past Cuthbert though he tried to hold me back, I ran after Nikki and I saw she was panicking, streaking this way and that, too fast, sprinting blindly away—

She was headed right at the white strings.

I chased after Nikki. The awful tingling shot up my back, and just beyond the white strings a tornado was swirling up out of nothing, a dark pumping column materializing and rushing toward her—its wind sucked me forward too, my feet skidding across the ground until I wasn't running anymore. I was flying and I couldn't stop—the shiver blasted through me—

Nikki went across the white string.

The tornado flipped Nikki's little body into the air, and she was sucked up into the sky. She was gone.

No.

Everyone was screaming behind me.

No—

I went over the white string too.

It was like plunging underwater. The sound of everyone shouting was suddenly silenced. The shiver gone. Colors gone. I hurtled across silent gray fields, numb with cold electricity, feet barely touching the ground. I tried to breathe, I couldn't, I was lost, sucked into the dark, spinning around, blind, the tornado whipping me, grabbing me, tossing me high up in the air—the tornado ripped my headphones off my neck, snatched away my Walkman, Nikki hurtled past me and I grabbed at her, my fingers brushing her for a second—

My eyes met her terrified animal eyes.

The tornado sucked us both in.

Outside the tornado was whirling gray. Inside the tornado was pure black. Outside I was peppered with flying dirt and stones. Inside nothing touched me. Outside the tornado's sound was like a speeding freight train. Inside all was silent. I was floating in the gentle soundless void and far below I saw Nikki swirling down into a grinning mouth.

I was being flushed down into the same mouth.

I couldn't breathe. The mouth was death.

Nikki went in.

A blur of violence and Nikki was gone.

I swirled down into it too and then giant cold lips were all over me, I was in the mouth now, it was chewing me with icy teeth, I shouted out for help, for the tornado killer to help me, tornado killer, and then blue and green stars were flashing—

A face took shape somewhere in the mouth.

Someone grabbed me and I screamed, I couldn't hear anything but then I could hear myself screaming, I was yanked out of the darkness and silence and numbness—I slammed into the ground and then I was on my back, out of the tornado, for a moment I thought he had done it, that the tornado killer had seen me in trouble, that the tornado killer had come and rescued me.

I opened my eyes.

It was Mr. Z.

I was in Mr. Z's backyard somehow. I lay in his overgrown grass, gasping, cut and scratched all over. I was back on the safe side of the white strings.

Not safe.

I heard my friends yelling, far away.

My head was in Mr. Z's lap for some reason. Where was Nikki? Nikki was gone. Had the tornado killer saved me? No. He was nowhere.

But here was Mr. Z.

Mr. Z bent over me, his nightshirt open, the skin of his wrinkly chest spattered with liver spots and moles.

He whispered, "What are you doing here?"

My body couldn't move. Mr. Z's phone kept ringing, ringing inside his house. I closed my eyes but then I saw again Nikki flushed down into that cold mouth at the bottom of the tornado. Who knows what happened to her then—shredded across the field, cat guts all over the place, I couldn't think about it—

Where was the tornado killer?

Mr. Z stared into me with his dark glasses. The black tornado loomed up behind him, strangely still.

Mr. Z held my hand, patting it.

"Are you okay?" he asked.

I tried to take my hand back. Mr. Z held it tightly.

Everything inside me yelled, Get out, get out.

"Let me go," I managed to say.

"What's your name?" said Mr. Z.

I couldn't move. The wind blew harder. My friends were shouting somewhere but they sounded far off. And Mr. Z was gruesomely, intolerably near.

"Actually, I know your name," said Mr. Z.

He brought my hand up to his lips and kissed it.

My skin crawled.

My friends were yelling but I couldn't see them anywhere.

"*I'm jest a girl who cain't say no,*" sang Mr. Z softly, like it was our own little song. "*Kissin's my favorite food.*"

He kept smiling, eyebrows raised above his dark glasses, looking at me as if he expected me to sing along. His voice slurred—the entire world seemed to slow down as he sang on: "*Wurthur wurthurt dor murstleturr, urmindu hurlirdurr murd.*"

I couldn't think, couldn't move.

"*Urthur gurrsurr korrand hurdtur gretch, burtatha gurrsurr harvurn arnifrun,*" sang Mr. Z. "*Everrturn aye lurza wurzzlin murf, arharva furna furrin durr aye wurn.*"

I spotted Cecilia running at us, hurtling across Mr. Z's yard, eyes filled with rage, and then she was on us yelling, "Get away from her!"

Mr. Z spun quick as a rattlesnake.

His hand struck Cecilia's jaw.

Cecilia went down in the dirt, holding her face, crying out. Everything was confused then, the other kids charged in right behind her, they were everywhere all around me—somehow in the free-for-all someone pulled me from Mr. Z's grip but I heard him laughing like he didn't really care and the wind was whipping hard now, the sky was black and green and the tornado had come back around, it was pushing at the white strings, straining at them so it could come even closer, closer than I thought was possible, the tornado was twisting sideways, its mouth open and roaring over our bikes, sucking them all up like a giant vacuum cleaner.

The tornado reared up, gulping our bikes down.

All our bikes were gone.

Then it snaked back around.

Coming for us this time.

Everyone scattered. We were all running for our lives now. Cecilia and Irene were half carrying me and I tried to keep up, I stumbled as fast as I could, blinded by the flying dirt but I kept seeing it happen again, Nikki getting sucked in—Nikki was gone—Nikki was gobbled down by that tornado and now it was coming for me—

"*Zurr I can feel the undertow, urnurvur murka cormplurnt,*"

Mr. Z sang, his voice unslurring. *"Turl it's too late for restraint—turninny wannoo, I cain't—"*

Even through the noise, I heard his phone ringing.

"I cain't . . . say . . . no!"

—————

It was eleven o'clock by the time Cecilia and I got home, bursting into our kitchen filthy and scratched up and shell-shocked after running all the way from across town. I had barely been able to talk the entire time, it was mostly Cecilia urging me to keep going although I found it hard to walk at first, I was too shaky and hurt and my head was buzzing and I kept seeing Nikki's helpless body twisting, then flushed away, and hearing Mr. Z singing—

Mom and Dad had waited up for us, of course. The first thing I said when we came in was "Nikki's gone, Nikki's dead," but they blew right past that.

They just yelled at us about the white strings.

Mom and Dad had already heard from our friends' parents—our friends had come home freaking out, blabbing everything that had happened. I was leaning on Cecilia and I couldn't say a word. Cecilia was talking too fast, furious and passionate, expecting Mom and Dad to be on our side at least a little.

They weren't.

"What did we tell you about going to those strings!" yelled Dad. "You're lucky you weren't killed!"

"That's not the point!" Cecilia shouted. "I'm talking about Mr. Z, the man's insane, he slapped me—"

"And what did you do to him?" said Mom sharply.

Cecilia looked at Mom like she'd been slapped again.

"Nothing!" stammered Cecilia. "You have to call the police on him, he—"

"We're not calling the police," said Dad firmly.

Mom said, "And if you think you're going to that concert tomorrow, forget it."

"*What?*" screamed Cecilia.

I was shaking. I couldn't say anything. Nikki was gone. Everything that was happening with my sister and Mom and Dad was just noise. Nikki was gone.

"That's not fair!" shouted Cecilia. "You *have* to drive us tomorrow, you promised!"

Dad said, "You should've thought about that before you went out to the white strings."

"We never get to do *anything*!" howled Cecilia, really hysterical now. She kept arguing with Mom and Dad but that was a mistake, because that gave them a reason to really lay into her—Mom and Dad didn't yell at me as much, maybe because of Nikki, maybe because I was so banged up and they could see I was kind of in shock—they just let me go to bed but downstairs I could hear them still hammering away at Cecilia, Mom and Dad shouting that if they ever caught either of us near the edge of town again, messing with the white strings, especially near Mr. Z's house, we'd both be grounded for the rest of the summer—and no, they *weren't* going to call the police on Mr. Z, even if he *had* hit Cecilia, and anyway how did they even know Cecilia was telling the truth? She'd lied about where we were going out tonight, and they could smell vodka on her breath, who gave her vodka?

I just lay in bed, listening to them screaming.

I shut my eyes.

Cecilia slammed her door. "I hate you!"

My Walkman and my headphones had been swallowed by the tornado too. I had nothing to block out my family. I just lay in bed and listened to them fight.

That night I dreamed about being in the city.

I was walking the streets at night and seeing the lights around me. Nobody knew me, but the tornado killer was there too, but he wasn't the tornado killer, he and I were just two normal people, he wasn't watching me from far away, in fact we had never met before, we were just two people who were dancing in a dark room together. I had seen dark rooms like that in magazines, places where people in the city danced, living in a more intense and vivid and better part of the world than mine, and I loved it because I could lose myself in that place, and so would the tornado killer, in the beautiful dancing crowd, but something began to feel wrong—there weren't so many beautiful people in the room anymore, the dance club was emptying. The tornado killer and I were still dancing, but slower, and there were fewer people around us, then all the strangers were gone and I recognized who was left behind.

There were four of us. We were all standing still in the dark. Each of us was the same distance from the others, like the corners of a diamond.

Me.

The tornado killer.

Mr. Z.

And one other person.

I knew her. But I couldn't look at her.

I woke up in the middle of the night, sweating, my heart beating too fast like it was going to break into pieces. The house was silent. Everyone else had finished screaming and arguing and were now asleep. I reached for Nikki.

She wasn't there.

I got up and walked around the room, breathing hard, saying okay, okay, okay. I took a deep breath. I wanted to cry. Okay okay okay. But I was finished crying. I looked in the mirror. Okay. Okay. I closed my eyes. Okay.

My heart wouldn't stop pounding.

Why was I dreaming about the tornado killer? Where was he, after all, when I was in trouble, when I was actually about to get killed by a tornado? Why did I even care about him, how had the tornado killer gotten in my head? I had gotten myself excited for nothing. For an embarrassing fantasy I had made up myself, for something that didn't even make sense. I didn't like being here in this town, I didn't like the people around me, I didn't like the person I was becoming.

The next thing I did, I was kind of doing it automatically at first. In a way I didn't even notice what my hands were doing. Sorting through my clothes, stuffing them in my bag. But then I did realize it, I realized what I was doing, and I thought: yes, do this, keep doing it.

I was running away.

THE AMATEUR RUNAWAY

You can mess up running away. You can make a fool of yourself if you don't plan it out right. Everyone remembers when Gary Ackerley had tried to run away back in eighth grade. He'd snuck out of his house late one night, but after he got a few miles from home he realized he had to go to the bathroom. There was nowhere for him to go, and so he ended up taking a dump on somebody's front lawn.

Gary hadn't brought anything to wipe with, but someone's sprinklers were on a few yards over . . . anyway, that's how the police found Gary, crouched with his underwear around his ankles, scooting back and forth over the rotating pulsing sprinkler as it fired water up his ass.

Nobody ever let Gary forget that.

I'm just saying: have a plan.

———

As soon as I made my decision to run away, my frantic feelings settled down. The world snapped into a different focus. I felt free. Not an exciting free. Just a calm recognition that nobody could stop me. Not if I really wanted to do it.

I felt cut off from myself.

But I preferred this new me. The cut-off me.

I wanted to be cold. Cecilia always told me that I looked *cold*. That I turned people off because my face was always the same, because you couldn't always tell what I was feeling, because I didn't always look like I was having a splendid time. Cecilia had said: At least fake looking like you care, people like talking to somebody who feels something.

As if I owed the world some emotion. Or the thing Cecilia called emotion.

I felt plenty, thanks.

I stuffed my backpack with clothes, a toothbrush, toothpaste, soap, a notebook, pens, all my money, toilet paper in honor of Gary Ackerley, Nikki's mouse toy to remember her by, my little pearl-handled knife in the side pocket, and my ticket for the concert.

Mom and Dad wouldn't drive us to the city? Fine, I'd take the bus on my own. Was the concert why I was leaving? Not really, but it gave me a destination. The concert was tonight and I was going. With Cecilia? No, Cecilia would complicate matters. I won my ticket alone, I'd use it alone. I'd get in trouble alone.

Trouble didn't feel like such a big deal anymore.

I left no note. Mom and Dad clearly hadn't felt bad about Nikki getting killed, so let them feel bad about me disappearing for a few days. Anyway, what's the worst that would happen? When I came back, they couldn't ground me forever. Twenty years in the future, this would all just be an anecdote we'd roll out at Thanksgiving or whatever. Remember the time I ran away from home? Big family joke!

Or maybe no joke.

Once I was gone, I could also pass on making the return trip.

Thrilling. Cut-off feeling. Cold.

I had never, ever done anything like this in my life.

I was angry enough not to come back. A ton of submerged anger I didn't even know I had was cracking through and it surprised me. But maybe it didn't surprise me so much. And something else, the thing that made me wake up in the middle of the night, sweating, blinking in the dark, out of breath . . . the feeling of being watched, of having his attention, of . . .

Get out.

I said goodbye to my bedroom, just in case it turned out I really was running away forever and I didn't realize it yet. Suddenly I didn't like the way my bedroom looked—like the way you see your house differently when a new friend comes over, the way a stranger would see it. Now that I was leaving it, I realized it was a crappy room. The dents on the walls, the worn-out carpet, hand-me-down clothes from Cecilia, a bunch of kids books that I didn't even read anymore, a bunch more books that I had never read at all because they were stupid. I had been living a crappy life in a crappy room.

I thought to myself: I am leaving this.

Nothing stirred in me.

I thought it again to myself, the actual words: *This might be the last time in my life I ever see my bedroom.*

Nothing. Cut-off feeling.

I went downstairs to the kitchen. Morning sun was streaming in. Everything neat and in place. I grabbed a box of breakfast bars and some crackers and raisins and put them in my backpack. I saw Nikki's bag of shrimp snacks, next to the sink.

That gave me a teetering feeling. Not an actual emotion. Just a little ill feeling. I wanted to feel excited about running away.

I had a stomachache.

My ten-speed was lost to the tornado, so I lugged my old dirt bike up from the basement. It was awkward carrying it up the stairs. I ended up knocking over Nikki's litter box.

Kitty litter scattered everywhere on the steps.

Whatever. You know what? Mom could clean it up. But what would Mom say, what would Dad say, when lunchtime came and went and I still wasn't there? They'd eventually get worried. They'd start calling around, sure. By dinner they'd be frantic. Police. Crying. Cecilia too. What did we do wrong? We shouldn't have yelled at her so much!

Kitty litter was strewn all over the stairs. Nikki was gone.

I tried thinking it hard, underlining it. Really trying to feeling it. *Nikki is gone.*

I felt nothing.

I hauled my bike up into the garage, already sweating. The tires were low on air. I found the pump behind the lawn mower. Stale oily smell. Nobody else awake yet. Pumping. I checked the pressure. Kept pumping. Birds singing outside. I was waiting for my emotions to catch up with what I was doing. I was running away! This was an adventure! I should feel eager. Maybe afraid. Sad, at the very least.

I didn't feel anything.

I kept pumping.

Done.

I came out of the garage. The morning felt new and fresh. I'd always wanted to do something bold like this, right? Now I was doing it . . . Jesus, what was I doing? I stopped as I rolled my bike down the driveway. Maybe this was the last time I'd see my house.

I felt nothing.

I got on my bike and started pedaling. I didn't look back.

The sun had risen. The morning was bright and silent.

Last time biking through downtown, I thought.

Nothing.

Last time I'd ever see the pet store. Last time, movie theater. Last time, drugstore.

Nothing.

Mom and Dad and Cecilia were probably waking up now.

Wind whipped through my hair.

⚊

Bus ticket prices had gone up. Now a one-way ticket to the city was all I could afford, not a round-trip ticket, with barely any spending money left over. Even worse: nonrefundable. So I was locked in now. I ended up not even telling the clerk the story I was inventing right then, on the fly, to make it seem not so suspicious that this high school girl was buying a one-way bus ticket to the city. When I paid for it my hands were trembling.

The clerk didn't care.

Now I had my ticket and an hour to kill.

I looked around the bus station. So many times I'd thought about leaving town from here. But I'd never actually been inside this building. I should've expected it wouldn't be much. Scuffed gray linoleum floor, line of orange molded-plastic seats, low drop ceiling with flickering fluorescent lights. Dead plant.

There were a few other people but they looked like they belonged in the bus station permanently. An old man in a wrinkled suit. A middle-aged woman asleep on one of the chairs, holding a big dingy purse. A pudgy guy with a beard and suspenders hanging out near the men's room.

There was an old coffee vending machine and a pop machine that said ICE COLD. Storage lockers too. Some of them had keys, some didn't. Some were rusted shut. Probably never cleaned out.

Who locks up their stuff at a bus station? I guess I'd find out soon. I was a bus station person now.

When I went to the bathroom, I saw that weird symbol scratched inside the stall door.

I'd never gotten to the bottom of that little mystery. I guess it would remain unsolved. For old times' sake I took out my little knife and carved my own symbol next to it.

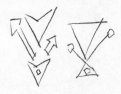

When I was done carving I thought, that's that.
I'm done here.

Half hour left until the bus leaves.

I couldn't stand the smell in the station anymore, the stink of old cigarette smoke and the sour chemical smell of whatever nasty cleaning product they used, which didn't erase the cigarette smell but only masked it with something even more disgusting. So I walked outside.

The fresh air smelled good. The weather felt stuck between spring and summer, the sky was somehow dim even though it was sunny and the air hummed with kinked energy, feeling damp but electric. I walked around the bus station a few times, then wandered out into the field of muddy grass.

There was a sputtering wind. The tornadoes weren't swarming around this part of town yet so there were only a few white strings out here. But inside I had overheard the clerk telling the wrinkled-suit guy that white strings would be going up near the bus station tonight. That after today, even this road—the last road out of town—would be blocked off.

That meant I had to leave today.

It was now or never.

The clouds bent and folded into each other, twisted all out of shape, making jagged foamy landscapes. The storm trembled in the distance, holding itself back with a mounting expectancy. As though, when the storm finally did come, it would surely bring some huge revelation with it.

I was fine with missing that revelation.

Last night, after I'd woken up from my dream, I had gone into Cecilia's room. It was dark in there but I knew she was awake.

I sat on the edge of her bed. She couldn't sleep either. But seeing Cecilia so freaked out and defeated felt weird. We talked for a long time, about the concert, about the tornadoes, about Mr. Z, about the tornado killer, even about that night in Archie's house that New Year's Eve, the woman with Archie's mother, the gigantic naked lady from my nightmares who I thought of as the Horrible Woman. I didn't tell Cecilia I was running away, but I did tell her I felt like there was something inside me that would get all twisted up if I stayed in town, and that I appreciated her saving me from Mr. Z, and that she was a good sister, and that I liked hanging out with her, and that I loved her, until I realized I had been talking for a while, and she hadn't responded, because at some point she had fallen asleep.

Just as well.

It was almost time. I was alone in the grassy field outside the bus station, trying to get myself excited for what I was about to do. In the distance I saw my bus coming. The sight of it made leaving town feel real. I felt a little weak. I would get on that bus and go. Not sure how I could even get back.

The wind changed. A fresh rainy smell blew over me and I felt the electric tingle of the coming storm. Plastic bags chased each other over the field, across the white strings. My bus was almost here.

I saw a figure moving, far away in the distance. Out beyond the strings, walking in the grassy fields.

The tornado killer.

He stopped walking. He turned toward me.

I felt the tornado killer staring at me, far away.

He wasn't coming any closer.

His green and blue eyes needled me from across the fields.

I looked away from them.

The bus was almost here. I thought of my concert tonight, in the city. I had my ticket. The glittering stars and skyline and dancers on my ticket would become real tonight, because I was making it real. That's what I wanted. What did the tornado killer want? I didn't even know. What did I want?

I waved goodbye to the tornado killer.

He raised his hand. But he didn't wave.

There were men between us in the middle distance, at work with surveying equipment. They were the same men I'd seen carrying the tornado killer's wooden box into my school. Now these men were driving wooden stakes into the ground and putting up more white strings.

My bus pulled into the station.

People got off. Other people began to board.

The tornado killer kept staring at me, his hand up.

I realized I had never seen the tornado killer up close. Well, now I never would. I was getting out of here. See you, tornado killer.

I stood on the edge of the grass.

The tornado killer was about a football field away.

He and I stared at each other.

The bus was waiting for me. My head rushed, my heart was beating hard. I kept moving toward the bus as if I were in a dream. My imagination had been secretly making up ideas about the tornado killer, was it curiosity? I was kind of curious about him, yeah. But I wanted him to be curious about me too. I wanted his attention. Who else in town was paying attention to me? Nobody. In the city, would anyone pay attention to me? Probably not. Why would they? I wanted someone to pay attention. I wanted them to *pay* it. The tornado killer wasn't paying anything. He was just watching me for free. But maybe there wasn't anything about me to understand. Maybe there wasn't much to me at all. What did the tornado killer want then? Did he just want to prey on some boring girl?

Did I want to be preyed upon?

Maybe more than I wanted to admit.

He was still staring at me.

I stared back.

I still hadn't boarded the bus. The bus driver was saying something impatient to me. Then he was kind of yelling it. Move it, kid. Come on. Are you getting on or what?

The tornado killer was saying something to me too. I didn't know what he was saying exactly but I wanted to know. His lips were moving. His eyes were saying it too. It almost tickled inside my ear, our own private sound maybe.

I wanted him to be saying: *Please stay.*

I stood at the edge of the grass, trying to hear him say that.

I stayed there, standing in the dirt, watching him. I stayed there after the bus door closed. I stayed there as the bus pulled away. Then the bus was gone, disappearing down the highway.

That night, the last of the white strings closed in.

THE LAST REAL SUMMER

My last real summer was the worst tornado season ever.

After that day at the bus station, after the last white strings went up, the tornadoes hit with full force. It was like we'd been told: nobody could leave town. Every day tornadoes whipped across the fields at brutal speeds and lunatic heights, prowling city limits like sharks, nibbling at the white strings, sometimes scattering into light breezes—but if anyone was stupid enough to cross the strings, those breezes would swirl up again into full-blown twisters, tear you apart in a second flat.

The tornadoes were death. Everyone knew it.

Nobody could stop watching them.

People would drag their lawn chairs out near the white strings and watch the tornadoes swirl and shriek. The tornadoes seemed to have different personalities: ferocious or shy, blustering or crafty, and from behind the safety of the strings people took turns guessing how close each tornado would dare come to town, what the tornadoes would do, and how they'd fight against the tornado killer.

People got used to the tornado killer. It was as though the tornado killer had been around town all along. Maybe that's the way it's supposed to be, people said. He's out there fighting tornadoes so we don't have to worry.

But there were so many tornadoes that summer, it was hard not to worry.

As bad as it got, though, the tornadoes never broke into town. That was all thanks to the tornado killer. The tornado killer worked hard—everyone had to admit that. Even those who'd thought he was just a freak at first.

I watched him every day.

I'd go to the edge of town and I'd spot him in the distance—a tiny figure in the fields, striding out to meet the tornadoes, waving his arms, punching and kicking the air. He would advance, threaten, engage, press against a tornado, pull back, strike suddenly, and the tornado would career, lash out, teeter, lurch, wobble, and topple, collapsing into vapor. Occasionally he had to fight two, even three tornadoes at a time, and they'd fight back, they'd beat him up sometimes, he would be on the ropes, but he'd always come back somehow—no matter how desperate and bloody, he always won. He'd kill them all.

It was better than a fireworks show, people said. A show that happened nearly every day, every night. Families would spread out their blankets in the fields near the white strings and bring picnic baskets full of fried chicken, mashed potatoes, cookies, and lemonade, and use their binoculars and telescopes to watch the tornado killer. It was a rough sport but he was a pro. Little kids punched the air and danced around, saying that they wanted to be tornado killers too someday. The radio played special music to accompany the tornado killer's fighting. At first the weathermen gave a play-by-play too, but the weathermen didn't really understand anything the tornado killer was doing, so the radio station replaced them with baseball commentators. The baseball guys didn't know anything either, but at least they were entertaining.

But it wasn't just entertainment.

It was life or death.

Because when the tornado killer was losing, when the wind picked up and whipped through the streets, papers and trash flying, electricity flickering, then we'd all feel that awful shiver in our spines, as though the entire town was getting sucked across the white strings together—we'd see the tornadoes looming too close, straining against the white strings, and that's when everyone would rush to the safety of their basements and turn on the radio, to find out if the tornado killer really could fight them off this time.

The tornado killer wasn't invincible. He'd get exhausted. He'd get hurt. Limping away from a fight, wiping blood from his face. Close calls. I wondered how he did it, how he kept fighting on, day after day.

I wondered how it felt.

I stood at the edge of town and watched him. Every once in a while he stopped, and turned.

Even though he was far away, I knew the tornado killer was turning to me.

———

I had a new plan. The tornado killer couldn't come to us. Okay, I got that. I understood. He couldn't cross the white strings. That was against the law.

But maybe I could cross the white strings. Maybe I could figure out where he lived, out there in tornado country. Maybe I could find a way to talk to him. Maybe I could figure out why the tornado killer was watching me. What he wanted.

What I wanted.

Maybe I would go to him.

I began taking walks at night.

Just to get out of the house, I told myself. To get away from the after-dinner cooking stink and Mom's nagging to clean up and the television blaring while Dad watched it with an empty look and Cecilia chattered on the phone. Our house was too small, too crowded. I didn't fit there the same way anymore.

I had changed that summer.

I liked the change and I felt the change sharpest when I was alone like this, walking through the dark neighborhood, breathing the warm night air, feeling my legs move, my arms swing, my brain hum, everything more vivid. As if until this summer I'd been like a radio whose dial had been slightly off, coming in staticky. But now my dial locked in on precisely the right spot and at last my signal streamed in pure and clear.

And then I would see his eyes.

Green and blue, flickering in the black distance.

Keep walking. Pretend not to notice. Past the dark houses with lights on. People moving in lit rooms, the bright squares of other people's lives. The flicker of televisions spilling out onto lawns. Insects trilling all around.

I would walk differently, knowing I was being watched.

The eyes would follow me, interrupted by houses, filtered through trees.

I would come out into a grassy field near the white strings. I'd look out across the prairie into the darkness. Feeling the hot summer night air.

I'd stare at the green light, the blue light.

Who are you?

Cecilia and I began to be friends again.

Nobody wanted to run at the white strings anymore. Archie's clique was mostly broken up now, and of course there was no way Cecilia, and by extension me, could go back to hanging out with Lisa Stubenberger, Sadie Hughes, Danielle Lund, that whole group. I heard Cuthbert Monks had made himself the head of what was left of Archie's clique. Turning himself into a kind of new Archie.

They could have him.

Cecilia and I went back to hanging out just the two of us.

Sometimes Cecilia acted like we were doing a project together. She pretended she didn't believe Nikki was really gone, and so she made us go all over town searching for Nikki, putting up homemade LOST CAT—REWARD posters.

I went along with it. We both had to ride around on our old junky pink and purple dirt bikes, since Cecilia's ten-speed had been eaten by the tornado too. On those days Cecilia would choose some random spot on the map, and she'd say: Okay, today we bike out here. Always the deserted edges of town, places nobody else went.

It wasn't really about finding Nikki.

While I packed lunches, Cecilia would secretly fill up her bike's water bottle with vodka or gin or whatever she could scrounge from Mom and Dad's "saloon," and then we'd bike out, maybe stopping at the pet store to play with the puppies and kittens, and then we'd head down to the overgrown train tracks where an old caboose was rotting away, and we'd drink there, and then once we were buzzed we'd ride out again to the edges of town, by the white strings, riding around tipsy, wobbling, a few times we almost fell off or crashed into each other, laughing, until finally we'd find a good spot and then Cecilia and I would lie back, watch the clouds above us curl into all kinds of strange shapes from the exotic tornado air and we'd feel the Earth turn beneath us and hear the thunder murmuring far off, we'd see the lightning flash miles away, and the rainstorm that never quite came, and we'd just talk and do not much at all, just feeling good. It was easy to be lazy and let the summer slip away, hanging out drunk with Cecilia.

One day Cecilia said, "You know what's weird?"

"What?"

"Archie never writes."

"So?"

"It doesn't seem like him."

"Why not?"

"I don't know. He was so into the idea of being a nice guy. Doing the right thing and whatever."

"Do you write him?"

"No."

"Well, then."

"I don't have his address. He said he'd write me with it."

I closed my eyes. "You don't really care."

"I can tell *you* obviously don't."

"You don't either, though."

"I don't, yeah. But it's still weird."

"At least Archie got out of town."

"Oh, boy. Back to you talking about running away again."

"And you want to stay here forever?"

"Hell no. Of course I want to go." Cecilia sipped from her bottle. "Tell you what, let's make a pact. We'll leave town together."

"A pact?"

"Yes. A pact."

"Who makes pacts?"

"We do. A *blood* pact."

"I'm not getting up to do a blood pact."

"Okay, but let's say we have a pact."

"Fine."

"A *blooooood* pact."

"Christ, you're drunk."

"I like being drunk," said Cecilia. "I like being drunk with you."

———

Here's what I knew about the tornado killer.

He couldn't dress. He always looked like he was wearing whatever wrinkled laundry he found on his floor that morning. A T-shirt with a random logo on it. Shorts that looked like he'd taken scissors to some old pants. Beat-up sneakers.

He was always alone. Though sometimes the local news crews would stand at the edge of the white strings, shouting questions at him.

The tornado killer never answered.

He ate the crappiest food. When he brought a lunch out to his tornado killing, it'd always be a bag of fast food hamburgers, chips, a candy bar, whatever.

I wondered how the tornado killer felt about us. About me. About how we were safe behind the white strings while he was getting beaten up by tornadoes. Maybe he was jealous of our soft lives. Maybe he had contempt for us.

No. Not contempt.

He watched us all the time. Fascinated.

I watched back. Planning.

I joined the picnicking spectators near the white strings, watching the tornado killer. I listened to the baseball announcers' commentary on an old transistor radio I found to replace my Walkman, and I listened to his fights as I biked alone on the edges of town, and I stayed up late listening in bed too. I felt like I was keeping the tornado killer company, like he knew I was listening, and when I was half asleep I would close my eyes and feel like I was with the tornado killer, like we were out in the dark fields together.

At night, I left my window open. My lamp on. The wind blew into my room.

You can watch me if you want, tornado killer. You can watch me.

Watch me.

＝

The school year had been cut short but Mom and Dad still wanted Cecilia and me to learn stuff. Math, history, science, whatever, anything to make up for the classes we'd missed.

As per usual they approached the project in their half-assed way. Dad checked some math books out of the library, but they were too easy for us and he never got around to finding anything harder. Mom's idea was for us each to read a novel a week and write summaries. Cecilia and I just handed them our old book reports from school and they were none the wiser.

They also insisted we memorize poetry, an activity so stupid that even our real teachers didn't make us do it. It worked for Mom and Dad, though, because it was easy for them to check. All they had to do was sit, poem in hand, while Cecilia and I tried to recite the poems by heart.

Pointless.

Even still, it gave Cecilia and me a kind of private language, and verses that we'd thought were particularly pretentious or absurd would pop up in our conversation, especially with others around, like a secret code. While we were getting drunk at the edge of town occasionally Cecilia would stand up, face the wind, and declaim poetry dramatically, any random poem, gesturing with great swoops, her hair floating epically, affecting a plummy accent that did not exist anywhere on Earth:

> *I'm nobody! Who are you?*
> *Are you nobody, too?*
> *Then there's a pair of us—don't tell!*
> *They'd banish us, you know.*

The picture of the woman who wrote the poem was kind of terrifying. Her eyes, nose, and mouth were too big for her little delicate face. Her hair was too severely parted, slicked down, old-fashioned. She was an alien. According to the bio in the book she rarely left her room and didn't like to meet people.

I could see her point of view.

Cecilia drank more vodka and chanted the rest:

> *How dreary to be somebody!*
> *How public, like a frog*
> *To tell your name the livelong day*
> *To an admiring bog!*

"I don't get it," I said, although I kind of did.

"How public, like a frog," drawled Cecilia, and that became a kind of shorthand of disapproval for us, when, say, Cuthbert Monks or someone would do something particularly gross, Cecilia would mutter "how public, like a frog," or if Dad made some flat-footed pun I would whisper "how public, like a frog," or when we saw Darlene Farley totally making out behind the cruddy bowling alley with Theo Wagner, we didn't even have to say it, it was so awkwardly public, like a frog.

"I'm nobody," I said, laying back in the grass, my eyes closed, as the unsteady world floated under us.

===

Cecilia wanted to get her driver's license so Dad took us to empty parking lots to give her driving lessons. He took me along and taught me too, because he "didn't want to have to do the whole thing twice."

We practiced in the bus station's empty parking lot. No buses were coming or going anymore, but the bus station was still open for some reason. When Dad left us in the car and went in to ask the guy if it was okay to use the parking lot, I said to Cecilia, "You ever wonder what people keep in those lockers at the bus station?"

"What lockers?"

"You know. The lockers in the bus station."

"I've never seen them." Cecilia sounded put out. "When have you ever been to the bus station?"

Uh-oh. "Um. A while ago."

"Why?"

"Just looking around." I hadn't expected Cecilia to sound so displeased. Like she was jealous I had gone somewhere she hadn't.

The next day Cecilia and I biked together to the bus station.

When we went inside it was just as before. Grimy. Stale stink. Nobody there except for the same clerk behind the ticket counter. I hadn't been back since the day I'd tried to run away.

The clerk looked up at us, then went back to his paperwork. "No buses."

"We know," said Cecilia absently, browsing the lockers. About twenty dented steel boxes, rusted and scratched up, each about the size of a microwave, with a slot to stick a quarter in so you could take out the key. Some of them were missing keys.

Cecilia put in a quarter, took the key. "This one."

That afternoon we went to the hardware store and made a copy of the key. We tied our twin keys on strings and wore them as necklaces under our shirts. It made me feel like Cecilia and I were secretly on the same team. And I liked that it enclosed a small space in town that nobody else could touch, a place that was Cecilia's and mine alone.

≡

Did he want to flirt with me, was he already flirting with me? Had the tornado killer ever even met a girl before? Where had he been all those years, before Tornado Day?

I was restless again, another late night in my room, listening to the tornado killer fight on the radio. It was after midnight and the tornadoes were on the attack. The wind blew strong through my open window, moving papers and things around. The announcers droned away tinnily on my little radio, making the tornado killer fight sound almost soothing. I was slipping in and out of sleep, sometimes waking up a little, wondering if the tornado killer was looking at me again.

His blue and green eyes flashed in the distance.

Then I was out on the prairie somewhere, I was near the tornado killer and he was sitting on a blanket, having a picnic like the families who would watch him.

He was with some girl. They were talking, he was laughing, she was laughing, they were having a good time. They seemed to know each other so well. I stopped walking toward them, overcome with embarrassment and jealousy.

The girl turned to me.

The girl was me.

Not-me and the tornado killer looked at me. Not-me gave me almost a challenging look, a smug look, as if to say: you think you can steal him from me? And then she and the tornado killer turned to each other and cracked up, as though it was their private joke. I looked at the tornado killer, the way he was laughing, the way not-me was responding to him. Like she and I had always known him.

I didn't want to dream of the tornado killer anymore. I wanted the real thing.

I wanted to be that not-me.

Nikki appeared from behind the tornado killer and not-me and stared at me. I had dreamed of Nikki before, but not like this.

Nikki gave me a disappointed look.

I couldn't look back.

When I woke up I reached instinctively for Nikki but of course she wasn't there. All I saw was that disappointed look. I had never disappointed Nikki, not even in my dreams.

＝

Cecilia knocked on my door. It was already ten but I hadn't gotten out of bed yet, I didn't want to. I felt Cecilia waiting on the other side. She knocked again. I knew she wouldn't open it herself. We had an understanding about barging in.

Finally I said, "Okay."

Cecilia was holding some of her LOST CAT—REWARD posters. She probably intended to come bounding in with some goofball plan for tracking down Nikki that day. But come on. We both knew what that tornado had done to Nikki. She was trying to make me feel better by pretending otherwise, and I guess it had helped at first. But now I was just humoring her.

When she saw my red face, my teary eyes, she stopped.

Cecilia said, "If you don't want to go looking for Nikki . . ."

I said, "You know Nikki is gone."

Cecilia sat on the edge of my bed. For a long time we sat there. Cecilia didn't hug me. She knew I didn't want that.

She put her hand on my knee. That was enough.

Finally Cecilia said, "I guess we have to have a funeral."

"What?"

"And we have to eat the Martian penises."

"*What?*"

"To honor Nikki," said Cecilia firmly. "We have to get drunk, and we have to eat those nasty moon-man wangs of yours in her memory. You didn't throw them away, did you? We have to eat every single one."

She couldn't be serious. "The shrimp snacks?"

"Don't pretend like you've never wanted to do it," said Cecilia. Oh my God she was. "I don't want to . . ."

"You must eat tiny alien dongs," bellowed Cecilia. "You know it's true, so don't even fight it, I am going to get us tequila and we are going to eat the rest of those Martian penises, Nikki would want it that way, it's the only way we can truly honor Nikki, you have to eat Martian penises, Nikki forever, admit it, eat the Martian penis, say it, say it if you ever truly loved Nikki, eat the Martian penis, say it, *say it*, SAY IT," shouted Cecilia, grabbing me, hissing it in my face, until I said it, laughing even though I was still crying. That night she arranged everything. Cecilia and I went out after midnight and we made a bonfire in a field and I told some stories about Nikki and Cecilia gave a totally insincere eulogy and then we ate those cat shrimp snacks, all of them, the whole bag. Cecilia made me wash them down with tequila and later we threw them up, both of us barfing a million Martian penises.

Did you watch me doing that too, tornado killer?

It was a windy sunny morning and I was standing alone at the edge of town, near the white strings. Waiting.

A strong wind blew behind me, waving through the grass, blowing my hair into my face. I brushed it away from my eyes and then I saw him.

The tornado killer was out across the prairie, standing in the hills. Beyond the white strings. He was as close as he could come.

I was as far as I could go.

There were no tornadoes that day. He wasn't fighting anything. He had just come to see me.

I had come to be seen.

It was really windy.

On the way there, I had picked a flower from someone's garden. I didn't know what kind of flower it was, I'd never really paid attention to flowers. But looking at this flower now, really looking, it was so complicated, there was so much going on in it, large red petallike things that seemed to flare backward but embrace the delicate little yellow filaments flying forward, like the flower was lunging in two directions at once.

I had picked it for him.

I threw the flower at the tornado killer, into the wind.

It didn't fall.

Somehow it kept flying.

The wind carried it away until I couldn't see it anymore.

There was an old café on the edge of town where hardly anyone ever went. Cecilia and I liked to go to that café in the afternoons, after we'd sobered up a little, and buy hot dogs and pop and listen to the miniature jukeboxes that were right on the tables, and talk to the waitress and wonder about the lonesome-looking people who came there.

The waitress liked us too. Everyone called her Mrs. Lois. For the record, I never saw a Mr. Lois. Maybe she was divorced, maybe a widow. I never asked. I think she lived alone in a little apartment just above the café that couldn't have been more than two or three rooms.

Sometimes Mrs. Lois would give Cecilia and me our hot dogs for free. I believed she liked me in particular—she gave me a certain look. I appreciated how she ran the café, how she pulled off this difficult thing, day after day, keeping the place up. She was no-nonsense.

When I saw she'd put up a HELP WANTED sign in the window, I wanted to apply.

I needed money, of course. I'd wasted all my savings on that stupid bus ticket I never used. But there was another reason.

Because there had to be a way through the white strings. The café, and other restaurants and grocery stores I guess, they had to receive food deliveries somehow. Fresh milk and meat and whatever—it had to come from somewhere. A secret way to get past the white strings. If I worked at the café, maybe I'd learn that secret way.

That secret way could also get me to the tornado killer.

I didn't think twice. I just stuffed the application in my pocket before anyone noticed. Especially Cecilia. I didn't want her to think I'd rather work at the café than hang out with her.

The next day I ditched Cecilia.

I left the house before she woke up and rode my bike to the

library. It was full-on summer now and even morning was boiling hot. I was already sweating by the time I got downtown and it wasn't even eight o'clock.

The library was just opening when I arrived, so there weren't many people there. But it was cool and quiet in the old stone building.

I was there to research the tornado killer.

I mean, there had to be something about tornado killers at the library, I thought, if tornado killers had always been around town like people said. I looked in the periodicals section for old newspaper articles about tornado killers. Or reports of when tornadoes had hit town. Or how much damage the tornadoes had done . . .

There wasn't much. But I noticed that some issues of newspapers were missing, or pages from them, around the times that storms had happened. As though someone had removed them.

I flipped through the card catalog drawers. There were a handful of locally published books about the tornado killer and some materials in their "special collection."

But all those books were checked out.

I said to the librarian, "Who checked out all the books about the tornado killer?"

"I can't tell you who he is," tutted the librarian, but not unkindly. "Are you doing research for a project, or . . . ?"

She let the rest of the question hang there, and looked at me funny.

"No." I felt uncomfortable, the way the librarian was looking at me now. She wore one of those ugly necklaces like Mrs. Bindley's.

The librarian noticed me looking at the necklace and gave me a strange smile, as if we were both in on the same joke.

Of course, it wasn't so weird that all those books were checked out. The tornado killer was big news. People naturally wanted to learn more.

But the librarian had said "I can't tell you who *he* is." As though there was just one guy who had checked out all the books himself, all at once.

Who, then?

I said, "The card catalog says you have other stuff about the tornado killer in a special collection . . ."

"The special collection is closed while we restore the materials." The librarian indicated behind her. There was a window into a staff-only back room. Laid out on a table were a bunch of colorful note cards, torn and dirty.

Hey. I knew those cards.

"Aren't those from the speech the tornado killer made at school?" I said.

"The materials were damaged in the tornado," said the librarian. "When they're done being restored . . ."

She kind of trailed off. Not smiling anymore, and looking at me differently now. I realized I was being dismissed. I thanked her and started wandering around.

Why couldn't I just go look at the cards?

Why would they even keep the tornado killer's speech notes at the library?

The librarian seemed to have her own questions. She picked up the phone. A few seconds later she was talking to someone on the line, still looking at me.

I didn't like that look. Maybe it was time to leave. I had skipped breakfast and I was getting hungry anyway. I didn't want to be obvious about leaving, though. Maybe because of the way the librarian was looking at me now. I went into the stacks and took a roundabout way to the front door and ducked out.

It was blazing hot outside. I was thirsty too, so I went to the vending machine that was chained outside the library, right next to the employees' entrance. That door was usually closed, but today someone had propped it open.

I had already put in my quarters and pressed the button and heard my can rattling down the pathways inside the machine when an idea came to me. By the time the can *thunk*ed down I had made my decision.

I didn't know if I could do it.

The cold can sat in the vending machine slot, ready for me to take it.

I left it there.

I went through the employees' entrance.

I had never been in the back office part of the library. I crept in quietly, carefully. It was mostly empty, just a bunch of offices and a break room. I felt more nervous than I expected. After all, I'd explored lots of places where I shouldn't have been. But those were always abandoned places. If a real person, if a librarian or whatever, came down the hall and saw me, and asked me what I was doing there, I wouldn't know what to say.

I came into the room where the tornado killer's colorful note cards were laid out. I glimpsed the back of the librarian's head.

I stepped into the room, silently.

The librarian was still facing away from me.

Whose idea was it to gather up the tornado killer's speech notes after the tornado destroyed the school? They must've had to search through a lot of wreckage for it. Why? The speech had just been nonsense.

But it had been interrupted.

So maybe there was extra stuff that he hadn't said yet.

I came up to the table where the cards were laid out. The room was quiet except for the hum of the computer. I looked up. The librarian was still facing away from me. I glanced over the cards—torn, dirtied, but still readable. Typed out using an old typewriter. I saw phrases I recognized.

```
BUT HOW DID YOU KNOW I WAS YOUR CHOSEN
ONE?
```

I glanced up. The librarian still hadn't noticed me.

```
MY UNCANNY ABILITY TO SOOTHE THE WINDS,
OR WHIP THEM INTO A FURY
MY RAW POWERS INSTINCTIVELY GRAPPLED WITH
THE RADIO WAVES
```

I grabbed some cards, stuffing them in my pockets. Strange words flashed by.

I looked up.

The librarian was staring right at me.

My heart lurched. The room pounded all around me, getting smaller. I backed away from the table.

Beyond her, men were entering the library. The same men who had brought the tornado killer to my school. They saw me. One of them pointed and said something. They started coming for me.

They were wearing the same necklaces as the librarian.

I ran through the back offices and burst out of the library into the blinding heat.

I grabbed my bike and pedaled out of there fast. I didn't know anything about those men. But the look in the librarian's eye was uglier than what I'd expected.

Still, she didn't know me by name. I was pretty sure about that. She didn't know where I lived. Nobody caught up with me, or followed me, I thought.

I got home safe but my heart was beating fast, even after I'd run to my room, shut the door and the window, and laid down on my bed with the fan on.

I lay there for a long time, the fan blowing on me.

———

I took out the cards.

Some were torn up and I had to jigsaw-puzzle them back together. Most of them were from parts of the speech I'd already heard, but there were other parts. New parts, strange parts, things he hadn't yet gotten to say.

I pieced together the shreds of one card:

```
FORBIDDEN TO TOUCH ANY OF YOU, TO
PRESERVE MY EXALTED PURITY
```

And this one:

```
THROUGH PURITY AM I BORN AND REBORN, FOR
THE DEFENSE OF THE IMPURE
```

And this:

```
I AM HIS YOUTH AND HE IS MY AGE, AND I
SHALL BE HIS AGE AND HE MY YOUTH;
```

```
HIS PURITY IS MY PURITY, HIS
CONTAMINATION IS MY CONTAMINATION
```

And:

```
CONTAMINATION IS PURIFIED ONLY BY THE
DEATH OF THE IMPURE
```

And:

```
ONLY THE PURE CAN KILL A TORNADO
```

I read and reread them.

It felt unpleasant. It put me in the mood of church stuff. Mom and Dad weren't religious, even though they had both been raised in religious families. Our family didn't really go to church, except maybe for Christmas and Easter every once in a while, at the big church downtown. A few years ago Dad had some midlife spiritual crisis, though, and for a few months we did go to church every Sunday, and Cecilia and I had to go to Sunday school.

By that time, Cecilia and I were too old for any of the teachings to take root. Since we hadn't grown up religious, we'd never really paid attention to what people believed. It was just stuff we'd heard about secondhand. And so when it was all actually explained to us, it made zero sense. Cecilia and I would look at each other as the Sunday school lady rambled on—people didn't *really* believe this stuff, right?

Here's the secret of the world: nobody really believes it. Not even the priests, not really. There's a special way people talk when they're saying something that they don't really believe, and you don't really believe, but you've both agreed for some reason that you'll both pretend to believe it. That's what the stuff on the cards reminded me of. The creepy stuff our catechism teacher would recite to us, in tones both complacent and anxious.

When Dad's religious phase wore off, we stopped having to go to Sunday school. I didn't miss it.

I did notice something else about the cards, though.

One of them was a kind of title card. According to the date printed on it, these cards had been typed up thirteen years ago.

Back then, the tornado killer would've been three years old.

So he couldn't possibly have written that weird speech he'd made.

Who had written it, then?

———

I noticed more people wearing those necklaces. The same ones as Mrs. Bindley and the librarian. It was hard not to. Cecilia said those necklaces were ugly, and she was right—overly intricate chains with fussy ruffles and filigrees and a little complicated box hanging off, like a pendant or a charm.

People wore the necklaces outside their shirts, as if to make sure you saw they were wearing them. Even people who normally never wore jewelry were wearing them. I wondered if they had always been wearing these necklaces under their shirts, and only now wore them outside their shirts.

One day Cecilia and I were hanging out at the café (the HELP WANTED sign was still in the window, but I hadn't worked up the courage to submit my application to Mrs. Lois) and I saw a middle-aged man wearing one of those necklaces. An everyday guy, like somebody's uncle, beefy and wearing a flannel shirt and work jeans. But he had this ornate necklace hanging around his neck. I asked him why.

He gave me a gross once-over, then chuckled. "Well, just in case, kiddo."

"Pffft," said Mrs. Lois.

"You got a problem?" The guy twisted around. "I didn't ask you."

Mrs. Lois just kept doing her waitress stuff.

"You don't like it, I can take my business elsewhere." The guy turned back to me and Cecilia, and his harsh tone turned to what he might've thought of as fatherly. "Do you think you can guess what I keep in my locket?"

Cecilia seemed just as grossed out as me. "I couldn't guess, I just literally couldn't guess," she said.

"What is it?" I asked.

"Well, get this," said the guy. "Inside this locket right here, I've got something special."

He just looked at us, nodding. He was really milking my interest, really ramping up the drama to force me to ask again what was in it so I'd be half on board with whatever he said, regardless of whether or not it was interesting. He needed me for that. Mrs. Lois wasn't buying it, and Cecilia clearly was over this whole situation since she was already fiddling with the little tabletop jukebox. Maybe this guy was a salesman of these little necklaces. He looked at me steadily, still quiet but nodding, grinning as if he were about to close a big sale. I gave in. "Okay, what's in your locket?"

The guy smiled. "A chunk of a tornado killer."

I started.

"What?" Cecilia said.

"A tornado killer's *nose*." The man tapped his own nose, as though we needed a visual reminder of what a nose was. "I have bits of a *nose* of a real tornado killer locked up safe in this locket of mine."

Cecilia stopped messing with the jukebox.

I cleared my throat. "Why?"

"For protection," continued the guy, nodding. "Tornadoes can't abide tornado killers—stands to reason, doesn't it? Well, even after they die, the bodies of tornado killers stay special. This tornado killer died a hundred years ago, but you know what, his precious nose still protects me against tornadoes."

"How public, like a frog," said Cecilia.

"What?" said the man.

"I mean *gross*."

Mrs. Lois clunked around loudly in the kitchen.

"So if you were wearing that necklace, you could walk out into the middle of tornado country, and a tornado wouldn't kill you?" I said.

The man frowned. "Well, now . . ."

"Full of crap," Mrs. Lois said under her breath.

"I've had just about enough of your lip, miss," said the guy, turning again. "That's what's wrong with everyone these days. Everyone thinks they know everything. Well, I say that's why we're having so many problems with tornadoes! Think about it."

He got up, and gave me a look as if to say *you think about it too*. And then he was out the door. He didn't leave a tip.

I saw more and more of those necklaces around town. It wasn't clear where they came from. People claimed they just "found them again," stashed in an attic or forgotten in a drawer. That the necklace had belonged to an aunt or a grandparent or whatever.

At home, Mom and Dad would make fun of the sort of people who wore the necklaces. But I noticed that they weren't so mocking in public. Soon their attitude began to change. They seemed a little more worried, a little less outspoken. Once I was on the couch, watching TV, and Mom and Dad were talking in the kitchen, and in the brief silence between commercials I overheard Mom say, "It's not really going to happen, is it?"

Then they were both quiet. Something strange about Mom's voice kept me frozen on the couch. Aching for the TV to drown out whatever they were going to say next.

A few days later I woke up and the sunrise was glowing orange and yellow beyond my open window.

A wild wind blew through my room. I felt it on my face before I opened my eyes. I turned over and felt something cool and leafy on my cheek.

I opened my eyes and discovered I was surrounded by flower petals.

I sat up in bed. It was covered in flowers.

Dozens of flowers on my windowsill.

Flowers all over my floor, my dresser, my desk.

A hundred flowers lay all around me, shifting in the breeze.

The tornado killer had answered.

This wasn't a dream.

It was real.

Me and him—it was real.

Nervousness fluttered in my stomach. I was afraid. But I liked this kind of afraid. What did these flowers mean, what was I being invited into, what was I getting myself into? I didn't know what he'd do next.

I didn't know what I might do.

I cleaned up the flowers before anyone came into my room. I didn't throw them away but stuffed them in bags under my bed. There was no way I wanted Cecilia or my parents or anyone else to know about this secret.

This was mine. He was mine.

⚏

The faster and freakier the tornadoes twisted, lurching like enormous drunks across the prairie, the more fascinating they were.

People would stop whatever they were doing and watch the sky, entranced. Drivers would pull over and get out of their cars, standing in the fields, staring at the clouds. People washing dishes would catch a glimpse out the window and leave the water running as they slowly walked into their backyards, their eyes fixed on the hypnotic sky, the tornadoes pulsing, multiplying and swelling, thicker and darker, squeezing us down, penning us in, coming for us, but there was nothing we could do, the tornadoes were terrifying, the tornadoes were death and yet we couldn't stop staring, and I felt them staring back, like the tornadoes wanted to come close, like they had something to tell us.

And then I had the dream.

THE BRIDES IN THE YARD

I didn't feel like I was dreaming.

Cecilia and I were at Lisa Stubenberger's house with the rest of the old group late at night for a sleepover.

Obviously, that was unthinkable. I doubted Cecilia or I would ever be welcome at Lisa's again after Cecilia's bad-mouthing of the old group. It had been at least a year since I was at Lisa's house, but in this dream every detail was vivid, from the green patterned carpet to the fake wood walls. We were sprawled around on bean bags and pillows, surrounded by greasy empty pizza boxes and crusts. Lisa had turned off the lights and we were watching horror movies.

In real life Lisa was totally normal—in fact, according to Cecilia she was boring. There was nothing weird about her. But Lisa Stubenberger in my dream was different, she picked movies the real Lisa Stubenberger would never pick, and was creepily enthusiastic about these movies in a way the real Lisa Stubenberger never would be. In the dream, Lisa had chosen truly terrifying videos, low-budget freakouts from foreign countries, the actors speaking a language I didn't know and the subtitles in an alphabet I didn't know, and I couldn't tell if the tortures were special effects or real life, like was I watching actors or was it real people actually getting tortured?

But everyone at the sleepover was so exhausted that by the middle of the second movie they had all fallen asleep.

Except for me.

I felt alert all over. In the dream I was still awake, and still watching the hideous movie with the volume muted, in the dark, with Lisa and Cecilia and Sadie and Danielle and everyone asleep around me, but as the movie went on—I don't know if it was because I was up late, or scared by the movie, but I felt sharp and *ready*, I couldn't say for what, and in the movie a witch was tearing out some poor guy's spine and gobbling it down; thousands of worms were busily bursting out from behind a second guy's eyeballs, and the witch laughed; here was a third guy getting shredded in a grinder of giant knives, gleefully operated by the witch . . . Where did Lisa *find* this stuff, I thought to myself, what *is* this . . .

A noise.

Someone was outside the house.

Lisa's basement had a sliding glass door that opened out into a sunken backyard patio. Out of the corner of my eye I glimpsed someone on that patio. Someone at that door.

Someone watching me.

I kept my eyes locked on the television. The witch, a very old lady covered with slimy sores, was eating the brains straight out of some mustached guy's head. My body clenched tight. The someone was still at the door. I saw them out of the corner of my eye. Now another man was melting into a soup of blood and muscle, and the witch was licking it up with a black tongue, babbling to herself in her horrible language.

I turned.

He was gone in a flash of white.

I got up.

Outside the glass door there was nothing. Just the dim reflections of my friends. Beyond it, darkness. But if there really was someone out there, I thought in the dream, then I had to make sure the door was locked. In the dream I moved through my friends and reached the sliding glass door. I looked at my dim image. Then past it.

The television silently flashed colors and shapes.

I rolled the door open.

A flood of summer breeze floated in, heavy and sweet.

I stepped outside.

The night in my dream was sultry compared to the stiff chill of Lisa's air-conditioned house. Everything was dark. The stars were walled off behind clouds. Someone had put the moon away for now. I couldn't see anything but I knew Lisa's backyard. A brick patio, then a grassy field, breaking up into dirt and swallowed up by the forest.

My bare feet felt the change between the carpet's bland springiness and the uneven brick of the patio. I looked out blindly, listening to the whir of summer insects, as steady and shrill as a gym teacher's whistle.

He could be anywhere.

I took another step. Another. More steps and then I was far from the dimly glowing glass door, lost in burning summer darkness, but it wasn't darkness, it was a witchy light of its own, I was scalded by black light but I didn't want to stop feeling that way, the night wrapped me up and carried me forward like a shadowy river, deeper into the hot darkness.

He was near.

I didn't feel rough brick on the soles of my feet anymore. Now it was the prickling of grass. The night smelled warm, damp. Alive.

I couldn't see. He could be an inch away.

Then I knew.

I knew for certain he was so close that if I stretched out my hand I'd be touching his face.

The bugs were screaming.

I turned around slowly. Trying not to seem like I was panicking. Wet grass on my feet, moving.

Go. Start walking back to the house.

Calm. Steady.

I knew he was following me.

I wanted to run. The ground changed beneath my feet in reverse. From grass to brick. Brick to carpet. Broiling night to refrigerated house. The difference made me shiver. Inside, the horror movie still silently threw shifting blue and white lights over my sleeping friends.

I stood in the middle of the room.

I didn't turn to close the door. I didn't dare turn around.

I waited a long moment.

Then I heard the door roll closed behind me.

I turned, and I saw the tornado killer.

In this dream he was different than I remembered. Leaner. His skin browner. He wore a ragged white T-shirt, green shorts, and sneakers.

He was beautiful.

We couldn't speak. If any of my friends woke up, I knew the tornado killer would be out of there in a flash, bounding off into the night like a spooked deer.

He might do anything, I thought. I didn't know the first thing about this tornado killer. Not really. He might be dangerous.

I stepped toward him.

He tensed.

I wanted to reach out and take his hand. I could see his heart pounding, a delicate vein pulsing in his neck.

I wanted to put my lips on that vein.

I didn't move toward him. I moved back down, sinking onto my heap of pillows. The movie witch was using a jeweled, curvy knife to force a guy into a tank of razor-toothed octopi. The water turned red and black with blood and ink.

The tornado killer came closer to me, sat down with me.

Very close.

He looked me in the eyes.

Then we both looked at the movie.

Then the really scary part of the movie happened, something I don't even want to write about, not even now. All of my friends slept through it, but in the dream the tornado killer and I saw it together, and when the whole movie was over, we were lying very close together and my heart was beating hard. The credits rolled on forever. We were both kind of pretending to be asleep, pretending we didn't realize how close we really were, and then the videotape ran out and there was nothing but static, the TV a silent cage of billions of furious black-and-white bees giving off a gray swampy light that made our skin glow like moon creatures. His head was in my lap. I ran my hands through his soft brown hair. That's all I wanted. It was enough.

———

I woke up late after that dream.

I was eating breakfast that was more like lunch when Cecilia came into the kitchen and casually said something I didn't even process at first. I asked her to say it again.

"Lisa Stubenberger invited us over tonight," said Cecilia. "She's having a sleepover."

I was stunned.

"I know, I know, we don't have to go," said Cecilia. "I bet they probably just have some stupid revenge planned. I'll call her back and tell her no."

No, no. I had to go.

I had already dreamed of going there.

⸺

Be careful.

I remembered when Cecilia was around twelve, how she was crazy for boy bands. The music sounded terrible to me but Cecilia would tape posters of famous boy singers to her wall, boys that always looked like plastic nothings to me, distant zero people. They weren't real. They weren't even supposed to be real. They were just shapes and sounds for Cecilia to pour her want into.

I didn't want to pour my want into shapes and sounds.

Cecilia and her friends would go to school sports too. To watch boys play basketball and football and baseball. She wasted so much time watching boys do things.

I realized I was now a girl who watched a boy do things.

I shook myself out of it. I said to myself: I am through watching. I am through dreaming.

I took out the café application again.

⸺

Mom and Cecilia went out shopping that afternoon.

That gave me a chance to visit the café on my own. I was still half inside my strange dream as I biked over to the café. But it was more than a dream, because this morning, out of nowhere, Cecilia and I *had* been invited to go to Lisa's for a sleepover, just as I had dreamed. Why would Lisa want to hang out with us again? But if that part of the dream was coming true, then maybe the tornado killer part might come true . . .

Stop thinking of stupid dreams.

I had the café application in my pocket, folded and wrinkled and doodled on with my symbol and other things. In a way, I hoped that the job had already been taken. I was nervous about it.

When I looked in the café window, the HELP WANTED sign was still there.

I thought: here goes.

The café was empty except for Mrs. Lois.

When I came in, she gave me a funny look. Maybe I still looked weirded out from Cecilia telling me about the sleepover.

But I knew that look. Mrs. Lois had given me that look before.

I said, "I want to apply for the job."

Mrs. Lois said, "You finally filled out that application?"

I hadn't expected that. "You saw me take it?"

Mrs. Lois looked amused. "Let me get you something to drink."

"What are you drinking?"

"Coffee."

"I'll have that, then, please."

"I've never seen you drink coffee."

"I drink it sometimes." Actually I'd never tasted coffee in my life. But coffee seemed like the kind of thing a waitress should know about. I wanted to be on the same page as Mrs. Lois. But she probably could totally tell I was lying . . . maybe not a good job interview move. Wait, was this a job interview now?

"I have a fresh pot," said Mrs. Lois.

She went to pour me a cup. I sat in a booth, flipping through the songs on the tabletop jukebox. Maybe if I got the job, I could change out these crappy songs. Nothing good here. Just corny oldies, country music, show tunes . . .

I'm jest a girl who cain't say no.

I said without thinking, "Do you know Mr. Z?"

Mrs. Lois paused filling up my cup.

I didn't know why I had said that. I didn't talk much about Mr. Z with Cecilia. Definitely not with Mom and Dad, especially after they took Mr. Z's side against us. But seeing that song Mr. Z had sung at me on this jukebox made me feel weird. Like part of Mr. Z was inside the jukebox, staring at me.

Mrs. Lois brought over my coffee. She sat in my booth.

She ignored my application on the table.

She said, "Why are you asking me about Mr. Z?"

I hesitated. After all, Mrs. Lois was an adult. But she was different, right? She'd been so friendly to me and Cecilia. So I started talking. And when I started talking I realized I needed to talk. And then I couldn't stop talking, not just about Mr. Z, but about everything.

She listened.

No other customers came in. When the phone rang Mrs. Lois ignored it. It kept ringing as I told her about wanting to run away, and how I secretly went out with Roy Hetzler, and how the tornado killer had stared at me at Archie's party, and how I wanted to find the tornado killer.

Mrs. Lois was easy to talk to.

At first she seemed to be listening in that withholding way adults do. Like they're just letting you say dumb things because you're too young to know better. But then her face began to change, like something large was passing behind her eyes. I told her about how we used to run at the white strings to feel that addicting shiver, and about how the tornado had killed Nikki, and about how Mr. Z had slapped Cecilia and kissed my hand and sung that song at me, the very song on this jukebox, that's why I had asked about it, and I told her about how I dreamed about the tornado killer, and the tornado killer had filled my room with flowers, and . . .

Mrs. Lois looked like something was breaking open inside her.

I kept on talking and I even told her about that one time, in Archie's house, when we'd seen Archie's mother and the Horrible Woman, both of them staring at me—

Mrs. Lois put down her coffee.

I thought she'd put it down to answer the phone, which was still ringing.

But Mrs. Lois ignored the phone. She looked again at my application. She seemed to see something there for the first time. Something was dawning on her.

"Of all the people," she said.

I asked her if this meant I got the job.

"You've got the job all right," she said.

It did not sound like a good thing.

The wind suddenly blew the door open.

I turned, startled—when did it get so windy? It hadn't been windy like this when I'd biked over. But now the wind was blowing really hard. I saw tornadoes looming close against the white strings, a wall of howling dirty air. Raindrops spattered the windows.

A group of men was coming up the road.

It was the men from the library. The men who had brought the box to school on Tornado Day. The men who had been putting up strings around the edge of town.

Mrs. Lois saw them too. Her eyes hardened.

"Looks like we're in for some rain," she said.

She didn't sound like she was talking about rain.

I said, "Who are those men?"

She said, "Have you met the tornado killer?"

I didn't know how to answer that. Had I?

"Face-to-face?" she said. "Have you touched him?"

"No—"

"You said you wanted to run away." Mrs. Lois looked at the men coming up the sidewalk. Her tone turned urgent. "Do it. Now."

"What?" This wasn't the kind of thing adults were supposed to say.

"Don't let him, don't let the tornado killer—" Mrs. Lois stopped, then grabbed me. She pulled me up and pushed me to the back of the restaurant, through the kitchen.

I'd never been in the kitchen before. It didn't look the way I expected. Mrs. Lois reached to the back of a shelf and slid out a package, wrapped tight in greasy black paper.

I heard the men coming in to the café.

Mrs. Lois grabbed my jaw.

I flinched but she held firm. She tilted my chin up and stared in my eyes.

"Get away from the tornado killer," she said. "Don't touch him. If you touch him it's death."

I couldn't talk. She was gripping my jaw too hard. Her face was desperate and ferocious. I tried to pull my chin away.

She wouldn't let me.

She said, "If I'm wrong and it's not you, then you're lucky, but if it is you—if they put it in you, then you'll have to drink the whole thing, drink it all down, if you want to clean yourself out."

My face quivered in her grip.

"I couldn't do it," said Mrs. Lois, and then she let me go, pushed up her sleeve, and on her forearm I saw this tattoo:

I recognized it. That symbol was carved on the bus station bathroom stall. I started to tell her that—

Something shattered in the front of the café. Plates and glasses breaking.

Mrs. Lois cursed and ran back out of the kitchen.

She left the black package on the counter.

What was I supposed to do?

My face still hurt from her grip. In the front of the café I could hear Mrs. Lois's voice and the men's voices getting louder, angrier.

Her tattoo—

I grabbed the black package and dashed out the screen door in the back. It slapped shut behind me. Now I was outside, by the trash cans. The black package was heavier than I'd expected, sticky with kitchen grease. I still heard Mrs. Lois talking inside, sharp and hot-tempered. The men hostile, aggressive. An argument. Like the men were demanding something, and she wasn't giving it.

Storm clouds rolled black across the sky. Drops of rain tapped my skin. I threw the package into my bike basket. My hands were oily from touching it. I felt like I'd get in trouble for having it somehow.

I pedaled away fast and didn't look back.

I rode hard through the dark.

It was still only afternoon but black clouds blotted out the sun. Storm sirens were wailing. I had always thought that whoever invented those sirens made them sound way more eerie than necessary, like a huge lonely monster crying far away up in the sky . . . Raindrops spotted the sidewalk now. Windy blackness was rolling over everything. I biked through the empty downtown, slashing through puddles. I took a shortcut through the alley.

Everyone was off the streets. I had to get inside too, quick. You can't stay outside when the alarms are screaming, it meant the tornadoes might break through any second. That the tornado killer was having a rough time. I wondered where he was right now, how badly the fight against the tornadoes was going. I had to get to a basement, away from the storm.

In my mind I saw those men coming into the café. I saw the way Mrs. Lois reacted when she saw them, when she hustled me out as though she knew—

Nikki flashed across the street.

Nikki.

I skidded to a stop. Hot and cold snakes writhed together in my belly. I pushed down on the pedals again. Rain spattered my face.

But Nikki was dead—

Nikki! Darting down the alley, out of the corner of my eye—

I swerved around. "*Nikki?*"

My heart pounded. The storm siren rose and fell. The rain was really bucketing down now, soaking me. But Nikki was out in this storm too. Wind rushed through the alley.

Nikki streaked between the trash cans—

Then the rain came down all at once, I couldn't see through the flying water, it was dark but then lightning lit up everything, a huge thunderclap went off like a bomb, I was forced off my bike and had to push it through the dark rain, I was running down the sidewalk, drenched and looking for any store that was open, where the lights were on. I pushed open the nearest door.

It was the pet store Cecilia and I used to visit, to play with puppies and kittens before we went out for our get-drunk sessions. The clerks knew us here and they just barely tolerated us.

"Can I come in?" I was already wedging my bike through the door. "The storm—"

"Yeah, yeah," said the clerk. "Just shut the door, get in!"

"Can I bring my bike in too? I don't want to—"

"Shut the door!" said the clerk, who was too busy taking care of the animals. They were all upset by the storm and the siren, squawking and barking and hissing. The radio was on too, the tornado killer announcers talking confusedly, I couldn't tell what they were saying. I rolled my bike to the back of the store, tracking water in.

"Hey, um," I said to the clerk. "Have you seen a black cat around here lately? White paws, white front?"

"No."

"It's my cat," I said. "Her name is Nikki. She's missing, I had thought a tornado had gotten her but I think I just—"

"Yeah, I've seen your signs," said the clerk, who was clearly busy and didn't really care.

The sirens trailed off as though dying, then wailed back up again. Out the windows it looked like the pet store was underwater. Thunder cracked right overhead as everything flashed, the lightning was on top of us, and the siren kept howling underneath it, the storm was so wild I couldn't even see what was going on outside. Maybe the entire town was getting washed away except for us.

Nikki was outside in that.

Was the cat I saw even Nikki, though? And what had happened with Mrs. Lois, what did those men want from her? Was the tornado killer out in the rain right now, fighting the tornadoes?

The radio announcers didn't know. They kept shouting at each other, frantic.

Then the signal broke into static.

An hour later, the radio station was still off the air. But the storm had stopped. The rain had tapered off but the radio crackled white noise, as though the storm had washed the airwaves clean of human activity. The storm alarm kept wailing. The clerk had barely talked to me the whole time. I felt trapped. But you can't go outside if the alarm was still sounding, everyone knew that—

I heard the tinkle of the bells over the door.

The store door opened.

Melanie Fripp entered with her parents. I knew Melanie from school, she was my year. Right now she and her mom and dad were dressed up as if they'd just come from church.

But it wasn't Sunday. And there was a tornado. Or at least the storm was finished but the sirens were still blaring, so what were the Fripps doing outside? Even still, here they were, all dressed up. I'd never seen Mr. Fripp in a suit before. Usually you'd just see him in a dirty T-shirt, doing yard work in front of their house. Now he was dressed up in a bad-fitting blue blazer and gray pants, and Mrs. Fripp wore a dowdy middle-aged brown dress with weird gold buckles.

But Melanie—I'd never seen her like this. At first glance she looked beautiful, wearing a white lace dress with elbow-length white gloves and white stockings, her hair elegantly done up. Like she was a tiny bride.

Then I saw her face.

Her mouth was frozen in a stilted smile. Like someone had cut a lunatic grin off someone else's face and pasted it onto her mouth. Her eyes were wide open but blank. Melanie was not there.

All three of them wore the necklaces.

Mr. Fripp said, "Go ahead, Melanie. Pick a puppy."

I'd hung out with Melanie Fripp in this store before. She came for the same reason Cecilia and I did, to play with the puppies or whatever, because her parents didn't let her have one. She had told me she'd begged her parents again and again, but they'd always put their foot down: no way, no puppy.

Melanie didn't seem to see me now.

"Any puppy in the store," said Mr. Fripp.

Melanie just grinned, horribly.

"Come on, Melanie. You wanted a puppy, huh?"

I couldn't look at Melanie's face anymore.

Mr. Fripp turned to the clerk. "Okay. What's the best dog you've got here? I want the best goddamned dog in the store."

"Alan," whispered Mrs. Fripp.

"What's your most expensive dog?" said Mr. Fripp.

"She doesn't want one," said Mrs. Fripp in a broken voice.

I was standing in the aisle, caught between Mrs. Fripp nearly crying, Melanie with that empty smile, and Mr. Fripp, who took the clerk aside and whispered fiercely, "Just the best goddamned dog in the store, you hear me?"

The clerk showed Mr. Fripp a black Labrador puppy. He was a wobbly, enthusiastic little guy, who squirmed around as the clerk picked him up out of the cage. The clerk put the puppy in Mr. Fripp's big, hairy hands.

"There! We got a dog," said Mr. Fripp.

Melanie didn't even look at the dog. She just kept smiling at nothing. Mrs. Fripp put her arm around Melanie. Melanie didn't seem to notice. Mrs. Fripp led Melanie out the door, with Mr. Fripp following.

"We got your dog, okay? All right?" Mr. Fripp called after them. "All right? What?"

Mrs. Fripp turned around. "You're just making it worse—"

The Fripps were out the door.

The clerk wasn't meeting my eyes.

What on Earth had happened to Melanie?

I wheeled my bike down the aisle, following the Fripps out. If the Fripps could go outside, I figured I could go outside now too . . . The siren kept wailing. But there was something else in the siren's sound.

Something insinuating, mocking. Like the siren knew something I didn't.

I came out into the street.

I saw Janice Whaley. She too was all dressed up in a white fancy dress, like a bride. Her face was normal, though. She didn't have Melanie's creepy smile. Mr. and Mrs. Whaley came up behind her.

Janice spotted Melanie. Her mouth opened as if to scream. She tried to get away, but Mr. and Mrs. Whaley held her back. She twisted and kicked and now Janice was trying to say something but the Whaleys covered her mouth and pushed her on. The Fripps kept on walking in the opposite direction.

Melanie didn't react.

"Melanie!" shouted Janice. "*Melanie!*"

Then I saw Irene Bellardini wearing a little wedding dress.

Mr. and Mrs. Bellardini were right behind her.

Darlene Farley came around the corner too, stone-faced, also dressed like a bride.

Mr. and Mrs. Farley were behind her.

They were all wearing the necklaces.

I followed them on my bike, keeping my distance.

The sirens continued to wail. The brides and their parents didn't acknowledge me. I kept after them, pedaling slowly. The rain had petered out but the wind was still strong. A dozen girls and their parents were all heading to the edge of town.

I knew where they were going.

This is what I saw.

Twelve girls in white wedding dresses stood in line outside Mr. Z's house. Their parents stood behind them, holding their daughters' shoulders. Everyone was still. The only sounds were the storm siren and Mr. Z's ringing, ringing, ringing telephone.

Mr. Z's front door opened.

Mr. and Mrs. Stubenberger came out with Lisa Stubenberger. Lisa was wearing a white dress too. Mr. and Mrs. Stubenberger looked relieved. But Lisa's expression was empty, like she had seen something that had broken her eyes.

She had the same frozen smile as Melanie.

The Stubenbergers took Lisa by the shoulders and walked her forward. They tried to talk to her.

Lisa didn't respond.

Lisa and her parents moved past the other girls and their parents. Some stupid part of me remembered the sleepover that was supposed to happen at Lisa's tonight. Then Tina Molloy, wrapped up like a little white present, was guided toward Mr. Z's door by Mr. and Mrs. Molloy. They entered Mr. Z's house.

The door closed.

The Stubenbergers led away smiling, empty-eyed Lisa. I felt like the sky was getting closer, pressing down heavier and squeezing thicker around my head, shrinking into a tight painful dot, everything flying fast-forward all around me, the line of brides at Mr. Z's house brilliant white against the gray sky, the breeze playing with their dresses and their hair, and I had a queer feeling, like I had gone through the rear door of the world, that I was seeing some backstage thing I wasn't meant to see.

Or maybe this was the way the world had always been, and I was only finding out now.

Ten minutes later Tina Molloy and her parents came out of Mr. Z's house. Tina's face was also plastered with an empty grin. She stumbled and her parents caught her. They all kept walking.

Mr. Z's phone continued to ring.

═══

I pedaled home fast through the still-empty streets. The siren was still braying nonstop. I threw my bike down in our garage and ran into my gray, empty house.

Nobody was home. Everyone was probably still locked down where they were. Dad at work, Mom and Cecilia out buying clothes. A note taped to the refrigerator said Mom would drop Cecilia off at Lisa Stubenberger's sleepover right after shopping, and that I should find my own way there.

I kept seeing Lisa's bizarre grin.

What happened to her?

I didn't see a sleepover happening at Lisa's tonight.

═══

I didn't know who to call. I didn't know what to do.

I couldn't stop thinking about those girls at Mr. Z's house.

An hour later the siren stopped. I still didn't want to go outside, but I felt trapped in the house. It didn't feel like my house, somehow. It was like the time I'd realized that one day Cecilia and I would grow up and move out, that Mom and Dad would move out too or die. Some family of strangers had lived in this house before us. Some other family of strangers would live in this house after we went. It wasn't our house. We were a replaceable part that got swapped out, like light bulbs.

I wanted out.

The girls in the wedding dresses had been lined up outside Mr. Z's and everyone just seemed to accept it. Even those who struggled, it was like they were struggling against something they'd known all along. That they knew this would happen to them sooner or later.

I saw again Lisa walking out of the house with that grotesque grin.

Her eyes a million miles away.

I went into the garage. Mrs. Lois's black package was still in my bike basket. I didn't like the way it looked. What had Mrs. Lois said about it? Why had she given it to me?

I didn't want to open it.

But I couldn't throw it away, either.

I would bring it to the café tomorrow, I decided. Yes. I'd ask questions. I'd return to the café tomorrow, definitely. Mrs. Lois had something more to tell me. Because of her tattoo. She knew something. She was in the club. She would tell me.

I hid the black package behind Dad's toolbox in the garage, where I knew it would never be found. I had never seen Dad fix anything.

It got dark.

Nobody came home. The sky spit random drops but it wasn't really raining anymore. As though the clouds were holding themselves back for round two, waiting for something in particular.

Lisa's empty white eyes. Her death grin.

Mr. Z's house, opening up for the next girl.

I called Lisa's house. Her sleepover couldn't possibly still be happening. Could it? After whatever had happened to her?

What *had* happened to her?

I hung up before anyone answered.

I felt like Lisa was contagious. Like maybe even just talking to Lisa on the phone would give me her infection, and then I'd have to go to Mr. Z's too.

But being home, all alone, was also freaking me out.

At last I got out my backpack. It was still packed for running away but I didn't bother unpacking it. I just stuck in my toothbrush and clothes for tomorrow and a random black T-shirt and gray sweatpants for pajamas. I hitched my sleeping bag to it and slung it all over my shoulder.

I went to the garage and got on my bike.

I rode back out into the wet, empty streets.

I had to bike past Mr. Z's on the way. My legs didn't want to keep pedaling but I forced them to do it. I coasted as Mr. Z's came into view again.

Nobody was there anymore. No brides, no parents. It was just a dark gray field with a lonely house. You might've thought it was abandoned. But his phone was still ringing.

I pedaled hard again.

The world got darker.

I swung into Lisa's neighborhood.

A car honked. I looked back at the headlights and saw it was actually Mom's car right behind me, coming to drop Cecilia off at Lisa's. They pulled up level with me and I saw Cecilia in the front passenger seat. I wanted to tell Cecilia about what had happened to Lisa at Mr. Z's house but Mom's car chugged ahead. When I caught up with Cecilia, she was already at Lisa's front door and the car was idling in the driveway. Mom rolled down her window—she wanted to tell me something.

I saw a half dozen bikes at Lisa's house, lying on the lawn and leaning against the fence.

That meant the other girls were already there for the sleepover.

I listened to Mom talk. She and Dad were going out tonight and she wanted to give me contact information in case I changed my mind about being at the sleepover. She wrote it down. I took the slip of paper.

I didn't know how to tell Mom what I'd seen. When was the last time I had confided in her at all?

How was this sleepover even happening? Why was everyone here, as though nothing was wrong? Maybe Lisa was in bed recovering from Mr. Z and the other girls were helping out.

"What's wrong?" said Mom.

"Nothing," I said.

"Okay then, have fun!" she said and her window rolled up. Mom pulled out and drove away. When I joined Cecilia on the front porch she'd already rang the doorbell. There was laughter inside, the television was on.

I turned to Cecilia, to tell her what I had seen. But then the door opened.

It was Lisa.

She looked completely normal.

———

Wait. What?

Cecilia and I came out of the dark and into the Stubenbergers' bright house. Lisa chattered on about all she'd planned for us that night. Some princess cartoon movie was on the TV somewhere inside. Everything was full of light and warmth and I smelled baking chocolate chip cookies and in the other room I heard girls talking and laughing. Lisa said she was so excited, her eyes bright and alive, giggling, saying that this sleepover was really going to be a lot of fun!

I didn't know what to say.

———

I had definitely seen Lisa Stubenberger at Mr. Z's. I had definitely seen her parents taking her into his house. I had definitely seen her stumble out with a frozen smile, her eyes as blank as though her core had been scoured out.

I had definitely seen that.

I was not crazy.

———

Lisa's basement was just the same as in my dream.

Sleeping bags were spread out all over the patterned carpet. The fake wood walls, the television, the bean bags, the sliding glass door. The pizza and pop and candy. Cecilia went over to Sadie Hughes, tentatively at first. Was our old group taking us back, really? How long had it been since we'd hung out with them? I looked over. Cecilia and Sadie were already talking and laughing.

I hadn't seen any of these other girls at Mr. Z's. Only Lisa.

So none of them knew what was happening.

But I knew.

Lisa knew.

The party went on around me. I felt like I was in some creepy copy of the world. All of the girls were wearing those ugly necklaces. Cecilia and I used to make jokes about those necklaces, like Mom and Dad did, about the kind of gullible people who wore them. I noticed Cecilia wasn't wearing our string-and-bus-locker-key necklace anymore. I was still wearing mine. It suddenly felt ridiculous. I took it off before anyone noticed and stuffed it in the side pocket of my backpack. My backpack was stupidly big, still filled with stuff for running away, not a sleepover. Did anyone even notice? Probably. I felt my social standing dwindle. Girls weren't talking to me, they were talking in new codes I had to catch up with. Now Danielle Lund was letting Cecilia try her necklace on. Cecilia just wanted to be part of the old group again. If everyone was wearing those necklaces now, then fine, Cecilia would do it too, even though deep down she really thought they were ugly. She and I were the ones who had been out of the loop.

I took Lisa aside. "Are you all right?"

She laughed. "Um, yeah? How about you?"

"You can tell me."

Her laughter fell away. "What?"

"I saw what happened."

"What happened?"

"At Mr. Z's house."

"Come on," Lisa said with a smile, as if I had said something that we both knew was dumb, and she was being nice by letting it pass.

She went off to talk to someone else.

It was as though the white dresses, the empty eyes, the creepy smiles had never happened.

But it had all happened.

I tried talking to the other girls. Something was wrong. They had changed into pajamas now, and their pajamas seemed childish to me. Lisa wore actual pink pajamas with footies, I didn't even know they made pajamas like that for people our size, our age. The other girls were watching some cartoon movie about a princess and they were eating their cookies, giggling about stupid stuff.

It was as if, during the time Cecilia and I had been out of touch with these girls, they had all made some decision to go back to being children.

But we weren't. These were the same girls I'd seen drink alcohol, that I had seen pairing off with boys, the same girls who used to intimidate me sometimes. Now they were acting like third-graders in pink pajamas.

I sat with my black T-shirt and gray sweatpants and felt out of it.

───═══───

I fell asleep in Lisa's basement. And dreamed again that I was in Lisa's basement.

It was the same basement but the tornado killer and I were lying together on the couch, watching TV.

But I was not me.

I watched not-me from across the room. Just like the dream before, the tornado killer's head was in not-me's lap. Not-me was touching his hair.

The other girls, Cecilia and Lisa and Sadie and Danielle and everyone, were lying in the darkness. But from here I could see, in the shifting light of the television, that they were not as asleep as I had thought. In fact, they had known the tornado killer was there all along. Their eyes were open and empty. They had fixed grins on their mouths.

They all stared at me in the television's flicker. I realized I was where the television would have been. In fact, I was inside the television. I looked and saw I was holding a jeweled, curvy knife.

I knew this knife.

I watched not-me and the tornado killer. The tornado killer turned to not-me. His eyes had an inviting look.

The tornado killer and not-me did not speak.

He and not-me got up.

There was a new door in the corner of Lisa's basement. Not-me and the tornado killer moved toward the new door. They went through it and they were gone.

I wanted to go through that door but the eyes of all the other girls were frozen and vicious.

* * *

Someone was shaking my shoulder. I woke up. Everything was dark. The other girls were in their sleeping bags but they were all awake too. I saw the clock. Two a.m.

Something was tapping against the window. Something moved outside. A face.

Cuthbert Monks.

THE PEOPLE MADE
OF NIGHT

Cuthbert Monks had a car.

He had invited his buddies over for a sleepover too. They had snuck out to take his brother's van for a joyride. The van was now parked down the street from the Stubenbergers', a junky brown monster, the lights off, the engine rumbling. The boys wanted us to come out.

Lisa's parents were asleep. They wouldn't miss us, Cuthbert said, if we went out for just a little while.

I didn't like the look in his eyes. The girls pretended to be mad at Cuthbert for butting in on our sleepover but I could tell they weren't really mad. Now things were going to get interesting.

I didn't want to go anywhere in Cuthbert's van but I couldn't stay at Lisa's alone. And going home was out of the question. So I went along with it when all the girls changed out of pajamas back into normal clothes, and we all sneaked out the sliding glass door, into the backyard and then down the street, leaving behind the Stubenbergers' house, and we got into the van.

The seats had been torn out of the back of the van. We sat on the bare metal, which was corrugated in such a way that you really couldn't get comfortable.

The back of the van didn't have windows. The van was moving

now but none of us knew where Cuthbert was taking us. It was rattling and shaking so loudly we could hardly hear each other. There were five boys in the van, and the six of us girls, and all the boys were wearing those little necklaces too.

A big bump. We all popped off the floor, came down hard on the metal. Cuthbert was taking us into a part of town I didn't know so well. A bottle was being passed around in the back, I smelled the alcohol and I didn't want any part of this, I wanted out of this van, something bad was going to happen, we were going to get in trouble or someone would get hurt and I squirmed up to the front, into the passenger seat, which for some reason nobody was sitting in, and told Cuthbert I wanted to get out.

"Why don't you be cool for once," said Cuthbert. "And a smile wouldn't kill you."

I don't have to smile around you, I said, and let me out.

"Oh, but you don't want to miss this," Cuthbert said in a voice I could never tell if it was sarcastic or not. "I'm taking you somewhere awesome."

I asked him where he thought he was taking us.

"She wants to know where we're going," shouted Cuthbert back to the boys, and they all cracked up, and Cuthbert added "We're going to tornado country," and the laughter stopped. The van was quiet. That wasn't the plan, the boys said. Hey, let us out, said the girls, that isn't funny, if we're going to tornado country then we want out too. A bottle rolled around in the back, clunked in the silence. We were supposed to go skinny-dipping at the quarry, said the boys, that's what you said, and then everyone was saying at once we can't go to tornado country, come on, that's suicide, remember what happened with the tornadoes last time?

"Yeah, but last time we didn't have these necklaces," said Cuthbert in his breezy voice that made me want to hit him. He twirled his locket. "Aren't these supposed to be stuffed full of the bones and teeth of dead tornado killers? Aren't they supposed to protect us?"

But you're not supposed to test the necklaces, they were saying in the back, my grandma said that's not right, my dad said that's blasphemy, a necklace is like a promise of protection, you have to wear it in good faith, the tornado killers in our necklaces died to protect us, not to be tested just for fun, for no reason.

"Oh, we're going for a reason," said Cuthbert.

The van swung around the corner and Cuthbert hit the gas. We were rocketing down the street, headed for the city limits. My insides clenched. I saw the white string stretched across the road, just a few inches above the pavement. It was one of the roads that had been closed off when tornado season started. Nobody had driven on it for months. Dead branches scattered across the pavement. The white string rushed at us.

I braced myself for the shiver.

It never came.

The van sailed over the string and we were rolling through tornado country.

Nobody in the van even had the chance to get really scared. Some hadn't even realized we'd already gone over the white string. Our van rolled through the flat plains, through forbidden tornado territory, no trees or hills for miles, just empty dirt, as alien and silent as if we were zooming across the surface of the moon.

I said, where are you taking us.

"To the tornado killer's house," said Cuthbert Monks.

There was a moment of incomprehension, everyone still startled by not feeling any electric tingle or dizzy blindness or floating feeling when we crossed over into tornado country, everyone was surprised that no tornadoes had appeared, waiting for the other shoe to drop, but when Cuthbert Monks said we were going to the tornado killer's house it sounded like a joke, ha ha, they were saying in the back, that's a good one, like you actually know where, nobody knows where the tornado killer lives. But I looked at Cuthbert and I knew he knew. We'd opened the windows and cool night air was blowing through the van, the smell of fresh rain coming. Cuthbert turned the wheel and we were off the road, bumping over stones and ruts, and in the back everyone was bouncing around on the painful floor and saying hey, what's going on, where are you taking us really?

"To the tornado killer's house," said Cuthbert Monks.

We drove on, rattling crazily across the uneven ground and it felt fun and dangerous, oh crazy Cuthbert, what'll he think of next, he can't possibly mean that, and the others were drinking in the back, a new bottle passed around, we could do anything, we were in tornado country and nothing had happened to us, maybe we might all die any second, but for now we were cheating death, daring the tornadoes to get us.

Cuthbert Monks and I watched the empty land roll toward us. I glanced over at him. He looked different. He had changed, maybe, since the last time I'd seen him. That was weeks ago. Maybe I didn't even remember him right, but he seemed older and I almost respected Cuthbert now, almost, though it was an irritated respect, really I was irritated with myself, because I'd imagined the tornado killer was my own thing. Because I expected I'd discover where the tornado killer lived on my own. Because I thought I'd secretly find him, that I'd visit him secretly.

But Cuthbert had actually done it. Cuthbert had figured out, on his own, where the tornado killer lived.

I couldn't believe I'd been outsmarted by Cuthbert Monks.

He stopped the van. We were looking over a dry riverbed too steep to drive through. On the other side was a house.

I knew that house.

"There it is," said Cuthbert.

But, I said, and I couldn't believe what I was seeing, that looks just like Mr. Z's house. The same house, but in a different place.

"Of course they live in the same *kind* of house," said Cuthbert. "They're both tornado killer houses. Mr. Z is the retired tornado killer. Now it's the new guy's turn. Didn't you know that?"

I didn't know that.

"You don't know much about anything, do you," said Cuthbert, not accusingly, just stating a fact, and I hated him more because he was right.

Hated him because, for a half second, his coarse face didn't totally repel me.

Cuthbert must've been the one who'd checked all the tornado killer stuff from the library. He'd gone through the trouble of figuring all this out for a reason. Because he didn't like the tornado killer. Because he wanted to do something bad.

Because, I suddenly guessed, Cuthbert wanted to do something bad at the tornado killer's house *tonight*.

The side door of the van rumbled open. Cecilia and Danielle and Sadie and everyone got out, but cautiously, as though the tornadoes might come roaring back at any moment. Cuthbert Monks jumped out with his usual cockiness. But playing a different game than the other boys, now. Something sharp lit up behind his crudeness.

I didn't know what he had in mind. But I didn't like it.

And yet I wanted to see what was inside the tornado killer's house just as much as anyone.

Maybe the tornado killer was home right now.

Everyone was making their way to the house. I hung back, watching their shadows move across the dry riverbed. Cecilia shouted "come on!" but the scene before me was otherworldly, it looked as though Mr. Z's house had been plucked up and flung miles away to this strange moonlike place. All the lights in the house were off but the van's high beams lit up the riverbed, making my friends into sharp silhouettes, closing in on the house like they were people made of night. We were far away from the town and the sky glittered with a ridiculous number of stars, so many stars so intimately close I felt I could reach out and touch them. I heard a small noise and Lisa Stubenberger was discreetly vomiting behind the van.

"I'm sorry," she said to me with a weak smile, and added, unnecessarily, "I shouldn't have drank so much."

Then she saw the tornado killer's house.

Her smile drained away.

Lisa said softly, "I'm going to stay in the van. Can you stay with me?"

I told Lisa again that I had seen her and her parents at Mr. Z's house.

Lisa said she didn't want to talk about it.

I asked Lisa what happened to her in Mr. Z's house.

Lisa said she didn't want to talk about it, she didn't want to, she didn't want to talk about it.

I said she shouldn't be quiet, that whatever Mr. Z is doing to her, to our friends, we have to do something, we have to say something.

She said there was nothing anyone could do.

I asked her why did the tornado killer and Mr. Z live in the same kind of house?

She said I'd find out soon enough.

I told her I wanted to know now.

Lisa shouted at me to go away, why was I still talking about it, couldn't I let it go, just leave her alone, she was going to stay in the van, I should just go on into the house with the others, she didn't want me there anymore, her sleepover was ruined, she was wasted, she'd never been wasted before, this is what being wasted feels like, her parents were totally going to find out, they probably already knew we were gone, they probably were in the basement right now, wondering where we'd all gone, maybe even calling the police, we were all in big trouble and nobody cared about what happened to her, she was just trying to have a nice sleepover, she couldn't even have that, even after what happened.

I asked her what had happened.

Don't worry, she said, you'll find out what happens inside Mr. Z's.

I said What.

She said Every girl has to go to Mr. Z's sooner or later.

The others had already run ahead to the tornado killer's house. Lisa sat tight in the van.

I said, slowly and carefully, What do you mean, every girl has to go to Mr. Z's?

You'll find out, Lisa said, you'll find out everything you want to know, you'll learn plenty, and I swore for a second she actually smiled, but not the empty smile when she came out of Mr. Z's, this smile was different, it was knowing, vicious, Lisa smiled the nastiest smile, just before she rolled the van door shut.

I stood alone outside the van.

———≡———

I started toward the tornado killer's house. I had to scramble down into the riverbed and then back up again to get there, and I was out of breath when I came up. The others were standing around the house. The screen door was swinging open. Cuthbert had gone in. Nobody else.

The phone was ringing inside, just like at Mr. Z's.

Cecilia and the other girls and boys peered into the dark doorway. I heard Cuthbert clunking around in there. I asked the others what was going on.

Nobody answered.

I brushed past them and went in alone.

———

I don't know what I expected to see in the tornado killer's house. It was just a little one-bedroom bungalow. It smelled like a boy. There was a rumpled, unmade mattress and clothes lying on the floor. I saw the clothes the tornado killer had worn when he visited our school. The refrigerator was mostly empty. Junk food. The furniture looked like it had been donated or bought from the thrift store. None of it matched. There was a hole in the couch. The phone kept ringing. How did the tornado killer put up with that ringing? But it didn't feel like the tornado killer spent much time here, somehow. Maybe sleeping and eating and that was it. I heard Cuthbert creaking around in another part of the house. I looked for the ringing phone but I couldn't find it. Cecilia and the others were coming into the house now too, looking around warily, whispering at first but then getting louder. I ran into them in the hall. We couldn't believe we were actually in the house of the tornado killer. The house was so ordinary. I think some of us expected the tornado killer to be home. Or if he wasn't home, we at least expected him to live in an interesting place, a nightmare house or a crazy house. But this was just a house. There was really nothing much to see here. Somehow that was more unsettling. The tornado killer was just this random boy who lived alone in a copy of Mr. Z's house in the middle of the countryside . . . The phone kept ringing and I tracked down the ringing, it was coming from behind a locked door, it was the one room we couldn't get into, like a second bathroom or a closet. We found a radio and turned on music to drown out the phone. The music was loud and some of the boys were eating the tornado killer's leftover takeout from the refrigerator, they'd brought in beer from the van and they were drinking, it was a party, we were partying at the tornado killer's house, it was getting wilder, I was drinking too, even though the tornado killer might come home at any moment, the tornadoes too, but it hadn't happened yet and it felt fun and dangerous, Keith Merkle was pretending to be the tornado killer, dancing around the kitchen the way the tornado killer fought, but like an idiot, kicking and punching the air, he was an idiot but somehow it was funny, everyone laughed and egged him on, he jumped up on the kitchen table and jumped and kicked some more, he liked the attention, he took off his shirt and we all hooted and he did a jump kick at an imaginary tornado and he landed off-balance, he was about to tumble off the table but he didn't, he somehow righted himself at the last second, and he lifted his hands in the air, wobbling slightly, but almost like a gymnast, and we all cheered. I wasn't drunk, or I didn't think so, but it was intoxicating, I liked this, the tornado killer's house felt like a ship on a stormy ocean, tilting through the waves, we didn't care, the ship might hurtle down into a whirlpool but for now we were having a good time, I was having a good time with my friends, these were my friends, the phone kept ringing and someone said, turn up the radio I'm so sick of that phone, I don't know how that tornado killer even handles it, the party spread out throughout the house and I was sitting next to Cuthbert Monks, he put his arm around me but I didn't move away, I thought to myself, maybe I haven't been giving him credit, maybe there's more to Cuthbert Monks, he was smart enough to figure out how to find this place, and I asked him how he found out about all this, and he said you'd be surprised how much is in plain sight, and he looked at me, intensely, he was close, his casually brutal face, his big hands and I thought, oh my God, I'm actually about to kiss Cuthbert Monks.

He pulled me to my feet. The floor felt like it was spinning. There was a gap between two songs on the radio and I heard the phone ring, faintly, and I said who's calling? And Cuthbert said something like, the tornadoes are calling. We were dancing but it was going too fast, I was feeling like I was floating away, like I was running at the white strings, dancing close, my hands on his broad shoulders, his thick hands on my waist, and I heard myself say, but why are the tornadoes making telephone calls, and Cuthbert was answering me, but his eyes were so weird now, I hardly heard him, he said the tornado killer lives with a ringing phone he's never allowed to answer, we were slow-dancing in the kitchen, my hands clasped around the back of his neck now, so close, his hands sliding down my waist, everyone somewhere else in the house, we were alone, the music was loud the silence between us was huge, silence pulling me toward him and I said why can't he answer the phone and Cuthbert said because the phone tells him the truth, and now I couldn't believe I was so close to him, I said if you were the tornado killer would you answer it, if there was a ringing phone that told you the truth about yourself, Cuthbert looked at me seriously, he said that phone is ringing in your face every second.

The song was over. I moved out of Cuthbert's arms. Holding his hands.

I said Let's go answer that phone.

Cuthbert said The door is locked.

I said I bet you could break that door.

He said What?

I said You heard me.

The party was still going on around us, people coming back into the kitchen but Cuthbert and I were still close, the others saw us but I didn't care, we might actually kiss now, we could if we wanted to, how drunk was I, raindrops spattering on the windows, something was happening outside, I wondered how long we'd been there, Cuthbert said wait here for a second, he let my hands go, I'm going to get something, he went down the hall and I heard a girl snicker about me and Cuthbert and I thought, what the hell am I doing, what is going on, I can't believe I was almost kissed by Cuthbert Monks.

I was walking down the halls but the halls were unsteady. My eyes felt soft, the music was too loud, I had to grab the wall to stay on my feet. I opened a door and I was in the tornado killer's bedroom. There were some girls and boys on the mattress, Cecilia was one of them, they pulled up the sheet and said get out of here. I turned and went out, I left the door open, I didn't know where I was going now, the tornado killer's house had seemed small before but now I was lost somehow, everything was taking a bad turn, the party was going wrong, I came around another corner and there was a window.

A space had been cleared out from the clutter on the windowsill. There was a vase and in the vase was a flower.

Red petals flaring backward. Yellow filaments flying forward.

My flower.

I smelled something sharp and foul. There was a dribbling sound. I turned and saw Keith Merkle was here too, still shirtless, and peeing on the carpet. Someone's hogging the bathroom, he tried to explain to me, as if this was totally reasonable, as if this were a valid reason to pee on someone's carpet—and it broke on me, we shouldn't be here, we were trashing the tornado killer's home, and what was worse I was one of the people doing it, I turned and stumbled down the hallway and then I was at the door that had been locked before, but it was broken open now and Cuthbert Monks was there and he said, Where were you, I came back to the kitchen and you were gone, look I broke the door, I opened the room.

The phone was still ringing.

I saw the phone.

I said, Let's get out of here.

He said, Come on, and it was the old Cuthbert Monks, that bullying voice, he was impressed with himself, I hated myself for being part of his stupid party trashing the tornado killer's house, I hated him. He'd broken open the door and the room beyond was small, barely as big as a bathroom with just a little dusty window and a little table with a green rotary phone on it. The phone was still ringing. Cuthbert and I looked at it. I wanted so bad to be back at Lisa's, safe at her sleepover, or back home, because this was out of control, the loud music and the disgusting smell of piss and they were breaking things in the other rooms, I heard a bottle shatter and the boys whooping, Cuthbert's hand touched the phone that was still ringing and I said Don't touch it.

Cuthbert said Oh so now you're scared.

I said I'm not scared but we have to get out of here.

Cuthbert said I don't get you.

I said I hope not.

He said What's wrong with you all of a sudden.

I said Don't answer that phone.

He said Watch this.

Cuthbert picked up the phone and put it to his ear and opened his mouth but he never even got out a hello—just before everything changed, his eyes went wide, he jerked back as if punched, as if the phone had poured some electrocuting truth into his brain.

The power went out.

Nobody made a noise at first. The lights went dark, the radio silent, and in an unreal moment we all felt it together, that tingling in the small of our backs, oh no please no, it was spreading and getting pricklier, all of us really were going to go down that whirlpool together, the shiver blossomed through my spine then blasted throughout my body and we were all seized by it, our bodies rattling, we were crashing into walls, falling on the ground, trying to get away from it, we were tickled by invisible fingers that wouldn't stop and the wind was suddenly deafening and we were all shouting, screaming, drowned out by the howl of tornadoes whipping out of nowhere, and the wail of police sirens, the air flew out of my lungs, I couldn't breathe, the air was sucked straight out of us, then it streamed itself across the fields, swirled up into these impossible colossal monsters, these tornadoes, we were blindly pushing each other over, trying to get out of the house, and I felt them in the room with us too, whispering, their hands on my neck, squeezing the air from me.

I ran outside, we all ran outside, my heart leaped up my throat and I gasped but nothing came in, my lungs were empty, the tornadoes were rushing down the prairie at us, fat black columns of spinning air. The police were coming too, like every police car in town was charging across the prairie, I didn't know why but I could barely think, stars blinked in my eyes, I couldn't see, like being deep underwater, I'd never get to the surface in time, I was going to die, everyone was rushing for the van, tripping across the riverbed, we couldn't hear each other over the tornadoes and when I got to the van it was already moving, Cuthbert was already driving the van away, leaving me behind, but Cecilia reached out of the van and pulled me in just before a huge blast of wind slapped the van into a tailspin.

We were screaming but nobody could hear, the shrieking wind cut our eardrums wide open, Cuthbert was trying to drive but the van was smacked from side to side, he couldn't find his way back to the road, the rain was pelting and splattering down now, so hard I couldn't see out the window but we all felt the tornadoes pick up the van, the van actually left the ground, it crashed back down, then it was lifted again. We were going to die. This was it. Sirens wailed against the gut-roaring tornadoes, gleamed out of the watery darkness, the van banged down again and I looked over and saw Cuthbert wasn't even driving, he was knocked out, his head was smashed against the window and blood was smeared on the cracked glass and his eyes were closed.

I yanked Cuthbert out of the driver's seat and wedged myself behind the wheel, shoving him to the floor. Lightning flashed and in the rearview mirror I saw the tornadoes bounding up behind us and I gunned it. The van took off and I saw at least a dozen blue police lights flashing and white headlights swinging at me.

I veered, grazing a tree that sprang up out of nothing, plunging toward I didn't know where as rain poured down full blast, wind roaring, thunder cracking. I couldn't see out the window and then—I hit a puddle, the van spun, and now I was driving in the opposite direction somehow, all of a sudden I was driving *toward* the tornadoes rushing toward us, the police lights flashing from behind, sirens getting closer—

The tornadoes.

Four slender funnels stretched up forever, lined up in a row, looming in front of us, swirling majestically in place. Cecilia shouted something but I couldn't hear. I yanked the wheel as hard as I could to the right. The van skidded over sheets of water and I pressed down the gas, leaving the road and taking off through the muddy field. Cecilia yelled at me from the passenger seat, the sirens surrounding us, the sucking roar of the tornadoes, everyone in the car screaming.

Then I saw him.

The tornado killer was up ahead, blazing up from the van's mud-splattered headlights. His back was to us, his hands thrown wide, making the tornadoes sway in rhythm with his movements, like they were marionettes yanked back and forth with miles-long invisible strings. I had never seen the tornado killer move like this before, so unnaturally, not beautiful but terrible, his arms and legs spiraling and pumping, flying out at impossible angles.

He turned around, toward us.

His eyes, a tiny green dot and a tiny blue dot, burning across the field.

Inviting.

I drove straight into the tornado.

Cecilia screamed.

The van was yanked off the ground and reeled into the sky. It spun around, around, around, faster and faster, flinging off everything, shivering, cracking apart, the back doors flew open and then Cecilia and Cuthbert and Lisa and everyone else were sucked down away into the clouds, but I was still in the driver's seat, the van was pointed straight up into the sky, shooting upward through seething darkness, rocketing toward a distant swirl of gray light.

Everything was silent.

The van burst through the swirl.

The van was floating over a field of clouds stretched like rolling plains in every direction. Above me were only the naked stars, the black sky, and the mellow burning moon.

The van floated silently.

I looked back. The van was empty. The back doors hung open. Everyone else was gone. I saw clouds flowing by, far below.

I looked out the front window.

He was there.

In the clouds. Watching me. Floating only a few yards away.

Green and blue eyes. That unfriendly look. But not an unfriendly look. More like he couldn't believe it. Like I was the one who was cornering him. Like he'd started something and he hadn't expected it to go this far.

Like he was in over his head.

Mrs. Lois: *Don't touch him.*

Only the pure can kill a tornado.

I opened the door.

He watched me.

No noise up here. Just a giant silence that ate all sounds.

I was drenched, scratched up, my clothes muddy and torn. My feet squishing in my shoes but my heart flying wildly. I was flying, insanely high up above the world. I looked down. Clouds rolled and stretched in every direction like a fluffy, frozen ocean, bulging and curling and spreading in a cottony sea, swelling up into fragile eruptions of billows and swirls.

Cecilia, the others—

I looked up at the tornado killer.

Even closer now.

Curious. Reckless. My brain blinking and buzzing. Didn't care about the risk.

I stepped out of the van.

The van gently tumbled away.

I was in the clouds. The tornado killer and I were so close. Almost touching. Floating together, the tornadoes far below somewhere, too silent to speak, his eyes up close, curious and nervous, my heart going crazy and then a cloud floated right at us, we slipped deep inside, I couldn't see anything buried this deep in the cloud, just a hot glowing whiteness, I was waiting and my hair was wet and a lock hung in my eye but the tornado killer took my hair and tucked it behind my ear. I shivered. He came closer. I couldn't see him, I was just waiting for him to kiss me and he kissed me, his lips softer than I thought lips could be, we slipped out of clouds, my hands on his waist, his thighs, his chest, he kissed me again, I kissed him harder, and we went on kissing until we were out of the whiteness and in the open and the clouds spread out below us like a map of heaven.

THE KID WHO DIDN'T
COME BACK

Now I am different.

The sun was breaking out across the horizon when I climbed back into the floating van, high up in the clouds, the sky soaked in pinks and yellows. Then the van plummeted before I could even put on my seat belt and I was plunging out of the sky, I saw the tornado killer dwindling far above me, laughing high in the clouds but I was whistling down fast and the ground roared up toward me and then the wind blasted the van sideways, came down with a rattling bump at one hundred miles an hour, hurtling down the highway. I hit the brakes with my bare foot but I couldn't control it, the van roared back over the white string, I yanked the wheel, turned the corner, clipped a mailbox, swerved, ran over the sidewalk and was suddenly back in town, laughing, sweaty, happy, astonished, I slowed down and then I was driving around normally, in a blinking daze, not sure where I was going, still buzzing, until I realized I was heading back to Lisa Stubenberger's house.

I was awake.

I felt new. My hands on the steering wheel of the van were new. The neighborhood houses flying past me on either side were new. A crying kid running across the street was new.

I wasn't thinking of the others who'd been in the van. There wasn't room in my brain for Cecilia or Cuthbert or any of them.

Should I have done it? I shouldn't have done it.

I had done it.

I didn't feel the way I expected to feel. A bewildered blankness. Fireworks going off inside me, but they didn't feel like anything. Not a good or bad thing. Just a new thing.

The tornado killer and me.

I had gone looking for him. I had found him. Gotten him.

I wasn't telling anyone.

I wanted to tell everyone.

Nobody would understand.

This is how life changes, I thought. This is how it feels. My entire life was going to change now. Everyone would know. Maybe they could tell just by looking at me. Maybe my body was going to turn into something else. Maybe I would turn into a tornado killer. Or a tornado. Maybe my body was about to explode.

I was already kind of exploding.

Still too astonished to feel afraid.

How long had I been up there? I almost hadn't thought of anybody else, in a way not even about the tornado killer, he was just a boy and at some point he wasn't even a boy, his body just became a door I wanted to get through, then I went through the door and he was a monster, I was a monster too, taking and using. Making myself blank.

Now I was blank.

It was over. I was through the door and back out again, bruised and exhausted and only now really wondering what had happened to Cecilia or Cuthbert or anyone else.

Selfish.

But when the tornado killer and I were so far above the world, in a blinding white so huge we could barely see, in a silence so total we couldn't speak, I didn't care, I just saw his lips, I saw his lips move. He was saying my name.

Now I am different.

I was naked on the nasty fake leather seat of Cuthbert Monks's van, my heart pumping hard, my brain buzzing on autopilot. My clothes must have been tangled in tree branches somewhere, or lying on someone's roof.

Driving through town I saw an early-morning jogger pounding the sidewalk. Then I saw a woman opening a café. Today was business as usual for them. I was from another planet. My body was banged up, head cleared out, split open and new. I felt new but like I had touched something very old.

I turned the corner.

I saw Lisa's house.

Then I saw the police, ambulances, reporters, Cecilia and Lisa and Cuthbert and the rest of my friends, and my parents—they all saw the van, they saw me too, my stomach dropped and I realized, oh crap.

We were all in deep trouble.

They all came running toward me. When I got out of the van the police reached me first. They wrapped me in an emergency blanket and then Mom and Dad were hugging me, but hugging me too hard, shocked hugs, angry hugs. The wrong emotion. I wanted to keep feeling what I was feeling, I wanted to figure it out, I wasn't done with it yet. Dad was crying but Mom just looked stunned, freaked out. Asking me if I was all right, what happened to me.

The police took me aside. They talked to me very seriously.

Medical people were checking me out. I didn't hear them. A force field of blankness separated me from everyone else. I was safe in it. Insulated.

"What's so funny?" said the policeman.

I saw Cecilia and Lisa and the rest of the boys and girls, scratched up and dazed. Paramedics were examining them too. Lisa had a broken arm. Cuthbert Monks was in a stretcher. Everyone was alive but they were out of it. It was like when the tornado had wrecked the school, except this time, instead of tossing everyone out onto the playground, these tornadoes had spewed Cecilia and everyone out onto the hoods of the police cars that had been chasing us, police cars that had jammed their brakes just in time, spinning out in astonishment as our van was yanked up into the sky.

Everyone had thought we'd been killed.

I knew why we'd survived.

The tornado killer.

It was illegal to cross the white strings. The police knew that we'd broken into the tornado killer's house too, they knew that we'd trashed it. The juvenile prosecutor wanted to throw the book at us but somebody's dad knew a judge. In the end we were all released to our parents, who were supposed to punish us in their own way.

Cecilia and I were grounded for the rest of the summer.

Everyone else in the group was grounded, too.

After Mom and Dad were finished crying and saying how worried they had been, they took turns yelling and lecturing. We could've been killed. It was a miracle we'd survived. We'd put the whole town at risk. Things were going to get stricter in this family, life was going to change.

I smiled.

"Oh, so you think it's funny," said Mom.

I did!

I said nothing.

"What happened to you?" said Dad, half angry, half concerned.

I said, "I don't remember."

Cecilia looked at me like, You better tell me later.

I gave her the same smile.

Mom and Dad kept lecturing but their words sailed right through me.

I sat there and glowed.

———

Cecilia stood in my doorway and said, "Keith Merkle is missing."

It was after midnight. Mom and Dad were asleep. They'd made me spend all day alone in my room, to "think about what I'd done."

Yes.

I did think about it.

Dinner had been quiet. Whenever I spoke, Dad kind of cringed. Mom just stared at me as though every word I said only got me into more trouble. Cecilia just sat and looked at her food.

Cecilia and I hadn't really talked until now. We were in solitary confinement in our bedrooms for the first time since we were little.

But now that Mom and Dad were asleep, she came to me.

"Did you hear me?" Cecilia whispered in the dark. "Keith Merkle never came back."

She stood there in the door, wanting me to invite her in. Wanting to talk it over.

"I just talked to Jessica," Cecilia went on. "And Danielle and Jimmy. Mr. and Mrs. Merkle are totally freaking out."

We were grounded from the phone too. But Cecilia had snuck out of bed to secretly call the others. Everyone was calling each other, I learned later, the ringers on their phones turned down low, picking up before parents could hear. I knew Cecilia had been on the kitchen phone, whispering. Whispers connecting them all over town, trying to figure out what had happened.

Cecilia sounded impatient. "Are you even listening?"

I said, "Did you come in here just to tell me about Keith Merkle?"

"Don't you care?"

"No."

"*No?*"

Even I was surprised at how mean I sounded, actually, when it came out. But it was true. Keith Merkle was the one who'd been pissing on the tornado killer's carpet. You know what? Keith Merkle would be fine. He'd find his way back.

I was done faking it for other people.

I had my own thing now.

I was insulated.

"Everyone came back home but Keith." Cecilia's face was in darkness, her voice on edge. "The tornadoes let us all go but they kept him."

I didn't know what Cecilia expected me to say to that.

"Well?" said Cecilia.

"Uh-huh."

A long silence.

Cecilia said, "What's gotten into you?"

I just wanted Cecilia out but she kept standing in my doorway.

Cecilia said, "Why were you naked when you came back?"

"I don't remember."

"You're lying."

I turned toward the wall so she couldn't see my face.

Cecilia said, "Something weird happened to you."

"Something weird happened to all of us."

"Everyone got sucked out of the van except you. Everyone got hurt except you."

"I got lucky."

"You were gone for like an hour."

I didn't say anything.

"What happened?"

"Nothing."

"You're different."

"Jesus, Cecilia."

She came in. "Did you see the tornado killer?"

I tightened, still facing away from her. I felt Cecilia sit down on my bed.

"You saw him with those tornadoes," she said. "You drove at him on purpose."

I didn't say anything.

"Why did you do that?"

We were both silent. Then Cecilia started making little noises. I didn't realize until a few seconds later that she was almost crying.

"Why won't you *talk* to me?" said Cecilia, her voice breaking. "I don't get you—Keith is gone, maybe he's dead, it's like you don't even *care*, and Danielle was saying something bad happened to Lisa and Melanie and Irene, they won't talk about it, something about their parents making them go to Mr. Z's house, he's doing something to them, something bad, nobody will say . . . what if that's actually true, what if . . . what is *happening*?"

So she knew. Just yesterday I had been afraid of Mr. Z, too.

Now I wasn't.

There was a force field around me.

"You're different," cried Cecilia. "Something happened to you."

━━≡━━

Selfish.

I shut up.

In the old days Cecilia always wanted to talk to me about her relationship with Archie. To analyze why Archie said this, why Archie did that. To figure out what Darlene meant when she said that Archie wanted to go to some dance, to agonize over whether she should wear this skirt or that blouse to that dance . . . and then, after the dance, Cecilia would spill all the details to me, she'd even tell me the gross sex stuff, her voice low and serious, as though she was telling me nuclear codes that could blow up the world. I listened, repulsed and thrilled. Reports from another galaxy.

It was my turn now.

I gave Cecilia nothing.

Cecilia and I stopped talking. But Mom and Dad and the policemen and the reporters all wanted to know what happened, too. Where had I been? How did I survive? Did I remember anything?

Yes. I remembered everything.

But not for them.

━━≡━━

The next morning a bright gloom hung over everything. The skies were packed with dark clouds but the sun still shone brightly through a gap, making everything glow with alien brilliance.

I woke up early.

I sat out on the front porch.

I saw everything with new eyes. Under such a black sky the grass seemed a little too green. A passing school bus full of loud summer campers looked too yellow for its own good. The house across the street was an improbably vivid red.

I searched for him in the distance. Tornadoes were idly blowing around outside town, but they seemed listless. As though they didn't know what to do without the tornado killer either.

The world looked too bright to last.

I heard Mom and Dad and Cecilia having breakfast inside, getting ready for the day. Mom poked her head out and chirped "There you are!" and asked me if I wanted breakfast with a kind of apologetic cheerfulness. Like she wanted to make up for how harsh she'd been yesterday.

I said later.

I was separate.

All that day I listened to the radio, hanging out in the yard alone. My giddiness mellowed. I let the sun shine on my skin, making me glow as weirdly as everything else. I waited for another sighting of the tornado killer to be reported on the radio.

Because as soon as that happened, I wouldn't hesitate. I'd run away for real. I'd run off this porch, I wouldn't even pack, I'd rush straight to wherever the radio said the tornado killer was.

He'd be ready for me.

We'd run away together, I thought.

———

The tornado killer didn't show up that day.

Or the next.

The day after that, the radio announcers got nervous. They said the tornado killer wasn't at his house. He wasn't out in the hills.

He wasn't anywhere.

A forced twilight hung over everything.

The tornadoes were confused, skittish. In the morning they moved cautiously, shrinking back into the hills, as if suspecting some trick; but in the afternoon they roared back angrily, steaming across the prairie, chewing asphalt off the highways, snapping telephone poles, spitting rain and hail, plowing up ground all the way up to the white strings.

I cleaned my room. It felt good to throw stuff out, old clothes, old books, drawers full of schoolwork, stuffed animals in my closet. I boxed it all up and got rid of it. I cleaned out my desk, dusted my dresser. I wiped down my window and my mirror. I cleared out everything from under the bed, even the old flowers the tornado killer had blown to me. Scrubbed down the walls, got the stains off. Vacuumed. Opened my window. Let the fresh air in.

I kept going back to the window. Looking.

No tornado killer.

Just tornadoes, lurching back and forth.

I took a long shower. Then I dried off and I lay on the fresh sheets of my bed in my clean room.

I stared up at the light fixture.

The radio announcers said that the white strings would only hold up for so long. If the tornado killer didn't show up soon, they claimed, one of the tornadoes was bound to break through—and if that happened, the rest of the tornadoes would gallop right in after it, and we'd all be sucked up into the sky—

—he and I naked, blur of hot white clouds, arms and legs tangled, his green and blue eyes close, his lips on mine, whispering in my ear, his smile, my hands on his back, in his hair—

Lying on my bed, feeling it all over again.

Mr. Whaley said screw it, he'd take his chances. I watched from the porch as the Whaleys packed everything into a moving truck and pulled out of there.

I heard about the rest on the radio. The announcers said that the minute the Whaleys crossed the white strings, their truck was flipped up in the air, whirled up into a cyclone, and shredded to bits.

The Whaleys were in the hospital now.

Nobody was going anywhere.

I was sitting out on the porch again with a book, drinking lemonade, feeling the sun on my skin. Dad was at work. Mom and Cecilia were out somewhere.

Where was the tornado killer?

```
FORBIDDEN TO TOUCH ANY OF YOU, TO
PRESERVE MY EXALTED PURITY
```

Whatever.

```
ONLY THE PURE CAN KILL A TORNADO
```

Uh-huh.

But maybe the tornado killer wasn't so pure anymore. Maybe I had scuffed him up, maybe we had scuffed each other up. I listened to the children laughing in the next yard over. Maybe he wasn't coming back ever. My fault, maybe. I remembered how tentatively he moved at first. Everything so confused, dissolved in the clouds, ecstatic, scrambled. How astonished he seemed. How careful when we touched. How he held himself back, like he was afraid of giving something away.

How I took it from him.

How we both took it, then. And then we were both giving, giving, giving away everything like we were millionaires.

I felt my warmth. I felt the warmth of the sun on my skin.

Then I felt cold.

I opened my eyes.

Down the street, the men were turning into my neighborhood. They were emerging from around the corner, six houses down. Coming down the street in a purposeful way.

I couldn't move.

The men walked along. They were unhurried and deliberate, spreading to both sides of the street. All business. They moved steadily from house to house, knocking on doors.

I scrambled up, knocking over my lemonade.

The mother of the kids playing the next yard over saw the men. She called the children inside. The children didn't pay attention at first. She called them more sharply. After the children scurried inside she slammed her front door. The window shades went down.

All along our street, people went inside.

Doors and windows closed. Like nobody was home anywhere.

I abandoned my spilled lemonade, abandoned my book on the porch, dashed into the house. I locked the front door. I leaned against it, breathing hard. I didn't hear anything outside. I edged over to the narrow window next to the front door and peeked.

The men were coming along my sidewalk.

One of them began turning to me.

I ducked back behind the curtain, heart pounding.

Slow footsteps came up our front walk. I was alone in the house. What was going to happen? The men stopped on the porch. I was only inches apart from them now. Separated only by the door.

Knock. Knock. Knock.

I crouched down, trying not to breathe. My back was pressed against the door. I felt the vibration of each knock.

I heard the men shifting around.

The door handle jiggled. It moved just a little, gently.

Then the handle stopped moving.

The men still didn't speak but I heard them leaving the porch. Heard them walking around the side of the house.

I sprang up. I skidded into the kitchen, to the unlocked back door.

I locked the back door.

Seconds later, I heard them gather on the other side of the door.

Knock. Knock. Knock.

A silence.

Slowly the doorknob turned. It stopped against the lock.

They were trying to get into the house. If I hadn't locked the doors they would be in here already. Maybe they were looking for something. Maybe looking for the note cards I had stolen from the library. Maybe looking for the black package Mrs. Lois had given me at the café.

Maybe looking for me.

The men and I waited, tense, on either side of the door.

Did they know I was here?

Any second I expected them to kick the door open. To smash the side window.

A minute later: still silent.

I crept to the front of the house. I peered out the curtains.

The men were leaving our yard, continuing down the street.

Wait.

One man was still standing on our front lawn.

He stared at all our windows, one by one.

He couldn't see me, I told myself, hiding behind the curtain.

He came closer.

I backed away from the window, into the shadows. He was at the front door now.

Something scraped near the door.

Then I heard the man walking away. Out the window I saw him go, already walking down the street.

I approached the door and cracked it open. A pale blue booklet fell through the doorway.

The booklet's cover had a stylized picture of a family enjoying a picnic in a field. The daughter and son were playing with tame animals while the wife gazed up at her husband, who had his hands on his hips and was looking off into the distance with a purposeful air. In the background there were some tornadoes, but they had the hesitant curve of tornadoes held at bay. The graphic design was out of date, the paper musty and brittle, as if it were an overstock that had been packed away in a warehouse for years.

I had seen this booklet before.

I had forgotten the afternoon I'd first seen this. The memory started to come back.

I felt my brain straining against it.

But holding the booklet, a switch in me flipped.

═══

It had been maybe five years ago. It was a day like this one, overcast and oppressive, and then too I was alone in the house.

Mom and Cecilia were out shopping, and Dad was gone at a convention, and so the house was empty and lonely in that depressing autumn late afternoon way, like when the lights have turned on in the other houses up and down the dark street, and other families are sitting down to dinner together, but you haven't thought to turn on the lights in your own house because you're alone, and you're wondering why you feel so gloomy and meaningless.

Just that afternoon I'd seen something on TV about kidnappers. I hadn't told anyone I was scared, but right after Mom and Cecilia pulled out of the driveway and the garage door closed I made sure every other door and window was locked. I shut myself in my bedroom, peering out my window.

Then I saw Archie's mother on the sidewalk.

She was moving from house to house in the twilight, ringing doorbells. She had a purse full of booklets she was giving out. Sometimes she'd manage a minute of conversation out of whoever opened the door, but usually the doors shut in her face. She couldn't even give away her little booklet. I felt sorry for her.

Then Archie's mother looked toward my house.

She stared right into my eyes.

I almost felt like she was in the room with me. I backed away from the window.

A minute later I heard the front door open.

"Toodle-loo! Don't worry, it's just me," sang out Archie's mother. "I'm just going to come upstairs for a little while and we can have a chat, if you don't mind."

But I had locked that door. I was sure I'd locked the front door against kidnappers. Nevertheless, before I knew it, Archie's mother was bustling into my dim room. She didn't even turn on the lights but just sank down at the foot of my bed, this vague gray lady I never liked, and she exclaimed, "Whew! All day on my feet—sure takes it out of me!"

Archie's mother in my bedroom was wrong. She didn't belong in my bedroom. Her haziness, her colorlessness, her bustling but deadened voice. Now she was rummaging through her purse, her stacks of pamphlets, cards, and envelopes stuffed with ragged receipts, but it didn't seem she was finding what she was looking for. "Just trying to get the word out. Youth outreach, you know, but I thought I had a booklet, or a pamphlet, for you, a leaflet . . . *Well!* It's so nice to take a rest, if you don't mind, I've been going door to door all day and would you believe nobody invited me in for a cup of coffee, or tea, or a muffin, or anything?"

A leaden feeling crept over me as she talked, like Archie's mother and I were the only two people in the universe and everything else was gray. Archie's mother chatted about the weather, I couldn't understand why, then I shook myself—time had passed, I didn't know how long she'd been talking. Had I been asleep? I thought she was talking about the weather but . . .

"Now, what it all comes down to is this. Have you ever stopped to think about the *wind*?"

I lay in my bed in the gloomy room and didn't know what to say to this suddenly very strange woman.

I coughed.

Archie's mom got excited.

"Oh, oh, do you *feel* the wind? Right now? Really, really, feel it? You know—here?" Archie's mom reached over and, with little fingers as limp as worms, touched my stomach.

I was startled mid-cough. Her repulsive fingers came alive, kneading away energetically at my stomach, squirming and turning, and she murmured: "Yes, you do feel it . . . don't you . . . ? You're a lucky girl, don't you know . . . yes, it's . . . why, you could be the bride of the tornado."

I didn't know what that meant.

I tried to say stop it.

"Ah, that's what *you* want," said Archie's mom, her hands working my stomach hard. "But maybe the question isn't what *you* want all the time. Have you ever thought of that?"

Her hands were quick and busy on my stomach, pinching, poking, rubbing. A nasty wriggling sensation spread inside me. Like thousands of tiny arms and legs coming to life under my skin.

I tried to get away. She wouldn't stop.

She was talking. I wasn't listening. My body didn't move. Not my body, it wasn't my body now. The real me was on the ceiling, looking down at not-me and Archie's mom.

Thrashing around inside.

"Yes, *he's* all around us." She nodded, though I didn't know who she was talking about, who *he* was. "In fact"—and here she leaned in conspiratorially—"he's even inside us. *This very minute.* Or is it that *we're* inside of *him?*" she chirped in wooden wonderment, as if the idea just occurred to her. "*He* knows what we're doing. All the time! *He* never sleeps, like you or me! Ah, ah, ah . . ." Her hands were squishing my stomach furiously now, like she was looking for something, and then she stopped, she was staring into my eyes, as though astonished that she'd found just exactly she was looking for.

The garage door rumbled open.

Mom and Cecilia were home. I'd forgotten that such a thing was even possible. The trundling of the garage door pushed me back into real life and it fully struck me how messed up it was that Archie's mother had been sitting here in the darkness and rubbing my stomach and talking to me for hours. Hours? Yes, I realized she had actually been in my room for hours, and my head throbbed, she had been doing something to me I didn't even remember, but now Archie's mother looked alarmed, panicked, so panicked that even before the garage door had finished opening she had already stood up, shoved her papers into her purse, glanced around—"Oh, the time! I hope you don't mind—I think that I'd be best if—your parents probably wouldn't—wouldn't—" She opened my window, removed the screen, and swung a leg over the sill—"Well, I think I'll just go out your—it seems more convenient—there's a, why, would you look at the time?" she said, pulling herself up onto the windowsill.

Mom was walking up the stairs. Archie's mother's skirt was hitched up, she had one leg already slung over the sill, her body halfway out the window. She awkwardly heaved herself over—and then she was gone.

"Why are you sitting in the dark?"

Mom switched on the lights. The sudden yellow gush yanked all the colors back into reality. For a moment I was startled that the world was really so vivid; sitting in the gray with Archie's mother, it felt like the whole world was as drab as that gloomy little woman.

Now, surrounded by the gaudy reds and lush greens and oceanic blues of my room, looking at my own normal mom, the gloominess disappeared, and the notion of Archie's mother, which a moment ago was so hypnotically huge she took up every corner of my brain, dwindled until I wondered if she had even actually been there at all; she hadn't been there; she had never been there; I had imagined it; and then, eventually, I didn't even remember thinking I had even imagined it.

With the booklet in my hand now, I was jerked back into that dreary world.

That had been five years ago. Already my mind was trying to scrub the unearthed memory away. Like when you try to recall your dream in the morning and the vividness melts, the storyline scrambles. Your brain doesn't want you to remember.

But now I remembered: a few days after Archie's mother's visit, I had found a copy of this very booklet under my bed, and spent a dull rainy afternoon trying to read it. It was mostly the kinds of nonsense things Archie's mom had been saying to me. And it had the same moldy, solemn aura as those little necklaces—somber, complicated, and poisonous.

I had to show this booklet to Mrs. Lois.

Don't touch him, Mrs. Lois had said. Touching is death.

Well, we had touched plenty. And I wasn't dead yet.

But maybe the tornado killer was?

I had to go to Mrs. Lois. I had to ask her what was going on. I barely knew anything about her but I knew she could help me. She knew about the tornado killer, she knew about Mr. Z, she knew about those men. She had that tattoo on her arm, the same symbol from the bus bathroom. She recognized my own symbol on my application. We were both part of something bigger. We were in the same club.

She had given me that black package.

Where was *Mr.* Lois, anyway? Was Mrs. Lois a widow?

I went down into the garage. I opened the door and there was its usual stuffy gasoliney smell. The black package was where I left it, still hidden under Dad's tools. I unwrapped the greasy black paper.

Inside was a cardboard box sealed with duct tape. I used a blade from Dad's toolbox to cut it open. Inside was more black paper, tissue-thin, slightly damp.

Nestled in it was an ordinary supermarket jelly jar.

Its label had been removed. But instead of jelly in the jar, there was a pale white oil. The tin lid was twisted on tight, then sealed with white wax. Still, some of the oil must've leaked out, because I could smell it. The unnatural stench of burnt plastic. I had the beginnings of a headache. My stomach was crawling like it was full of bugs.

If it is you, then you'll have to drink the whole thing—

It felt like homemade evil.

I put the jar back in the box.

It took a long time to wash the toxic smell off my hands.

―――

That night I asked Mom if we could go to the café for dinner. She didn't know what café I meant at first. When I explained where it was, that it was the café Cecilia and I used to visit for lunch on our bike rides, she seemed surprised. In the end Mom and Dad agreed to take us, maybe because they wanted to rebuild some good feelings around the house.

Cecilia and I hadn't been talking. Cecilia looked at me now as if to say, it's your move. She wouldn't lower herself to asking me why I wanted to go.

I didn't blame her.

We all got in the car and drove to the café. It didn't feel like a fun family night out. We were all quiet and strained. We took a road that skirted the edge of town, where tornadoes were hurling themselves against the white strings, swirling around, charging back again.

The white strings were fraying.

I sat with Cecilia in the back. She wasn't mean to me but she wasn't nice. I watched the road whip by. Cecilia and my parents were trying to keep up a conversation with each other, trying to find some way to click again, to feel like a family. Temporary truce.

I had the booklet in my pocket. I had planned out all my questions for Mrs. Lois. I would ask her about the men coming to my house too. I would tell her about them knocking on the front door and back door. I would tell her about the men trying to force their way in.

I hadn't told Mom or Dad or Cecilia about that.

I felt like admitting the men had come to our house would get me in trouble.

———

I had never been at the café at night. Everything looked both darker and brighter, the hard light of the interior fluorescents pushing out against the dim windows. The café was usually nearly empty during the day but now it was crowded, it felt like a different place, silverware and plates clattering, blazing streetlights, loud conversations, the car headlights sweeping through, clashing greasy smells, the sound of night insects buzzing in the parking lot—I didn't associate any of this with the sleepy daytime café I knew. It was the wrong café, a bad copy of my café.

We sat down at a booth. I looked around for Mrs. Lois.

There was a different waitress.

I got back up. My heart was in my throat. Mom asked me where was I going. I lied that I had to go to the bathroom. Mom said she'd come too.

I said no, I wanted to go alone.

Mom looked nervous.

A few other diners noticed me as I walked past. Not really looking at first. But then an unfriendly glare.

Everybody in the café was wearing those ugly necklaces.

I bumped into the new waitress as she was coming out of the kitchen. "Excuse me, um . . . miss?" I said.

"Can I help you?" said the new waitress. She was wearing a necklace too.

I said, "What happened to Mrs. Lois?"

"What?"

"The other waitress? The one who's here in the daytime?"

The new waitress was distracted, busy with silverware. "I just started last week, hon. The day shift girl is gone."

It took me a second. "Gone?"

"Left in a hurry." The new waitress looked at me impatiently. "I don't know anything else."

I felt the situation slipping. "Doesn't she live upstairs?"

"Not anymore."

"Do you know how I can contact her?"

"I just started." Brusque now, moving past me. "Didn't really know her."

I tried to say something else but the new waitress was already off to another table. She had a job to do. I returned to our table in kind of a daze. For some reason I had thought Mrs. Lois owned the café. But in actuality, she was just the "day shift girl." And now she was gone. Mom and Dad and Cecilia were talking but I wasn't really paying attention.

Mrs. Lois was gone.

The café felt even more alien. Lighting out of whack. Colors harsh. Outside the windows wasn't a warm summer night but a weird void. This was not the café Cecilia and I loved, it was a substitute. The waitress was a substitute. Everything looked bright, brittle, unreal.

Cecilia said, "Why is that man making that face at us?"

Dad said, "Eat your hamburger."

Mom said, "We shouldn't have come."

Cecilia's voice got tense. "What is going on?"

I looked. Our family was getting weird looks from all the customers.

"Ask for a doggy bag," said Mom quietly. "We should just go."

Dad said to the waitress, "The check, when you get a chance."

Cecilia and I glanced at each other.

We both understood. Everyone in the café blamed us. Keith Merkle was still missing, and why? Because of me and Cecilia and our friends. Because of our recklessness, because of what we'd done. And what's more, the tornado killer was missing too, because *we* had crossed the white strings, *we* had trashed the tornado killer's house, so *we* had made the tornado killer disappear. Who was going to fight the tornadoes now?

Poison eyes all over the room.

My food tasted weird. I didn't finish my hamburger. Dad paid in a hurry. We left our food on our plates. On our way out of the restaurant someone yelled something after us. I didn't hear what but Dad turned around angrily. Mom stopped him.

"Please don't," whispered Mom. "Let's just go, please let's just go home."

From the parking lot, I could see people in the café staring.

Death eyes.

On the drive home none of us talked. The world outside the car was pitch-black. We were hurtling through a hostile vacuum. Maybe it *was* our fault. We listened to the tornado announcers on the radio. Dad wanted to turn it off but I said no, keep it on. With no tornado fights to narrate, the announcers were just taking calls from anyone. Hysterical callers who were freaking out about the tornadoes, terrified callers who were afraid to die, angry callers who blamed us for driving away the tornado killer, Keith Merkle's heartbroken family and friends begging folks to keep an eye out for Keith Merkle, even a call from some crackpot who said hey everybody, don't worry, problem solved, because he'd actually figured out how to fight tornadoes all by himself, no need for the tornado killer anymore, in fact anyone could do it, all you had to do was learn his system, a system he'd figured out in his garage, using a humidifier and a dehumidifier and the principles of kung fu, and we listened to the play-by-play on the radio as the crackpot actually ventured out beyond the white strings and tried to fight the tornadoes during our drive home, and we heard the announcers describe the last part, just as we were turning into our neighborhood—the man *popped*, he was facing down a tornado and the tornado lashed out and the next second the man's body literally popped into a cloud of red mist.

The announcers kept describing it. They wouldn't let up.

Dad shut off the engine.

We sat there in silence for a minute, in our driveway.

The tornado killer had to be in trouble. He had to be hurt. Or dead. He wouldn't leave us alone. Not this long. He wouldn't allow amateurs to die trying to fight tornadoes, jackass impostors trying to do his job.

The tornado killer wouldn't leave me.

We got out of the car. I searched the distance for the tornado killer's faraway eyes.

Nothing.

We went into our house. The front door was unlocked.

But Mom had locked all the—

A man burst out of the laundry room.

He came at us screaming. Wild long frizzy red hair and in a dirty gray T-shirt, screaming that yes it was our fault, mine and Cecilia's fault, we hadn't respected the tornado killer, we'd desecrated the tornado killer's house, and now the tornadoes would have their revenge, Keith Merkle was only the beginning. The man lunged at me, grabbed me, but then Dad socked him and they were rolling on the ground, punches connecting with dull, horrible sounds. I'd never seen Dad actually punch another man. Mom screamed, she shouted out the window for the neighbors to help. Nobody came. They must have heard but were staying out of it on purpose. Cecilia and I ran and hid in the bathroom, we locked the door, Cecilia was crying, she said it wasn't worth it as police sirens wailed, then flashing lights strobed through the windows—outside the bathroom we heard scuffling, then we heard the police overpowering the guy, handcuffing him, and dragging him to the police car all while the guy yelled that he wasn't alone, he wasn't the only one, that others would come for us too.

Two policemen stayed behind to guard us. They would be stationed at our house from now on, they said.

One of the policemen said it was the same with the families of all the other kids who had gone out to the tornado killer's that night.

That night the threats started. Every time the phone rang it was another nutcase saying awful things.

We took the phone off the hook and left it off.

Five days, now.

The tornado killer was still missing.

My fault.

⹀

A memorial for Keith Merkle went up.

It was an improvised thing at first. The Merkles laminated

pictures of Keith and tacked them to the trees and the fences at the edge of town. They wrote and typed up anecdotes about Keith and posted those there too, little by little making a little shrine. They hauled out Keith Merkle's sports trophies and even some of the art he did as a kid. Friends added pictures and stuff of their own to the memorial. They arranged it all there as if to prove something. As if to say to the tornadoes: look, Keith Merkle was a person. This was his life. He was somebody. People cared about him. Give him back, tornadoes. Even if it's just his body.

The tornadoes just kept shrieking.

Late one night Cecilia came to my room and said, "Cuthbert's on the phone for you."

I was in bed. I turned away from her. This was the third time Cuthbert had called. I had overheard my parents talking to Cuthbert Monks on the phone. No, Cuthbert, she can't talk to you. She's not just grounded from going out, she's grounded from the phone too. No, Cuthbert, not even if it's urgent. Cuthbert, we've already told you.

Cecilia, impatiently: "He asked me to get you special."

"Why?"

"I don't know." She said it flat, like she was delivering a message to a stranger. I felt like garbage. I wished I'd told Cecilia everything from the beginning. But it was too late now. I didn't know how to reconnect.

Cecilia said, "Are you coming or what?"

I got up and followed her downstairs.

"So, um," I said. "Is there anything new about Keith Merkle . . . ?"

"Don't pretend to care."

I caught the sting of alcohol on her breath.

"Hey, are you all right?" I said.

Cecilia didn't answer. We went down to the dark kitchen, where our yellow rotary phone was attached to the wall. I saw the receiver in the shadows, off the hook.

I could feel Cuthbert waiting on the other end.

"Go on," said Cecilia, irritated. She probably wanted to call someone else. I was cutting in on her secret midnight phone time. I didn't even know who Cecilia would be calling. We were disconnected. I looked at her. Her face was blotchy, her eyes exhausted.

I picked up the phone. Then I hung it up.

Cecilia started. "Why'd you do that?"

"I don't want to talk to him," I said.

Now she just looked exasperated. "Then why'd you even come downstairs?"

I could have said something smart-ass like "So I could have the pleasure of hanging up on Cuthbert Monks."

But I should've said "Because I want to talk to you."

Because I needed to talk to her. Cecilia and I were out of sync. We didn't know how to be sisters anymore. I should've just let her talk, let her say anything. And if she wanted to hear me talk too, sure, I could just start talking, in fact I'd tell Cecilia everything. Did she have her string necklace with our bus locker key anymore? Mine was still in my backpack. I hadn't opened it since the sleepover. Maybe Cecilia had lost her key. Or thrown it away.

Just ask.

But I was scared of the dullness in her eyes.

I went upstairs.

After a few moments, I heard Cecilia going down into the basement, to the "saloon."

Cecilia. No.

Midway down the stairs she paused.

Cecilia, I thought.

But she went the rest of the way down.

<hr>

I tried to listen to Electrifier. But he had changed or I had changed. The music that had felt so fascinating and dangerous was cheesy now.

Not just Electrifier. Scrambled eggs at breakfast were rubbery, alien. How had I ever eaten eggs before? Mom made me a ham sandwich for lunch but the ham was like sweaty skin. Fruit tasted rotten. At dinner we had chicken but cutting around the bones and the cartilage and the muscle made me feel like I was eating a baby.

Where was the tornado killer?

After dinner, Mom and Dad were still at the table and Cecilia was washing dishes, they were all talking, the radio was on in the background, I was still sitting at the kitchen table, trying not to look at my fetus-chicken, trying not to throw up, and then the radio interrupted for a special report.

There was a body in the sky.

I looked up. Heart stopped.

"*What* did they say?" said Mom.

Cecilia turned it up.

I stood. Unsteady.

We gathered around the radio.

The radio said some guy had been scanning the outskirts of town with his binoculars, watching the tornadoes, when he spotted a body flying in the sky. The guy's girlfriend had called the radio station and she was on the phone with the announcers right now, breathless, repeating everything the guy said, repeating his description of what he saw, where it was.

Dad grabbed his binoculars. We all dashed out into the backyard.

Others had run out of their houses too, looking at the sunset sky, pointing.

There *was* a body, high up in the clouds. It was caught inside a tornado, tumbling around in circles . . .

It wasn't the tornado killer.

"He's alive," said Dad, looking through his binoculars. "His eyes are open! He's trying to say something, he's—"

It was Keith Merkle.

===

The tornado was on the move. It held Keith up high as it lurched across the prairie, snaking and wobbling around the perimeter of town. Against the purple and yellow of the sunset, the tornado looked like a monstrous shadow come to life, bloated to gargantuan scale. And yet it moved with a ceremonious air, carrying Keith Merkle delicately, like someone walking across a room while balancing an egg on a spoon.

It got dark. We watched late into the night on TV. Local news trucks followed the tornado, training their floodlights on Keith Merkle. The only thing you could see, turning from channel to channel, was different views of Keith's body tumbling through the black sky, as if he was trapped in some nightmarish outer space.

Then the tornado stopped.

It stopped at Keith Merkle's memorial.

The tornado churned in place, right outside the white strings.

People from all over town mobbed the memorial. Not just Keith's friends and family, but also strangers with lit candles and signs and stuff. Like this was their chance to personally confront the tornado. Even people whom I knew had never met Keith were holding up big pictures of his face, and poster boards that said KEITH, COME HOME and WE LOVE YOU, KEITH and GIVE US BACK OUR BOY.

Did they think a tornado could read?

But maybe this tornado could. The tornado seemed to have intentions. It dangled Keith Merkle over the memorial like it was trying to make a point, like it was trying to tell us something.

Keith twisted in midair, eyes wild, mouth moving.

Nobody could hear him.

Everyone at the memorial was acting crazier and crazier. The police had to hold the Merkle family back, to keep them from dashing out over the white strings. People in the crowd were waggling their signs at the tornado, shouting like the tornado could understand them. Everyone had become emotionally invested in Keith Merkle. The announcers on the radio and TV said stuff like "We are all Keith Merkle now." It felt like you *had* to go the Keith Merkle memorial, to show your support, to prove something to the tornado.

We didn't go.

None of the families of the kids who had trespassed in the tornado killer's house went. We stayed at home and watched it on TV. The look in the eyes of the people in that crowd was just like the people at the café. Or the red-haired man who had been hiding in our bathroom.

They hated us.

The tornado killer had to come now! said the announcer. To

save Keith Merkle! If there was any time for the tornado killer, it
was now!

I watched the TV all through the night, waiting for him to come.

I was back in Lisa's basement.

I was dreaming but it didn't feel like a dream. It was Lisa's
basement but it wasn't Lisa's basement. It had the fake wooden
walls and patterned carpet but there was something different.

In that basement the tornado killer and not-me were gone,
disappeared beyond that new door in the wall. All the sleepover
girls were lying where they were before, watching me with their
empty eyes and fixed grins.

But this time, I walked past them.

I went through the hole in Lisa's wall.

The room beyond was completely dark except for four people,
standing equally apart from one another as if standing at the
corners of a baseball diamond. Mechanical stillness. The blackness
was total. And yet all four people glowed.

I had been here before. I knew this place. The black place felt
like nowhere but I was connected to it, like a room in my own
house that I had never known was there.

The four people glowed.

The tornado killer and Mr. Z faced away from each other. They
were on opposite sides of the diamond.

The third person was Mrs. Lois. She stood next to me.

The fourth person, opposite me, was—

I couldn't look at her.

Some kind of dance started. Mrs. Lois moved away from me
and approached Mr. Z. She took his hands, guiding him so he was

walking backward, like they were doing a grave and elaborate tango. She looked deep in his eyes, a wanting look, advancing, guiding him backward toward the tornado killer.

And with every backward step Mr. Z took, he was getting younger.

The tornado killer was moving too, jerkily in step with Mr. Z, their movements connected like mutual marionettes. And as the tornado killer walked backward toward Mr. Z, little by little he wasn't a beautiful boy anymore. His face coarsened, step by step, into something harsher, older.

The tornado killer and Mr. Z passed each other, and at that moment they looked like two young Mr. Zs, or two old tornado killers. The twins looked into each other's eyes and with a kind of solemn do-si-do they turned and now they were walking away from each other. Mrs. Lois walked away from them both and passed me, as if I wasn't even there, disappearing into the darkness behind me.

Her part was over.

Mr. Z wasn't Mr. Z anymore, he was the tornado killer. He kept moving until he was a little boy. He kept moving. He was a toddler, he was a crawling baby. On the opposite side, the tornado killer had now fully aged into Mr. Z.

The dance was finished.

I stepped into Mrs. Lois's place. She had disappeared into the darkness behind me—where had she gone? I knew that if I turned around, I could see where Mrs. Lois had gone, the place where she went after I replaced her. But I didn't want to see what happened to her, I didn't want to turn around. That left me facing the other person, the fourth person staring at me across the room.

I looked at her.

The Horrible Woman radiated in the darkness.

The same monstrous woman I had seen with Archie's mother in that room waiting for me and Cecilia to come to them that snowy New Year's Eve, a hundred nightmares ago.

She smiled, and she showed me her curvy knife.

I was shaken awake by Cecilia. I was still on the couch. I had fallen asleep in front of the TV. Mom and Dad were there too. My head felt huge and buzzing and everything was confused, they were all talking at once. I couldn't understand what they were talking about.

Cecilia said it again: "The tornado killer is dead."

THE EYES BEHIND
THE WALL

It felt like the television was flickering at the other end of a long tunnel. The volume was up but everything was muted.

I was far away.

Something like this shouldn't be on a television. The screen I watched wasn't built to fit these images.

Growing up, when I wondered what the end of the world might be like, nuclear war, final judgment, asteroid crash—I tried to imagine how I'd really act. If I turned on the TV one day and saw it happening, the bombs dropping, cities on fire, if hell finally opened up and everyone was being rounded up and marched down there, what would I do? Would I cry, would I freak out? Would I freeze? What would I say to Mom, to Dad, to Cecilia? Goodbye? What would we do?

Now I knew.

Nothing.

When the time came, Mom and Dad and Cecilia and I didn't do anything. For ourselves or each other. We should've been closer. We should've talked to each other. We should've helped one another.

We just watched.

They replayed it again and again.

A slow pan of the Keith Merkle memorial from afar. The memorial was overrun with people but everything was dwarfed by the tornado, black and titanic, swirling monstrously slow. Just barely visible, Keith Merkle tumbled around inside the tornado, far overhead in the dim sky.

Unreal.

New shot. The camera was jostling in the crowd. People were as close to the white strings as they dared to get. Mr. and Mrs. Merkle were there, and Keith's friends too, and other people I didn't recognize, all blurred into one another in the chaotic footage. They were chanting at the tornado, singing. Crying, pleading.

Don't watch.

There was an eruption of surprise, the camera swung around—yells of "Let them through!" and "Thank God!"—and the men, those men from the school, the men who had tried to force themselves into my house, now they were pushing their way through the mob.

They were carrying that big painted complicated old box that they'd brought into my school.

The men put the box down. They opened it.

The tornado killer climbed out.

He must've known what would happen next. My chest tightened. I felt something invisible in me stretching out to him.

I saw the awful recognition in his eyes.

The crowd roared. More than just applause and shouts, it was like the mob broke open and something hopeful and hysterical burst from everyone at once. Everyone pushed forward to see the tornado killer. The men could barely hold the crowd back.

The tornado killer walked unsteadily through them.

He looked sick.

I was sick. My stomach tumbling.

I knew too.

The tornado reacted to his arrival. I could feel surprise in the tornado, as though it hadn't really expected him to come. The tornado swerved away, tentatively lowering Keith Merkle, almost letting him go.

The tornado killer stepped over the white string.

The crowd went nuts. Yes!

I should've left the room. I should've gotten up right then and walked out.

The tornado killer held up his left hand. Keeping his left hand raised, he sliced his right hand—

The tornado lashed out.

The tornado killer went sprawling facedown in the grass.

Don't watch—

The tornado killer scrambled up. He raised his trembling arms. With a clumsy lunge, he swung both arms through the air.

The tornado *reeled*—

The crowd whooped. The tornado killer was back! Yes, yes, he could do this, he was going to lick this tornado—

The tornado grabbed him.

Don't watch.

The tornado killer opened his mouth but he couldn't scream, because then it happened, the tornado yanked him around, flipped him, bashed him into a tree, stomped him into the ground and then it snatched him up again, it whipped him left, right, left. I saw the tornado killer's legs twist, then break, his arms were wrenched out, they popped right out, flopped around, bloody, he clawed the air, his face, his strange and beautiful face, I knew that face, I had kissed it, but it was all panic now, he knew what was about to happen, I knew it too, the tornado had him upside down, throttling him, he was struggling to escape the tornado's grip, and then the final thing happened—the tornado twisted the tornado killer's body hard, like wringing out a rag.

He wasn't moving anymore.

The tornado let him fall.

He hit the dirt.

He didn't move again.

Panic. Screams. Everyone was trampling one another, trying to get away.

Up in the tornado, Keith Merkle reached down toward his family. Desperate eyes.

Mrs. Merkle's voice: "Give my baby back!"

The camera was knocked sideways as everyone tried to escape. The memorial had fallen. Pictures and letters were fluttering everywhere.

The camera swung, off-kilter, back to the tornado—

The tornado tore Keith Merkle in half.

The tornado split Keith down the middle and threw the gutted halves into the crowd. Mom and Dad and Cecilia and I watched. The tornado gave him back, sure. Everyone screamed. Blood on faces. I still watched. A gush of meat, intestines wildly unspooling, splattered onto everyone.

The replays repeated all night. You could watch it as often as you liked.

The next day was beautiful.

The bright blue sky was empty, scoured of clouds. The sun was hot and happy and carefree.

My parents drove Cecilia and me to Keith Merkle's funeral. We didn't talk. Our car's air conditioner was blasting but I sweated. My head pounded. My eyes were dazzled. I watched the shimmering world pass outside the window. Numb.

Keith Merkle was dead.

The tornado killer was dead too.

Cecilia was next to me in the backseat. She faced out the window. I wanted to talk to her but she had turned herself off. Because I had shut her out. I hadn't cared enough about Keith Merkle. Now Keith was dead. Cecilia didn't want to deal with my crap.

I felt hollow.

After the tornadoes killed Keith Merkle, after they killed the tornado killer, everyone expected the tornadoes to blast through the white strings right away and kill everyone else too. Demolish our town once and for all.

The opposite happened.

One minute the tornadoes were straining hard against the white strings, churning dust into hideous shapes, reeling a furious ring around us, about to blast through, gobble us up, destroy everything—

Then they all reared back, folded up—

And were gone.

I had come out onto the porch, still shocked. Mom and Dad and Cecilia came out too. The TV showed what was happening, but we had to see it for ourselves. It was happening everywhere—the tornadoes were slackening, losing contact with the ground—one by one, the tornadoes stretched themselves out into long, wavy, thin lines of steam, flopping over, poof, entire monsters of smoke and steam vanished, one after another.

For the first time that summer, the prairie was silent.

The tornadoes were gone.

We got to Keith's funeral early but the church was already packed. We only barely squeezed into a pew. People kept coming. Eventually people filled up the aisles too, and the vestibule, and they even gathered outside on the grass, crying over Keith Merkle. Maybe also crying with relief, because the tornadoes were finally gone.

Nobody cried for the tornado killer.

Mom and I had fought that morning over breakfast. I couldn't make myself even touch the bagel slathered with gluey cream cheese. Cereal looked like a bowl full of scabs and dead insects. If I ate anything I was sure I'd vomit. But I was so weak. There was nothing in my body.

I was going to faint.

Just about everyone at church wore the necklaces. For the first time Mom and Dad seemed self-conscious about not wearing them. I saw it in their conversations with other adults before the service. Dad was talking to some other man and the man's eyes flicked down to Dad's chest, just silently noting that Dad wasn't wearing a necklace. Even though nothing was said, the message was clear: get with the program, buddy.

When a tornado killer dies, did they cut up his body right away and stuff the pieces in lockets, to make more of those necklaces? Had they already cut the tornado killer up? Whose job was that?

The questions rattled around emptily.

I was too drained to feel any of them.

The organ droned. The world was swimming around me, the church a claustrophobic nest of gloomy woodwork and stained glass in muddy browns, olives, and grays, like we were trapped in a jeweled walnut, the windows spiderwebbed with lead so thick hardly any of the blazing sunlight broke through, except for the odd blot of purple or green splashed across the floor, glowing dully on the red carpet.

I felt eyes on me.

When I caught someone staring, I stared back. They always looked away. But I wanted to stare them down. Because I was mad at them for being right. They had been right about everything. They told us not to do it but we did it anyway. Touching is death. Now Keith was dead. The tornado killer was dead. You were right. So fight me.

I wanted to fight someone.

Punch a face. Any face at this funeral.

The funeral was half-assed, as if even the pastor didn't believe in what he was doing. Other priests were at the altar too, and Deacon Terry, the youth minister, an exhaustingly cheerful guy with a haircut fifteen years out of date, someone Cecilia and I had spent way more time with than we would've liked, because Mom and Dad always sent us off to church camp, it being cheaper than regular camp. Since we only belonged to church in a Christmas-Easter, weddings-and-funerals way, Deacon Terry was eager to make us feel welcome, to create a positive atmosphere, which inadvertently brought out the jerk in us, we were awful, Deacon Terry didn't deserve it, like when Cecilia and Jessica and I had smuggled a pack of condoms into church camp, of course we had zero intention of actually using them, it was just for giggles, the boys thought it was funny too, they inflated them into balloons, but when Deacon Terry discovered the opened condom packets he gathered us together and he was very concerned and understanding, and had said to Cecilia, as delicately as he could, "Are you sexually active?"

Cecilia said, "Vividly."

"What have you done?"

"Oh, you know. Orgies." Cecilia deliberately pronounced it with a hard *g*.

Deacon Terry corrected her automatically, but without condescension: "Orj-ees."

Cecilia: "What?"

"It's orj-ees, not org-ees."

Cecilia, slight frown: "No, I'm pretty sure it's org-ees."

Deacon Terry, impatiently: "No, I'm sure it's orj-ees."

"Oh, uh, you're sure? *Absolutely sure?*" Cecilia said, opening her eyes wide, leaning forward, and Deacon Terry realized he was sitting there arguing with a teenaged girl about the correct pronunciation of *orgies*.

I looked at Cecilia now. Her raunchy goofiness was gone. All of our other friends were miserable too. The other families in church glared at us.

Come at me, then.

The funeral went on forever. I stared at the life-size Jesus on the cross behind the altar. It was too gross, too real. It had always creeped me out. You could actually see the nail entering the top of his plastic foot on one side and then coming out the sole of the foot and then going into the cross—ugh, too much blood, of course he was in pain, I get it, he was nailed to a cross. But it had always felt to me like when you looked at that crucifix, you were being invited to *savor* the pain he was in. And I didn't like how Jesus seemed to be fearfully glancing over his right shoulder either. As though he was startled by something he'd just noticed. As though he'd sensed some approaching thing and was afraid. As though, even though he was in agony, he was even more terrified by what was behind him.

I kept my eyes on Jesus anyway. I was trying not to pass out during

Deacon Terry's eulogy. I barely recognized Deacon Terry's version of Keith Merkle. Everyone knew Keith Merkle was never really that nice, he was not that smart, not that kind. Now Deacon Terry was praising Keith Merkle for volunteering at the senior citizens' center. Everyone knew that those service projects were required by school. I thought of shirtless drunk Keith Merkle pissing on the carpet in the tornado killer's house—there's your real Keith Merkle, Deacon Terry. My head throbbed. Now Deacon Terry was reading some crappy poem Keith Merkle had written in eighth grade. My parents were crying. This funeral was schlock. Deacon Terry was overselling Keith Merkle's poem, blatantly trying to make people weep. I was light-headed.

Above the crucifix, a little door slid open.

A dark square was revealed beyond.

Two eyes stared out of it.

Brown eyes. A woman's eyes. Staring at me.

I sat up, electrified.

The panel shot closed.

Nobody else reacted.

Wait. I couldn't have been the only one to notice it.

My heart pounded.

The service ended, everybody shuffling and sniffling. That panel had always been there, above the crucifix. But I'd never seen it open before. I got up too quickly, went dizzy, found my footing, and tried to make it over to the altar.

Two brown eyes.

I knew those eyes.

Behind the altar you could enter a kind of backstage for the church. I wanted to get behind the altar, behind the crucifix, to find out whose eyes those were. But I couldn't get anywhere near.

Nobody was allowed back there. Still—I recognized those eyes. There were too many people. I was woozy. I looked for anyone from our group across the church but they had all had ducked out when the last song started—

Brown eyes behind the wall—

Some people were being quietly taken aside.

In the vestibule one of our neighbors took Dad aside and said something to him. Not a big speech. Just a half minute. But Dad's expression changed. In the parking lot a kindly older lady touched Mom's elbow and said a few words.

Mom's face changed.

Mom and Dad didn't talk on the drive home. Cecilia was still crying. I still wanted to fight but I was exhausted. They wanted me to mourn Keith Merkle but all I could think of was Keith acting like a jackass at the tornado killer's house, shirtless on the table, doing a jump kick, nearly falling off, righting himself as everyone cheered.

Nobody had mentioned the tornado killer.

When I got home I went straight to my room. I shut the door and fell into my bed, still in my clothes.

Brown eyes followed me into my dreams.

―――

When I was younger I found a certain book at the library.

It was a book that I happened upon one day but never saw it again. I didn't even try to check it out that day, I was afraid of it. But when I got my courage up a few days later, the book wasn't where I'd originally found it, and it wasn't on any of the nearby shelves either. Even though I looked for it all throughout the stacks, there were too many books there, I couldn't find it at all. I couldn't even remember its name, or even if it had a name, or even what the cover looked like, so maybe I dreamed that book and it never actually existed.

But I remembered it. The book was written in an alphabet that didn't look like any alphabet I'd ever seen. It was handwritten, not printed, in a way that was cramped and weird, like something from an old foreign hymnal. I had no idea what the words and symbols meant but the pictures were awful. Every ten or so pages (pages that were super thin, like you only see with old Bibles) there was a kind of old-fashioned woodblock print illustration of something ghoulish, something that made me feel sick and ashamed just looking at it. But I kept looking. The picture I remember was of a woman's naked body lying on a dinner table, but her body was split open, neck to navel, and she was disgorging all these meats and fruits. Her face was still smiling. There was a family of three gathered around this woman's body, a mother and father and son leering around her hungrily, holding knives and spoons, like they couldn't wait to dig into her, like this was going to be the best meal of their lives. Their faces were inhuman. But the thing that made me shiver most of all was that the split-open woman's face had the sweetest, most relaxed, most blissful smile.

I never found that book again. Maybe I had never seen it. Maybe I had just invented it in my dream now, and then some weird synapse in my brain fired to make it feel like a memory, like I'd seen that book long ago, but there actually had never been any such book. But no. That book did exist.

I recognized that naked split-open woman.

And I knew that family too. I recognized them. They were—

Brown eyes grew larger in my mind, obliterating all of it.

———

I woke up. Sunshine filtered through my curtains, groggy and dim. I had been in and out of sleep all day, feeling sick. Being in bed while the sun shone made me feel even sicker. Light trying to break into my room, through my curtains. I turned over and faced the wall. Someone was knocking at my door, probably Mom, maybe Cecilia. I was too sleepy to care.

In the early evening I woke up for real. I took off my gross clothes and changed into clean pajamas.

I moved the curtain aside and looked out into the night.

The two policemen stationed at our doors stared back at me.

I got back into bed. I stared at the wall again. The brown eyes weren't just behind the church wall, they were behind every wall, the eyes were invisible and everywhere . . .

When I woke up next it was long after midnight. Wide awake. Still weak but I didn't feel hungry anymore.

I felt light and clean and a little unreal.

My window was slightly open. Wind blew in the dark, moving my curtains, different than wind I was used to. Blowing harder, rustling through the trees and leaves.

Everything felt new and vivid.

The brown eyes burned in my mind. They were familiar but a bad familiar, like when I was ten, when Cecilia and I would look at each other's faces upside down for a long time, until for one horrible moment Cecilia's face would seem to reverse—her nice eyes suddenly vicious, inhuman, conniving, an upside-down secret face that had always been secretly there, riding along with her; and I knew she was looking at my own upside-down face too, she saw my own vicious upside-down eyes, and I realized Cecilia and I had always carried around these secret faces, my reversed eyes silently conspiring with hers.

I turned my bedside table lamp on.

I wasn't afraid of the dark. But tonight's dark was a different dark. If I spent too long in this dark, those brown eyes above the cross would appear for real.

I got out of bed. I went to my window, pushed the curtains aside, and opened the window some more. I opened it all the way.

Wind rushed into my room.

I heard voices. The kitchen window was open too. Just below me, I could hear Mom and Dad's low conversation. I tried to make out words but I only caught their tone. Tense. Strained.

It was four a.m. and I stood still at the window, looking out into the dark, letting the wind blow through me. I felt new and strange, like the night was shining through me. The wind was fresh and pure. Then I noticed something.

The policemen were missing.

The policemen who were supposed to be guarding our house—they weren't at their usual spots.

Now there was silence downstairs.

Mom and Dad weren't talking anymore—

The back door *snick*ed shut. Then a moment later Mom and Dad were crossing the lawn, quickly and stealthily. They were sneaking out.

I watched them go, startled.

I ran to Cecilia's room.

"Cecilia!" I shook her shoulder. "Wake up!"

Cecilia opened her eyes. "Uhhh, no, uh."

"Mom and Dad just left. They left the house." I pulled at her sheet. "Something weird is happening, come on, let's go!"

Half asleep: "What?"

"Come on!"

"I don't want to, don't anymore," mumbled Cecilia.

I smelled the gin. Saw her bottle.

No time.

I dashed downstairs, shoved my shoes on.

I ran into the night in my pajamas, alone.

It was too late to catch up to Mom and Dad. I didn't see them anywhere. But other adults were out on the streets too, all silent. It seemed like every adult in town was slipping out of their houses, all of them moving along in the same direction.

There was no moon. I kept to the shadows, following the adults by darting through dark backyards and catching glimpses of them between houses, cutting through little patches of trees and gullies.

They were all headed to the church.

I hid behind a car, catching my breath.

Why church? We had all just been there in the afternoon for the funeral. Why only the adults? But I remembered the whispered conversations after the funeral. The neighbor who stopped Dad in the vestibule to say a few words. The old lady in the parking lot, whispering to Mom.

I was close to the church now. Something was happening in there already. I couldn't tell what. The lights were barely on, a dim glow behind the stained glass. I saw shadowy figures moving around inside. More people were filing in, joining them.

The church was full.

The last of the adults entered. The church doors closed.

The street was empty now. I crept up to the high wooden doors. There was no sound but the nighttime chirp of insects, a few early-morning bird twitters. The church so quiet that if I hadn't seen all those adults go in, I would've thought it was empty.

Something in me said: Get out of here.

I moved closer. I tested the doors.

Locked.

Get out of here now.

Most of the windows were stained glass but there were clear windows a little bit higher. Too high. I could maybe touch them if I stood on a partner's shoulders. But I didn't have a partner anymore—Cecilia had drunk herself to sleep. I circled the church, looking for another way up, and I saw in the back, near the tangle of electrical generators and air-conditioning stuff, a tree growing right next to the wall. I climbed onto the humming hardware, grabbed a branch, and pulled myself up through the tree.

I edged over to the window.

A rustling below—I twisted around. I stared out into the darkness, listening to the night.

Nothing. A raccoon.

I turned back and looked through the window.

It was dim inside the church. It took a minute for my eyes to adjust. Adults filled the pews. The hinged kneelers had been lowered and everyone was on their knees, their heads bowed.

I looked for the priest. He wasn't at the altar. Then I spotted him: the priest was kneeling in the pews like everyone else, wearing regular-person clothes. Deacon Terry kneeled next to him, also in ordinary clothes.

This wasn't their show.

Whose show was this?

The little door above the crucifix slowly slid open. The square hole beyond was black but then two brown eyes glowed. They stared out over the crowd impassively.

The Horrible Woman.

It was the Horrible Woman who had the brown eyes, and who

sat in the room behind the crucifix, staring out of that hole, scanning the congregation as though searching for someone. I recognized those eyes from that snowy night at Archie's house, the Horrible Woman with Archie's mom in the closet . . . The men were there too, standing at the doors and in the aisles. But not like ushers. They weren't helping anyone to their seats.

A shape was moving among the pews. I hadn't seen the shape at first because it had been right below my window, but now it came into view and it was Mr. Z. He was wearing his dark glasses even though it was night. He was pacing up and down the aisles, shaking his head, nodding and talking to the people he passed. Occasionally Mr. Z would stop, lean over, and talk to someone, and they would nod, still kneeling, head still bowed. Mr. Z then would straighten up, pat their back, and start walking again, talking as if to himself, and one of the men would sidle up to that person and speak, and the person would nod some more, and then sometimes a man with a pitcher of something black would come and fill up a paper cup.

Then that person drank.

This happened again. And again. I couldn't always see who Mr. Z was talking to. I didn't see Mom or Dad. But they had to be in there. Mr. Z might have spoken to them. They might have drank.

I didn't know what that drinking meant.

I looked to the front of the church again. Startlingly, Mr. Z climbed to the top of the altar. He was perched atop it like a malevolent ape on a table, gripping the edge, staring around the room.

I looked at the pastor, expecting him to object.

The pastor kept his eyes fixed to the ground.

The men came down the aisles. Mr. Z began to beat the altar rhythmically. The glowing brown eyes above the cross glared as the men approached.

The men removed the giant crucifix from the wall.

Mr. Z beat the altar faster. The brown eyes from above the crucifix watched stonily as the men took it down and laid it on the floor.

The men removed Jesus from the cross. Now the detached Jesus just had his arms spread out for no reason, like an exaggerated shrug—*What am I supposed to do now?* he seemed to say.

Mr. Z froze on the altar, as though he were about to relish a rare sight.

The men began to disassemble the cross. This was wrong. I disliked this church, I didn't believe the stuff they believed, but this felt wrong. And yet the men were taking the cross apart with businesslike skill, like they had their own long-agreed secret use for it. Maybe this was the real use of the cross all along, maybe I was the one with inaccurate information.

With the same diligence, they split the detached plaster Jesus down the middle like Keith Merkle. Something was hidden inside his hollow body.

Movement.

A twitch out of the corner of my eye. Something was moving in the window opposite mine.

I looked.

It was Cuthbert Monks, glaring back at me.

Startled, I almost lost my grip—

Commotion broke out below. I looked back down as a confused roar went up, a scuffling. Adults in the pews were rising, pointing up at my window. I couldn't move. Mr. Z slapped the altar and hopped up and down, hooting in rage. More people were getting up from the pews, looking up at me. The ceremony broke into chaos. The men were pushing through the crowd for the doors. They couldn't recognize it was me, I knew, I was too far away—I was only a blurry floating face in the dark—

The Horrible Woman stared right at me.

Furious.

Cuthbert Monks's face vanished. Below I heard the church doors rattling, unlocking. I ducked from my window—

I couldn't move my foot! My shoe was jammed into the cleft of the tree. I yanked my foot clear out of the shoe, then I dropped, scrambled, half fell out of the tree, onto the electrical equipment. I reached up and grabbed my shoe, wrenched it free—brain frantic, heart in throat, I heard the church doors opening, the men coming around somewhere behind me. I took off, the men were running after me, I ran shoe-sock, shoe-sock, shoe-sock, into the neighborhood behind the church, one foot dry, one wet, getting wetter, and turned the corner. I was near the Zendermans' house, I saw their station wagon up ahead and I remembered how Mrs. Zenderman used to drive us all to the movies, how the door to the way-back never locked, the car always full of kids, me and Cecilia and Eric Zenderman and Archie and Lisa and some others, me in the way-back and Mrs. Zenderman had complained how the lock in the back was broken, that anyone could break into the station wagon whenever they wanted, and we all laughed, because who would want to break into the Zendermans' car, which was famously dirty and always full of crap?

I grabbed the Zendermans' station wagon's back door. Like magic it opened. I jumped in and shut the door just as the men's flashlight beams came swinging through the dark. They'd be here any second.

Then I saw Cuthbert Monks.

He was running down the street, not seeing me.

The men were going to catch him.

Cuthbert Monks stared around wildly. Flashlight beams stabbed through the dark around him.

I opened the door. "Cuthbert!"

His eyes found me. He hesitated. As though getting in the car with me would be worse than getting caught.

A yell from the men.

Cuthbert ran over, scrambled in with me. I shut the door just in time. Flashlight beams zapped through the windows, illuminating the crap strewn all around the car.

Men's voices came closer, angry, confused. I pulled a blanket over Cuthbert and me. The men's voices became clearer as they neared the car.

Flashlights swept around. More footsteps.

Don't even breathe.

Cuthbert Monks was so very, very close.

He stank. His breath smelled like Dad's breath before he quit smoking, like when I was very little and Dad and Mom would get dressed up and go out dancing with their friends and they'd come home smelling like smoke, like alcohol, like glamour, and Dad would come into my room and kiss me when he thought I was asleep. Mom and Dad would have been out doing who knows what with other adults, dancing, flirting, the secret part of them I'd never see, and I knew that Dad's kiss, which I had been waiting for all night, was just an afterthought for him, sometimes he didn't even kiss me, he'd forget, and I never liked his bristly cheek and his smoky alcohol breath, but I actually longed for it, and I hated Cuthbert Monks for having Dad's smoky breath, or I hated him for other reasons but his smoky breath made me hate him more.

The men's voices faded to a murmur. Cuthbert and I were too close, face-to-face under the blanket, staring at each other, not daring to move.

Cuthbert looked different. Damaged. Wary. He didn't want to meet my eyes. It was hot under the blanket and cramped and everything stank of Cuthbert Monk's smokiness, his boy armpit smell.

The voices were gone.

I whispered, "What happened?"

Cuthbert moved to open the door.

"Hey." I grabbed him. "What just happened in there?"

Cuthbert twisted away. "Don't touch me."

I held on. "You know what's going on, tell me!"

Cuthbert tried to shake me off. "I don't know."

"You do!" I said. "Why'd you come out?"

"Why did *you* come out?"

I still had his arm clutched tight. "Because my parents sneaked out. I saw them. I followed them. Isn't that why you came out? All the adults were—"

Cuthbert narrowed his eyes. "No other reason?"

I stopped. What was he getting at?

Cuthbert said, "What do you know about the tornado killer?"

A switch in tone. Not scared anymore.

Insinuating.

We were out from under the blanket but we were still closer than I wanted to be. The heat from our bodies made the windows foggy.

"I just saved you," I whispered. "You owe me! Tell me what's going on, I know you have something to tell me!"

"Why do you think that?"

"Because you've called me like three million times this week—"

"And why didn't you talk to me?"

"I didn't *want* to talk to you then."

Cuthbert pulled his arm away. "Well, I don't *want* to talk to you now."

"You know something! You checked those books out of the library—"

"Books?"

"Don't act dumb, the books about the tornado killer—you checked them all out!"

Cuthbert didn't answer me at first. He just looked at me for a long time.

Then he put his finger on the foggy window, and drew.

He looked at me, waiting for a reaction.

I felt my stomach falling. I tried to stay blank-faced.

He kept drawing.

"You've seen these?" said Cuthbert.

I kept my face neutral.

"Do you know who's doing them?" said Cuthbert.

Say nothing.

"And this one?"

Stay blank. Don't tell.

Cuthbert said, "That one is yours, isn't it? It's you."

Get away from him.

Cuthbert kept his finger on my symbol. Like he was touching *me*. He traced the larger triangle on top. "You've seen her before. Those brown eyes at the funeral. Who is she?"

The Horrible Woman.

I swallowed. "I don't know—"

"You're lying."

Damn him. Cuthbert Monks always took control, always steered conversations where he wanted them to go, to somewhere I couldn't go. But I couldn't talk to him about the Horrible Woman in the little room in Archie's house—watching me in the blackness, glowing in my dreams, now in the church, the eyes behind the wall—

"You know who she is." Cuthbert was much too close to me now. "The night we went to the tornado killer's house, what happened to you?"

"If you already think you know—" I started, but then I realized there was something even more threatening than the Horrible Woman. Something that was dangerously near. As close as if we were boyfriend and girlfriend.

His face so close, so demanding.

Cuthbert said, "You touched him, didn't you?"

Don't give him anything.

"You did." I could feel Cuthbert breathing. "What did you do?"

"Stop."

"That's why he's dead." Cuthbert trapped me against the seat. "That's why Keith is dead too. You didn't know."

"I knew."

Cuthbert stared. Too close.

His voice had a new edge. "You know?"

Oh no. No.

Just shut up—shut up get out—

Cuthbert grabbed me. "Are you one of them?"

I struggled. "Let me go!"

"Do you know what Mr. Z does to girls in his house?"

Crushing me against the seat. "Stop—"

"Did he already get you?" said Cuthbert.

"Stop!" I tried to scream.

"Shut up!" Cuthbert put his hand over my mouth, my neck. "Shut *up!*"

I choked.

"You know why the tornado killer never answers his phone?" said Cuthbert in my ear. "The tornadoes *talk*."

Get out—

"When I picked up the phone, they told me everything."

Do anything, get out now—

"You wanna know what the tornadoes said will happen to *you?*"

I kicked, broke free of his hand. Cuthbert shoved me back and the back of my head banged the rear window, hard. My head burst in pain and I saw stars, and I felt how big he was, how much bigger than me, too big. If he wanted to really hurt me—

I tried to squirm away but couldn't. We were tangled up in the blanket, kicking around, and then he was on top of me, pinning me down, demanding answers.

"Why'd you come out?"

I strained against him.

"The tornado killer, is *he* why you came out?"

"Get off!"

"You don't know who you are, do you?"

"Let me go!"

"Maybe the tornado killer doesn't know what he is either."

"I don't even know—"

"I think you do know—you, them, you're all the same thing, that's why the tornado didn't kill him at first—"

I was crying. "They *did* kill him! He's dead, you saw!"

"Wait, you really don't—" Cuthbert was still holding me down, but his face changed and there wasn't anger in his eyes anymore— more like a stunned pity—

He said, "Don't you know you're the bride of the tornado?"

I rammed my knee up in between his legs.

Cuthbert Monks yowled. I threw open the back door. Dogs were barking up and down the street. Lights flickered on. I staggered through the empty street, ducked between houses, ran into the woods. Voices shouted behind me. People were coming out onto their porches. I didn't know if Cuthbert escaped or if he got caught in the Zendermans' car.

I didn't care.

I ran. I ran until I couldn't run anymore, until I stumbled to a stop, in some neighborhood I'd never been to. I wandered for about an hour in the dim daybreak, my mind frazzled, buzzing.

Where could I go?

I couldn't stay here. Not after what I saw at the church. Not after what Cuthbert had said. Even though I didn't understand it—

It didn't matter. Leave town now. Even if I had no money. Even if I couldn't take a bus. The tornadoes had stopped anyway, who knew why. So now there was nothing keeping me from just waltzing across the white strings. And once I got far enough away from town—

Just get out of here.

═══

I stood in front of my house for the last time.

It wasn't my house anymore. It wasn't the house that I used to eagerly run home to from school, the house Cecilia and I and other kids used to play ghost in the graveyard around, the house that held all my Christmases, Thanksgivings, and birthdays.

This house was an alien place.

The policemen weren't around. I'd spotted them in church with the rest of the adults. I guess they were taking their time getting back.

I let myself in through the back door.

I moved swiftly, quietly. Mom and Dad and Cecilia were all asleep in their beds. The house was silent in the fragile way it is in the early morning, when everyone is just about to wake up. Had Mom and Dad seen me at the church? Had they noticed my bed was empty when they got home?

No time to wonder.

I slipped into my room.

There was my backpack.

Grab it.

Get out before anyone wakes up.

I had everything I needed now. It was impossibly good luck that the policemen were off duty or whatever, that Mom and Dad were still asleep. But that kind of good luck doesn't last.

Get out now.

Wait—the black package Mrs. Lois gave me. The jar of pale oil. It was still behind the toolbox, in the garage.

Mrs. Lois must've given it to me for a reason.

There was still time. A second later I darted down the stairs. I swung around the corner and opened the interior door to the garage. Always creakier than any other door in the house . . .

Slip in.

I went to the toolbox. The black package and jar were still there, where I left them. I unslung my backpack, unzipped it, and stuck the jar inside.

I zipped it back up.

Okay. Go now.

Who makes pacts? We do. A blood pact. I'm not getting up to do a blood pact. Okay, but let's say we have a pact. Fine. A blooooood pact. Christ, you're drunk.

Cecilia.

Damn it.

I couldn't leave Cecilia. I went back into the house. But would Cecilia even listen to me? Would she be too hungover even to understand? There was no time to explain. Grab her, get both of you out. Explain later.

I opened Cecilia's door—

Empty bed.

The sound of the shower turning on in the bathroom.

Damn it damn it damn it Cecilia.

Mom and Dad's bedroom door was opening. They were awake now. It was too late for Cecilia. I just had to get myself out now, get past them and not let them see me. Dad walked past Cecilia's door. I held my breath on the other side. Now he was going downstairs . . .

I opened Cecilia's door and stepped into the hallway.

Movement behind me. Mom was creaking around in her bedroom. I dashed down the hall, tried the bathroom door. Locked. Jesus Cecilia, you don't have to lock it.

Mom was coming.

Get out of here before she sees you. Run downstairs, stay quiet, just get out.

Dad was in the kitchen—wait, no, he was coming my way—

I slipped through the half-open garage door.

I closed it behind me.

Creak.

Footsteps behind the door. Dad's humming grew louder.

No no no, why is he coming to the garage? Look around. Nowhere to hide. Get in the car?

I scrambled around, tried to open the car door—

Nowhere to go, trapped, *damn it*—

Dad passed the door and kept on walking to the laundry room.

I gasped in relief.

Then the automatic garage door jolted to life.

I dropped my backpack. The garage door opened. Sunlight streamed in.

The policemen were back on duty, standing in the driveway. One of them had the garage door opener. They waved hello and smiled.

I was trapped.

THE GIRL WITH THE
NECKLACE AND THE SMILE

When I came back into the house from the garage, shaking, Dad yawned and Mom said good morning as though everything was normal. Neither suspected anything of me. I could tell from their eyes that they didn't know I'd seen them sneak out to the church last night.

But there was something else in their eyes.

I didn't like it.

Cecilia was still in the bathroom, taking the longest shower in the world.

I shut myself in my room and stared at the walls for a while.

Then I heard Dad calling me.

———

As soon as I walked into the living room I knew something was wrong.

Dad closed the door behind me. Mom sat on the couch with a kind of pained smile. Dad remained standing, shifting his weight from foot to foot.

They were both wearing those necklaces.

Mom said, "We have a present for you."

"Here you go," said Dad, and gave me a wooden case.

I opened it. Coiled inside like a metal snake was another one of those necklaces. A twisty silvery locket hung from a complicated chain, inlaid with pale stones.

"What do you think?" said Mom.

I remembered what was supposed to be inside that locket. "Oh. Thanks."

"Why don't you try it on?" said Mom.

"Not right now," I said.

"Just for a second," said Mom.

I said, "Why are you giving this to me?"

There was an uncomfortable pause.

"Well, you know," said Mom, "there *have* been a lot of tornadoes around lately. And your father thinks, and I agree with him, that there are some important choices we have to make."

Dad cleared his throat. "Some folks we hadn't seen in a while, but decent folks, they took us aside and when they were done talking, what they said made a whole lot of sense, especially when you think about what's been going on around here with tornadoes lately."

Why were you at the church last night? How long have you known this would happen?

Who are you?

I said, "You used to make fun of people who wore these necklaces."

"I don't know about that," said Dad. "I don't know if that's exactly true."

"Actually, we've always had your necklace lying around," said Mom quickly. "We shouldn't have ever put it away. That was our fault."

"Your grandmother wore it, actually," said Dad.

Mom said, "Your great-grandmother, too."

I said, "I don't want it."

Dad looked impatient. His hand twitched.

"Oh, but why not?" Mom laughed nervously. "It's pretty. You don't even have to wear it outside your shirt. You can keep it underneath."

"No, thank you."

"Now listen, you're going to wear it," said Dad. "Cecilia wears hers."

"Yes, yes, *Cecilia* wears hers." Mom nodded, as if she had scored some point. "I gave it to her yesterday. She's wearing it right now."

Cecilia came in. She was done with her shower and was dressed for the day. Sure enough, she was also wearing the ugly necklace, although she had clasped it in such a way that it hung differently, more fashionably than I'd seen it on others. This kind of touch was instinctive on Cecilia's part; she almost made the necklace look good.

"Just put it on," whispered Cecilia. "We're in enough trouble."

"No."

I expected Cecilia to be irritated with me but she just looked uneasy. Mom came at me with the necklace, trying to put it around my neck—"Just try it on once!"—but I twisted away, backing toward the door. Mom was left holding the necklace in midair.

The phone rang.

"Wear it for *me*?" said Mom.

I walked out. The phone kept ringing. I had a drained feeling, like they weren't my parents. Like I wasn't myself either. Like we were all reciting lines from a script that had been written for other people, acting in roles that weren't really us.

I came into the den.

I saw someone out the window.

Jessica Hauser was walking down the sidewalk with her parents. She was wearing a white, low-cut, gauzy dress with chiffon trimming. Her mother and father were directly behind her. Jessica's father held her elbow. Her mother's hand was on her shoulder.

They all looked straight ahead.

Our phone kept ringing.

Then it stopped.

I picked up the phone in the den. Mom had already answered it in the kitchen. A man was talking to her.

I listened to them.

Then I put the phone back on the hook. In the other room, Cecilia asked who was it. I watched as Jessica Hauser and her parents walked down the street.

Cecilia had gotten the call.

≡

When Mom told Cecilia that Mr. Z had called for her, Cecilia blanched, her hand flew to her necklace, and her eyes exploded into a kind of cold, obscenely eager glitter; my parents, as if they had been waiting for this, grabbed Cecilia and dragged her upstairs, and my sister snapped out of whatever had come over her and kicked and swore and howled that she didn't want to go, that they couldn't make her, that they were lying and Mr. Z must've called for me, not for her, don't, please don't make her go.

I wanted to run out of the house but I couldn't because the policemen were still at the doors. I ran down to the basement and into the storage room, just trying to find somewhere to hide. I could still hear Cecilia screaming upstairs, and the sound of a slap. That couldn't have been my parents slapping Cecilia. My parents never hit us. But then there was another slap, my mother yelled something, and *thump*—everything went quiet.

I threw open the big Christmas box, scrambled in, and let the cardboard lid flop down on top of me.

Our washing machine had come in this box. Ever since I was little I remembered this box being in the corner of the basement storage room, full of Christmas bric-a-brac: rolls of gleaming wrapping paper, a big plastic plug-in Santa for the porch, fake holly wreaths with fake red berries, shimmering tinsel ropes, tangled heaps of lights, glittering silver and gold ornaments and homely wooden ornaments and gingerbread men sprayed with some kind of creepy fixative that made them last forever—you kind of wanted to eat them, but you couldn't, which was weird because you'd had this vague desire to eat the same inedible gingerbread man every Christmas since you were four years old—and lying loose on the bottom of the carton, a nativity scene that we hadn't put out in years. The figures were broken and some were missing, one and a half wise men, baby Jesus held together by tape, a bunch of chipped farm animals. My parents kept putting it out every year until Cecilia finally said, "you know, in the Bible, Joseph has a head," which shamed my parents into buying a new one, but they kept this old one in storage anyway, because it feels weird to throw away a nativity scene.

When I got in trouble when I was little, I would sometimes hide in this big box. Somehow I'd thought that if I hid here, nobody would find me. It smelled safe. I hadn't hidden in this box for years but for some reason I had gone straight for it—I burrowed under the plastic holly and string lights and didn't move.

For the first time in my life I was afraid of my parents.

At some point, while hiding in the box, exhausted from lack of sleep, I drifted off.

When I woke up the house was quiet.

I was still inside the box, curled painfully under the Christmas decorations. My head felt huge and foggy, my mouth as foul as a dead animal. My back ached.

I peeked out of the lid.

Nobody was in the basement.

I climbed out of the box. I looked out the small windows, high up on the wall. It was light out. I didn't know if I'd slept for just an hour or all the way to the next morning.

I crept upstairs.

The house was empty.

I went into Cecilia's room.

It was wrecked. Her window was broken, clothes and furniture were thrown all over, posters were torn down. Fingernail tracks ripped through the wallpaper. There were streaks of what looked like blood.

I looked outside.

The policemen were still posted at our front door.

They stared right back at me. The message was clear. I wasn't going anywhere.

I went to the bathroom and locked myself in.

An hour later I heard the garage door opening. My parents and Cecilia, back from Mr. Z's. What would I do when Mom and Dad came for me? I felt like I was in the deepest of trouble, even though I'd done nothing wrong. Nothing that deserved this. But maybe it *was* my fault, somehow, my fault Cecilia had been called to Mr. Z's

. . . because I wouldn't wear the necklace? Or was it something else I'd done? Something even I didn't know about?

I couldn't stay locked in this bathroom forever. How long could I last? Maybe a long time . . . really, all the necessities were here. I had a sink, so water's taken care of, and a toilet, okay, and I suppose I could sleep on the floor—although there wasn't any food. I could eat toothpaste, maybe the potpourri Mom kept in the cabinet—could you eat that?

I heard the front door slam shut downstairs. My parents were moving around the house. I heard them go into Cecilia's room. After a while I heard them come out of her room.

I didn't hear much else. At no point did they call out, "I'm home!" like they usually did. But they didn't seem to be actively looking for me either. I stayed locked in the little bathroom, wondering what they would do next.

They didn't do anything.

The sounds from downstairs were the normal daytime sounds of our house: in the kitchen the microwave hummed for a while, then stopped with the usual *beep-beep-beep*; the refrigerator clicked open and thumped shut; the screen door to the patio scraped open; the lawnmower fired up. Mom turned on the television and watched the news. Dad finished mowing the lawn. I heard him clunking around in the garage.

I unlocked the bathroom door.

I stepped out into the hallway.

The house was wrong. The hallways had been shortened, the color of the carpet tweaked. The ceilings were lowered. Floors and walls tilted slightly. Or maybe our house had always been like this. Maybe I was just realizing for the first time that our house was wrong.

I moved down the hall to Cecilia's room.

I opened the door.

Her room was dark. It had been straightened up. The blinds were pulled down.

I saw a lump on the bed. The sheet was pulled up over it.

The wind blew outside, making the blinds rattle.

A soft noise came from the bed.

I moved closer.

The lump under the covers didn't move. The wind blew harder. The lowered blinds knocked back and forth. Papers in Cecilia's room fluttered around.

I pulled the sheet away.

Cecilia was naked except for the ugly necklace. Her face was frozen in a vicious little smile and her eyes were wide open and blank and her face stayed stuck in her horrible grin, as if she was enjoying some repulsive secret pleasure.

THE MONSTER IN
THE HOUSE

I ran out of Cecilia's room.

I dashed out the front door, pushing past the startled policemen. They shouted after me as I ran away from my house. Mom and Dad were yelling somewhere behind me too, but I didn't stop, I didn't look back.

I darted around to our backyard. The policemen were chasing me now. I cut across the next yard, then the yard after that, and then I was out of the neighborhood, into an empty field, wind blasting in my eyes, sirens shrieking up out of nowhere—

Tornado sirens—

The world tilted, rushed to meet my face.

My chin slammed into the mud. Tackled. One of the policemen was on top of me, flipping me over, shaking my shoulders, yelling, I couldn't hear anything, I only saw his frantic face—then sound surged back into the world, keening sirens and a turbulent roar, and I saw the policeman's partner running to catch up, waving his arms—a colossal churning darkness swooped down behind him—

A tornado.

The tornado engulfed the running policeman and he vanished, sucked up into the furious clouds. The policeman on top of me tried to shield me but then the tornado was upon us and he was ripped away, slurped up into the sky—the tornado blasted through my body, sucked the air out of my lungs, popped my ears, I was swirled up, throttled, smacked down and then the tornado was gone, leaving whirling wind and garbage and mud in its wake, hurtling away across the sky with a piercing shriek and a bottomless howl.

I couldn't breathe, couldn't see. I lay flat in the mud, my body crushed, my eyes mashed into the dirt.

The world spun under me. I waited for another tornado to finish me off.

Mist settled.

I opened my eyes. I spit dirt. I looked around.

Everything was mud, churned almost to a froth.

Both policemen were gone. I was alone on my back on the scoured prairie, watching the sky boil with impossible colors.

The tornadoes were back.

Tornadoes had crossed the white strings.

Tornadoes were *in town*.

I wobbled to my feet. Looking down what used to be my street, I saw tornadoes roaring through downtown, wrecking it, eating it, sucking it up into the sky, the sky flashing green and black, vomiting paper garbage all around, hamburger wrappers and shredded newspapers fluttering, romping up and down, tossing cars and dumpsters and school buses, whipping and wiggling as though putting on a show, pirouetting like mammoth demented ballerinas—

Then reversing.

Veering around.

Coming back my way.

Run—

I didn't know where to run. My house was gone. My street was gone. All of my neighborhood had just been blown away, gobbled up into the hungry sky. Pieces of houses from my street were shredded up and strewn about. I saw my own last name, in reverse, my own mailbox upside down, jammed into the mud, its ripped post sticking up into the air, quivering.

My house wasn't here anymore.

The tornadoes had erased my home.

I didn't see Mom or Dad or Cecilia. Had the tornadoes erased them too? Maybe not. I was still here—

Where was here? *Here* was gone.

The tornadoes were barreling back toward me.

I ran, I fell and got up, I kept running. I didn't know where to run but if I didn't stop running I'd be dead. Mom and Dad and Cecilia had been in our house. But our house was gone now.

My family was gone.

I kept running.

On its hill, in the distance, Archie's old house sat untouched.

Tornadoes howled behind me. Electricity zigzagged up my back.

Keep running. Maybe could I make it to Archie's house.

Tornadoes whipped around my ankles and neck, pulling me backward. My world was gone, or made bizarre—I passed a single metal fence post speared clean through a tree trunk, a chimney with no house, a soccer goal wrenched out of the ground and twisted into a corkscrew. Everything was collapsing around me, bursting apart, but if I could just make it to Archie's—

A refrigerator zoomed overhead.

I stumbled, staring up in shock. A tree lifted right out of the ground, roots and all, and blasted off into the sky like a rocket. I turned around, out of breath, just as a house disintegrated in front of me, fluttering away like someone blowing a dandelion. I didn't know where I was going. It didn't matter. I stumbled and spun and saw a man trying to run, but a tornado picked him up, whirled him around, faster and faster, spun him so fast he was ripped apart by the centrifugal force, his torn-off arms and legs and head splitting apart and flying north, south, east, west—

I staggered back.

A bathtub crashed down inches in front of me, burying itself into the mud.

Screams. I turned.

It was a girl screaming. I ran through a flurry of flying garbage and there was the Hausers' house—

And another house that had fallen from the sky, smashing right on top of the Hausers'.

I saw Jessica Hauser, just barely hidden under debris. Jessica had been trying to crawl out of her bedroom window but the window frame had collapsed on her. Now she was squeezed tight, pinched under the wreckage. The crashed house weighing down the top of her house shifted, collapsing a little more. Jessica was still in the wedding dress from when her parents had taken her to Mr. Z's. She stared up at me, her face smeared with blood, as though begging for something.

I grabbed her arms and pulled.

Jessica squealed and gasped. She couldn't speak. I couldn't quite move her from this position. But maybe if I tried another angle . . . I got under her, hooked her shoulders under my arms, pulled—

Crashing noise. The house on top caved further into the Hausers' house. Jessica cried out as I scrambled away—

The Hausers' house collapsed onto her.

Jessica was gone.

Don't look.

I ran. I kept running. Don't look back again, don't stop now, don't try to help anyone, just try to save yourself—

Everything was shaken up and swirling. I stumbled down the street. Everywhere trees were uprooted, splintered, stripped of their branches. One tree had been torn out of the earth, flipped upside down, and plunged straight back down into the ground, its roots flopping around twenty feet in the air like unruly hair.

More tornadoes were looming, closing in. I kept seeing Jessica's face, right before it was crushed. I tried not to see it.

I kept running.

Then I spotted Cuthbert Monks running down the street.

He saw me too. Began shouting at me.

I bolted in the opposite direction. I cut between houses. He yelled at me to stop.

Maybe Cuthbert Monks was offering me shelter.

He could keep it.

I knew where I was going.

I spotted a bike jammed through the branches of a fallen tree. I grabbed it, yanked it out, branches and spokes breaking. I jumped on it and I mashed the pedals down, again and again. Cuthbert came at me but I blew past him, swerving away before he could grab the bike. He shouted after me.

I raced out of his neighborhood. I plunged into the woods, up the snaky road to Archie's house.

I skidded into Archie's front yard. The storm was behind me, taking the world apart. I flung the bike away. I was drenched, scratched up, muddy, my chin bleeding. I stumbled onto the porch. I didn't know how I'd get inside, nobody lived at Archie's anymore, the door had to be locked, but the door unexpectedly swung open and I staggered into the foyer.

Cuthbert Monks was shouting outside behind me. He was running up Archie's driveway.

I turned and slammed the door.

Locked it. Bolted it.

Cuthbert rattled the doorknob. Pounded on the door.

Yelling at me to open up.

It didn't sound like he wanted to come in. It sounded like he was *warning* me.

I ran deeper inside Archie's house.

Three things surprised me about Archie's house.

The first was that everything was still there. The furniture hadn't been moved. The pictures were still on the walls. The piano was still in the living room. You'd think when Archie's family moved out they would take their stuff with them. But they hadn't taken a thing.

The second was the silence. Even with the tornadoes pulverizing everything outside, shrieking across the prairie, ripping up neighborhoods, shredding through the trees, it was quiet inside Archie's. As if it was in a different world.

The third was the half-conscious boy covered in blood, sprawled halfway up the main staircase.

The tornado killer.

He was alive.

I didn't know first aid. I didn't know anything about how to help an injured person. I rushed up the stairs, knelt down, talked to him, touched him, shouted at him.

He was out of it. He was dying right in front of me.

How long had he been there?

What was he *doing* here?

I dragged the tornado killer up the stairs, smearing a trail of blood. I heaved him into Archie's parents' bed and rushed to the bathroom.

The tornado killer gasped, bleeding all over the bed. He was babbling, delirious. He didn't even see me. I grabbed bandages, disinfectant, and towels from the bathroom.

I cut open the tornado killer's clothes with scissors and ripped them away. He was in bad shape. Worse than I'd thought. Scraped, cut, bleeding all over. There was a chunk taken out of his side and a long deep gash up his leg. I had seen the tornado killer's body, I knew this body. It wasn't the same body.

This was a wreck of scrambled meat.

I tried to clean him up, scooping out the dirt from the largest cuts. He twitched and moaned, kicked, tried to get away. I held him down, pressed a wet cloth to the wounds to stop the bleeding.

He calmed down. Breathed more steadily. I didn't know how to disinfect him the right way, I didn't know how to stitch him together, but I tried to help him, I stayed with him, I watched him, I held him.

He opened his eyes. He stared at me in bewildered pain.

"Who are you?" he rasped.

He could barely speak. His mouth was cut up, his tongue mangled. His eyes tracked me fearfully, as if at any moment I might murder him. I wanted to help him but I couldn't understand the way he looked at me, so confused and scared. Meanwhile the tornadoes spun, wrecked, and devoured everything outside. Rain kept lashing the windows. There was no getting out. When I changed his bandage he flinched as if stung, looking at me with baffled fear.

Maybe shock.

"Don't you remember me? You saw me at Archie's party?" I said. "The party here, at this house? You were watching me?"

The tornado killer shook his head.

"And then I came to your house with those other kids, and there was a storm, and you saved us from the tornadoes . . . In the van? In the clouds, you and me, we . . ."

He winced. Blank.

He didn't know me.

But I wouldn't let him die.

He was mostly unconscious at this point but he flinched every time I touched him, as if I was hurting him. I tried to feed him old canned soup I found in the kitchen. But even if I managed to get the food in his mouth, most of it trickled down his chin.

He peed the bed. Crap dribbled out of him. I had to clean up after him. I had to change the fouled sheets. The tornado killer had seemed magical to me before. He was no mystery now.

His body was just an object. A leaky slab of flesh.

And he didn't know me.

Maybe I wasn't the only girl the tornado killer had taken into the clouds. Maybe I was one of many girls.

The tornadoes raged.

They wanted in. I wanted out.

Nobody was going anywhere.

I took care of him for three days.

When the tornado killer was asleep, when I had a break, I walked around Archie's house.

It was strange to be back in this familiar place. I had thought I'd never be in here again. Now I had all the time I wanted to explore it, although it felt like there were parts of Archie's house that would always elude me. The place went on and on, a convoluted hive of dark wood paneling, dusty portraits of great-aunts and great-uncles, and creepy, twisting hallways—I remembered what we used to do in here, the sleepovers, the parties, the fireworks, but there was still so much I didn't know about Archie's house, it was vast and beautiful but there was something wrong with it, like it was infected with some disease, some architectural cancer that made the house curl in on itself, mangling the rooms and spawning senseless hallways out of control, whole floors of nothing but hidden passages and closets, turning inside out and having a fever all around me, growing inward on itself in unhealthy ways, sudden staircases going nowhere, triangular and trapezoidal rooms with sharp corners, sloping ceilings, a rust-clogged dumbwaiter stuck in its shaft, yellowed curtains as frail as tissue paper, thick with dust—but then the cramped labyrinth would suddenly open up into a huge space, a cavernous dining room, a garage big enough for a dozen cars, a grand echoing chapel. I loved Archie's house, I loved how creepy it was, its secrets, a little garden of mushrooms in the cellar, rooms with peepholes into other rooms, one-way mirrors, secret passages, and on the third day I even happened upon that jeweled curvy knife, the knife I'd seen with the Horrible Woman in that blazing room in a dark hallway on New Year's Eve, when she and Archie's mom were staring at Cecilia and me like they were expecting we'd come, the same jeweled curvy knife I'd dreamed about at Lisa's house—I found that exact same knife on the mantel, sitting innocently above a fireplace.

I looked at the knife warily. As though a piece of my dream had come loose and accidentally fallen into the real world.

I took it.

It felt correct in my hand.

———

The electricity was out. There was only darkness and the never-ending storm.

On my first day in Archie's house, I found candles in the basement and made a fire in the fireplace and kept it going. I found more food in the pantry. Canned stuff, rice, beans. I cooked them over the fire. Mom flashed into my mind, cooking canned ravioli for me. The grossest food, but when I was five I loved it.

Where was Mom?

Over the next few days, I tried to spoon the soup into the tornado killer's mouth. He wouldn't eat. I also found a flashlight and some books and I would I read aloud to him in the darkness. No response from the tornado killer. I thought of how Dad used to read to Cecilia and me, at bedtime. But Dad and Cecilia were probably dead now. Dad liked to say that at bedtime I always demanded a story, even though he wasn't good at telling stories, but that I'd cry if I didn't get one, and when I started crying I wouldn't stop—

There were tears on my face. Wait, was I crying? Yes, I was crying and I hadn't even realized it.

"Stop touching me."

I wiped my eyes, startled. "What?"

The tornado killer said, "Don't touch me."

"I'm trying to help you . . ."

"Get away," he slurred. "Get out."

I stared at him, uncomprehending. It was my third night taking care of him. But this was the second time he'd said anything to me other than "Who are you?"

Well. Who was I?

I sat in the dark and didn't know why I was doing any of this.

All the lights in the house suddenly switched on.

The electricity was back, unaccountably. The room was jarringly bright. The tornado killer had just been a shape in the dimness before but now I saw too clearly his bashed-in face, his crushed eye, his torn mouth.

All the appliances clamored to life too. In other rooms radios were blaring at full blast, televisions gabbling, dozens of things beeping and whirring. I backed away from the tornado killer. He was staring at me in an almost threatening way.

I left him there and went from room to room, turning things off to stop the din.

Until, abruptly, everything went dark again.

What was happening? I reached out blindly through the unlit hallways. I was lost for a couple of minutes, making wrong turns in the pitch-black maze of the house. But somehow I found my way back to the tornado killer's room.

I paused outside his door, nervous. Something felt different.

I didn't trust him. I was scared.

I went in.

The room was dark again. The tornado killer wasn't moving. I saw his eyes, shining now, green and blue, glowing horribly in the dark.

Staring at the ceiling.

He slowly turned to me—

I was caught in his blue and green eyes and I had that rushing feeling, the feeling of the tornado killer drawing me in, I was swirling deeper and closer, sucked in, I felt lightheaded, weightless, I was going *into his eyes*—

I broke away.

I left the room and didn't look back. Behind me I heard an unexpectedly vicious sound—the tornado killer making a rattling lizardy hiss—

I slammed the door behind me.

I dragged a bookcase from across the hallway and blocked the door. He was a monster. I went back down the hallway, found a couch around the corner and pushed it down the hall until it was blocking the door too. I had to protect myself. I wedged the couch between the bookcase and the wall.

I was panting now, sweating. He was penned in. I was safe from him.

His eyes were two horrible holes.

They were invitations.

———

I had to get out.

But this was what you wanted, isn't it? To be with the tornado killer? Now you had it. Isn't it what you always dreamed?

I had to get out.

More days went by. The tornadoes wouldn't stop. And during those days it felt like there was someone else in the house with me, someone who wasn't the tornado killer. I heard a scuffling behind the walls, like there were squirrels or rats who had fled from the tornadoes and were living in the house too—a rustling in the attic, maybe bats? I heard a clunk or shuffle far away on the other side of the house but when I went to investigate, there was nobody.

I was going crazy.

I had been cooped up in Archie's house for a week now. I estimated how much longer I could live on the dwindling canned food his family left behind. Maybe another week. Two weeks if I was careful. I wasn't feeding the tornado killer anymore but he didn't seem to need it. I would stand outside his door and listen to him moving around. Still alive. But not calling for help. He didn't need me. He didn't even know who I was.

I kept thinking of his eyes. Two glowing invitations.

Get out.

I kept the curvy jeweled knife close to me. I felt better when I had it near me. Not because it made me feel safe. The opposite. It was a sharp, merciless thing. But when I gripped the handle I felt like my body was complete.

I grazed its tip along my skin. It left behind a strange feeling.

I wanted to use it.

———

After the tenth day, the tornadoes stopped.

All at once they gathered up their whirling vapors like skirts and ascended, floating silently up into the clouds. They seemed to sulk, crowding out the sun, hovering over the world, just out of reach but still massive enough to sink down and crush everything.

A little sunlight broke through.

The rain dwindled.

I stood on the roof of Archie's house, watching through binoculars.

For the first time since the tornadoes broke through the strings I got a good look at town. I saw people crowded around the church. Some trailers and hastily built wooden structures and tents had sprung up around it, like a kind of emergency camp. Maybe Mom, Dad, and Cecilia were alive. Maybe they were there. It was still possible. I could hope for it.

But from this distance I couldn't see them.

I swept the binoculars and saw concrete walls ripped in half, twisted rebar sprouting out in crazy angles, a flipped-over truck with windows blasted free of glass, piles of brick and wooden boards and crippled furniture, a surprised-looking traffic light lying in the street, a filthy playpen, a steel filing cabinet, a metal highway sign wrapped around a utility pole, dirty shoes and clothes, a mangled swing set, half a couch . . .

And my house.

At first I didn't recognize it. The geometry of it was impossible. But it was my house. And then my perspective shifted and it made sense.

My house was just on the opposite side of town from where it belonged.

And it was upside down.

I stared at my upside-down house. Yes, it had been picked up and thrown across town. But somehow it was unharmed. Not even a broken window. Just upside down, lying on a slight angle.

I also spotted our car in a nearby soccer field. Seemingly intact.

I looked back and forth from my house to the car. Back to the church. Back to the house.

A plan was coming together in my mind.

At first I felt it was too risky.

But I had to do it.

I had to leave Archie's house. I had to leave the tornado killer. I was going to ditch him, and then run across town to my old house—because I knew Dad always kept extra car keys in the top drawer of his desk, and that was the plan—but were Dad or Mom or Cecilia dead? I couldn't bear to think of it, I pushed the thought away, I just concentrated on my plan—yes, if the desk was still there, I'd get the car keys, grab my backpack from the garage, take whatever else I could scavenge, run to the soccer field where the car was, and if the car still worked I'd drive out of town.

Just leave.

When should I do it?

Now.

Go ahead. Leave now.

The tornadoes had stopped. I didn't even know why. They could start again any minute.

Right now was probably my only chance.

The sun was setting. Perfect. Better to pull this thing off at night, when nobody could see me.

I waited for night to arrive. I didn't want to leave Archie's house messy, so I made my bed, swept the floors, washed the dishes, put everything back where it belonged. I intended to do this properly. I got my stuff together.

I hesitated over the curvy knife. Was it mine to take?

Yes.

On my way out, I stopped at the barricade I had put up outside the tornado killer's room. The couch and bookcase were still wedged against the door, blocking him in.

I was too frightened to check if he was alive or dead.

It didn't matter. I had to leave him. I had to *go*.

But what if he was still alive? Even if he didn't recognize me, it didn't mean he deserved to die in Archie's house, with no hope of escape.

I pushed the couch out of the way. I shoved the bookcase aside.

I hesitated before I opened the door.

Anything could be behind that door. Maybe he'd transformed into something totally different. An even deeper kind of monster.

I opened the door. I peeked inside, my heart beating fast. The room was dark but I saw his green and blue eyes steadily burning in the gloom. He was still lying on the bed where I left him.

I shined my flashlight on him.

He had changed.

His body looked perfectly normal now.

It was as though he had never been hurt.

I stared at him. This didn't make sense. I remembered what he'd been like when I left him. Half dead. A mangled thing.

Now he looked perfect.

How could that be?

What was he? What was he *really*?

I saw him breathing. Chest rising, falling.

His glowing eyes were staring blindly at the ceiling.

Invitations—

No. Just go.

He murmured something I couldn't quite hear.

Don't listen.

His clothes were on the ground where I'd left them after I cut them to pieces to stop the bleeding. I picked up his ripped-up shorts.

Something fell out of his pocket.

I saw it on the carpet. A gray limp thing that used to be a flower. The flower I had thrown to him, so long ago.

His green and blue eyes stared at the ceiling.

I came closer.

No. No. This was my last chance to leave. Go now.

His eyes glowed in the dark.

"Who are you?" I said.

His lips moved. What was he saying? He wanted to—

Don't listen. Don't look. Just go.

Something moved on the other side of his eyes.

No. Don't. No—

I looked into his eyes.

Something dizzying swept through me, and I exited my body.

THE SECRET WATCHERS

I was in a pickup truck with Mr. Z.

It was a hot afternoon and we were rattling down some bumpy dirt road outside of town, going too fast, the windows open and the air rushing in and Mr. Z was yelling, "Goddamnit, stop crying, boy, all you ever do is cry" and my face was wet, my heart pounding, but this was not my face, this was not my heart, and I was scared because I knew where Mr. Z was taking me.

My first tornado swirled up ahead.

Mr. Z braked and shoved me out the truck. I hit the dirt as the tornado churned up the road, coming at me fast, then Mr. Z slammed the door and threw the pickup in reverse, spun around and drove away.

I was alone on the prairie, six years old.

I was the tornado killer.

The tornado hurtled toward me.

I watched it through the tornado killer's eyes. I felt his panic.

I didn't know what to do. "Nobody does, either you're a natural or you're a dud," Mr. Z had said back at home, before he forced me into the pickup. I'd kicked and fought, because I knew what he was doing, where we were going, but I didn't want to, I was scared, I couldn't do it and he snickered, "You *should* be scared, son, you wouldn't be the first tornado killer who couldn't cut the mustard" and I didn't like the way he said that, I asked what would happen to me if I couldn't kill the tornado and he said "Take a wild guess" and I said "What?" and he stared at me with his dark glasses and asked me, did I ever wonder about all those bits of tornado killers inside those little necklaces?

"I've seen it happen." Mr. Z chuckled. "Takes about, oh, five seconds for a tornado to rip your ass apart. Then folks in town'll come scurrying out, they'll gather up your bits, a toe here, tongue there, a pancreas, bits of spine, and stick 'em in their little necklaces. You think we're the only ones? There used to be so many tornado killers, so many brothers . . . Anyhoo, enough chin music, let's see what you're made of."

The tornado weaved across the prairie, tremendous and beautiful, a whirling black tower. But then it saw me and switched direction. It came rocketing straight at me, faster than I thought possible. I felt how angry it was.

How hungry, how desperate.

How lonely.

I put out my hands. At once the atmosphere thinned around me, the air pressure, the humidity, the heat—I felt them all. I moved my hands and I felt how they changed, how air currents reversed. I knew how to do this, but *how* did I know? I just did. I squeezed the air, I stretched it, I swirled and counterswirled, I nudged the tornado, it jittered, I shoved it and the tornado staggered sideways, startled. I touched the tornado's brain—it had a brain?—yes it did, and it abruptly unspooled under my touch, I didn't expect that, the tornado didn't expect it either, it panicked, I panicked, I sliced my hand through the air and the tornado twisted into itself, imploding, crumpling, terrified—the tornado begged me, cried don't, don't, please—

I killed the tornado.

When I finished, Mr. Z wasn't waiting for me. He didn't come back in the truck to pick me up. I walked what felt like miles back to my house, alone.

I didn't get home until late that night.

I lay in bed and thought about the tornado's scream, and how I had made it stop.

<hr />

I tore myself out of the tornado killer's eyes.

We were back in Archie's parents' room and I was out of breath, my heart squirming and spasming. It was storming now—wasn't it calm before? How long had I been out of it? And the tornado killer was intensely awake, awake with *me*, looking like he wanted something from inside me. I felt the push and pull between us, a teetering, and with a collapsing pleasure I let the balance tip, I let my brain open up, I felt him rush in and vanish into me as he was caught up in some memory of my own from long ago—but wait, why *this*, of all memories why was my brain showing him *this*—

<hr />

In fifth grade Cecilia got the part of Mrs. Cratchit in Mrs. Papadakis's combined fourth/fifth grade production of *A Christmas Carol*. I squeaked in as Martha Cratchit, the daughter. Neither role was very big but I was thrilled by my five or so lines. Mrs. Papadakis assigned roles by drawing names out of a hat. Her reason was so everyone got a fair chance, so that the same usual "best" kids didn't get to be the stars of every production (but of course the part of Scrooge went to Archie, not some dodo like Jimmy Switz) and anyway that randomness was how Seth Dingle, who'd always been small for his age, was cast as Bob Cratchit, but

Ron Wofford, already a mammoth kid, was somehow cast as Tiny Tim. When your Tiny Tim is twice as big as your Bob Cratchit, it's comedy gold, as Cecilia would say, people will laugh, and now I remembered that performance, the part when I was offstage with little Seth and big Ron right before our big scene, peeking out into the dark auditorium, the blinding lights. I was so ready, I was giddy, I almost felt like I was famous, but Ron had stage fright. He wouldn't go on. Ron was crying.

The tornado killer was with me. Inside my memory. Watching, fascinated, through my eyes.

I hadn't thought of this in years.

"It's just stupid, I don't even want to do it," said Ron, and Seth (who was half his size) was impatiently like "We've done this a million times" and Ron wept, saying "This is different, everyone's here" and Seth said "Come *on*, you baby" and Ron said "I'm not a baby, there's just so many people" and Seth said "Yeah, like, my whole family's here too, so just do it" and of course Ron and Seth acted like I wasn't even there, because boys and girls kept to their own separate worlds, even though I actually liked Ron Wofford, because he ran a Dungeons and Dragons campaign during indoor recess that winter, and even though no girl ever joined them, I always sat nearby, kind of jealous, listening, I liked to hear Ron say stuff like "okay, you're in a vaulted stone chamber" or "the kobold takes four damage" or "clutched in his bony fingers is a bejeweled key," but now Ron Wofford was crying offstage, in danger of holding up the scene, and I wanted to help him, and so even though what I was about to do was totally taboo, I took his hand in the dark.

I felt Ron flinch.

The tornado killer felt it with me.

The tornado killer wanted to see this.

He wanted to see more.

Ron didn't look at me. But he didn't take his big hand away. I heard Cecilia's cue for me to enter ("What has ever got your precious father then?") and I squeezed Ron's hand and let it go, and I went out as Martha.

MRS. CRATCHIT: What has ever got your precious father then? And your brother, Tiny Tim? And Martha wasn't this late last Christmas Day by half an hour!

(MARTHA enters.)

MARTHA: I am here now, Mother!

(The younger children cheer, surrounding her.)

MRS. CRATCHIT: My dear Martha, how late you are!

MARTHA: We'd a deal of work to finish up last night, and had to clear away this morning, mother!

MRS. CRATCHIT: Well, you are home now! Sit down before the fire, dear.

BELINDA: There's father coming. Hide, Martha, hide!

(MARTHA ducks under the table. CRATCHIT enters, carrying TINY TIM with a crutch. The family happily greets them.)

Mrs. Papadakis made us follow the script as written, which meant Bob Cratchit had to enter the scene actually *carrying* Tiny Tim on his back—that is, gigantic Ron would be getting a piggyback ride from little Seth, even though it looked absurd. Nevertheless, Ron and Seth had actually managed this feat in rehearsal, a freakishly huge Tiny Tim piggybacking on a teeny-tiny Cratchit—but now this was the actual performance, and both of them lurched onstage, off-balance, Ron riding Seth and waving his crutch wildly, almost whacking Cecilia in the head, she ducked just in time as Seth staggered under Ron's weight—the crowd roared, this was great, they loved it!—but then they both collapsed, Ron tumbling off Seth's back, to huge laughs but gasps too, and I was still under the table hiding as Martha when Ron crashed down. Ron just stayed there, face on the floor, he wouldn't get up, he was humiliated. He was only a few feet from me. Everyone was laughing. I didn't know what to do, so I whispered, "The kobold takes four damage" and Ron looked up, he gave me the strangest look.

I felt the tornado killer smiling in me.

CRATCHIT: Why, where's our Martha?

MRS. CRATCHIT: I'm afraid she won't be coming for Christmas.

CRATCHIT: Not coming? Not coming upon Christmas Day?

MARTHA *(coming from under table)*: Here I am!

(Martha and Cratchit embrace. The family cheers.)

Did I actually care about Ron Wofford, then? I kind of did. Seeing Ron in this memory, from when I was in fourth grade and he was in fifth, and seeing Cecilia, Seth, Archie, and the rest of us— it was like watching us all in some nicer parallel universe, because of course now it's six years later and these days Ron Wofford's burnout hair is gross and straggly and he smells like leftover french fries and he listens to music that sounds like pigs getting thrown off of buildings, but back then we were all fresh and happy and silly, and now that I'm thinking about it, why was this was the only play I ever acted in, because I had loved acting, when I popped out from under the table and declared "Here I am!" the tablecloth half came off with me, as if anything more could go wrong with this play, the plastic plates and utensils tumbled to the ground, but I hadn't cared because it drew attention away from Ron and Seth, and I actually got applause—anyway, why had I stopped being in plays, how did I get so shy, what happened?

The tornado killer drank my memory.

Seeing me. Knowing me.

Wanting more.

> MRS. CRATCHIT: And how did little Tim behave in church?
> CRATCHIT: As good as gold, and better. Somehow he gets
> thoughtful sitting by himself so much, and thinks the strangest
> things you ever heard. He told me . . .

After the performance all the families went out for ice cream, and in fourth grade it was thrilling for our entire class to be out together at night, eating ice cream with our families, running around the ice cream parlor with each other and freaking out from the sugar and the special-occasion feeling of it. It was snowing outside and Mom and Dad were proud of me and Cecilia was laughing with me about our scene and I felt happy to be there with my family, with my friends, and Ron Wofford was there, he studiously ignored me and I totally ignored him, but the next indoor recess I saw that Ron had put out an extra chair, and I played Dungeons and Dragons with his group the rest of that winter and nobody objected.

———

I broke away from the tornado killer.

I was so close to him, lying next to him, almost but not quite touching, in Archie's dark strange house.

The tornado killer lay back, exhausted, his eyes closed.

He didn't say anything.

I was wide-awake, wide-eyed, exhilarated. The tornado killer had been in my head. He had lived my memories. He had been me. I had lived his memories too, I had *been* him too . . . and when the tornado killer turned back to me, when he looked at me again, I felt it all starting over, I was falling into his eyes, I thought I wasn't ready but then I was, I wanted to do it, even if the tornado killer saw something embarrassing about me—I didn't care, I wanted to show him everything, especially the embarrassing stuff, I wanted to let him inside.

Did I even want to escape this house, anymore?

"What are you?" I said.

Outside the sky darkened. The wind blew harder, raindrops pelted the windows, and then the tornadoes were lowering themselves out of the clouds again. Now we were truly trapped in Archie's house together, in the tornado killer's bed, but I wanted to be trapped, I wanted to be in his eyes again, his curious eyes deep in mine, searching for something in me, and I let him have even more, I went ahead and gave up everything I had in a luxurious freeing rush.

It is something to be truly and totally seen.

I got on my bike and swung out onto the road.

The sun poured down hard and happy. It was summer of last year. I was alone, headphones on, Electrifier pulsing in my ears, nightlike and hypnotic, strange to hear in the bright morning. Cecilia was supposed to come swimming that day but she'd ditched me. Far away there was black buildup of storm clouds but right now it was too hot, the air clammy and boiling. I glided down the street.

But this time the memory was different.

I felt the tornado killer invisibly riding with me.

I whirled the pedals, flying out of town.

I had forgotten about this day, too.

I liked being alone but I didn't want to be alone today. Cecilia and I had planned to ride out to the quarry pool together but at the last minute she bailed to hang out with Archie. I felt free but lonely, but not as lonely now, because the tornado killer was living it with me, I was sharing it with him, look at this, this is my life, I'll show you what I have, you can look at all of it, we were coasting down the last hill together, into the forest together, listening to Electrifier together.

I passed Archie's house on the way. It was still morning but it was already hot and hazy and Archie's house was half hidden behind trees and only revealed itself in pieces as I biked toward it, shambling out of the woods like a grand shaggy beast made of bricks, windows, drainpipes, and shingles, shaking off the leaves and pushing aside the branches.

I shot past.

Nobody was at the quarry pool when I got there. Good. I was sweaty and ready to swim. I took my headphones off. Now there was no sound but the static of cicadas.

I felt the tornado killer move inside my mind.

Listening. Watching.

I leaned my bike onto a tree and came to the edge of the pool. There was a ten-foot drop. It was so hot. Everyone's parents warned us about swimming at the quarry, they forbade us to go anywhere near it because there were jagged underwater ledges and old machinery at the bottom and the sides were too slippery.

We swam there anyway.

I stood there for a while in my memory, the empty blue sky here but the storm gathering far away with its distant rumbling thunder. I listened to the buzz of insects, I smelled the trees and weeds and dirt, I let the warm morning air linger around me. Nobody else was here so it was okay to take off my clothes. A couple dragonflies were buzzing around. I felt free. I'd never swam here on my own before. A squirrel poised on the branch of a plum tree, considering a nut in its paws, turning it over and over like he was reading it. The tornado killer was silent inside me. Some birds fluttered and swirled in the sky.

Then I hopped off the ledge, I hung in the air, the world blurred past and suddenly I was underwater, fresh and cold and roaring, I splashed back up into the sunshine and then I saw the tornado killer.

He was swimming in the quarry with me.

Not inside my mind anymore.

He was somehow *right there*, treading water, looking at me.

This wasn't part of my memory—

But it was happening now. The tornado killer was swimming closer, he was laughing and I said "How are you doing this?" but he didn't answer, the storm clouds rolled overhead and rain pelted down around us, he came closer with his green eye and blue eye so real that I felt my memory changing, like my real past was changing, like this was how the day had actually happened, we really had skinny-dipped together that day, the tornado killer was coming toward me in the rain and the clouds rolled over and it got darker and my feet touched the sand below and my back pressed against the rough rock and then he was close, his skin on my skin, our mouths met and it didn't matter that this had never happened in real life, this was happening now.

The storm boomed outside Archie's house. The tornado killer closed his eyes again. His chest shuddered. He winced from trying to move. He was still so delicate, so hurt. But I wanted to push back into his mind, and I wanted him back in mine, I wanted to force it even, because my heart was freaking out, I saw the delicate vein on his neck beating so fast too, his heart going as fast as mine, faster than I thought human hearts could go.

There was something I wanted to find in him.

I felt myself getting closer to it.

He could feel it too.

I woke up in the tornado killer's little house.

I was the tornado killer again. I rolled off my mattress and pulled on some shorts and a T-shirt I'd left on the floor the night before. Mr. Z's horn was honking outside. I grabbed a cold slice of leftover pizza from the refrigerator and ran outside.

I liked being in a boy body. I liked the tornado killer's lankiness, his lean sides, the easy energy in his legs and arms, perfect.

Tornado killer memories flickered through me. I killed tornadoes all the time now, I learned as I went, I learned on the fly, I had to learn or I'd get hurt. I got used to being hurt. I tested myself. I pushed myself. I walked straight into tornadoes, I let them swallow me whole so I could kill them from the inside out. Inside a tornado, I'd feel its power whirling all around me, power that could shred me if I made one wrong move, but I kept steady, I slowly and carefully throttled the tornado, I choked the tornado down until it was nothing, until I was standing on an empty field on a clear sunny day, as if there hadn't been a tornado at all—and then I'd hear a slow, sarcastic clap from where Mr. Z was sitting in his lawn chair.

"Whoop-de-doo," he shouted. "Nobody cares if you do it fancy."

Mr. Z came over to my house every morning. I'd hear his pickup roll to a stop outside. He never got out of the pickup, he just sat there and honked. But I knew if I didn't get out there quick, there'd be hell to pay. Ever since I was little I trained with Mr. Z, riding around in his rotten-smelling pickup outside town, hunting down tornadoes and killing them—Mr. Z treated me like dirt but he did know what he was talking about, the man knew how to kill a tornado.

Mr. Z came early every morning. I woke up earlier. Up until I was ten years old Mr. Z actually lived with me—on a day like this, he would've woken up before me, he'd already have all my clothes laid out, my breakfast already made. Those days, I'd put on my clothes and eat and talk to Mr. Z. And when I was little, he actually wasn't so mean. Mr. Z had been tender with me.

At night I'd sit and watch TV with Mr. Z. When I was a very small there were more people who took care of me, there were even children I played with, but as I grew older it seemed that part of my life was over. I didn't even remember those people anymore. Now it was just me and Mr. Z and the TV. It was lonely but I sensed my isolation was why I was improving every day, why I felt the back of my mind invisibly complicating, why my body was getting stronger, why every night I would lie staring at the ceiling in a blissful haze, cataloguing with pleasure all the new knowledge pouring into my brain, the new things my body could do.

When I was about nine years old, playing checkers one night with Mr. Z, I said, "Why can't I ever go into town?"

Mr. Z said, "That's the way it works for tornado killers. It's not allowed."

"But you go into town," I said.

Mr. Z gazed at the TV.

"Don't you want to do something other than kill tornadoes?" I said. "Why do you want to be cooped up in the middle of nowhere with me?"

Mr. Z looked up at me sharply. "Are you bored?"

"It's just that you're the only person I know. I don't even know my parents."

"You don't have parents."

"Everyone has parents," I said. "And I don't have friends."

"I'm your friend."

"No, I mean—" I stopped, exasperated. "I want to meet other kids like I used to, why can't I go to town?"

Mr. Z didn't reply.

I said, "How can I fight tornadoes for people if I never even get to see them?"

Mr. Z said, "Have you ever *tried* to see them?"

Then he looked at me with a hard gleam in his eyes, as though he'd hinted at something forbidden.

He began cleaning up the checkers.

"Game's over," he said. "Go get some fresh air."

I went outside.

Inside Mr. Z turned up the TV. I heard the laughter and the applause, a rerun of some old variety show. He would spend the rest of the night watching reruns.

I wanted to watch something else.

I gazed across the prairie, at the distant town that I couldn't enter. I didn't see anything different.

But I felt something new. A tugging behind my eyes.

For the next few nights, after killing tornadoes all day and eating dinner with Mr. Z, I'd climb up on the roof and stare at town, and I'd feel that little tug behind my eyes. The town was just a distant blurry glimmer, but as I stared, it seemed to edge closer, bit by bit, and the tug got stronger—and as I kept looking, over weeks, I sensed something changing—until one night behind my eyes I felt a subtle *click*—

And with an exhilarating rush distance collapsed, my vision zoomed, and all at once it was as though I was *in* town.

My eyes were telescopes. I could see anywhere in town. I could see all the way into downtown, if I wanted. It was dizzying, I felt like I was there myself—I was among the people, I was side by side with a bunch of kids running down the sidewalk, I was with a family coming out of a restaurant, then a car passed startlingly close to me, a man in a suit came around the corner and brushed past me—if I moved my head the world would jump, a kaleidoscope of so many different faces, so close, but I could adjust the focus, the range, and it almost felt like I was part of their world—

After that, I watched the town all the time.

The town was like a huge party. But I wasn't invited to this party. I was outside it, watching from the other side of a window. Watching kids playing, watching families eating dinner, watching people walking hand in hand . . .

I started watching her.

———

Me.

It was me.

When I first saw myself in the tornado killer's memories, I almost didn't recognize myself. I looked like some old photo of me walking around. But the tornado killer was definitely watching me. He was curious about me, drawn to me, but guilty too, confused, tracking me as I rode my bike around alone, as I stood on the roof of Archie's house watching fireworks, as I wandered the forest . . .

The tornado killer had been watching me for a long time.

I didn't know how I felt about that.

I felt the tornado killer resisting me in his mind. He didn't want me to see these memories. He was embarrassed.

Why had he been watching me? How much *more* of me had he seen?

And now his memories swerved into something else—I felt the tornado killer get flustered, we were on the verge of a memory he was ashamed of, that he didn't want me to see—

I felt myself getting closer to what I was looking for. He struggled against me but it wasn't a real struggle. He was scared but deep down I knew he wanted to give me everything.

Give it to me.

———

I was the tornado killer again.

I was nine years old, it was dawn and I was walking home alone after an all-night tornado slaughter. I had killed dozens of tornadoes in the blind darkness and now I was exhausted, scratched up, bruised, hungry.

I limped inside my house yelling, "I'm home!"

No answer.

No Mr. Z.

I looked through the house. I went from room to room, more and more confused. Then panicked.

All of his stuff was gone.

I shouted again for Mr. Z.

There was no answer.

I ran outside. Mr. Z was in his truck. The headlights were on. I saw all his stuff piled up in the back. He was already pulling out onto the road.

I ran after the truck and grabbed the side mirror, as if I could stop a moving car with my nine-year-old strength. He slowed down, but not much, and I had to trot next to the car as I yelled, "Where are you going?"

"Who, little old me?" said Mr. Z, mock innocently.

"Yes! Why are you leaving?"

"What, you thought you'd get to hang out with me till the day you die?" said Mr. Z. "Too bad. You're all groweds up now."

"You can't just go away!"

Mr. Z shrugged, speeding up a little.

I scampered after, frantic. "But, but I don't have anyone now!"

"You'll always have me deep inside," cooed Mr. Z. "And that little girl you've been spying on, I suppose."

I nearly tripped. Mr. Z hit the brakes. The truck lurched to a halt.

"Oh ho ho, don't look so surprised," said Mr. Z. "I know every little thing you do."

I was breathing hard from running. But I still felt myself blush.

"Shut up," I panted.

"And that's why we keep you out of town, lover boy," said Mr. Z. "Now listen sharp. Stay clear of that girl. You got that? Don't touch her. Don't even go near her."

How did he know?

"I'll do what I want," I managed to say.

"Uh-huh, you go and do that," said Mr. Z, nodding. "And the minute you do *that*, I'll find you, and you can be sure I *will* find you, and I'll cut off your balls, and trust me those won't be the first balls I've cut off, nothing I like better on a Saturday afternoon than cutting off balls, sure, balls and balls and balls, just a backyard full of cut-off balls of the little shits who've crossed me, whaddya say, now how does that sound?"

I tried to sound tough. "I'll—kill you."

"Wrong again, you go and try to kill me, hell, try to kill any tornado killer, see what happens—yeah, and you too," said Mr. Z. "Even those poor ripped-up tornado killer losers trapped in those necklaces, they're still alive—did you know that? Wriggling around, in pieces. Not comfy. You'll learn. Hell, you don't even know who we are yet. Sure, you, me, and big old brown eyes, we've always been around, I'll introduce you to her later—I used to be like you, I thought I was just a kid, hey, ha, you think you're actually just a *kid*?"

I didn't know what to say.

He said, "Our last day, I'll teach you what we really are."

There was something in his tone, in the way he looked at me, that chilled me.

"I know who I am," I said.

"Well, I guarantee you will know one day," said Mr. Z. "And I guarantee one day you'll be teaching tornado killing to the next brat, and that brat will be crying just like you are now, boo-hoo— and when that happens you're gonna remember this conversation, just like I'm remembering it now, and I want you to remember *me*," and he grinned, and this revolted me, because it was a conspiratorial grin, like Mr. Z and I were secretly on the same team, and my face was reflected in the window, and I saw it for a second.

Mr. Z and I looked so much the same.

"Oh and by the way, you just turned ten," said Mr. Z. "Happy birthday."

Mr. Z drove off into the sunrise.

I went back into the house.

I didn't know what to do. I was alone. But I didn't want to be alone. Mr. Z could be awful but at least he was someone. With all of his stuff gone, the house was worse than empty. There wasn't enough of me to fill this house.

I shut myself in my room. I pushed my bed against the door even though there was nobody who wanted to come in here anyway. Nobody other than Mr. Z even knew that I existed. Nobody cared whether I lived or died. I felt the tears starting to come even though I didn't even like Mr. Z, he taunted me, he hurt me, I was crying over someone who didn't even love me. My face was a mess of tears and snot and I let out a ludicrous moan that embarrassed me even though I was alone.

But I wasn't alone.

Someone knocked on my bedroom door.

Impossible. I had spent my tenth birthday crying alone.

But that memory was different now.

I knew who was knocking.

I pushed the bed away from the door.

When I opened it, she was waiting on the other side. A ten-year-old version of her. She came into my room.

She smiled and said, "I guess I can do this too."

She held me, and I let myself break completely.

The tornado killer was awake.

He was awake. He knew me now.

He could move, but not much. He couldn't walk yet. I managed to put clothes on him from Archie's closet. He looked up at me, grateful. He couldn't speak more than a few words at a time or it would rip up his throat. That was okay. We spent most of our time in each other's memories anyway.

I went along with him killing tornadoes, I walked with him on the deserted prairie at night, and he inserted himself in my memories too, playing video games with me at the bowling alley, exploring the storm drains with me . . . When I remembered that muggy rainy day at the quarry pool now, kissing him in the water, my skin on his skin, now it was like I'd always swam with him that day, it was impossible that it had gone any other way.

We were colonizing each other's pasts. We were making it like we had always known each other. We *had* always known each other. We were each other's secret, each other's hidden half.

Still, we couldn't touch when we were awake. If I touched him then, he'd lose whatever little tornado-killing power he had. FORBIDDEN TO TOUCH ANY OF YOU, TO PRESERVE MY EXALTED PURITY; ONLY THE PURE CAN KILL A TORNADO—that was true. But as long as we didn't touch, his tornado-killer powers were slowly building back up. And once the tornado killer was strong enough, once he could kill tornadoes again, then we could do what I'd planned in the first place—except we'd do it together—we'd go to my old house, we'd grab the keys to my parents' car, and we'd leave town. He needed to be able to kill some tornadoes for us to pull it off, so he had to rest up first to rebuild. But once we were far away from here, he'd never have to kill another tornado again.

And then—and then we could—

In bed, in the darkness, the tornado killer and I stared at each other.

So close.

I wanted so badly to put my hand on him.

Another week passed like this. We had been in the house together for almost a month now, safe from the never-ending storm outside. I went around the house foraging, finding more canned and boxed food in out-of-the-way places, stuff that I liked trying to make real meals out of.

Because I wanted to cook. Because I liked taking care of him. Because this was our hidden place and I liked pretending that I was his weird little wife. It was a new and strange feeling and I did not dislike it.

There were also some things that he didn't know I was doing.

Whenever he was asleep I went off to a little room in the attic where I hoped he wouldn't find me.

I brought the curvy knife with me.

I felt like I knew what the knife was for. I had an idea of what to do with the knife. To him. When I couldn't sleep I sat and stared at the knife in the attic, watching it gleam in the dark.

Downstairs his powers were flowing back into him, the powers he'd lost by touching me. Not just powers for killing tornadoes—he was using his powers to heal himself too, to knit his internal organs back together, to regenerate something important inside him. The tornado killer would look asleep but he'd actually be awake, just turned inwards, doing some mysterious psychic surgery on himself.

During those times I went to the attic with the curvy knife. I let the tip of the blade rest of my skin. It felt right. The blade was so sharp even sliding it lightly down my thigh left a little cut.

The cut felt good. It meant something. Like I was starting to write a word. I wasn't ready for the word. But if I kept going, I knew the word would appear, a word I wanted badly to read.

The tornadoes kept raging, churning up and down the prairie, slashing through town, burrowing deep into the ground, leaping far off into the sky, and the tornado killer and I loved it, he was just healed enough to walk around now and we opened the windows to let rain and wind blast through the house, curtains flying, papers fluttering, we played together even though we couldn't touch and he couldn't really speak, we hooked up the record player to the house's intercom and we danced up and down the halls to scratchy records, we danced so close, I felt his breath, his heat, we played ping-pong in the attic, we rode the creaky elevator up and down the crumbling brick shaft, we chased each other through the wildly winding hallways, we climbed onto the roof where the wind whipped us as the stars winked and glittered, we swam in the creek that flowed through the backyard as the rain pelted down all around us, watching each other's bodies, each other's eyes, coming close, don't touch, don't touch—he ran ahead of me into the darkness and I followed him, and we went further and deeper into the house than we'd ever gone before, far enough to disappear entirely.

When we both disappeared, in the dark we'd come close, lips almost touching, we were still kind of strangers, too close, on the verge of something—

And then thunder rolled and midnight lightning suddenly lit us both up, and we'd jump up and down on my bed, both of us as pale and alien as something lurking at the bottom of the sea.

Five weeks in Archie's house.

It was the middle of the night.

The tornado killer was asleep.

I wandered the dark hallways alone. Tonight Archie's house didn't even feel like a house, it was like I was inside something alive, a twisty, huge, cramped, dark organism breathing and quivering around me. I was swimming around inside it, inside the veins of a vast diseased dragon.

I carried my curvy knife.

The tornado killer was now sleeping in the bedroom Cecilia and I had slept in back on New Year's Eve. I thought about my old life in this house, my long-ago normal life with Cecilia and Archie and everyone in his house . . . the two worlds superimposed in my imagination for a moment, and I almost felt like I might turn the corner and see Archie again, or my friends, or even myself, or maybe I'd see Cecilia and me sleeping together in that bed, because I was a ghost drifting through my own past, I was watching myself and Cecilia sleep—

Except Cecilia wasn't asleep. Her eyes were wide open. She was wearing that necklace, staring straight at me, and she had that hideous smile.

I bolted awake.

I was alone, in a different bed in Archie's house, sweaty, heart pounding.

I lay there for a while.

Then I went down the hall, to what used to be Archie's parents' room, where the tornado killer really slept.

He and I never slept in the same bed. It would be too easy to touch by accident. But I felt reckless now. I got in bed with him in the dark and lay next to him. The tornado killer's back was to me. I was close to him, too close. My heart going fast. Feeling crazy. Sick of waiting. I knew what I wanted now, I had an idea of how to get it. I looked at the angles of his back. Only weeks ago he'd been half dead, a bloody, bruised mess. Now his body was even more perfect than before. I was aching. The windows were open but the night was too hot. I came closer to him. We spent so much time in each other's memories but I didn't know him enough in real life. We still had barely said a word. Maybe I wanted him to remain a stranger. I was hungry for being on the edge of something new with a stranger.

We had lived each other's memories. I could give him more of that.

But now I wanted to take.

I wanted to take his secret.

I came closer and I smelled the back of his neck, foreign and addictive, the oil in his hair and sweat, and then I began to realize he wasn't asleep either, he was awake, I had woken him up, or maybe he had been awake for a long time, waiting for me to come into his room, waiting for me to slip in bed behind him, to come closer. I could feel the doors inside him unlocking.

Then he turned to me.

Green and blue eyes glittering in the dark.

I'm ready, I said.

He said, Ready for what.

I said, Ready to get out of here. You can kill those tornadoes. Let's go right now.

He looked at me for a long time, and before I could say what I wanted to say, he said it first.

<hr />

We celebrated our last night at Archie's house.

Archie's house had a weird chapel in it. We rummaged through the closets and found a suit that fit him, and I found a white dress that fit me, and we went down to the chapel, with some champagne from Archie's dad's cellar, and we drank in that musty chapel with no windows except its little lozenges of colored glass.

It was almost like we were pretending to get married. It was kind of a joke. But behind his eyes I saw maybe he wasn't joking. Maybe I wasn't joking either.

We were lounging on the chapel pews now, me in my antique white dress, him in his old-man's suit, passing a bottle of champagne back and forth, maybe drinking too much, but then the tornado killer turned over and put his elbows on the pew, his head in his hands, and he stared at me with his strange green and blue eyes.

Eyes getting bigger, somehow growing—

Eyes somehow bigger than his face—eyes bigger than him, eyes bigger than me, horrible eyes, I was inside them again, drunkenly falling in, I was somewhere else, but too fuzzy, out of control—

<hr />

I was in a little room. I recognized this room. It was dark and cramped, barely as big as a bathroom. From the small dusty window I saw it was night outside. A little table with a green rotary phone rang shrilly next to me, drowning out the two voices on the other side of the door.

It was Mr. Z's voice. And the tornado killer's voice.

I was at the tornado killer's house, in his little phone closet.

"Say it again," said Mr. Z's voice. "Make me believe it."

"*I am your chosen one*," said the tornado killer.

My skin prickled. I didn't want to see Mr. Z. I didn't even want to hear him. The doorknob was locked on my side of the door. Mr. Z and the kitchen were right on the other side. But Mr. Z couldn't get me, because this wasn't real, I was only inside the tornado killer's memory—I was safe—

Mr. Z snorted. "Chosen one? Phhht, you sound like the knucklehead who bags my groceries. Again."

"*I am your chosen one!*"

"Put your weight on it or I swear I'll take my next shit straight down your throat. Go!"

"*I am your CHOSEN ONE!*"

"Still sound like you're about to wilt on a scented sissy couch. Tornado killer? Hell, you don't sound like you could wound a grasshopper's fart. Never forget, deep down they hate you, or they *would* hate you, if they knew what you really were, so you gotta make it clear who's boss from the get-go or they'll turn against you, they'll tear you apart, so kindly take the daisy out of your ass and read it right."

The phone kept ringing.

"This speech is dumb," said the tornado killer. "I don't want to read—"

"You'll read it, and you'll read it word for word, by God, or I'll knock out your teeth and shove 'em up your nose, merry Christmas. And don't think you can get away with changing a word, I wrote it this way for a reason, the men who're boxing you up and taking you into school will tell me if you do any ad libs—depend on it."

A pause. "Boxed up?"

"Jesus, *sure* you'll be boxed up—what, you wanna lose the power you've spent your whole life building? Lose the power that I spend all my goddamned time giving you? Not gonna happen. Hell, I was boxed up too, before I made my own speech. The second you touch one of them you're leaking power, you understand me?"

"You touch people."

"I'm retired, I do whatever the hell I want. You're the tornado killer now, God help us all. Read the damned script."

The tornado killer took a deep breath. "*But what was I chosen for? What mysterious aristocracy do I belong to, that no mortal may look into my eyes without sublime—*"

"Christ on a stick. No, no, don't even bother reading it again, just keep on going."

"*But how did you know I was your—*" The tornado killer stopped. "I can't read this."

There was a dangerous pause.

"Go off script again, I invite you," purred Mr. Z. "As a favor to me, I *want* you to go off script, I want you to discover the wonderful things I'll do to you, I've flossed dipshits like you out of my baby teeth. So, oh please, oh jiminy, oh hummina hummina, give me a reason, *please* say anything other than the words on that card, I'm dying for it."

A long pause.

"*But how did you know I was your chosen one? Take your pick from the multitude of signs and wonders that attended my birth . . .*"

There was hardly enough space in the room for both me and that ringing telephone. It was ringing in my ear but I still felt fuzzy and muddled, I could only hear snatches of what Mr. Z and the tornado killer were saying—

And then I realized that I had found, at last, what I was looking for inside the tornado killer.

This phone.

What if I picked up this phone?

Cuthbert Monks had.

When Cuthbert put the receiver to his ear, it had changed him. It had looked as if he was being electrocuted but it had changed him. And now Cuthbert seemed to know things. Cuthbert had said the telephone was the tornadoes calling.

You know why the tornado killer never answers his phone? The tornadoes talk.

When I picked up the phone, they told me everything.

Whatever it was, Cuthbert knew more than I did. But then again, this phone wasn't real, this was only a phone in a memory—

I reached for the phone anyway.

The tornado killer said, "I can't even sleep, that phone is ringing all the time now."

"Suck it up," said Mr. Z. "There used to be a lot more tornado killers. The difference between us and them? They answered their phones."

"But there's got to be a way to—"

"Wait a second," said Mr. Z suspiciously. "Somebody else is here."

What?

I heard a chair slowly being pushed back.

Wake up wake up.

Footsteps coming closer.

This was just a memory, right? Nothing bad could happen to me here, not really—

Mr. Z chuckled, just on the other side of the door.

Like he could hear me thinking that. Like he found it funny.

"So you're keeping each other company now?" whispered Mr. Z to me. "How's it feel this time around?"

This time around?

But this is all just in my mind, in his mind, Mr. Z couldn't get me for real, I was just playing games inside the tornado killer's memories—

A key slid into the lock.

"*I'm jest a girl who cain't say no . . .*"

I stumbled backward. The doorknob was turning. I staggered,

knocked against the phone table. This wasn't a memory.

This was real.

The phone kept ringing.

The tornado killer lives with a ringing phone he's never allowed to answer.

Why can't he answer the phone?

Because the phone tells him the truth.

If you were the tornado killer, would you answer it, if there was a ringing phone that told you the truth about yourself?

My hand stopped on the ringing phone.

That phone is ringing in your face every second.

I couldn't do it. I couldn't pick it up. I turned instead, I forced open the window, just as the closet door was opening behind me I scrambled out, I heard Mr. Z's snarl and his hand was on my shoulder but I broke free, I hurtled out the window, I dropped to the dirt, I was outside running through the grass, running across the empty night prairie, but then I wasn't, I was running down the halls of my school, toward the auditorium, no I was in the auditorium, everything was getting mixed up, I was sitting next to the tornado killer, heart pounding, and we were watching *A Christmas Carol*.

The tornado killer sat right next to me in the audience. He was absorbed by the play. It was the part with Archie as Scrooge in the spotlight, asking a question of Todd Vanderwald as the Ghost of Christmas Present, and Todd wore a big fake beard and a laurel of holly and was draped in huge purple robes.

There was a movement within the robes—

SCROOGE: Forgive me, Spirit, if I am not justified in what I ask, but I see something strange, and not belonging to yourself, protruding from your skirts. Is it a foot or a claw?

leaves and rain splattered in my face.

The wall of tornadoes rushed toward us.

Cuthbert Monks shouted over the noise, "There's too many, we're not going to make it—"

The back doors of the van flew open.

I turned.

The tornado killer was gone.

Wait—what?

I heard a bump on the van's roof—

I turned back to the front. "Look out!"

A tornado dove in at us, hungry, snarling—

The tornado disintegrated.

We blew through it like it was steam.

Cuthbert and I stared. The tornadoes kept flying at us, attacking us, but one after another they were cut in half, turned inside out, choked to nothing, boiled, twisted, exploded, sliced to ribbons, slaughtered—

The tornado killer was on the roof of the van.

He was fighting.

"Insane," whispered Cuthbert but the tornado killer wasn't insane, he was amazing, he was fighting the tornadoes and I felt the baby-thing inside me syncing up with his power, I was helping too, heightening his power. Tornadoes hurled themselves at us but every tornado got caught, strangled, butchered, wrecked. The air sizzled. I was the tornado killer too, I was riding on top of the van, my muscles taut, my brain sharp, my body moving with precision. I smelled the storm and we were invincible, we were doing it together, we were perfect together, standing on top of the van as it sped seventy miles per hour, killing tornadoes, eighty miles per hour—

A coldness came over me.

GHOST OF CHRISTMAS PRESENT: It might be a claw, for the
little flesh there is on it. Look here!

Todd pulled aside his robe. Out came Cecilia and Cuthbert
Monks from six years ago, dressed as London street children.
Cecilia had gotten to double up her roles, because her role of Mrs.
Cratchit had so few lines, but this was the only role Cuthbert
Monks had been cast in, with zero lines, since he was such a pain
to Mrs. Papadakis—

SCROOGE *(alarmed)*: Spirit! Are they yours?

Cuthbert Monks onstage stared straight at me. It was young
Cuthbert Monks from six years ago, but somehow it wasn't young
Cuthbert—his eyes were just like his eyes now, his stare intense,
accusatory—

GHOST OF CHRISTMAS PRESENT: They are yours! And do you
not know them? This boy is Ignorance. This girl is Want.

I grabbed the tornado killer's hand next to me.
His hand was cold, clawlike.

GHOST OF CHRISTMAS PRESENT: Beware of them both, and
all their kind!

I had thought it was the tornado killer sitting next to me. I had
thought that the hand I had grabbed was his.

This hand felt different.

GHOST OF CHRISTMAS PRESENT: But most of all beware this boy, for upon his brow I see written the word DOOM—

Cuthbert Monks pointed at me—no, not at me, he pointed at the person next to me, whose hand I was holding. But it wasn't the tornado killer.

I turned to him.

Mr. Z was sitting next to me.

He squeezed my hand and grinned.

I screamed. Everyone in the auditorium turned to me, their faces feral and leering. I scrambled out of my seat. The lights were still off, the play was still going on, but everyone was staggering at me, grabbing at me, everyone's parents, even Mom and Dad were coming for me with ferocious smiles, hands all over me, but I broke free, I burst out of the auditorium and I was running, running down the hallways of the school at night and I turned left and right and then I was in the gymnasium—it wasn't night, it was morning, and now I wasn't even me—

I was the tornado killer, standing at a lectern, reading off of Mr. Z's cards. "But what was I chosen for? What mysterious aristocracy do I belong to, that no man may look into my eyes without sublime terror?"

I was up on the small stage, with hundreds of hostile kids watching me from the bleachers. The boys were separated from the girls, all of them dressed up in suits and dresses.

"Ass," shouted someone.

"For this reason: I am the tornado killer!"

"Ass!"

"But how did you know I was your, ah, uh, chosen one?" I said, reading from my cards too quickly, tripping over words; my voice broke on "chosen one" and kids giggled; I hated this script, I could feel it turning the audience against me, I knew I was failing but I swallowed, read on: "Take your pick from the multitude of signs and wonders that attended my birth! There was, of course, the matter of my unsettlingly beautiful *eyes*."

I looked up into the crowd for her. She went to this school, I was sure of it. Why couldn't I find her? Too many people. I had never been so close to so many people.

I said, "Or my uncanny ability—"

"—to be an ass," said Cuthbert Monks, and minutes later this same Cuthbert Monks was beating me up in the darkness, his two friends holding me down, my power draining away, dwindling every time they hit me, just like Mr. Z had warned, I tried to wriggle away but they dragged me up the stairs, they stuffed me in the janitor's closet and locked me in, laughing, I kicked the door and screamed, nobody heard, nobody helped, and when the tornado came and destroyed the school I barely had enough power to kill it and then run away.

I ran away.

I lost myself in town.

I wandered the streets alone all day and into the evening. Terrified. I had watched over this town all my life, I had spied on it, I had ached to be here. Now I was actually walking its streets, I was in it for real. But the streets were too narrow, the looming buildings were hemming me in too close on either side. People walking by almost brushed me. I shrank away from them, overwhelmed. I knew that the men were in town too, looking for me. I spotted them patrolling, searching for me. They wanted to put me back in the box. I moved quickly, slipping through streets and parks and buildings. I was close to this world now, not just watching it from afar, I was smelling it, feeling it. When the men appeared I ducked around the corner, into a store, behind bushes, in an alley—

I was looking for her.

Finding her house was harder than I thought it would be. There were too many buildings boxing me in, getting in my way. Too many people confusing me. Sometimes I'd come across a place I recognized from watching her. The library she'd visit. The pet shop she and her sister liked. But the places were never where I expected.

When I finally found her house, it was too late. She wasn't there.

Wait—not too late! I spotted her, down the road.

Biking away with her sister.

I followed them.

When I arrived at the party at the big house at the edge of town it was already night. I watched from the outer darkness, in the trees, at the little island of light that was the party in the backyard, the Christmas lights and tiki torches and the tornado piñata and the kids milling around, dancing, laughing.

Then I saw her.

She saw me.

I felt it. I knew she felt it too.

Then I looked up.

Other eyes were watching me from an upstairs window. A gigantic woman alone in that house, watching out that window, while everyone else was outside at the backyard party. Nobody seemed to notice her.

She had two brown glowing eyes.

I looked back to the party. The girl wasn't looking at me anymore. They had blindfolded her. She was swinging a baseball bat at a piñata.

Nobody was watching the piñata.

Everyone was watching her, their eyes vicious.

———

I woke up in my white wedding dress, covered in sweat, my heart beating hard.

I was back in the chapel, at Archie's house.

Something was wrong. We shouldn't have entered each other's memories when we had been trying that champagne, when we were drunk. It had scrambled everything, taken me further and weirder than I wanted to go. Now the tornado killer was swaying over to behind the altar. There was a little door behind it. He stumbled, grabbed on to the door frame, swung himself in. He was gone.

I slid off the pew, onto my feet.

The twilight dimness in the chapel buzzed around me. I took a step, wobbled. I put my hand on the pew.

But we were supposed to be leaving soon. Leaving town. What time was it? Was it morning?

Our plan . . .

Whose plan?

I lurched after the tornado killer toward the open door. Beyond the door was a vague gray room. The light was like a thick gray smoke rising all around. I found my way through.

I don't know what I expected I'd find backstage at a chapel. Not God, obviously, but maybe something like that, something too special to be seen by just anyone—a secret golden throne, a claustrophobic shrine, a drawer with a little grinning idol.

It was a small drab room. It seemed to be a kind of lounge or storage room for the priest. The same carpet from the chapel continued into here. There were a half dozen metal chairs folded up and stacked against the wall, a wardrobe with a couple of priests' frocks, a stainless-steel sink, dry and dusty. Gray light limped in from the windows high on the wall, too high to see anything but an empty sky, long rectangles of colorless light. There was an electric socket in the wall. The whole room had a deadening feeling. A chalice had been turned upside down and left to dry on a dish rack with some spoons and a soup bowl.

The tornado killer had turned his back to me. He was in the corner, his hands busy doing something. I felt blurry. I sank to the floor. I felt like I was getting lost in a long dull complicated piece of music. The tornado killer was lighting candles. I heard a little ringing phone, just barely, coming from a tiny corner of my mind. I was lying down somewhere but I didn't know where. I didn't know how to work my own body, it had an unfamiliar shape, I couldn't feel where it began or ended or how to move it.

Where was my knife?

Something thin and cold was crawling across my skin. My eyes focused again and I saw candles surrounding me, tiny yellow flames everywhere, pressing in closer, like I was in the heart of a tiny sun.

The tornado killer had my curvy knife.

How did he have my knife?

He was dragging the knife down my thigh.

The tornado killer's face was very close, his eyes were so soft.

He cut me open.

———

Light poured out of me.

The tornado killer cut me again, the knife went in, like he put a nail through me—the nail blossomed into a hundred hallucinatory flowers, opening up into spirals, turning jagged into pulsing spikes, it was too much, the hot knife zigged and zagged through me like I was made of ice cream, tingling leaped around in its wake—I wanted him to keep cutting, I closed my eyes, I didn't care if I was shredded, the knife was singing into me, unzipping me, slicing me into pieces, I was laughing, I couldn't stop laughing and then I was standing outside myself, watching myself as the knife sizzled through my thighs, my arms, my stomach, my neck, bliss flooding and streaming through me, twisting together like a braid, turning and blending and then pulled tight like a quivering wire. My face was slick with tears, sweat. The tornado killer's face was close. I wanted to kiss him. I had never realized before how beautiful his mouth was. It made me feel he wasn't human at all, he was something else, a fascinating alien, an animal, how could you eat, how could you talk, with a mouth that beautiful? I knew he didn't know what he was doing either, we were discovering it together, he wasn't a human being anymore and neither was I, we were both monsters now. Little cuts opened up all over me and I could taste through the cuts, the knife curled in, left sweetened blood behind, fire was leaking off me, just keep doing it, please keep doing it, I was a gleaming, writhing blur.

The tornado killer's strong legs and bare chest, brown back twisting, hair falling on my stomach, pulling away and drawing me closer, his nose almost touching my ear, whispering on my neck, the knife in me, touching me with the knife. How did he get my knife, my knife, how did he know about it, but it wasn't a knife, it was a key, he was unlocking me, this was the thing I had been looking for, we were opening each other, discovering what was inside. I was going to find out his secret, no our secret, no the knife wasn't a key it was a pen, the knife left scorched lines behind, writing something on me, my body was covered with symbols and I knew those symbols, I remembered a whole secret alphabet, he was cutting a message into me, in a language we were inventing as we went along, a language that we'd made up together a long time ago. He moved in close, he pressed the knife in my hand, I took the knife and did the same thing to him, I cut him, he was gasping, eyes closed, I drew the symbols in him, the alphabet I'd forgotten but now remembered, I felt clearer than I ever had before, like my eyes had been cleaned of all the grime that had built up around them all my life. My skin was scrubbed clean of everything that came between it and the world, we were bleeding all over each other, into each other, becoming each other, there was no difference between our bodies, both of us carved with this ecstatic alphabet, and I was about to carve the final symbol on him when I paused—the symbol I had secretly carved all over town, in the places that were my own, because the tornado killer was my own now too, I was about to make it real with this knife, he whispered he was mine, I told him I was his, smiling into his ear, agonizingly close, his bare chest close to mine, and I cut my symbol at last into his arm.

A phone rang, loud.

I went cold.

I pushed away from him.

I realized what I had done.

For a moment the tornado killer's body changed—I watched him age at light speed from himself into Mr. Z, into an unthinkably old thing, an ancient monster covered with all the symbols. His eyes stared up at me helplessly, he didn't know what was happening either, he hadn't intended this, he didn't understand either—

An entire wall fell away and there was Archie's mother and the Horrible Woman, they were shrieking, laughing. We were naked and cold on the floor of the room behind the altar, surrounded by burned-out candles, panting up at the ceiling. Our bodies weren't cut up into anything, we were both helpless, Archie was there and Archie's father too but they were goblins with empty black eyes, they were grabbing me, grabbing the tornado killer. The Horrible Woman shambled over to me, draped in colorful sashes and robes with a red turban and gold jewelry and her monstrous breasts that were leaking some black liquid. Archie's mom eagerly sucked the black milk and spit it into a cup while Archie and his father sang some toneless, repetitive song, and Archie forced open my mouth while Archie's dad held down my arms and legs and Archie's mom poured the black milk down my throat. I choked, I spit it in Archie's mom's face, but Archie's mom sucked more from the Horrible Woman's teat, and let it dribble into the cup, and jammed the cup into my mouth, hard this time, everyone was swaying and singing now, I was drinking it, I couldn't help it, and they were all overjoyed, because Archie's family and the Horrible Woman had never gone anywhere, they had never moved, they had been in this house with us all along, watching us, delighted.

THE BRIDE OF THE TORNADO

The next thing I knew I was at home, lying on my bedroom ceiling.

I was in my own bedroom in my own house.

My bedroom was upside down.

A man and a woman came into the room. They had to step over the top of my doorframe to come in, because my bedroom was upside down. They stepped through the door and walked across the ceiling.

I stared at my carpet, which was overhead. The floor was where the ceiling should be. My dresser, my desk, my clothes, all my stuff was scattered upside down on the ceiling, which was now the floor. The ceiling's light fixture sprouted next to me, wrenched sideways. A cracked bulb was still in its socket.

Colors wrong.

Dark outside.

Air cold on my skin.

The man and woman had flashlights. Their faces flickered in the dark, in the flashlights' glare. It was Mom and Dad, but they weren't Mom and Dad—how could they be? The woman had to be an actress who resembled Mom, the man was clearly just an actor who looked like Dad, they weren't even good actors. The man looked shabby, the woman harsh and dour.

The man picked me up. He held me as the woman wriggled a white wedding dress onto me in a clumsy way. Both of them seemed to want this to be over with, to get this dress on me as quickly as possible. They weren't gentle. Nobody was fooled that they were my parents. Who could be fooled by them?

I was fooled, a little.

Mom and Dad picked me up and carried me through our upside-down house. I couldn't move. Something was wrong with my mouth. I saw conspiratorial glances between Mom and Dad— not Mom and Dad, I mean these crappy actors didn't even look like Mom and Dad, actually that's not true, they looked exactly like Mom and Dad, but I wasn't tricked, no wait, I totally was? These actors were geniuses! They really had me going, these actors. And I had me going too! Yeah, we were all in on it, we all got the joke, almost winking at each other, I knew we'd laugh about this at the cast party later—a cast party? Sure, there'd be a cast party after this show, and just to prove I was a good sport, I tried to imitate me, but not really, I wasn't very good at it either, I was only attempting to play me, I didn't feel like me. I was not-me.

The real me was somewhere else.

Mom and Dad carried me out of our upside-down house. The air was crisp, cold. When did it become fall? Hundreds of people were outside, gathered in front of my house. When Mom and Dad carried me toward them it was like coming onstage. But it wasn't a show.

Nobody clapped.

My mouth wouldn't stop smiling.

The colors were wrong. Grass red as blood. Sidewalk shimmering rich purple. Everyone's faces were blinding silver, impassive masks of gold, black holes for eyes and mouths. Mom and Dad carried me through the crowd. Neon-colored tornadoes whipped and whirled far away, their glows smeared across the dark horizon. Candy-pink and lime-green twisters pulsing through the black, ropes of light slowly whirling out like huge rainbow jellyfish.

Mom and Dad carried not-me down the road.

My frozen smile hurt.

Girls followed us, all wearing wedding dresses, as we moved through the neighborhood. It was a parade, but nobody seemed very happy to be in it. It felt like every girl in town was following me. It was my first time going to this place, but the other girls had done it already. I knew that. It had happened dozens of times. They had all rehearsed.

I smiled at everyone.

I had always known I would go to Mr. Z's.

The careful way Mom and Dad carried me, the way they looked down at me now, with so much emotion, I thought, these actors are terrific, I wouldn't be surprised if they really *were* Mom and Dad! I looked around for the tornado killer, too, or for whoever was playing him. All I saw were wrecked houses, ripped-up roads, big old trees shivered and blasted apart. The tornado killer wasn't in this scene, apparently. Who was running this show, who was the director? I stared up at the stars, twinkling red and purple and yellow. Hot-pink leaves on the trees, passing overhead. Burnt-orange sky. Neon-green moon. Strange colors, strange weather, the air was too cold.

November cold.

Then we were at Mr. Z's house, standing on his front porch. I'd never actually stood on Mr. Z's porch before. Had there been a rehearsal? Maybe I'd missed it. Then again, I knew my way around this place. It was the same design as the tornado killer's house.

Inside, the phone was ringing.

Lisa Stubenberger's sleepover felt like a lifetime ago. That night that we'd driven Cuthbert Monks's van out to the tornado killer's house, and partied there, and drank and danced, that was a lifetime ago too. All of my life had happened to somebody else, not me. Summer had never happened, my whole self had never happened, I was just something I had read in a book once. This was the fall.

This was real life.

There was a fresh tattoo on my left arm:

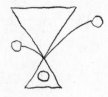

I had seen that symbol before. Where?

I couldn't remember.

But not-me absolutely knew.

Dad-not-Dad rang Mr. Z's doorbell. Archie's mother opened the door—wait, what was she doing at Mr. Z's house? I smiled my frozen smile at her. Archie's mother's eyes moved over my wedding dress, my face, my body, examining me. Bigger than I remembered her. Behind her the phone rang again and again.

I entered Mr. Z's house, smiling.

The house smelled sick and mildewy. The actors playing Mom and Dad looked uncertain, glancing around as though hoping for an excuse to exit the scene. Mr. Z's house's floor plan mirrored the tornado killer's house, but it was different, because the tornado killer's house had been bare except for a mattress in the bedroom, the refrigerator, a kitchen table, a couch, some clothes lying around, but Mr. Z's house was crammed with grandpa crap, porcelain figurines and yellowed magazines packed on overloaded zigzagging bookcases, cluttered broken tables and slanting shelves stuffed with knickknacks, a piano heaped with papers and dead plants. It looked like nothing had been dusted in years. Everything was ancient and moldy feeling, with the stale lizardy smell of an old man.

Archie's mom brought me into the parlor. She sat me on a chair. Mr. Z sat across from me on a yellowed sofa.

He had Nikki.

Nikki sat in Mr. Z's lap, staring at me intently.

Nikki.

Archie's mom stood behind me. Her hands rested on my shoulders. Mr. Z watched me from behind his dark glasses, tongue slightly out of his mouth.

Had Mr. Z been keeping Nikki here all this time?

My frozen face just smiled at Mr. Z.

There was a table between me and Mr. Z. It had a plate of little cookies on a doily. Two cups of tea in saucers. Dust on the cookies. A motionless fly in my tea.

Nikki regarded me calmly.

I thought desperately at her: Nikki?

She didn't react.

I glimpsed movement in the unlit hall behind Mr. Z. A shape stirred in the darkness, a bulky entity larger than a person, passing through the shadows in the other room, like something massive moving way down at the bottom of the ocean.

Two brown eyes moved past.

Then the hall was empty.

The phone was still ringing. Behind Mr. Z, beyond the hallway, the ringing phone sat on a table in the little closet-like room. I remembered that, at the tornado killer's house, that room had been locked.

Here at Mr. Z's, the phone room was wide open.

Mr. Z moistened his lips.

There was an old-fashioned record player in the corner, softly playing some old show tune. Nikki hopped off Mr. Z's lap and stalked around the room, ignoring me and him and everyone, as though nothing unusual was happening. The phone kept ringing. Everything looked like a bad copy of itself. Faces in masks. Wrong colors. Something was beginning to happen outside. Behind me, Archie's mom's hands gripped my shoulders. Mom and Dad sat in the corner, in metal folding chairs. Outside the window the psychedelic neon tornadoes were syncing up, pulsing up and down in a jerky nightmare rhythm, locking into a pattern, their howls crossing, harmonizing, building to—

Mr. Z said my name.

My name sounded bad in his mouth. Nikki investigated a dust ball in the corner. Mr. Z rose from the couch and came around the table, closer to me. I didn't want to smile but not-me couldn't stop smiling. The record playing the show tune skipped. Mr. Z's mouth was slack. My parents didn't move from their chairs, I could barely see them. Mr. Z's face came closer, a face that was not a face, it was a great pale mushroom mottled with purple liver spots, gray bristles, quivering holes, swelling until it filled my whole vision, yellow teeth behind wet lips, dark glasses—a diseased moon on which I was, to my nauseous shock, just about to land.

Mr. Z gripped my chin, hard.

He forced my teeth apart, he forced my smiling mouth open. He turned on a little flashlight and pointed it down my throat.

"Let me see now," murmured Mr. Z.

Mr. Z stared down my throat for a long time. His breath smelled like a dead bird I once found in my backyard. Scratchy music played from the record player.

"I see some comfy spots in you." Mr. Z's voice was nasal, sentimental, as though he was making fun of the words he himself was saying. "I'm going to find a comfy spot."

His grip loosened.

"Are you going to be a soft mommy?" said Mr. Z.

I glanced at the ringing phone. Mr. Z watched my face in the dark. His wrinkly hand petted my cheek.

"That's just the tornadoes calling." He winked, as though we were both in on the same joke. "But we don't need to listen to what a tornado has to say, do we?"

The tornadoes outside were a kaleidoscopic smear of thousands of colors, spinning past the window, one after another. I felt like I should be answering Mr. Z. Some voice inside me was shouting suggestions, a line, an action. But I couldn't do anything. I didn't even know how to feel anything. The record skipped again. I couldn't move. The black milk they had made me drink froze me.

I couldn't get this smile off my face.

The shouting voice inside me said, how about trying to answer that phone?

It was an idea. It might surprise Mr. Z, I considered, and Archie's mother, and my parents . . . Something unscripted by me might add juice to the scene, might shake things up, an improvisation, in any case the voice in me wouldn't stop shouting about it, because hadn't Cuthbert Monks answered that phone and learned the truth?

I had to answer that phone.

Something sharp pricked the small of my back.

I still couldn't move my arms or legs. The black milk had hardened in my joints, gummed up my bones. But when Mr. Z grabbed my chin, he had shifted my weight, and inside the rickety chair's upholstery something must've sprang loose, because now a sharp nail or screw under the cushion was driving itself into my back.

I blinked.

The jab of the sharp thing cleared the fog. Hurt me but woke me up a little.

This wasn't a dream.

Show tunes were still playing on the record player. Black milk soaked my brain. This wasn't a play. My head lolled to the side, still smiling. My body slumped that way too—but I let it slump farther, on purpose, to press myself harder against the sharp thing in the chair.

It hurt.

It woke me even more.

The room swam into crisp focus. There were no actors here. Mr. Z was standing over me, real. That was Mom and Dad for real, sitting in the chairs behind Mr. Z, they had always been real. They were scared. There was no prismatic ring of tornadoes out the window.

Just masses of raw and ugly twisters, hungry.

Stop smiling.

No. Smile more. Fake it.

I moved my left big toe.

Archie's mother grabbed my head, twisting it back so that I was smiling at Mr. Z again. But Mr. Z wasn't in the room anymore. Something happened in the few seconds I wasn't looking.

Where Mr. Z had been was now the tornado killer.

Really?

Yes, the world was getting blurry again but I could see it was now the tornado killer sitting across from me, dressed in Mr. Z's clothes. The tornado killer was wearing old-man Mr. Z makeup, he looked just like Mr. Z . . . actually there wasn't a switch at all, it had never really been Mr. Z! It had been the tornado killer all along, disguised as Mr. Z!

The tornado killer did a dead-on Mr. Z impression and said, "You know what I'm going to become now? A baby tornado killer."

Then the tornado killer looked at me, expectant.

Hilarious! He really nailed that impression!

He said, "Doesn't every baby need a mommy?"

My mouth was frozen. I couldn't answer. Big-band music played.

The tornado killer repeated, crossly, "I said, doesn't every baby need a mommy?"

He grabbed my chin again, crushed it in his grip, forced my mouth open. My face sang with pain, my eyes teared up, I couldn't see. He jerked my head up and down, making me nod.

I hadn't answered fast enough, maybe.

The tornado killer's lips were in my ear.

"Doesn't every baby need a mommy?" said the tornado killer, doing his incredible Mr. Z impression.

My face hurt but my mouth was still frozen in that smile. I couldn't speak. I wanted to explain this to the tornado killer. He would certainly stop hurting me if he understood I couldn't speak right now.

Mom and Dad watched. They did not move to help me.

But I could move, just a little. The sharp thing in the chair was driving hard into my back, piercing my skin, cutting into me. I winced but the real pain woke me more. I moved my foot, secretly.

My paralysis was wearing off.

They didn't know.

The show tune on the record player ended. Another show tune began. Now it wasn't just my foot that was awake, but my whole leg. I moved it experimentally, a little pivot. Yes. Both of my legs were coming back alive.

"Your boyfriend doesn't even know what he is yet," said the tornado killer.

My legs were free. I looked at the tornado killer, in his ridiculous Mr. Z costume, the dark glasses, the wrinkle makeup—wait a second, had I honestly believed that was the tornado killer imitating Mr. Z? Come on! It obviously *had* been Mr. Z all along, pretending to be the tornado killer pretending to be Mr. Z! Because the tornado killer would never hurt me, it was just Mr. Z doing the world's worst tornado killer impression. As if I couldn't tell the difference right away, right? What did he take me for?

Mr. Z rolled up his shirtsleeve. He had a tattoo on his upper forearm.

Mrs. Lois's tattoo . . . my head was foggy again. I knew what that meant. It meant something. What was it?

The sharp thing drove in deeper. Waking me up more. Arms and legs free now.

The phone was still ringing in the other room.

The tornado killer lives with a ringing phone he's never allowed to answer.

Why can't he answer the phone?

Because the phone tells him the truth.

At last my face was thawed. I could stop smiling at any time.

Don't stop smiling.

Mr. Z took off his dark glasses.

"I'll tell you what I'm gonna do," said Mr. Z, blue and green eyes glowing. "I'm gonna make myself really small. And I'm gonna go inside you. And I'm gonna stay inside you until I'm ready to be born again because you're the bride of the tornado."

As he spoke, the Horrible Woman stepped in the hallway again, and beyond her the tornadoes appeared outside the window, excitedly pressing forward, whirling around the house so close, putting us in the center of a spectral geometry, an undulating power passing from the tornadoes to the Horrible Woman to Mr. Z, and now Mr. Z was becoming smaller, and smaller, still speaking in his wheedling nasal voice, smaller every second, the thing that called itself Mr. Z still looked like an old man but now he was half his original size, now a quarter, now he was doll sized, now even smaller, his clothes were too big, they rustled to the ground, and a little naked old man emerged from them and scampered across the floor.

I could move now.

I still didn't move. I faked being frozen. I stayed utterly still. I didn't move even as I felt the tiny Mr. Z crawling up my leg, crawling up my thigh, coming up through my wedding dress, and then he popped out from my neckline, from between my breasts, like some monstrous insect.

The tiny man stared at me.

Move. Move. Move.

Not yet.

Blue and green lights needling in.

Archie's mom gripped my jaw. She forced my mouth open—

The record skipped.

Whole new song.

I broke free.

I lunged out of the chair. Mr. Z tumbled off me, yelling as he fell. I staggered up, almost crushing him underfoot, I lurched at the hallway, at the room with the phone—

A hand grabbed me.

I ripped free.

Behind me, roars and shrieks.

I stumbled into the phone room, then I wheeled around— Archie's mom was chasing me into the room—my parents were on their feet, and the Horrible Woman was lumbering out of the darkness at me, furious brown eyes glowing—

I slammed the door.

Locked it.

Phone next to me ringing ringing ringing.

Bang bang bang, they were pounding on the door, rattling the doorknob. I lurched, clumsy from the black milk soaking my insides—I tilted, I hit the wall, I slid to the floor, bleary, the black milk foaming angrily inside me, the phone ringing ringing ringing.

Nikki was in the closet with me.

Staring at me.

They were breaking down the door.

I sneezed. The room was full of dust. I sneezed again, dizzy. The window was so caked in dust you couldn't even see outside. The ringing phone was covered with dust too, the continuous ringing agitating the dust around it. Sneeze. Black milk rose up in me, my arms and legs were locking up again—everything dimmed, out of focus—

I stabbed myself with my fingernails.

Scratched hard.

The world snapped back, barely.

The doorknob jolted. The door jumped in its hinges. Somebody on the other side was knocking the door down. My head was on the floor—wait, how did my head get on the floor? I had fallen. I couldn't get back on my feet.

I stared at the door.

In the gap between the bottom of the door and the floor, a tiny angry Mr. Z was wriggling in, crawling at me.

I screamed.

The phone screamed.

An axe blasted through the door. The door splintered. I had to get out. I lurched to my feet. I pushed open the grimy window.

Outside, the house was surrounded by people.

Everyone I had ever known in my life was staring at me.

Behind them multicolored tornadoes cavorted.

I grabbed Nikki, she yowled but I threw her out the window, go now Nikki, get out of here cat, you're free now, the phone was still ringing, I spun back but the room whirled too fast, everything dizzy, the axe punched through the wooden door again, splinters flying—phone ringing and Archie's mother's face stared from between shards of wood, phone ringing ringing—

I picked up the phone.

I put it to my ear.

I listened, and the tornadoes spoke.

The tornadoes spoke, and they told me everything.

———

The door broke down and Archie's mother came rushing in, and the Horrible Woman came after her, and Mom and Dad, they ripped the phone away from me and held me down on the floor as Archie's mother picked up Mr. Z and forced him into my mouth.

I gagged but Mom and Dad held me down, forcing my jaws open. Tiny Mr. Z slid down my throat. I choked. Archie's mother sucked more black milk from the Horrible Woman's giant breast and then spat it down my throat, dizzy stars, more black milk in my mouth, and then Archie's mother's lips were on mine, sloppy and soft, the black milk was bubbling out of her mouth into mine, I tried to spit it out and I couldn't.

I felt Mr. Z pushing my tonsils around until he found it. A tunnel in me.

Nikki screeched outside.

Someone replaced the phone on the hook.

It immediately began ringing again.

⚊⚊

They carried me out of Mr. Z's house.

The parade was waiting for us. The Horrible Woman was perched atop the back of a convertible driven by Archie's father, majestic in her robes and jewelry. Her head swiveled around, taking it all in. Her mouth did something like a smile.

She looked monstrously satisfied.

There were people everywhere, walking alongside the Horrible Woman's convertible, following my car too. I was laid out in the back of one of the "classic" cars Archie's father collected, a long black sedan with a grimy white leather interior, smelling of pipe smoke, rich and settled. Outside I could hear—cheers? Some kind of happy noise, anyway, it felt like an actual celebration now, a real parade, but I felt miles away from it, black milk gurgling in me, throbbing colors chasing each other, the tornadoes' voices from the phone still roaring in my ears, while the big brass band played in the parade, the high school marching band, drums banging and horns blaring.

The tornadoes on the phone had told me everything.

I knew what was going to happen now.

I knew where I fit in.

My stomach rippled, trying to eject tiny Mr. Z from my body, but the black milk clogged my throat. Mr. Z was digging deeper in me, wriggling his little body down through my belly, and then down beyond that, pushing around my insides, as though looking for some special place.

He sang to himself a song from that musical, in a slowed-down, garbled yodel only I could hear—"*Wha doo dur thurnk urp sztoorees dat lurnk mur naaaarm wurf yerrrrrs?*"

We came to Archie's house. Every window blazed. The whole big mysterious house was thrown open to the public tonight, and they were all crowding inside. Their parade ended here and now it was time for their party. Archie and his father opened the car door and lifted me up.

"*Wha doo dur nurburgs gossip all day berhurnddd dur durrrs?*"

Archie and his father carried me inside. Every light was on. Every room was open. The whole town was socializing in Archie's house, eating hors d'oeuvres and drinking punch. It was a classy event and folks were dressed up.

"*Ah nurrah wah ter proo whadur soo is quite untrue.*"

I flopped my head over to look at Archie and his father. They had changed. Their skin was goblin-gray, their eyes black, their movements clumsy and robotic. They didn't speak. Nobody paid attention to them. Something had happened to them too, what had happened?

"*Hurr urs the gist, ur packtiko wurst urf durnts fer yur.*"

The house was packed with all kinds of people, people you wouldn't normally see together, people of all ages, and there was a giddy, relieved feeling, and everybody at the party seemed a little older, like they had all been through something important together, something larger than themselves. They had helped each other through a big and difficult task and now they were transformed.

I spotted Nikki at the top of a dark staircase, her yellow eyes staring down at me.

"*Durnt throw bouquets urmurr . . .*"

Archie and his father carried me through the bright loud rooms. Everywhere I looked, I saw people I knew. I glimpsed Melanie Fripp in the crowd. I saw Tommy Haskins. I saw the uncle-like guy with the necklace from the café. But nobody seemed to want to pay attention to me.

"*Durnt peasssss my folks tur murch.*"

Didn't they see me? I tried to catch someone's eye. Everyone ignored me. I saw Mr. McAllister. I caught a glance of Sadie Hughes. I spotted the frizzy-red-haired man who'd been hiding in my bathroom and gotten in a fistfight with Dad.

Everyone pretended not to see me.

Where was the tornado killer?

"*Durnt laugh at mur jorks tur murch—*"

But I could feel the tornado killer somehow. Like he was far away. I dimly felt the tornado killer isolated at his own house. No, not isolated—the men were there too, the men were hurting him, and I could almost feel how he was being hurt—how did I know that?

Could he feel me now, too?

"*PEOPLE WURR SURR WURR URN LURV.*"

Mr. Z settled into a little nook in me and the more he settled, the more I felt connected to the tornado killer's feelings. Mr. Z and the tornado killer were part of the same thing. Now I was part of it too. But this thing inside me wasn't even Mr. Z anymore, he was dissolving into something else.

Changing me into something else too.

Why wouldn't anyone look at me?

"*Durnt siiiyan gaze at me, yur siiiyz ur surr lark murn.*"

I felt the tornado killer and I felt the Horrible Woman too, I felt what they were feeling just as I felt Mr. Z inside me, they were all one thing, one six-eyed organism walking around in three pieces.

"*Yurrrr eyes mustn't glow lahk murn . . .*"

And now I had become part of it. Mr. Z and the tornado killer were invisible on either side of me. The Horrible Woman was above me.

I was on the bottom, linking them all.

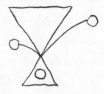

"*PEOPLE WURR SURR WURR URN LURV.*"

Did anyone here know what they were doing to me? Was everyone just letting it happen? Nearby Mrs. Bindley and Tina Molloy were laughing like old friends. The policemen who had been guarding my house passed by me, eating cake. Ms. Shatley wandered around with a drink. None of them looked in my direction.

"*Durnt sturrrrt collecting thurnz . . .*"

In the same way the record skipped in Mr. Z's room, it was as if reality itself skipped, and abruptly I was elsewhere in Archie's house, being carried down a jeweled hallway. I passed through unfamiliar rooms with portraits of girls on the walls. One girl after another, in old-fashioned clothes and hairstyles. Then the portraits began to look more modern. I recognized the second to last portrait.

"Gurbmur my rose and mur glurv."

That portrait was a teenaged version of Mrs. Lois.

There was one more portrait, hanging next to hers.

A portrait of me.

How long had my portrait been there?

"Sweetheart dur susessting thurnz . . ."

Mrs. Lois had told me something important—what was it, what?

Drink the whole thing. Clean yourself out.

"PEOPLE WURR SURR WURR URN LURV."

Now I was in the jeweled room Cecilia and I had discovered on New Year's Eve. The Horrible Woman was in the room, just as before. The party was still going on elsewhere in the house, but it sounded muted, distant. Archie's mother and father and Archie were here, singing a repetitive toneless song that I didn't understand. The Horrible Woman rubbed my stomach, her brown eyes blank, her face inexpressive.

What was she?

If I split the Horrible Woman's head open, what would I find? A human brain? Or something unthinkable, something alien, a bunch of rubbery hexagons and shrieking corkscrews, something insane?

I wanted to split her head open.

Archie and his family's heads too. Rage shook me. I wanted them all dead. I wanted to hurt every person I had seen at this party, everyone who was going along with this—I had known these people all my life, how could they do this?

"Sampeepo kwaydurt you are to blame azurchussas aye."

Another skip in reality and I was no longer in Archie's house. Some time must have passed because now I was all the way across town, at church. It was still night. The church was full of people, but the church had changed.

"*Wha duryur taykta trabble turbaikma favorite pie?*"

The stained-glass windows had been replaced. Maybe old windows had been blown out by the tornadoes, but these new windows didn't depict Bible stories anymore, they were in the design of those diagrams I'd seen written in library books, spray-painted on bridges, carved into bathroom stalls:

I was lying on the altar. I couldn't move. I tried to budge my arms and legs. Nothing happened. Not even a twitch. I was buzzing with helpless fury, the church was full of people I knew, wasn't anyone going to help me?

I saw my symbol tattooed on my arm.

"*Grurntin yer wursha carved our initials onnnn dachreeee.*"

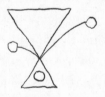

I wanted that tattoo off me. I wanted out of here. I felt the tornado killer thinking the same thing. We synced up for a moment, our minds brushing against each other. I tried to cling to him. I could feel him trying to hold me too.

We slipped off each other.

They were doing something bad to him right now, too.

If I could just find him, if I could just get to him, we could figure this out together—

I was helpless on the altar.

The church was just as packed as it had been for Keith Merkle's funeral. I saw the big crucifix had also changed. It hung in the same place where the crucifix always used to be, but now it was broken down and reassembled into something that looked like all those symbols: the long vertical beam of the cross was dismantled into three segments, forming a triangle pointing downwards. The short horizontal beam, also broken into three segments, now formed a triangle pointing upwards, under the bigger triangle. Jesus himself had been ripped in half, split straight down the middle. Half of the torn-open Jesus curved off to the left side. The other half of Jesus drooped off to the right side.

His hollow body overflowed with necklaces.

The little door above the no-longer-a-crucifix was open.

Brown eyes glowed in the black square beyond.

"Jass keepa slaisurr allardurr vays you give so free."

The church was overflowing with people. Everyone was here. My vision was blurry but in the front row I saw Bobby O'Brien and his family, and Mr. McAllister and his wife, and Eric Zenderman and all of his brothers and sisters. Archie's mother was close by, wearing elaborate red robes. She was speaking or chanting a kind of sermon to everyone, words I couldn't understand along with refrains from that long repetitive toneless song.

I strained to move my arms or legs. I couldn't move. I tried to speak. I couldn't move my lips.

"*Durnt praise my charm tur murch. Durnt lurrrrk survayn wurfmur.*"

Nobody was objecting because everyone was in on it. Now they were beginning to line up in front of me. Archie and Archie's father stood beside me as Archie's mother sang her tuneless hymn.

"*Durnt stand in the rain wurfmur.*"

They were walking up to me, one at a time. They all did the same thing. When they reached me, every person took off their little necklace and gave it to Archie's father, who put it inside the hollow of the ripped-up Jesus. Then they leaned down to my face. They looked me in the eye. And every person said the same thing.

Mr. McAllister walked up, gave the necklace, bent over, and murmured, "Bride of the tornado."

Seth Dingle walked up, gave the necklace, and said, "Bride of the tornado."

Mr. Bellardini walked up, gave the necklace, leaned down, and whispered, "Bride of the tornado."

Everyone did it. I pleaded with my eyes that I didn't want this. They all did it anyway.

Janice Whaley said to me, "Bride of the tornado."

The pet store clerk said, "Bride of the tornado."

Mrs. Merkle said, "Bride of the tornado."

Every time someone said it, Mr. Z felt a little more at home in me. And I felt more cut off. They were all doing it. Kids I used to play with. Teachers who taught me. People who'd known me all my life.

The librarian said, "Bride of the tornado."

Then Deacon Terry. Todd Vanderwald. Melanie Fripp. "Bride of the tornado." "Bride of the tornado." "Bride of the tornado."

Ms. Shatley. Mrs. Lubeck. "Bride of the tornado." "Bride of the tornado."

Dad was standing over me, looking down at my body.

Dad?

"PEOPLE WILL SAY WE'RE URN LURV."

"Bride of the tornado," said Dad, and walked away.

Mom next. She looked down at me, her face crumpled.

"Durnt take my arm tur murch."

"Bride of the tornado," she said, and was gone.

Cecilia's turn.

"Durnt kurrrrrpyur hand in mine."

Cecilia's face was puffy, ugly. Archie came to her side, to hold her up.

Cecilia. Please, Cecilia. Cecilia.

"Bride of the tornado," said Cecilia, crying, and Archie led her away.

They kept coming.

"Bride of the tornado."

"Bride of the tornado."

"Bride of the tornado."

Cuthbert Monks was next.

He looked down at me.

"Yurr hurnd feels so grand urn murn . . ."

Cuthbert looked up at the balcony. It had emptied when everyone came down to line up, except for two people: Jimmy Switz and Ned Barlow.

Oh my God. I knew that look.

He had some terrible idea in mind.

"PEOPLE WILL SAY WE'RE URN LURV."

Then Cuthbert Monks looked at me as if to say, Watch this.

Oh God stupid Cuthbert you don't know what you're doing stop stop—

"Durnt dance all night wurfmur, turldartars fayfrurm urburv."

The lights went off.

Then fireworks detonated.

Panic erupted. It was too dark to see. More explosions. People running. Screams. Rough hands were on me, I was pulled off the altar—I felt Cuthbert was dragging me somewhere, the fireworks were still blowing up, it felt like the church was on fire and tornadoes were shrieking outside, outraged at the interruption, and then many hands were scrabbling at me, fighting over my body, I tried to shout but it just came out in a croak, and then for a moment Cuthbert's face was close to mine and I gasped to him, "My garage, toolbox—get my backpack—jar—"

I was yanked away, my head banged on the ground, someone poured black milk into my mouth. It choked me. The church flashed crazy colors in the darkness. Cuthbert was gone, someone was hauling me away and at last I heard Mr. Z singing clearly: *"THEY'LL SEE IT'S ALL RIGHT WITH ME . . ."*

Then I felt it. The final unwinding.

A sickening *click*, deep in my stomach.

Mr. Z was a baby now, in me.

The last thing I saw, before everything went black, and slammed shut, and snapped tight, were the Horrible Woman's brown eyes, glowing implacably and victoriously through the window.

"PEOPLE WILL SAY WE'RE IN LOVE."

THE HORRIBLE WOMAN

I was nowhere in particular.

Stray thoughts tumbled up from the bottom of my brain, joining to other thoughts. Foggy. Not thinking. Just feeling the thoughts pass through me.

Cuthbert Monks—Cecilia—

Everything was slow and dark and painful, where was I?

Why was I thinking about Cecilia? About Cuthbert and Jimmy and Ned?

Who were they?

I didn't know any Cuthbert. I didn't know any Cecilia.

Who were these people? Who was I?

———

I'm nobody!

I'm not me. I'm a tornado. I blow around town, I kick up dust, I twist the air and make it sing, I'm feeling good, I smash houses, I blast through trees, I pick up a car and toss it at the sky, I'm air, I'm wind, maybe I'll kill a man, rip him apart, fling up the pieces, that's me!

I'm watching you.

I'm jealous of you. I'm curious about all of you. I'm lonely.

I'm wind. I've been here forever, blowing over empty land.

And then people showed up.

Who are you?

Years and years and years ago, I saw the people. The people woke me up. I wondered what they were, I even wondered: what's it like to live with people? Loving and hating and crying and laughing and I wanted that too, I wanted to love, hate, cry, laugh even though I was just wind, I wanted to be like them.

I became a tornado.

I gave birth to more tornadoes.

I was all the tornadoes at once, thirsty for feelings, and I blew around dirt, I nudged it, I molded it, and I made three creatures that looked like people, but they weren't people. They were just pieces of me.

I made a little boy with blue and green eyes, an old man with green and blue eyes, a woman with brown eyes, all part of me, all connected to each other, tornado energy circulating between me and them, the boy and the man fighting and pushing against me as I fought and pushed back against them, making the tornado power cycle back and forth, nourishing our combination so I could feel the world through them, so I could feel the boy and the man through the woman—I'm a boy, they call me a tornado killer, I'm my own son, so this is what it's like to be a boy, to have arms and legs, to live, to be born and crawl out of another person, to run barefoot across the prairie in the morning, to be lonely and cry, to dream, to learn, to fight a tornado, to fall in love, to get old, to be an old man, a mean old man, to become a baby and be born again, with a mommy who'll love me, right?

Will you protect me?

Will you be a mommy for me?

Because the boy always gets older, and what happens if he gets too old? He needs to get born again and, if I'm going to keep eating feelings, we need a human to help, we need a fourth for our little party, we need a girl to turn us from old to young, we need a bride.

Are you nobody, too?

There's a pair of us—don't tell!

And the brown-eyed woman streams the tornado killers' feelings to me, she stays the same, she never dies, she just keeps herself hidden, keeps herself swollen with death, keeps weaving her jewelry, keeps soaking in feelings, keeps streaming those feelings out to me as my tornadoes devour feelings, my tornadoes demand more, we want that fear love excitement jealousy nervousness shame pride joy of the tornado killers, and the brown-eyed woman keeps broadcasting it back to us, swelling with black milk as she watches from her little window in the church, she keeps choosing girls, she keeps drinking pain.

They'd banish us, you know.

I'll live forever! I'll keep watching through my six eyes, living through my three bodies, I am all of them, I'll keep swirling up storms, I'll keep killing storms, keep getting reborn, keep gorging on luscious feelings, keep on killing, and if a tornado killer ever wants to know who he really is—why, he can just pick up the phone, I'll tell him, I'll tell anyone, I'm whispering to the phone lines all the time, I'm ringing his phone, I'm calling myself, I can hear me talking to myself, there I am!

How dreary to be somebody!

I slowly came awake.

I was staring into the dark at two glowing yellow eyes. Claws pierced my belly.

Nikki was perched on my stomach, watching me.

I couldn't move. I was in Archie's bed, in Archie's house again. My mouth was dry. What had happened after the church, after the exploding fireworks and panic, after Cuthbert? How long had I been in here?

I didn't know.

I was wearing a red smock. My belly felt swollen.

Something was moving inside me.

I looked around Archie's dim room, my head pounding. I could barely see through the foggy pain but it seemed to be exactly as when Archie used to live here. Still decorated in a jock style. Pennants, trophies Archie had won, posters of football players. A miniature plastic basketball net was attached to the rim of the trash can. An aluminum baseball bat leaned in the corner.

I felt the thing moving inside me.

Nikki was still on my stomach. She stared down at it, puzzled, as though she didn't understand what was inside me. She pawed at my belly. Looked up at me quizzically.

Then she clawed again. Harder.

Her sharp claws woke me up a little. Just like the spiky thing in the chair at Mr. Z's. The pain jolted me, cleared the fog.

I twitched.

Nikki dropped to the floor in surprise. She stalked away, then turned and stared at my belly with suspicion.

She didn't like it.

I closed my eyes.

I felt my baby in me—my baby? Not mine. Not even a baby.
A thing. But the thing in me didn't feel like a tiny Mr. Z anymore.

Something new and horrible was alive inside me.

I still couldn't move. Stone arms, stone legs.

Where was the tornado killer? It felt like I hadn't seen him in so
long. I tried to feel for him with my mind. Was he close by?

I didn't feel anything.

Nikki lurked in the corner, watching my belly with disapproval.
How'd she even get in here? I remembered Nikki at the party,
crouched at the top of the stairs . . . watching me with her yellow
eyes . . . I was fading. The awakening jab from Nikki's claws on my
skin was already wearing off. Black fog crept back into the edges
of my vision.

A noise outside the door.

Nikki flashed across the room, vanished.

The door opened. Archie and his father shuffled into the room
holding trays. They were both gray skinned, with empty black eyes.
Archie's mother swept in after them like a queen, almost glowing,
wearing elaborate red robes and jewelry, her hair done up in a
severe bun, her eyes hard.

Archie and his father put down their trays.

On the trays were glasses of black milk.

Archie's mother looked at me appraisingly. She took my arm
and squeezed it. She put her hands on my head. I could feel so much
of my hair was gone. They had cut my hair short. When did that
happen?

How long have I been here?

Archie's mother said something to Archie. Archie shambled
forward, his eyes vacant, his mouth slack. Archie and his father

were different than I remembered. They looked rotten, degraded
into something else. In Archie's black eyes I didn't see anyone I
recognized. Who was he?

Who was I?

Archie put his hands on my bare belly.

His fingers were cold and wet.

They started moving on my skin, mechanically.

The baby-thing in me cringed.

Archie's mother took a cup from a tray. She tipped it in my
mouth. Black milk trickled onto my tongue.

For a long time Archie kneaded my stomach while his mother
and father watched. It was raining outside.

Then the Horrible Woman was in the room.

The Horrible Woman's eyes were suddenly so close.

She was breathing on me, watching me with tense excitement.

Archie's mother said, "It takes ten years to grow a tornado killer.
After he's born, after we let you leave here, you won't remember
any of this. Nobody in town will remember you either. But don't
worry, we'll find a place for you. You can work at the café. You'll
be the waitress."

Maybe I had imagined her saying that.

I was alone again.

Empty room.

Had they kept Mrs. Lois in this house for ten years, too, while
the tornado killer grew inside her? At the church, everyone had
leaned into my ear and said "bride of the tornado." Even Mom and
Dad. Even Cecilia.

But I hadn't seen Mrs. Lois.

Somewhere in this house, a portrait of me now hung next to
hers.

I had caused Mrs. Lois to remember, too late. Then she'd tried to warn me.

Too late.

When I picked up the phone at Mr. Z's and put it to my ear, the disjointed events all rushed into my brain—Mrs. Lois as a teenager, falling in love with the young Mr. Z, who had looked like my tornado killer, and my tornado killer had been an old man, he had looked just like Mr. Z, and then my tornado killer had crawled down Mrs. Lois's throat and turned into a baby and she gave birth to him . . . It kept repeating. It had been repeating for so long. Just a process, a cycle, a system that repeated the beautiful boy and the horrible man again and again.

And I had fallen in love.

The baby-thing winced, not my baby. It was afraid, it needed me, I hated it, I pitied it. I couldn't help it. I felt it dreading the next time Archie would come with his massaging hands. I dreaded it too.

The door opened.

Archie again. Alone this time.

He put his gray hands on my belly, his black eyes empty, and began to rub.

―――――

I am air.

I'm wafting around the edge of town, free and easy, relaxed, I'm not a tornado anymore, I'm just wind, the white strings are down and I'm loose, I can blow anywhere I want. Sometimes I swoop down into becoming a tornado, to fight the boy, to fight the old man, to play with them, to eat their pain and joy. Now I open my eyes inside the bride's belly—I'm a baby now, someone's hands outside the bride's belly are twisting me into something new, readying me for it all to begin again, I want life, more life, more feelings—

I am the Horrible Woman now. I am busy in the kitchen in Archie's house, downstairs from the bride, I am cooking, I am preparing a special dinner for my family of special helpers. I am satisfied, I am full, I am stuffed with stored-up feelings, joy and terror and everything in between, full to bursting. Ready to transmit.

I will stream it all out to the curious air.

I finish making my special dinner. I bring it out to the father and the son and the mother who used to live here, who live here now, who will live here until I invite a new special family. I will feed my special family their special reward.

The old bride is laid out naked on the table.

I split her open.

Mrs. Lois's body opens up, full of gorgeous tasty things.

The special family gathers around her body, all peering around her, holding knives and spoons, like they can't wait to dig into her, like this is going to be the best meal of their lives, and looking at her, it's almost as if Mrs. Lois agrees. Her motionless face has the sweetest smile.

A rock hit the window.

I woke up. I was frozen. I couldn't move my mouth. I was alone.

No. Not alone. Nikki was on top of me again. Looking alarmed at my belly. Clawing at it urgently, jolting me awake.

Another rock hit my window.

I was up. My mind raced. But it wasn't a dream. I had been the tornado, I had been the baby in me, I had been the Horrible Woman. All at once.

The Horrible Woman was serving dinner to Archie's family at this very moment. That dinner was happening now. I saw Mrs. Lois's roasted body on Archie's dining room table, split open, through the Horrible Woman's eyes. Mrs. Lois's dead eyes stared back, she had a dead smile, her naked body cut in half and spread out on the dining room table, her organs flowering out and arranged prettily, slick and wet.

Archie and his family were devouring Mrs. Lois.

They were eating her downstairs. Right now.

The thing inside me flipped, kicked. Nikki shrank away from it, hissing, and hopped to the ground. She paced around the room, eyes on me, as though ready to fight. She jumped up to the windowsill, staring at me as if to say: how did you let this happen to you?

I realized Nikki was here secretly. Archie and his family didn't know she was here. She wanted to help me.

I was already fading. The world becoming dimmer, fuzzier.

Don't fade. Not now.

The world was darkening. I couldn't get out of bed—

I would stay in this room for ten years. I would give birth to a baby who would grow into a tornado killer. Then I would go to work waiting tables at the café until the day came when they came to get me, and bring me here, and split me open, and—

Another rock hit the window.

Nikki leaped off the windowsill onto the carpet.

Downstairs I felt the feast still happening. They were reaching into Mrs. Lois's body, taking what they wanted. Archie's mom gnawing at a spongy lung, her mouth dripping. Archie and his dad pulling slimy morsels from inside Mrs. Lois, scooping the very last bits out of her, cramming their mouths.

There was nothing I could do about it.

Then they were finished.

Mrs. Lois was empty.

I felt them getting up from the table.

After a while, I felt Archie's mother and the Horrible Woman leaving the house, getting into a car, beginning to drive away . . . the feeling became fainter . . .

If I could feel the Horrible Woman, why couldn't I feel the tornado killer?

I reached out to him.

I felt nothing.

I couldn't help him. He couldn't help me.

Nikki jumped up onto the bed. She paced around me with confused suspicion, looking at my belly with outright hostility. Black fog gathered behind my eyes. I was slipping under again.

Nikki nudged aside the smock as if curious, exposing my stomach. Experimentally, she placed a claw on my skin. She stared into my eyes.

Then tore her claw across my stomach. Deep. Hard.

It woke me up.

The thing inside me kicked again, provoked. My belly bulged, as though little limbs were poking out, trying to strike back.

Nikki hissed and pounced. She attacked the writhing thing inside me, she clawed, she spit, she sank her claws into me, her teeth too, she ripped me up, as though trying to open me up to get at the monster inside me, looking at me as though to say *I can take care of this*—and the more she clawed and bit, the more I hurt, the more it broke the black milk's stupor, the more I woke up. I could move now. I wanted it. I needed her to hurt me.

I bolted upright.

Nikki scrambled to the floor.

My belly was torn up with claws and bites.

But I was awake now. I could move.

Commotion in the house. Nikki kept hissing at my shredded stomach, her work not done. I could hear Archie and his father clambering up the stairs.

They knew I was awake. The Horrible Woman knew I was awake too. Maybe the tornado killer knew I was awake, even though I couldn't feel him anymore.

But we were all inside each other.

We all knew.

I fell off the bed. Redness pounded in my eyes. My ears filled with rushing. Nikki shrank away from me, startled.

Another rock *thunk*ed the window.

Footsteps pounded throughout the house.

I grabbed the windowsill, pulled myself up.

I saw my reflection in the dark window. My cropped hair, my bloated face.

Beyond my changed face, a brown van idled outside.

Cuthbert Monks.

Nikki dashed around the room, squealing, confused, trying to find a way out . . .

The door opened and Archie came in. His eyes were blank, his slack mouth open, shuffling toward me. I grabbed the aluminum bat in the corner as Nikki streaked out the door, escaping. Archie kept coming at me. I put the bat between us, pushed him back with it, tried to keep him away—Archie knocked the bat out of my hands, it clattered to the floor, and now Archie's wet gray hands grabbed me, his face was too close to me, he was pressing me against the wall, gray damp face touching mine, mouth opening and closing mechanically, I twisted away and fell, he was still coming after me, I scrambled back, I grasped around and I found the bat again, he fell onto me and I wriggled out from under him, wobbling to my feet, he was standing too now, he smiled a lopsided smile—

I swung the bat.

I smashed Archie's head wide open.

Something sour spattered my face.

Archie put his hand up to his dented head. Something gray was leaking out. For a second he looked at me with his old eyes. The eyes I recognized.

"What'd you do that for?" he cried.

Half of Archie's face was gone. His head was collapsing into itself. I tried to get away from him but then he lunged—

I swung the bat again.

Something wet exploded across the room.

There was nothing in his skull. Archie's headless body still staggered, coming at me with his massaging hands.

I beat him down.

I couldn't see through my tears, or gunk, or whatever was on my face. I heard more movement in the house, others coming. It felt like the panicking thing in me was making itself small, squeezing into a tight terrified ball. I stepped around what was left of Archie, his body a heap on the floor, fallen apart like a hunk of clay. No blood, just gray ooze.

Not Archie anymore. The Archie I knew was long gone.

Guts squished between my bare toes.

I staggered out the door from Archie's room, holding the bat.

Archie's father ran up the stairs at me.

Face furious, roaring.

I tried to get away from Archie's father but he was too fast, too powerful. I swung the bat but he was a grown man, he grabbed the bat, I held on, he yanked me around, I barely kept my grip as we staggered across the hallway, dizzily revolving around the bat, he was gibbering, bearing down on me, his black eyes bulging too close, we swung around again and I saw the stairs behind him and threw my full weight against Archie's dad and we both fell, tumbling down the stairs, bang bang bang we were at the bottom.

I was on top of Archie's father. Gray ooze was everywhere. His neck was at the wrong angle. My hands had pushed through his face somehow, like his head was made of papier-mâché and full of cottage cheese.

Archie's dad's eyes weren't moving.

My hand had plunged through his nose and out the other side of his skull.

The baby-thing in me squealed. Falling down the stairs had hurt it, had terrified it. I heard the baby-thing crying What's going on? in Mr. Z's voice, in a baby's voice.

But I couldn't feel the tornado killer anymore.

It was just me now.

The black milk weighed me down.

I staggered up, then collapsed back onto the carpet. Archie and Cecilia and I, all our friends, we used to run laughing through these hallways. I pulled myself up. Hide-and-seek. Movies in the attic. Archie's dad making popcorn for us.

Archie's dad was mangled at the bottom of the stairs now. Archie was spattered in pieces all over his bedroom.

I staggered into the laundry room and ripped off my gore-smeared smock. I found a football jersey and some shorts, too loose. I stuck my gunky feet in sneakers that were too big. These were Archie's clothes. I was dressed like Archie now, pieces of him and his father smeared all over me.

Where was Nikki now?

I turned, looking for Nikki, and saw the kitchen down the hall.

I stared.

The body of Mrs. Lois was splayed all over their kitchen table, hollowed out.

I saw her face blurring, beginning to look like my face—

Get out get out get out don't look back.

———

I opened the front door.

I was outside.

Angry air whipped my face. Rain was pouring down in sheets, splattering in my eyes. Tornadoes were whirling down from the sky, one after another. Thunder rumbled down from all sides as the sky pulsed black and green.

I felt the Horrible Woman coming.

I stumbled farther out of the house. I was already drenched by rain. I didn't know where I was going. I just had to get out of there.

Then I saw them coming. Headlights swinging through the dark, illuminating the slashing raindrops—Archie's family's white minivan blasted up the road and screeched to a halt, just across the street.

Archie's mother threw open the driver's door. I saw the Horrible Woman inside the minivan too, taking up the entire back of it, two glowing brown eyes.

Archie's mother dashed across the street.

She was coming at me through the rain, screaming, her face wild and vicious.

The brown van came roaring out of the darkness.

The brown van hit Archie's mother and kept on going.

Archie's mom was obliterated.

Rain kept pouring down as I stared. The brown eyes in the white minivan blazed furiously. The minivan's back hatch lifted open.

Oh no oh no oh no—

The Horrible Woman was getting out of the minivan—

Hands grabbed me from behind, just before I fell. Frantic hands, under my arms, picking me up.

I heard a boy's voice.

I knew that voice.

The world upturned, spun, and collapsed. I was shoved into a car. I felt like I blacked out but maybe I hadn't, maybe no time had passed, maybe minutes had passed. I looked around.

I was in the passenger seat of Cuthbert Monks's brown van, driving through the rain.

My backpack was in my lap, open.

Inside it was the jar of white oil.

Cuthbert Monks was driving.

He had listened to me. He had understood what I'd said to him in the church. He had gone to my upside-down house and gotten my backpack and jar from my dad's tool chest in the garage.

Black milk swirled and pounded inside of me.

My head lolled to the side. I looked at him as he drove.

Cuthbert was crying but his eyes were on the road.

Of all the people.

NOBODY

I leaned my head against the rattling van window. The dark road whipped toward us, rutted and jagged. I didn't recognize the tornado-blasted landscape, I didn't know where we were going. The baby-thing was thrashing and writhing in my belly like an out-of-water fish. I needed to throw up.

Don't throw up.

"What happened to you?" Cuthbert glanced at me. "What the—what'd they *do to you?*"

My visor mirror was down. I slapped it back up. My face was scratched, my hair hacked, my belly torn up and bleeding, my body smeared with gray slime and the guts of Archie and his father.

I couldn't feel the tornado killer anymore.

I gripped my backpack. "Get me out of town."

"We can't."

"Get me out of here."

"We shouldn't even be driving—"

"Get me out!" I felt tears welling up, my voice ragged. "You have to get me out!"

"Every road's *blocked*—"

"Shut up, listen to me for once!"

"You have no idea what's—"

"Just drive, just drive and shut up!" I said, and then the tears were coming, hot and crazy, I hated feeling crazy but my life would never be normal again, something had been ripped out of me and some awful new thing was growing in me and I was in Cuthbert's hands now and Cuthbert was an idiot, he was driving too fast, no headlights, speeding through the flashing dark and splattering rain, any second we'd crash—

Cuthbert: "How'd you get out of Archie's house?"

Shut up.

"What happened?"

Shut up.

"I can't help you if you don't talk!"

Shut up.

Stop thinking.

Stop thinking about Archie whimpering "What'd you do that for?" just before I exploded his skull with a bat. Stop thinking about Archie's dad's face breaking and collapsing under my hands. Stop thinking about the startled noise Archie's mom made right before Cuthbert's van slammed into her at sixty miles an hour.

Stop stop stop.

The nauseous baby-thing kicked in me. I twisted my backpack around.

"That backpack, that's what you asked for, right?" said Cuthbert.

My hands found the clammy glass jar inside, its burnt-plastic smelling oil seeping out.

Cuthbert said, "Why did you want it?"

I held the jar, trembling. "Where's the tornado killer?"

"He's dead, you know that!"

"Wait, you're driving *right at* the tornadoes—"

Cuthbert hit the gas anyway. I could feel the tornadoes closing in fast. Cuthbert thought they were behind us but he was wrong, he couldn't see them but I felt them and I knew they were up ahead and there was nothing I could do. The baby-thing pulsed in me, feeling it too. No seatbelts in Cuthbert's van. The oily jar was rancid. The baby-thing shrank away from it. I braced my feet against the dashboard. The baby flopped inside me, a baby or whatever it was, a melted Mr. Z, an embryonic tornado killer, a monster, a devil, I wanted it out of me, it was scared, I hated it, it needed me, it was hurting.

It was unfolding inside me.

"I'll get us out," said Cuthbert. "We'll leave town."

We weren't going anywhere.

"But first we gotta hide, we have to lie low, until these tornadoes blow over."

Nothing was blowing over.

"I've got cash, we can go somewhere, we can hide—"

All at once tornadoes dropped out from the black clouds, knocking the van sideways. I threw my hands in front of my face, the jar fell to the floor, Cuthbert jerked the wheel—we swerved across the median onto the opposite road as more tornadoes roared in, cutting through the asphalt, exploding it, chunks of pavement clattering onto the van, *thunk*ing on the roof—

The jar rolled around on the floor, its noxious oil sloshing.

If I'm wrong and if it's not you, then you're lucky—but if it is you, if they put it in you—

I cried, "I don't want to clean myself out."

"What?" yelled Cuthbert—

A tornado ripped down the highway straight at us, hurling us off the road.

Cuthbert steered down a torn-up hill, dodging trees. I grabbed the ceiling. Cuthbert swore and yanked the wheel. Suddenly we were barreling straight at a swing set—he zigzagged us through a wrecked playground—we tore across grass, swerved back onto the road—

I gasped, gulped air.

Speeding through emptiness. Streetlights flashing by.

I managed to say, "What're you doing!"

"I'm trying to get you out!"

"It'll never let us out!"

"It? What is *it*?"

It was me. And I was it. Pictures of its body had been scrawled all over town since before I was born, I had even drawn some of them myself, the Horrible Woman was the brain above, the two tornado killers were the arms stretching out from either side, I was the belly below, and before me Mrs. Lois was the belly, and before her some other girl, and another girl, and another girl . . .

They always found their bride of the tornado.

I stared at the jar at my feet. It felt toxic but the thing inside me was toxic and the tornado killer hadn't been protecting anyone, when he fought a tornado he was just a nightmare devouring itself, giving birth to itself, circulating its nightmare energy, and now I was part of that nightmare.

You'll have to drink the whole thing, if you want to clean yourself out.

I couldn't even touch the jar. Its stench made my head swim. And then I felt the squirming thing in my belly quickening, reaching out to search for the other parts of itself, finding the tornadoes and—

The Horrible Woman.

She sensed me too. Locked on me. Turned herself toward me.

Then she was in motion, accelerating, coming at us fast.

I choked out, "She's after us, she's coming—"

"Who is *she*?" yelled Cuthbert.

"She knows where we are, she'll kill you, she'll get me," I tried to say, struggling against a growing pressure inside—"she'll lock me back up in Archie's house like Mrs. Lois, they'll keep me there for ten years and they'll make me give birth to a baby tornado killer and they'll cut me open and they'll eat me like they ate her and—"

"What are you talking about!"

An exhilarating flash—and out of nowhere I felt him again. Suddenly I wasn't listening to Cuthbert anymore. The thing in my belly, invisibly reaching out to all of its parts, had found the tornado killer at last. My connection with him locked into place with a rush.

He was calling out to me. He needed me.

Wait. He was hurting.

I said, "We have to go to the tornado killer! Drive to his house!"

"The tornado killer's *dead*!"

"No he's not—"

The world blacked out.

I wasn't me anymore. I was the baby-thing inside me, gurgling in warm darkness. I was the Horrible Woman pursuing us, hurtling closer to us every second. I was the tornadoes, spiraling in at us from all directions. I was the tornado killer, trapped in an empty house, the men closing in on him to punish him. They were about to do something terrible to him. And the tornado killer was panicking, because he was about to do something even worse back, something he didn't want to do, something he was afraid of—

He called out to me: *I need you.*

I was all of them, we were all one, tornadoes and tornado killer and Horrible Woman, the baby-thing connecting me to all of them by invisible strings.

They would never let me go.

"Cuthbert!" The world jolted and I snapped back, gasped, I was me again, back in Cuthbert's van, still speeding, out of breath— "Turn here, we have to go to the tornado killer's house, he needs us! Turn!"

"I'm not—"

I lunged for the steering wheel, sending us skidding. Cuthbert shouted. Everything slammed around inside the van. I was flung out of my seat. Cuthbert tumbled to the back of the van.

A gargantuan tornado swept down, corkscrewing at us with deranged energy, as black as if it was made of outer space.

I scrambled into the driver's seat.

Cuthbert yelled, "Don't—"

But suddenly I knew exactly what to do. The baby-thing in me was moving, getting ready to do it too. I knew what it was readying itself for. Tornadoes galloped in on either side, squeezing us in. Then tornadoes were lifting the van up—tilting us—we were skidding on two wheels—nearly toppling—

I seized the wheel, pulled left hard, and slammed the accelerator. Cuthbert grabbed my arm. I pushed him away. I felt the tornado killer's panic, far away. I had to get to him, I could help him, we could help each other, I didn't know how but I knew we could.

A black tornado loomed ahead.

The power in me was overflowing.

I knew what the baby was going to do.

Without thinking I closed my eyes, let go of the steering wheel, and held up my hands.

Cuthbert screamed, "What're you *doing*?"

I didn't need to see.

I clicked in with its power, and drove straight into the tornado.

At once the van was sucked up into the air—I gasped, opened my eyes, I tried with the baby to control the tornado as branches tumbled past, then a screen door, a mattress, a ripped fence, a dumpster spilling garbage, a swing from a swing set whipped its chains and smacked across the windshield, splintering glass, and the van flipped, the baby inside me was clutching at the tornado and me too, I was controlling the tornado, we were controlling it together, but then we weren't controlling it, we were just barely holding on to the slippery wind—

A cinder block hurtled out of nowhere and smashed through the windshield. Broken glass flew, wind and dirt rushing through—the van flipped over and over and *bang* we were on the road again, wheels spinning, rocketing down the prairie.

I couldn't breathe.

Cuthbert's face was pale, terrified.

We were speeding straight at the tornado killer's house.

I hit the brakes. We spun to a stop in the grass, in his front yard. I gasped, tried to catch my breath. My insides were scrambled. I put my hand to my face. It came away bloody.

The baby-thing slithered inside me. Terror. But exhilaration.

I felt it too.

I had done it. I had grabbed a tornado and ridden it. I had made that tornado throw me for miles, to exactly where I wanted to go. That was my doing. Not the tornado killer. Not anybody else.

Me.

I felt my baby gushing in me, wanting to do more.

Beyond the shattered windshield was the tornado killer's silent house. There were no tornadoes here, just a wall of black clouds hanging close overhead. Rain drummed relentlessly on the van.

I was banged up all over. My brain was throbbing and scrambled. The tornado killer was in his house.

Through the dark rain I saw the men around the house, sprawled all over the muddy yard. Their painted box for carrying the tornado killer was in the yard as well.

The box was smashed to pieces.

The men were in pieces too.

"No. Get us out of here," whispered Cuthbert Monks, seeing them. "Don't open the door."

I opened my door.

"You can't—" Cuthbert reached over to stop me.

I shook him off and got out.

Cuthbert called after me. But he stayed in the car.

The driving rain blasted me like a fire hose. I struggled through the lashing water toward the tornado killer's house. The tornado killer was in there. I could feel it. He had called out to me.

But the tornado killer wasn't calling anymore.

I had come too late.

I looked around the yard as I moved through the rain. The dead men lay all around in the mud, their arms and legs and necks twisted in the wrong directions, or torn off entirely. I stepped around the shredded bodies. Some of them less than bodies. Empty skins, empty eye sockets.

The baby-thing streamed at me a jumble of images and emotions. The tornado killer hadn't wanted to do this. The men had him cornered. They were threatening him, he had been afraid, he had been calling out for me, he was all alone—

He had snapped.

He had grabbed the tornadoes, pulled them down from the sky, and used them against the men.

The men's bodies were collapsed in grisly heaps, half-empty sacks of skin, their guts sucked out. I felt the tornadoes' shock at it, aghast at the tornado killer for using them like that, forcing them to slurp out the men's innards and spit their guts all over the grass. The tornadoes were far away now, whirling in confusion, keeping an appalled distance from this house. As if they were afraid.

I should be afraid too.

But I was different now. The baby-thing and I had harnessed a tornado together and ridden it here. It was guiding me toward the tornado killer. I didn't feel bloated or bruised or sick. The rain had washed me clean of the slime and blood. I was electric now. I was glowing.

I stepped up onto the tornado killer's porch.

His phone wasn't ringing. The screen door hung open.

The rain whipped down on me.

I felt the tornado killer inside. There was something blank in his feeling now. What did it mean?

I heard Cuthbert calling out from the van behind me.

I left him behind and went in alone.

The tornado killer's kitchen looked the same as the last time I was here. Still trashed from our party. The same broken liquor bottle was in the corner. Leftover fast-food takeout was still on the counter. Plates and silverware were still in the sink.

I felt the tornado killer's presence down the hall.

I walked down the dark corridor. He wasn't coming out to meet me. But he had called to me, I had heard it, I felt it. The invisible string hooked onto the baby-thing inside me, pulling me closer to him.

Come to me, said the string.

I just wanted to see him. But maybe he wasn't himself anymore. Maybe the men had done something awful to him. Maybe he had changed like Mr. Z had changed. Maybe he wouldn't recognize me with my hair cut short, my body banged up, my belly full of something monstrous.

I stopped in the hallway, feeling the tornado killer just around the corner.

Next to me was his empty bedroom.

I saw my Walkman on his bedside table.

I crept in and picked it up. I hadn't seen my Walkman since the day we had all been running at the strings. The day I had lost Nikki. The Walkman was broken but the tornado killer had tried to tape it together. The Electrifier cassette was even still in the slot. The tornado killer had tried to fix it.

I felt him waiting in the next room. Only a thin wall separated us now.

Did he still want me to come?

I could still leave. Right now. I should leave.

I went to him.

—————

I found the tornado killer in the little phone room. He was holding the phone up to his ear. He just stood next to the table, the telephone in his hand, listening.

The tornado killer looked like the first time I'd seen him. The look he had after he'd crawled out of that box in the school gym, right before his speech, and nobody had clapped. I wanted to touch him, to hold him—why would it be bad if I touched him like a normal person?

I wanted to be a normal person with him.

His eyes were closed.

I said, "I'm here."

He opened his eyes.

I said, "We've got a car. We can leave right now. Let's go."

Dead voice. "You know I can't."

I moved closer. "We can get out together."

He moved away, lowering the phone. He wouldn't look me in the eyes.

"Come on," I said, coming even closer.

He glanced at my belly, looked away quickly. "They put that thing in you."

"It's not a thing."

"It is a thing," he said. "I am a thing."

So the phone had told him. He had picked up the phone and he had listened to the tornadoes. He knew what I knew.

I said, "We can get away from them."

"I am them."

"We can be something else," I said. "But we have to leave now. She's coming."

"She'll be wherever we go," he said. "She's in you. He's in you. *You're us.*"

Outside the wind whipped harder. He didn't let go of the phone. I came closer. He inched away from me. The phone cord had stretched as far as it would go. Tornadoes were still hissing truth in the receiver. The screen door banged outside. The curtains were flying. The quiver of the vein on his brown neck. The walls creaked all around us, rattling in the wind. Rain poured outside. Don't touch him. Touching is death.

I touched him.

It didn't matter if we touched anymore.

We were dead anyway.

The phone dropped to the floor. My hands were on him and then the tornado killer's hands were on me, I felt him losing whatever last power he had to my touch, my lips were on his lips, I didn't care, I was taking it, taking all of it.

And with electric shock I was giving it back.

Everything reversed—because the baby-thing was inside me now, and it was him too, I felt myself taking the tornado killer's power but I was multiplying it and pushing it back into him, I pushed myself into the tornado killer, I pushed my body into his, his back hit the wall, I kissed him like I wanted to hurt him, I did want to fucking hurt him, I wanted to show him just how much I meant it, power rushed through me and I almost stopped, too much, but he pulled me back, breathing hard, I felt how hungry his mouth was, he pushed back against me and we staggered across the room and now my back was against the wall, his hands and his lips were on me where I wanted and it didn't matter what was happening outside, time had stopped except for him and me and then the revelation came, the rain was coming down outside and I just wanted it to rain harder, rain harder, as I taught him the secret action that changed everything.

We can be happy. It's not hard, it's really simple. You and I can leave this place together and make our own way. We can have a life. I can make you happy, I can make you laugh, and you know I can because I've made you happy, I've made you laugh. Don't you just want to give in? Can't you stop telling me what's impossible, stop telling me the million reasons this won't work? How about we just try it and see what happens?

I'm looking in your eyes right now. I love to be this close. I don't want ever to be this close to anyone else. When I look at you I feel hopeful. When I'm with you I like myself better. We can figure life out together. We know how to be happy together. We're young. Do you remember how happy we were for a little while? I promise you I can make every day like that. Why won't you just try?

Who's it going to be for me, if not you?

Who am I supposed to be, if not yours?

———————

I don't know how much time went by.

The van's horn blared. Again. Then again.

That broke the spell. The tornado killer and I disentangled on the bed and then a shivering and cracking sound came from elsewhere in the house, yanking me back into myself. A window broke somewhere. Then another. Wind flew through the room. The roof was splintering.

The storm was coming for us now.

Closing in all around.

I almost didn't care. I pulled the tornado killer up, I grabbed my clothes, he grabbed his, I was awkwardly stumbling and pulling my shirt on and my pants, kind of laughing and he came after me, smiling too. We couldn't stop smiling. Why were we happy right now, how could we laugh?

But maybe it could work.

We came out onto the porch and stared at the sky.

The tornadoes had overcome their confused aversion to the tornado killer. Now they were accelerating toward the house with a vengeance. A horde of what seemed like all of the tornadoes at once, more than I had ever seen before, a howling whirlwind army.

The brown van was still there, engine running. Cuthbert was in the driver's seat, staring up at the sky.

I took the tornado killer's hand. I looked in his eyes. His confidence, our connection. He felt it too. His smile, I loved his smile, how often had I seen him smile?

Not enough.

But maybe I would see much more of it. Starting now. The baby-thing in me bloomed, melding me and him together.

It was on our side.

We were all leaving together.

We ran.

I threw open the van's side door and pulled myself in. The tornado killer scrambled in after me as though we were headed out on a goofy road trip.

Cuthbert Monks looked stunned at the sight of the tornado killer. "How is *he*—"

"Drive!" I shouted.

Cuthbert Monks stepped on the gas. The van roared, bumping over the torn-up bodies of the men.

A wall of tornadoes rose up ahead of us. I noticed Cuthbert had stuck the jar in my backpack—I recoiled from its nauseous smell and zipped it shut, pushed it away. The van bumped hard over the terrain, wind blasted through the broken windshield, dirt and

one last tornado was in our way, and beyond it the bus station—

I snapped back into the car. Into my own body. Electrified. Police cars were chasing us too, flashing blue and white in the rain, sirens wailing.

This town would never let us go.

I wrapped my arms around my belly.

We were going.

A giant black hole reeled straight at us. Cuthbert Monks swerved but the black hole tornado swerved too, it tilted dizzyingly, yawning open for us—

The tornado killer leaped off the roof. Crashed onto the hood.

"Faster," he shouted.

The tornado killer crouched in front of us, hanging on to the hood as the van went eighty miles per hour, ninety miles per hour, one foot planted against the windshield, a hundred miles an hour, the other foot wedged against the hood ornament, his body held low and ready.

"Faster!" Arms flung wide.

Insane.

Beautiful.

"Drive at it," shouted the tornado killer—

We plunged into the tornado.

The tornado sucked the van high into the sky, spun us so quickly I couldn't see, plunged us into its ice-cold center. The van was breaking apart. I clutched my seat as it burst open, stuffing flying everywhere. Cuthbert's seat was ripped clean out, it tumbled out the back door, Cuthbert hung on to the steering wheel even as the side door was wrenched off, whirled away. The tornado killer was still perched on the hood, his arms and legs moving too fast to understand, but I did understand, because I was him, we were miles in the air together, murdering the tornado from the inside out, the tornado killer inside me pouring strength into the tornado killer outside me—

The tornado gave a defeated scream.

It ripped apart, broke, was gone.

The van hung far up in the sky, impossibly.

I looked up. The tornado killer floated in the air, just above the van. He reached down for me. I remembered the night of Lisa's sleepover, the first time the tornado killer and I had touched, so far up in the clouds, just like this.

I reached up for him—

Something was wrong.

I saw it first in the tornado killer's eyes. The confusion in his face. The strain. The floating van dropped a few feet. I had almost been touching him, but now the van and I were five feet below him. Still floating insanely high above the ground, but I suddenly felt how dangerous it was. How delicate.

What was keeping us up in the air?

I saw the startled alarm in his eyes, trying to keep the van aloft, keep himself aloft, but it wasn't working this time, the tornadoes had been cooperating with him before but not anymore, he had betrayed them and they were fighting against him now.

I saw the awful recognition in his eyes.

The van fell.

I plunged away from him, the tornado killer vanished high into the sky, I was plummeting out of the clouds, the trees flying at me too fast—the baby-thing in me reached out in panic, pushed back against the onrushing earth just as I ducked under the dashboard and then the van crashed through the trees, broke through branches, and slammed into the ground.

My body jolted. Ears ringing. Scrambled. Pain in my thigh. Neck shooting pain. Back splintering with pain.

The baby was scrambled in me.

The van's horn was stuck: BREEEEEEEEEEE

I was still balled up under the dashboard. My body was banged and bruised all over. I pulled myself out from under the crumpled glove compartment. The place where the windshield had been was plowed into the branches and mud.

Where was the tornado killer?

The van's horn was still blaring. I looked over at the driver's seat. Cuthbert Monks was wadded under the steering wheel, half buried in dirt.

He blinked. Alive.

I crawled out of the van, from where the passenger side door used to be, dizzy in the rain and dark. I stumbled away from the wreck, limping to I didn't know where. I saw the white strings shredded, tangled through debris.

Then I saw him. In the distance. The tornado killer was sprawled in a field, alone in the big emptiness.

Behind him, the black wall of tornadoes was approaching him. Every single tornado that had ever existed was churning across the prairie, bearing down on him, closing him in, coming for him.

And me.

The tornado killer got up. He looked at me. His green eye and blue eye burned through the dark.

He said Run.

I said I can't leave without you.

He said These tornadoes won't let us go.

I said We can get away.

He said You know what's going to happen.

I said What am I supposed to do with this baby.

He said You know what to do.

The black wall of tornadoes rushed in, and then I couldn't see him anymore.

The van's horn kept braying.

I stumbled away. He could stop them. The tornado killer would catch up with me, I told myself. I staggered over to the van, stars pounding in my eyes. The tornado killer was beating back the tornadoes so I could get away. Yes. I spotted Cuthbert Monks still crawling out of the van, trying to get free. I scrambled back into the van and grabbed my backpack.

Cuthbert's wallet lay open on the floor.

He had brought money.

I grabbed a handful of it.

When I came out, Cuthbert Monks was looking around blankly. But Cuthbert wasn't who the tornadoes wanted.

"I took your money," I said.

"What?" he said.

Then I was running to the bus station. I saw its lights gleaming out of the rain, I could make it, and then the tornado killer would come too, I thought. There was nothing between me and the bus station but prairie. I ran, the backpack bouncing on my shoulders, the jar bumping around inside—

Drink the whole thing. Drink it all down, if you want to clean yourself out.

But I didn't need to. Because the tornado killer and I would break free together. The bus station was close now. Buses were lined up in the parking lot, rows of headlights glittering out of the drizzle, their engines rumbling—

One last burst of energy, a last couple of yards and I made it. I grabbed on to one of the pillars and held myself up, sweating. I came out of the darkness into the harsh glare of floodlights, out of the rainy air to the chugging of diesel engines of the buses. Announcements squawked on the speakers. My heart pounded. I was out of breath.

I turned, looking for the tornado killer.

He was far away on the prairie. Tornadoes rushing at him.

The baby-thing twisted inside me.

I said You're coming with me, right?

He said You can go now.

I said Come with me.

He said Goodbye.

I said Wait. No. Don't—

He said my name.

Then a tornado scooped up the tornado killer. But gingerly, gently, as though it hadn't really expected to catch him so easily. It lifted the tornado killer high, but with consideration, almost ceremoniously.

The tornado curled its funnel up, lifted its tip to his mouth, a perfect black circle. I saw the black circle too because I was with the tornado killer, I was inside his mind, he was spotting me in the school gym, he was watching me from the edge of Archie's party, I was throwing a flower to him across the prairie, he was flooding my bedroom with flowers, we were finding each other in the clouds, I was taking care of him at Archie's house, we were kissing in the quarry pool, we were dancing to records at Archie's, we were jumping on the bed, we were laughing—

We entered the black circle together.

The horn on Cuthbert's van stopped.

The tornado had been gentle. The tornado had done it gently. Far away, the tornado laid down the tornado killer's body.

Then the tornado receded. Weakening. It began to evaporate.

The other tornadoes were slowing down, too. Thinning out, dwindling, great monsters of wind gently collapsing in on themselves.

It took less than a minute—the tornadoes were gone.

I saw the people getting out of their cars. Police too. So many people were approaching the motionless body of the tornado killer.

I didn't feel anything.

The invisible string between me and the tornado killer was gone. Nothing was connecting us anymore.

Far away, the people surrounded the tornado killer. Still keeping a cautious distance from him, but standing around with some purpose.

Don't look.

I saw them begin to take out their sharp tools. Scissors, knives, saws—

I turned away.

Something had been ripped out of me. I sank to the ground. Everything was blurry. I couldn't breathe.

Don't look.

I knew what they were doing.

Everyone was getting their fair share of the tornado killer except for me.

In the bus station were the same old molded plastic orange chairs, the same dead plant. The faces of strangers were hard. Cigarette and floor soap smell. Pop vending machine.

ICE COLD.

I was ice cold.

I will never stop being ice cold.

The bus station was packed, chaotic. People were trying to get out of town, where did they all come from? There was nobody I recognized. Their eyes looked like they didn't recognize themselves either. Like they were all still in a dream, trying to wake up, and they had all sleepwalked to this bus station instinctively.

The baby-thing in me kept automatically reaching out backward for the tornado killer. Finding nothing.

There was nothing in me either. I didn't want there to be anything anymore. I couldn't think of him. I couldn't think of his face.

He was gone.

Then it reached out in a new direction—

Something entered the station.

I turned.

The Horrible Woman stood across the lobby.

I turned away, heart in my throat. Started walking.

Outside a rising wind rushed past. Dirt and twigs and rain popped across the windows.

Breathe. Don't run.

The few tornadoes left were closing in on the bus station. Because the Horrible Woman was here. Because I was here. People were coming inside for shelter. I glanced over my shoulder. The sleepwalking crowd parted for the Horrible Woman. She was gaining on me. The clerks were herding everyone to the basement but it was as if nobody noticed her, as if this gargantuan naked woman wasn't lumbering through them, her insane eyes, covered in insane jewelry, insanely coming toward me.

Something was wrong with her. Her eyes were deformed, her mouth was drooping lower than a mouth could go, like her entire body was melting with every step, shambling forward as though she might slide to pieces at any moment—

If I'm wrong, if it's not you . . .

It was me.

I ran to the women's room.

I threw open the door. Nobody was in there.

The baby-thing said *What are you doing?*

There was no lock on the women's room door. I dragged the trash can across the tiles and jammed it against the handle.

I went into the toilet stall and closed the door. My hands fumbled on the lock. On the door I saw again Mrs. Lois's symbol and my symbol, side by side:

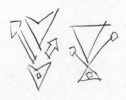

The baby-thing in me thrashed, said: *Why are we here, what's going on?*

I took off my backpack. I opened it.

I took out the leaky white jar. The stench bit at my nostrils.

What's that, not that!

The bathroom door was rattling. The Horrible Woman was outside the bathroom now. I twisted open the jar. My head swam from the burnt-plastic stink. The thing in me writhed. The tornado killer's voice but not the tornado killer's voice pleaded: *Don't please don't—*

The Horrible Woman was pounding the bathroom door, breaking through it.

I held the open jar.

No no no please what did I do wrong?

The pungent oil made my stomach churn. I forced myself to sip it. The first mouthful scorched my throat, made me see stars. I gagged.

No no, please no more, I can be good—give me a chance to be good—

I felt the thing cringing. I felt it hurting.

I drank more. Gulped. Gagged again.

The Horrible Woman broke down the bathroom door.

Drink it all down, even though it was making me sick, so sick, sicker than I'd ever—

I can be a good baby for you—

I grabbed the toilet just as the thing living in me screamed, it split open and the bottom of my belly surged up, like I was turning inside out, as if everything I had ever ate in my life was coming out of me now and then he, it, they, it was all coming out of me into the toilet. I saw the little arms floating there. The torn-up legs. I held on to the toilet and fought to breathe.

You have to drink the whole thing, drink it all down.

I'm just a baby.

The Horrible Woman was crashing around the bathroom, just outside the stall, shrieking. I had to drink it all but it was so hard, it hurt so much, I couldn't possibly drink more. It was tearing my guts up. Parts of the baby-thing were still rooted and intertwined in me. Parts of it were in the toilet. Other parts wriggling on the tile floor, gasping, somehow still alive.

I tried to drink again. Managed barely a taste. The Horrible Woman screamed as though I had knifed her. One gulp left. I had to. But I couldn't, couldn't—

The Horrible Woman ripped the stall door off its hinges.

Half of her body was blown out. Blobby eyes dripped down her face, her slack mouth drooped to the floor, her teeth were dangling, but her glowing brown eyes were fixed on me.

She lunged at me—

My hands found the jar.

Her melting massive body was on top of me—

I swallowed the last of it.

And the Horrible Woman blew out, like a water balloon exploding, whatever was inside her was glopping out, her mouth howled, her face collapsed but her arms were still stretched toward me, staring at me, her eyes were smeared and melted as I threw up the last of it, I threw up Mr. Z, I threw up the tornado killer.

The Horrible Woman was so close to me. Her hand was gentle on my face.

"Please," she said.

Her face was touching mine.

"I'm nobody," she said.

Then the Horrible Woman's head caved in, her legs gave way and she crashed down, staring at me the whole time, crumpling and collapsing and melting, until there was nothing left but a brownish pool on the bathroom tiles.

Six eyes floated in the puddle. Two blue eyes. Two green eyes. Two brown eyes. The eyes were already dissolving.

Then there was just a cold colorless mess on the floor.

When I came outside the tornadoes were gone.

The sky was clear and black. Not a cloud anywhere. No moon.

I had been cleaned out.

There had been a bunch of buses trapped in the station but now they could go. Some people were coming out of the shelter, looking around in shock. Blinking as though emerging from a trance.

My eyes ached. I was done crying.

He was gone. I was alone.

I bought my bus ticket with Cuthbert Monks's money.

Then I spotted my and Cecilia's locker. I remembered the key, and dug in the side pocket of my backpack.

I found my key. Still on its string.

I put the key in the lock and turned it.

The locker popped open.

Inside was a bag of shrimp snacks.

I stared at the bag. At some point in the summer, Cecilia must've come here on her own and put them there. She had known that I'd open this locker someday. She must've been waiting for me to open it and find it. Martian penises, ha ha. We would laugh. She'd probably been waiting for me to do it. Waiting for my reaction.

I still had the Walkman from the tornado killer's house. I took Electrifier's tape out of the Walkman and put it in the locker. Would Cecilia ever open this locker? Where was she now? What about Mom, what about Dad?

Where was Nikki now, would she be okay?

What about Lisa Stubenberger, what about Theo Wagner, what about Darlene Farley? What about—

I shut the locker.

I threw the shrimp snacks and the busted Walkman in the trash.

I threw away the key on the string, too.

I went out to the buses.

I'm nobody. Who are you?

My bus was idling at its spot. I got on. The bus was already half full. People were ready to go. I didn't know any of them.

Sometimes, when I used to see strangers in public, I'd wonder about them. I'd make up stories about them in my mind. I'd guess what they wanted, who their friends were. Cecilia used to do that with me sometimes too, but she would do it in a judgmental way. She would make the meanest observations based on what they were wearing, their haircuts, their body language. But I could never do that. I wanted to be hopeful about them. Whenever I saw someone, especially someone who looked like they'd messed up in life, like they'd made some bad choices, or had bad luck, no matter how badly they had gone wrong I always thought to myself, some mother had once held them in her arms and thought, the world is brand-new for you, you can do anything, you can have a great life. I am going to try my hardest for you.

I didn't feel anything for these people on the bus.

I sat in an empty seat.

He could've been sitting there.

The driver said we were leaving in just a few minutes.

The bus hummed under me.

Cuthbert Monks boarded.

He looked over all the people in their seats. Then he saw me and smiled. He looked relieved.

I didn't smile.

Cuthbert came down the aisle. He sat next to me.

The bus rattled around us.

"You can't go alone," he said.

I didn't respond.

"I'm going too," he said. "But I can't go alone either. There's no way we can stay in town, neither of us, not now, right? I don't see how anyone could. But I think now that it's all over, it might just feel like a dream to them . . . They'll wake up and they'll wonder what had happened to you and to me. But they'll never know what really happened."

I stared straight ahead.

"I know I was a dick, but if we're going to run away, we need each other. It's going to be hard. I'm not trying to be weird. I'm just saying . . ."

He was saying all the right things. If he was trying to say the right things, then sure, he could pat himself on the back. He was doing a good job.

Cuthbert said, "I don't know what just happened. You can tell me about it if you want to. But if you don't want to . . . I don't know, maybe you need someone who can at least try to understand."

Cuthbert Monks looked at me.

He took my hand.

My hand was in his hand.

"Wait a second," I said.

"What?" he said.

"Just wait here." I got up. "There's something I forgot. I have one last thing I need to take care of, before we go."

"But the bus is about to leave," said Cuthbert.

"Two minutes," I said and I got my backpack and went to the front and I said to the bus driver, "I just need to take care of something quick, don't leave until I come back, okay?"

The bus driver said, "Two minutes."

I ran to the ticket counter. I told the clerk I needed to change my ticket. Were there any buses leaving earlier? Like right now? Like right away?

That other bus in front of us in line—where was it headed?

Thank you.

I ran back out to the where the buses were idling.

I got on a different bus. It was only half full.

A minute later my bus swung out in one direction, and I watched as it left Cuthbert Monks's bus behind, and as Cuthbert's bus pulled out in another direction, and I felt light, so light it was like I was floating, looking out the window.

I had always wanted to get out of town.

≡

On the bus I had a dream, but not really a dream—a jumble of thoughts that you have when you're half asleep, the kind that come to you not when you're comfortable in bed but when your head is resting against a balled-up sweater on a rattling bus window.

Looking out the window at night, at the streetlights slipping past the window, and the reflections of the interior lights of the bus, and the lights of the cars streaking past us, and the dim lights of the lonely houses in the middle of nowhere, drifting in the distance, it felt like I was already in the city, walking down the streets. And even though I was dirty and exhausted and hurt, the lights felt inviting, I felt free and light and easy, I was walking at night and seeing the lights around me, nobody knew me and I was dancing in a dark room somewhere, the kind of room in magazines, where people in the city danced, a more intense and vivid and better part of the world.

I could lose myself in that crowd, in that music, and when the bus sped up and merged onto the interstate and its engine was too loud for me to sleep, the window rattling too much for me to even try, it didn't matter, because I would be awake forever, everything bigger and freer and fresher and colder, and I had a rushing, emptying feeling, like escaping from a tiny hot vicious universe made just for me into a whole world made for nobody at all.

ACKNOWLEDGMENTS

I am grateful to everyone who helped me with this book. First, tremendous gratitude to my agent John Cusick for believing in the story. Thanks to everyone at Quirk Books, especially Jhanteigh Kupihea for her insightful editorial guidance, Jane Morley for her sharp copyediting, Andie Reid for her beautiful cover, Paige Graff for her interior design, John J. McGurk and Mandy Sampson for their production work, and Nicole De Jackmo, Jennifer Murphy, Christina Tatulli, Jamie-Lee Nardone, Kate Brown, and everyone else in publicity, marketing, and sales for working hard to put this book in the right hands.

Thanks also to everyone who read and helped with the early drafts, including Christy Allen, Kate Babka, Eti Berland, Ronica Bhattacharya, Matt Bird, Arthur Bond, Emily Bricker, Vanessa Campos, Joe Cannon, Noah Cruickshank, Eileen Favorite, John Fecile, Dana Formby, Joe Fusion, Keir Graff, Amy Holland, St. John Karp, Kara Kennedy, Molly Ker Hawn, Rob Knowles, Megan Larson, Sam Malissa, Chris Norborg, Chris Norborg Sr., Heather Norborg, Jennifer Norborg, Ellen Palmer, Rory Parilac, Max Pitchkites, David Rheinstrom, Deb Ross, Marie Selavy, Alice Setrini, Abi St. John, Laura St. John, Melisa Swain, Nick Swain, Freya Trefonides, Theo Trefonides, Max Trefonides, and Brandon Will. If I have omitted anyone, I apologize.

Finally, thank you to my parents James and Priscilla, my wife Heather, and my daughters Lucy and Ingrid.